Karen Wehrstein

LION'S HEART

A Baen Books Original

Baen Publishing Enterprises
P.O. Box 1403
Riverdale, N.Y. 10471

ISBN: 0-671-72044-9

Cover art by Larry Elmore

First printing, March 1991

Distributed by
SIMON & SCHUSTER
1230 Avenue of the Americas
New York, N.Y. 10020

SIMULATION

My training got harder again. One day after winter solstice I fell wrongly, landing full on my sword-arm. There was a crack, then a gushing as if all my blood were pouring out, though I saw none. I began the usual leap, lifting the sword, and pain the like of which I had never known in my life threw me back to my knees.

I laid the sword across my thighs and felt for my wrist through my padded sleeve; when I touched it the falling snow went black and then grey. Bones were broken. All the while I was expecting warm strong arms across my back, leading me to hearth, and a healer. Instead, Azaila was shouting the same things as usual when I fell: "Chevenga! Chevenga! Where's the demarch?"

The sense of it came cold to me, ground in by training. In battle one might fall from a wall, be thrown by one's horse, or break one's arm a thousand other ways; yet that does not end it. I was not playing a child. War-training is all, or nothing.

I drew myself up, sword in shield-hand, just in time to parry.

Novels of the Fifth Millennium:

The Cage by S.M. Stirling and Shirley Meier

Book I

PROLOGUE

The story with which every Yeoli's story begins:

Once upon a time in the great Empire of Iyesi, there was a sect called the Athyel, who believed in no god but the God-In-Ourselves, and that humanity by nature is free. When the King 14th Jopal had risen to power, he sent his warriors to kill all who would not abandon their creed and pledge themselves to his. The Athyel refused. Nine days the streets ran with blood and the sky shone with flame, and all who were not killed fled into exile or into hiding.

Now it happened that a teacher in an Athyi school gathered together her students and fled away with them into the mountains. Although they soon were tired and hungry, and some of the children were lost or eaten by wild beasts, she barely let them rest as much as they needed, and at each choice of ways chose one without pausing, though she didn't know which way to go.

One day, near the end of their strength, they came to a deep wide valley. On the shore of a lake they found a woman fishing. The teacher fell on her knees and begged her aid.

"Many years ago," the woman said, embracing the

3

teacher, "the knowledge came to me that Athyel children would flee to this place, driven from Iyesi. So I prepared for you as best I could: the house is large, you see, the garden wide and the goats many. My name is Yeola. Come in! All this is yours."

So they went in and ate from the great pot of stew which hung waiting, then lay down upon the many mats and blankets, while she tended their hurts with medicines she had in plenty.

"Yeola, our benefactress," the teacher said, "we could never thank you enough. But every time our way forked, I chose without pausing, so it is entirely by chance we came here. How could you have known many years ago that we would?"

"Foreknowledge works outside of time," Yeola answered. "Had chance taken you to the next valley instead, I would have known to wait there. That is hard to understand, I know, for those who don't have a touch of it themselves; perhaps the best explanation is to say that the God-In-Me told me."

The teacher was overjoyed. "You are one of us!"

"No," said Yeola. "But I can speak the language of your thought. I believe in none of the gods as their priests would have me do, and believe in all of them as they are: the spirit of life as people feel it. I serve no god, for none has spoken and asked it of me; I serve all, because their presence asks, in all the wonders of life. I proselytize for no god, since each is part of the truth as nations are part of the world; but I speak the language of each, so that I may understand all people. To Enchians I would have said my prescience came from First Curlion, to nature-cultists, from the Hermaphrodite, to animists, from the mountain-sprites, to Fire-cultists, from the Twin Hawks. But you happen to be Athyel, so I said it came from the God-In-Myself."

"Well . . . I thank you for being so considerate as to speak in the language of our thought," the teacher said finally. "But I am curious to know where you believe it came from."

"I believe—I firmly believe—it came from all of them. Or none. Or me. Or out of the sky. I firmly believe I do not know. Also that I do not care. It came from the world of the unknown, which is wondrous because it is unknown. All the gods' names are names for it. Once given, such a name becomes Truth, the name of the Truth a people feel from the unknown. Yours is the God-In-Ourselves. So I used it, to give you from the unknown your Truth of where my prescience came from.

"Not that it matters a whit anyway. I hope this never ends up in some chronicle. You're here, there's food and bed, and you are invited to stay as long as you like."

So it was, they stayed. When they were strong enough they began the work of life, on the land, and continued their education from the many ancient books that Yeola had. Seek wisdom, she taught them, find the God-In-Yourselves: live by the ultimate law that is hardest to live by: that there is no ultimate law. For meanings their native tongue had none for, they invented new words; for settling their disputes and making their common choices they created new customs.

Years passed, and the children grew, built houses and had children of their own. Yeola grew old. In their thirtieth year in the valley, as their children were just beginning to have children, Yeola took ill, and it became clear she would soon die.

Around her bed the people gathered. "My children," she said, "you think I have shared everything I have with you, but in all honesty I have not. I see I must now.

"I could never choose your ways any more than I could think your thoughts. You will choose whether to stay in this valley or go somewhere else, to remain Athyel or take up some church, to retain your customs of being the other and of voting or return to your previous ways. Yet there is one choice I did dearly wish to deny you forever, pretending to myself in my foolishness that this peaceful garden in which we live was the whole world. There was one thing I hid from you. You must choose what has always been the hardest choice. It's in the chest where I keep my things, at the very bottom."

In the box they found a sword.

The sight brought back a thousand things to those who had fled Iyesi: the iron-armored warriors of Jopal, houses falling in flame, the cries of the dying, the smell of smoke and blood.

"Never did I want you to bear killing tools," Yeola

whispered, "and be so tempted to kill. But someday someone may come wanting to kill you, who has no ears for your words of justice or sense. Someday having it may save your lives, which I cannot deny you. You must choose, whether to take it up or not.

"I ask only this: see what I show you now." Opening the packet she showed them, they found five books of an age beyond thinking. The pages were darkened but the writing was visible, and made them start and shiver in their hearts. A human hand is unsteady, and will err; this writing was flawless, as could only have been done by the hand of a machine.

"I guessed Jopal would burn your libraries. So I took these, which the first Athyel collected from the ruins. They knew people would start doubting it was human-crafted fire that burned the world, for such power is beyond imagining today; so the proof must be preserved. These were written when such weapons existed, and speak of them.

"The knowledge to make them is lost—but only for now. Do you know what the common weapon of war was, 500 years before the Fire?" She cast her gaze to the sword.

"We won't have this thing!" one cried. "We'll throw it into the deepest lake we can find!" But another clenched his fists and said, "Are you mad? Someone will come, just as Yeola said, as Jopal did. If our parents had had swords, all would have been different!" A quarrel ensued, each side horrified at the other. "Yeola," they said finally, "we see this thing's two edges now, very well."

"You are forgetting something," she said. "This is not a good or evil thing, for it does not live. It's only a piece of steel. Never can it kill, without a living hand wielding it, and bare hands can kill without swords. What brought the First Fire, and will bring the Second, is not weapons or knowledge, but choices made in error. Remember that."

They swore they would, and Yeola died.

Once again they wept and clung together, and found strength; once again they felt a sunset, and a dawn.

They buried her beside the lake, and then all bathed naked in the clear water, to cleanse themselves. Later she became known as Saint, for having been divine in her humanity, and Mother, for having been mother in spirit to a people. Her sword, serving as a sign to all and belonging to no one, now hangs in the School of the Sword. In her honor, the people named the valley in which they lived Yeola-e.

I

Vae Arahi, Spring Y. 1554

Two days after I was born my parents carried me up Hetharin, with the two monks of Senahera to bear witness.

It was a fall day like ones I remember: the land lies sweet as after the act of love, the scent of ripened crops fills the mountain air, and in the sun the lowland trees at the peak of their fall-turning seem on fire. Along the path that follows the meltwater stream from Hetharin, they climbed with me to the naked heights, to where the air carries so little life one must breathe hard to draw it in, and nothing grows but lichen and flowers smaller than one's fingernail. It seems a place little worth the climb, until one turns around.

Assembly Palace lies small as a lidless jewel box, pale and shining in the sun, far below one's feet. Vae Arahi is a handful of gravel strewn in a circle, the School of the Sword a gold tinderbox across the way. Beyond the lip of the valley mouth the lake shows plainly its reputed shape, that of a wide scythe, with the city Terera piled about its tip. Only the mountain's siblings remain large: Haranin at one's face, Saherahin at its shield-side, Perin to one's own sword-side. Beyond them stand the white-helmeted peaks no one sees who doesn't make this climb, the shoulders of the nearer ones forest-green, the farther ones deep steel-blue, and so on, fading into distance out of mind, till they drop from the rim of this facet of the Earthsphere. Here one sees, clear as a stroke to the heart, the smallness of oneself alone, and the greatness of all things as one.

There is no praying for us. We cannot receive comfort from a voice in the sky. It was for my parents then as it would be for me six years later, when I entered the School of the Sword to begin my war-training. Asked did I will this, I signed chalk, yes; I could feel the ability I had been born with, as people can, and was to my mind obliged to defend my people. I put my hand on the sword of Saint Mother, as all the masters and novices watched: the hilt, worn down to nothing by the touch of generations of initiates and replaced uncounted times, the straight dark blade, never used, the same she gave us. Hanging by chains, it stirred at my touch, and then came up with my hands as I hefted it; all down the line of people there was whispering. It was then I felt lost and frightened, to have so easily moved something so sacred, and knew I had taken on something I did not understand. But we cannot pray to her who lived a millennium and a half ago. If we must ask the age-old question all Yeolis seem to at one time or another, "Would she have taken *me* in?", the answer will never come to us on the wind. Unless we feel our worth in our hearts, we are without it.

So it was for my mother: they must stand aside helpless, the curse and the duty of all parents; my strength unaided would decide it. I had had my fair preparation, a good birth and my two days of having them all to myself; now I must make good my claim to go on, alone. The Senaheral placed their feet astride the stream, marking out a length of water just below the cleft where it gushes out. My mother knelt beside it, unwrapped me from my wool, and laid me in.

We are called barbarian for this. Often it is by people who keep slaves and maintain tyrants, who practice human sacrifice or sport-killing, or whose custom is to cut off the tenderest part a girl-child has, thinking that for a woman to have pleasure is evil. Perhaps my reader is of such a people and takes offense; then, like two striplings caught rolling in the dirt, we must each be the other.

If I were a Lakan, then . . . *these Yeolis with their*

baby-killing, doomed—for what god would take into his hand a people who scorn paying the sacred blood-price, yet freeze to death babies without dedicating a finger-bone to the Almighty? Such impiety will bring down the Earned Fire upon them again. . . .

Or an Arkan: *without gods, giving their heirs to the whims of chance, as if chance has better judgment than a good sensible father! All Yeolis are milksops to their hairy-chested wives, without the testicular juice to choose which children they will keep, let alone correct or purify those women. . . .*

Having played you, I am in my rights to ask you to play me. Having so done we will both see truth: that barbarism is in the heart of the beholder as beauty in the eye. Who, therefore, am I to call you barbarian, or you to call me? If there is some race on the Earthsphere perfect by all standards, let them call the rest of us barbarian.

Let the custom be judged by its justice. It is true that many other Yeoli families have given it up, since we increased enough not to interbreed, and life got easier. But I was born to serve my people; should we not take customary pains at least to give them good? It was just to me too, to whom trials harder than most Yeolis' awaited. If I were too weak, why let my failure or my death wait till I was old enough to understand what failure and death are? This way is quick; the child dies unknowing; the parents are freed to try again, also best for a demarch.

Most unjust are those who say my parents could not have loved me, to have done such a thing. Their hearts lay in the ice-water with me, nameless though I was. I know from standing there myself. It was worst for my mother, who had carried me. How else can it be with parents? But they must think of others than themselves.

I've been told I'd think differently if I could remember it, the sight of them, standing still with calm faces while my flesh shrank and my breathing weakened, while the life in me, so new, first felt itself failing, and the air shimmering with the steel wings of Shininao the Carrier waiting to draw out my soul when it came loose. Perhaps a child is one who has not yet learned to see beyond himself, and so the world must have been nothing but pain and terror to me then. But I think better of myself, now I am an adult, than to let the memory stain my belief. Besides, I had reason to trust my parents. They had loved me all my life.

These are only words. I would prove more taking my own firstborn there in my arms. As we are grateful so may we be thanked.

In my own time, as I would so many times later, I fought without speculating. Afterwards they lifted me out limp and blue and went back to the Hearthstone. When I turned from blue back to pink and my heartbeat didn't cease, they voted on my name. By the hearth they made the signs of the rite, sharing one crystal, and took up chalk or charcoal, one by one, to choose.

The decision was not unanimous, but split three-to-one. (To this day I do not know which one of them voted against, and never will.) It was a risk, after all, one they only dared because my father was so well-regarded. Only three demarchs had ever borne the name, and none since the War of the Travesty, two hundred years ago. It was considered too rife with the sound of war and grandeur, invoking the beast that was named Monarch of Beasts even before the Fire, and her fighting spirit. It has a tinge of human domination too, being descended in meaning from the name of the king who united Iyesi and whom Enchians still worship, First Curlion, who took it from warrior-kings older still. In the pure ancient tongue Yeola made, "che" is heart, and "i-veng" is lion.

Thus they threw their die, and I grew into the cast. In full: Fourth Chevenga Shae-Arano-e, at that time Ascendant to the Demarchy of Yeola-e.

I have been everything and nothing. I am Athyi but to some have been God, and yearned a thousand times, God knows, to pray. I have been both the living hand that wields it and the dead steel itself; I have been torn down to the roots and raised again cell by cell, enveloped by fire and water. I have been measured beside Saint Mother, and my namesake Curlion; I did in fact feel the call of both, and pattern my life accordingly. Yet we seize life and it seizes us at once, like dancers, and mine danced down a path whose sign-stone could bear no name but one: Chevenga.

Like all Athyel, I had nothing to judge myself by ultimately but the heart's own measure: "Is it kind or cruel?"

If you mean to judge me, I beg nothing more than the usual observance. I need not be with you—you have my whole life-story in your hands, with every scene written out as full as would fit. You may know me better by reading this than in life; I kept some secrets there, none here. Perhaps you are not Yeoli and don't know our ways; no matter, this one is simple. One becomes the other, like an actor. Imagine what I saw, speak what I spoke, feel what I felt. A greater favor I could not wish.

II

My earliest memory is my mother's fire. A pair of square orange eyes with gold edges, I would see, or a monster with stickles in his spine made of fire-jewels—then the poker in Mama's great hand striking it, destroying all in a burst of sparks, and creating new.

My floor was warm sheep-fur that tickled my skin; my roof, the creaking base of her wicker chair; my door, her legs. The dogs would shove their noses at me until I took them in under my arms. A thread of yarn stretched twitching from the ball to above; she'd be crocheting socks, or a crib-blanket for the next sib coming, still in her womb. My blanket was all rich bright blues, purples and turquoises, in running patterns which, if you journeyed across them with your eyes as children do, predicted and reflected each other; there was the Vae Arahi pattern too, single and double stitches interlacing, to mean balance and transaction. I wore it over my shoulder like a warrior's chlamys, to the mirth of grownups, until I was six, and kept it all my life.

One day, when I was about four, she was big with child, but reading instead of crocheting. Objecting, since this made her oblivious to me, I twirled a lit twig to make light-trails in the air. "You know very well you are not to do that, and why not, yet you are doing it," she said. "Why?"

"Why aren't you making a blanket for the new one?" I asked.

Instead of upbraiding me for answering a question with a question, she said, "I'm doing something else for the new one."

I had always been taught strictly never to lie, punished far worse for denying I had done wrong than for doing it. Nor had I ever needed much training in reading faces. Not knowing what else to do, I asked her, civilly as I had been taught, "Mama, if you please, may I know why you're lying?"

She was a warrior who left the field to bear children; not one whose eyes went wide, or whose cheeks took a touch of red easily. Her eyes were so much like mine that I could always become her easily. Now as she looked into the fire I did, my chin and nose adult and female, love-locks brushing my face, the heat of tears in my eyes just enough to shimmer like faint sun on the edge of a cloud. Lie forgotten, I wanted to fling my arms around her; I had never seen her cry in my life.

"I owe you truth," she said finally, "but I can give you only very little. Why I'm not crocheting, you are too young to hear. I am sorry, Chevenga. Will you forgive me?"

I wrapped my arms around her neck and kissed her in answer, and never spoke of it again. The child died in the stream. They gave him his rites in the hearth, after the rest of us were in bed. I heard, and saw with my inner eyes at least, the flames curling around his body, his fingers, delicate as my tiniest sib's, crackling. I wept my pillow wet, then dreamed. Such dreams always slip out of my mind as I get close to them, like a faint star that one can see from the tail of one's eye but not looking straight on, or the Second Fire, too terrible for the mind to approach any way but circuitously.

But afterwards I understood it all. She had foreknown his death, but wanted to spare the rest of us the grief of foreknowledge. Only later did I learn her gift was known. To me nothing of this seemed out of the way, nor my having guessed it, though I could not know why.

I was three when the Tor Enchian war ended; by the time I was six, we were sending each other envoys. I got to see their delegation in Hall, these glittering creatures with pompous manners, wearing strangling collars, metal jewelry and the furs of animals too small to eat, something I had heard of but not believed. They were all men, which made me ask my grandmother if there were any Tor Enchian women, to her mirth. Strangest of all, since they had been born with it, was their hair; not loose-curled, or even wavy, but spear-straight, hanging from the crowns of their heads like the smooth flow on the lip of a waterfall. When the leader moved the ends swung like a curtain in the breeze, cut in a perfectly straight line, a sight to see.

They all carried knives in their sleeves, little straight blades with a tang of bile like fear about them. Even indoors, where one never wears arms; my father permitted it. "You've heard they carry them?" my grandmother said when I asked about it. "That's his way, to call to their honor by trusting them." She said it with neither approbation nor reproach, I recall, but pride thrilled through me. Being helpless, children know fear, so they love courage.

There was a referendum that year over whether to answer Lakan raids on the border with war, our borderfolk pressing for chalk. Some western fool cited the old augury, that in this century we would break our custom of warring only to our borders, and conquer a great land, and tried to entice my father that way. Of course he had no wish to be King of Laka. When his turn came to speak—I already knew the demarch always speaks last—he said only that to think of raids as war just because western farmfasts were getting too many children for their land was against our law. In the end the vote went solidly charcoal, and he was praised. But he had to say it to the faces of those children, and the bereaved. Once a rock was thrown at him; I remember the scar, splitting the end of one of his pale thick eyebrows into a fork. When I first touched it, he said, "Sometimes they forget what is right, and hurt you for doing it."

The great baths in Asinanai were proposed that year; the city council asked for five hundred *ankaryel*, and the vote went seven in ten chalk, giving them 350; my grandmother used it to teach me division, and I still think of the number sometimes, stepping into a bath. Politics was in the air around me, as weather is for farm children or wool for the weavers. I took a dutiful but distant interest.

Someday, I knew, I would be demarch; I would grow into it as into size, in some mysterious way become filled with sacredness, and start presiding in Assembly with a crystal in my hand; then all Yeola-e would love me as all the Hearthstone did now. In the meantime, there were trees to climb and games to play; I had all the love and comfort that lets a child be a child. With my present sweet and my future set, my heart went out to everyone else, for I could imagine no one in the world as lucky as me.

In that same year came my father's Renewal.

My grandmother made me ready in her room. She had been demarch for twenty years, her five brand-scars spread in a half-circle across her upper chest like a mayor's collar of office. Now that era bore her name, and many still called her Nainginin: Naingini who is a mountain. Someday, I was sure, I too would have a nickname, and an era.

She kept all her mementoes here; political things, sacred. Gifts from envoys: a jade horse and rider, rampant with mane and mantle flowing; an Arkan pen with ink contained in its shaft; a blue feather as long as a man's arm from some impossible bird; a samovar from Brahvniki; portraits, letters, crystals. Our sword Chirel, my father carried, but its stand was here. The best was the comb standing central on the mantlepiece, her retirement gift: it had ebony tines curving like the petals of a tulip cut across, a diamond for chalk and a black sapphire for charcoal. I would have given a day's meals just to touch it. On the morning of my father's Renewal I felt her tugging the knots out of my hair more gently than usual, looked, and saw she was using it.

The courtyard was filled with Hearthstone people, their ringlets brushed to shining and kilts bright-pressed. As we came to people they made the sign of respect to my grandmother, and patted me on the head saying, "Today the Ascendant gets the first glimpse." I would just grin, knowing only to be excited.

A hush fell: my father had come out in a white robe, with the Crystal of the Speaker in his hand.

When I was growing up I used to gaze into my mother's mirror of Arkan glass in search of his likeness, squinting sometimes, to fill it in with the brush of imagination. My chin and cheekbones eventually would sharpen into similar

lines, to my delight, and people say—to my everlasting
surprise, since in my inward eye his head keeps company
with the mountaintops—that I am as tall as he was. But
never did my nose come to equal his, and the dyes are all
wrong; his hair was white-gold, the pin-curls standing up
around his head like the sun's aureole, while mine is my
mother's black.

Now as he came out I saw the demarchic signet gone
from his finger, leaving a pale band of wrinkled skin. Had
he been impeached? No, or I'd have heard about it. It was
some part of the rite. His eyes were still as those of the
ancient meditating demarchs carved in stone; they looked
at me once, but did not seem to see me, austere and
distant as the moon. Yet his body sang with an invisible
brightness. He greeted no one, and everyone stood off,
even my mother. We are making him a stranger, I thought,
and he's accepting it, like one guilty. Why? A thousand
questions crowded in my mind.

In Terera the square was jammed, the roofs fringed with
people; overloaded boats nudged each other in the harbor.
On the pier stood five Senaheral, in full robe, with things
ranged out: I saw a spear and a brazier and others I could
not name. The wind was full of lake smells; waves lapped
on the docks.

One of the monks began to sing a full, rich, steady note.
Then his voice thinned, and a second note drew out of the
first, soaring upward from plateau to plateau like a bird on
mountain wind. He was a harmonic singer, trained to sing
with two voices. Foreigners are startled by this; to me,
who cannot remember hearing it for the first time, it was,
and will always be, the sound of sacredness.

He finished, and another monk began speaking. Not
understanding I ceased attending, and heard a woman
near me whisper, "You know, the second time is always
the hardest. He knows what it will be, you see." I thought,
that's what Renewal means: the second time. Whatever he
must do he succeeded at last time. Finally my father
stepped forward, naked now, and the crowd pricked up.
The monk raised his arms, and invoked us to call him out.

I could remember his triumph after the war, though
vaguely as an old dream: the chanting of his name, the air
filled with flowers and scarves and streams of wine, the
songs, the drums, the warriors clashing their wristlets

together; his smile, as he was carried on a hundred shoulders, and Chirel flashing in his raised hand. We will chant his name as he deserves, I thought, there will be some ceremony to satisfy the monks and bureaucrats, and then everyone will break out the wine and stop looking so somber. I drew breath to call in that spirit. But in the last instant something in the air made me listen instead.

Ten thousand voices roared out his name, not in adoration, but in demand. Stunned, I turned and looked; the faces behind me were faces no longer, but stone masks carven hard and merciless; the raised fists, weapons. These were not the people I knew, but strangers possessed; not with anger even, but with power, power above all feeling, above all forgiving, high and calm and untouchable as the tallest peak, that judges all the world and takes its abasement as its unquestioned due; as if All-spirit itself had turned against him, and demanded the final reckoning.

I went dizzy, terror and black rage fighting in me. Imagining myself him I felt it wash over me, turning my legs to water; yet I also thought, how can they so abuse him, after all he's done for them? He's demarch! Not knowing what else to do I seized my grandmother's leg, and took in a deep breath to bawl. With hardly a glance down she said, "You're just watching! Watch him, who is doing."

My father stood like a candle-flame. The people's call, roaring over the square and shaking my very bones twice more, did not cow him, but seemed to enter and fill him, fueling his shining brighter still. When the third call was done he went to his knees, his hand on his heart; not stiffly, as if against his will, but like water, with the grace of complete consent, so that it was no abasement, but pride itself. "All the world is as it should be," that motion said. I stood in wonder, my anger snuffed out. He turned, and stepped into the lake. The Senaheral followed him, with the spear and the torch, now lit, and the fire-dish on its tripod, which they set in the water before him. The Ritual Monk followed, carrying nothing.

As they placed themselves I saw him look down into the water. I did not know what he was going to do, then, but now I wonder what he saw there. The shimmering leather-and-steel wings of Shininao? A wall of blackness that he must knock down, or like me, a gate to pass through, beyond which lay the bright days of his next four years of office, strung together in a chain? I never had a chance to ask him.

He knelt so that the ripples lapped his neck; the monk planted the butt of the spear in the mud beside him; he curled his shield-arm around the shaft. In his sword-hand he took the torch and laid his wrist in the crook of the fire-dish, so that the flame burned above it. He tested his grip, set himself like a runner at the starting line. Standing behind him, the Ritual Monk laid her hands on his shoulders. Then she threw them up, to show he was free, and the crowd drew in its breath.

One's inclination is to take in a great lungful of air, as if one were diving; but if you forbear, it is over sooner. A pause came, in which he knelt still as stone, then he bowed his bright head into the ripples.

Silence deep as death fell. Among the poles where the workfasts hang their banners, a rod that had not been tied off well quietly clinked; somewhere a baby mewled, and was hushed.

I had learned by this time how to put my face under water without drowning; I imagined myself him, seeing the little stones in the brown mud, the wood of the spear-shaft smooth against my arm. I found myself holding my breath, and my lungs straining; when it was more than I could bear I heaved it out and took several long sweet draughts of air. Around me others did the same, reminding themselves they were not him. It's a breath-holding test, I thought. He stayed under. In fact he lowered his grip on the spear, to draw himself a little further down. Somehow it was that motion that made me begin to understand what they had asked him to do.

I watched with the horror of the helpless. Though a monk held the spear in two ridged arms, it began to twitch and tremble like a living thing. From a distance, it seemed, I heard my grandmother whisper, "Strength, my child of steel, calm, my child of water, don't fight, give in, give in . . ." She was talking to him, I realized. The people stood still, content to watch his death-throes; he would die in the silence of the Lake, his lips sealed, alone among enemies. The Ritual Monk put one hand down into the water, which was muddy over his bright locks, from his struggle. He is a warrior, I thought, who will fight to the end.

When he went still, all the world did too, for a moment; then his fingers relaxing let the torch fall into the fire-dish. A gout of flame leaped up, and the crowd loosed a roar. Now, the wine flowed and the flowers came out; now, having rewarded his shining generosity with death, they chanted his name.

I could hardly breathe, and felt tears coming. But I had seen how he took it. How could I do less, when I had only watched? So I raised my head and squared my shoulders, and put into my face his look. Let them do with me what they will, I thought; shame me, drown me; I will be stone, and let their power touch me as much as he did; I care as much as a dust-speck for them. My grandmother gazed at me for a little, but said nothing.

From the water, they lifted a dead weight. It hung limp in their hands as they carried it to the pier, long arms trailing, water-darkened hair pasted across empty face, all grace gone. A clutch gathered round, blocking my sight; I saw them bend as one, then one monk kneel and lean as if to kiss him, moving quickly. The crowd quieted and tensed; then I heard a gasping cough and several quick tearing breaths, and saw his face flushed and grimacing, his hands clutching at his quaking chest. Then he spat, and sat up, and grinned.

The cheering redoubled. As they steadied him up into the crowd I saw him wave just as in his triumph. But it all seemed distant and false; closer to my ears was the dark beating of leather and steel wings. They grew louder as I listened to them, and the rejoicing seemed like a jest in bad taste. More than anything I wanted to be alone, in a dark place. I slipped away when my grandmother turned her back. No one looked down to see me, and I ran full-speed all the way home.

I hid in the top of my mother's wardrobe. They called my name through all the rooms, and outside on the mountain. I stayed quiet; I wanted to see no human face. They had killed him before my eyes, joyful, then shown it to be false, still joyful. Any greater meaning had gone entirely out of my mind. And he played along, I thought, he my father. Why should I let them, any of them, ever see me again?

What brought me out finally, a good while after dark, was hunger. I had to ask in the kitchen for leftovers. In

the halls people all looked and didn't look at me at the
same time, so that every eye I saw peripherally like a
weapon behind me. But I didn't care. My mother gave me
her comb across my hand, for worrying her; my grandmother likewise, for giving her the slip. I bore it stone-
faced, looking away. I decided to creep to bed without
anyone seeing me; but as I tiptoed into my mother's room
I found my father sitting at the hearth.

His hair was still snake-curled from the water, dried but
uncombed; he'd gone up the mountain after for his vision.
You played along, I thought, and heard Shininao's wings
again. You are as bad or worse than the rest. Yet this
person still had the looks of my father, who had always
loved me: the white-gold pin curls, the broad shoulders,
the great hand with the signet on it again (that part of the
ceremony I had missed). I stood trembling, torn between
stalking away in anger, and running to his arms. Just then
he saw me, smiled, and beckoned me to him.

I sat by his sword-hand, lips sealed. Closer, I felt the
solemn brightness still on him, now cruel and cold. Anger
returned, now he was close enough to not be unearthly,
but human, parent, such as a child can lay claim to. When
he took my face between his hands, I kept it stony, looking over his shoulder.

"Mama said you were angry back," he said. His hazel eyes
were full of tenderness. It is almost impossible for a demarch
to get angry back, on that day; and he had been in my place
once.

He drew me onto his lap, and wrapped me in his arms.
As always I felt shielded. To think of what you might have
lost forever is one thing; to feel it all warm around you is
quite another. My feeling burst out; I buried my head in
his neck, seized two fistfuls of his golden hair and bawled
like a baby.

"You made me think you were dead!" I yelled, and "You
lied to me!" and even worse things a talkative child will
come up with in a tantrum. He said, "You would have
understood it all, had you stayed to listen." Then as he
saw I was not yet ready for reason he stroked my hair, and
said, "Shh, it's all right, my child, see, I'm here, I'm not
dead. Do I look dead to you?"

What I knew in my depths, I do not know. I recall
knowing nothing. But many times on hindsight I have

recognized the sharpening of an emotion by foreknowledge. This had the feel.

"Perhaps you don't like the idea for yourself, either,"
he said after a time, wiping my tears away with a callused
hand.

I knew now, of course, that I would survive it. But,
aware that every such play is full of the heart's truth, else
it would have no power, I remembered the cruel faces. "If
they want me dead, even a little bit," I said, "why should
I work for them?"

I know now, how he wanted me to have the life that
meant so much to him. But he showed nothing. "You need
not, if you don't want to. Nothing's graven yet. All it
needs is Grandma'am and I to speak against you and you'd
never be approved. Shall we?"

I had sent it out as an angry wish. Now offered back the
real thing, I saw my own heart more clearly. Having lived
for nothing else, I could imagine nothing else; without the
demarchy, it seemed, I would be nothing. As well, his
giving came back to me, that brilliant grace that feared
nothing, making dust of all other aspirations. I signed
charcoal, no.

He smiled. "Whatever your tutors say when you throw
snowballs at them, there's a demarch in there somewhere.

"Shall I explain, or your grandmother? She does better." I lifted his hand solemnly onto my shoulder. In
truth, I did not want to leave him. He smiled, and said,
"There's a story, so if you need to visit the midden . . .
no? You're sure? All right.

"In the olden days," he said, "demarchs could do what
they liked. I should say, you always had to do as the
people voted; but you could own money, or marry whom
you pleased without Assembly's consent, or even abdicate.
And no one questioned that the demarch would obey the
vote, because they always had."

On the hearth lay a long iron thing whose end reached
into the fire's orange coals; as he paused he studied and
shifted it.

"But when we took up the sword, everything changed.
Imagine, Chevenga, what would happen if the Tor En-
chains attacked us again, and it was not me who must
decide what to do, but Assembly. They'd make a good
plan, well thought out, yes? But we'd be in pieces before a

tenth of it was ready. A decision from the many is most just, but from the few is . . ." He waited.

"Quickest." I knew from my siblings; if I wanted to do proper mischief, I'd learned, I had to take things into my hands.

"Yes. That's why we relinquish our wills to our commanders, in war. Because the people would trust only the demarch with such power, it fell to us to command. Thus we became warriors.

"So, one must be the Hand of the People, subject to all due process, but First General First as well, giving orders while others relinquish their wills. Years of this, and one can come to think enough of oneself, that a demarch's bounds come to seem . . ." He made the sign of being in chains.

His hand fidgeted with the thing in the fire, and I knew as surely as if he'd said it that he'd felt this way himself. "War is a strain on the customs of the peaceful, you'll see. Go fetch me a bowl of cool water, a linen cloth, a towel and the aloe salve on Mama's night table, there's a good lad.

"Some ten generations ago there was a demarch by the name of Notyere. He was a great warrior and commander, and began to feel his leash too short. Forgetting all that he had been taught, and losing sight of the All-spirit, he tried to free himself of it.

"His friends were those who would do what he said; he feasted and gave them gifts paid for with the peoples' taxes—the demarch could take freely out of the treasury then—wore fine clothes and jewels, made himself rich as a foreign king.

"Next he started forgetting small duties, and those who protested he would buy off, or convince it had been necessary, or distract with talk of the Enchians threatening war. People grumbled, but forgave. Then a Servant of Assembly who often opposed him was found guilty of vandalism, and hence had to give up her position; when a similar thing happened to another detractor, people grew suspicious. When some proof was found, they began gathering signatures.

"From then, he took his own part in Assembly, which as you know is not done; then, seeing true danger, he set loose dark-workers. The petitioners would find their pa-

pers missing or their horses stolen or a town claiming they
had already come through. Lies were spread, people even
got beaten; but in the end, the vote went strongly chalk,
for impeachment.

"And everyone waited for him to stand up in Assembly
as is required, say, 'The people wills,' and step down. They
couldn't imagine otherwise; they were Yeolis. To them, it
was being stabbed in the heart from within the heart. How
is that possible?

"He'd had people ready, armed. He announced that he
was falsely condemned, so that justice left him no choice
but this, and struck down the Keeper of the Arch-Sigil
with his wristlet.

"Do you know the notches on the doorpost of the School
of the Sword; the ones that are framed? Notyere tried to
take it, very early; he knew the Teachers were against
him, and wanted them out of the way fast. By killing
them, yes. Merasha Kaili, the senior then, said to him,
'A heroic last stand you want from us, Notyere, no surrender, so you can kill us, without shame! Well, you shall
have it; but you are our students, who held the Sword
before our witness. We could never harm you.' They all
laid aside their swords and took up staves, except one who
carried the sword of Saint Mother flat on the backs of his
hands, and fought their way out without spilling a drop of
blood.

"Now Notyere's sister Denaina—yes, your shadow-mother
is named after her—who should have become demarch,
had slipped out a window. In Terera she called out the
people to right this travesty, which is how the war got its
name. They surrounded her, linked hands and made a
common curse of ostracism on anyone who tried to break
through. No one dared try. But the war had begun, and
these very corridors where you play naked saw"—he made
the sign of protection around us both—"Yeoli slay Yeoli."

My father looked into the fire, then with the cloth
washed a spot on his chest, and carefully towelled it dry.
Some final rite remained. The thing in the fire, I knew, I
had seen before.

I tried to imagine people shouting death threats to each
other in the offices where I now pestered the staff, drawing Yeoli blades on each other among these quiet hearths
and lintels whose running patterns I knew by heart, cut-

ting each other near my grandmother's sacred things. I could not. No sword-marks mar the posts of the Hearthstone; in this place where children are raised, they'd been effaced the moment there was peace.

"The war really lasted only six days. He guessed wrongly that the warriors who had served under him would follow him, to wade in the blood of their own. Most turned at the start, shocked and enraged. All-spirit working in us wards off blind obedience . . . In the end Denaina took office, and Notyere was tried. He and all who had stood by him to the end were cast out.

"Outside the court waited those whose kin he had caused to die. Though Denaina herself came out with her arms around him, and pleaded with them to stay true to the way they had preserved at such cost, by forgiving, they pushed past the guards and killed him with their hands, on the steps of Assembly Palace.

"So fell the demarch who would be king. But the heart of the people was not at peace. If it could happen once, why not again? 'What will bring the Second Fire,' they were thinking, 'is not weapons or knowledge, but choices made in error. . . .'

"Fallen must change. Those reforms to tighten the demarch's leash that went chalk still hold today. That is why I cannot be owner of any property, why I must beg so many things, why there are acts for which I would be impeached without petition.

"But not even then was the heart at peace. Denaina did a seven-day abstinence, but when she returned among the people she understood at once. They had seen power corrupt Notyere. They had lessened her power, but had to leave her some. She was still First General First, could still command those who relinquished their will.

"So she said: 'My people, I fear what every demarch has feared since the first bathed in the Lake has happened: you no longer trust me, because of my position. Is this so?'

"Some answered charcoal and some chalk. So she said, 'Even that is too many. All-spirit must be that: all, else it is nothing. Thus I believe, to the death. Ask me, my people, to do that which is most hard to do, and I will do it; thus will I prove to you that I am your Hand, and your will is mine.'

"At this an uproar of debate filled the square. 'Demarch,'

they said finally, 'this offer seems good to us, but the hardest thing to do is die, and we fear that if we asked you that, you might in your zeal succeed. If there were some way of dying without dying, we would ask that of you; but how can there be?'

"For barely a moment she thought. 'Call my name three times,' she said, 'with the feeling that is in your heart!' They did; and she strode into the Lake, and did what I did today.

"Then all were at peace, awestruck, her the most. Knowing it needed renewing, she did it again four years later.

"So it became custom—but never law. The secret of the Kiss of the Lake, Chevenga, is not that we do it, hard though it is. Its power is that we do it willingly, that Denaina began it freely. It seems like law, the way they call and so forth, but it's nowhere in the books. It is binding by honor alone.

"I chose to let them command me. You may decide if you wish it is too much to give; they might impeach you, but they'd have to take the usual trouble. As always, you choose."

Truly, I thought, that is giving. Suddenly from within myself I felt the ringing of a whispered note, like the harmonic singer's, or a faint deep wind, as if a mountain could breathe, and did in my heart. It lingered a moment, as if to say, "Don't worry, if you need me. I am in you." That was the first time.

My mother came into the room, and sat beside my father. "It's time," he said smiling, and pulled the iron thing a little out of the fire. Its patterned end glowed orange as the coals.

I knew where I had seen it before: on my grandmother's mantlepiece, always, near the comb. The pattern was the same, I realized, as that which she had five times on her chest and he once, marks I'd always thought part of both of them, things one was born with, not to be acquired. "We chose it all," he said, smiling at me. Grasping the iron firmly in two hands, he blew off the ash, set his teeth and turned the bright end inward.

I remember thinking, This is what the Iyesian Athyel must have smelled on the nine days, the hiss like meat searing, the steam. Most of all I remember his face, unmoving as in sleep, the pale gaze steady and wide as a fight-stare, the lips keeping their smooth curve without the trace of a twitch. If my war-teachers think they taught me to bear pain, they are wrong.

It seemed to last a lifetime. The muscles stood up all along his arms, the iron seemed stuck to him as if he were helpless; he first shone, then dripped, with sweat. Then just as suddenly his hands drew it away. On his heaving chest, next to the old mark, the new one glowed red. Then he lay down and let us tend him, his day's work done.

III

I cannot remember meeting Mana-lai Chereda; he seemed born my friend, and I his, as our hands were born our hands; our parents put us together as babies, since we came only thirteen days apart. When I was seven, he, Nyera Harayel, Krero Saranyera, Sachara Shae-Shaila and I were a clutch. Loosed at the end of the day, we five and the three of my sibs who were big enough ran up to our secret fortress on the mountain.

A pall had fallen over my family in the past two days. My mother, as I knew by eavesdropping, had been struck with terrible foreboding. It is the nature of her gift that she feels such without knowing why; her child dying in the stream she had guessed by the feeling's timing. Now she was not expecting, no one was ill or at war, and no dangerous time drew near. The only measures that brought her any relief were forbidding us all to do anything risky, and carrying a knife, so that whenever she hugged me I felt it, that little sliver of fear in the midst of her love, its hilt, ready to hand, like a knot against my ribs. It was only on the condition that we climb no rocks or trees that she let us go up the mountain today. Seeing her face, I swore on my crystal for all of us. She was wearing her white linen tunic with the tricolor border that day, turquoise, deep leaf green and orange twined in vines. I remember it like yesterday.

It was a spring day of the kind whose scent signals to children the coming of summer, calling them outdoors as strongly as musk calls the deer. The streams suddenly run wild and muddy, the air carries sounds again, and on every hillock and bank life unfurls in a thousand shapes and colors under bright sun; the world is set free once more, and no one feels freer. But when we were some halfway up, and I had long forgotten that there could be darkness or danger in the world, we heard hooves crash on the path behind us, and our names shouted through the trees.

It was my shadow-mother. She was in full armor, and on her face was what I knew right away was the look of the battlefield, though I had never seen it before. She snatched up my sister Artira and me, commanded the others to run back to the Hearthstone, hiding if they heard anyone in the woods, and spurred her horse to a gallop down the mountain while we clung.

The courtyard was turmoil; people ran out with weapons as if the Enchians had invaded, others called for kin, still others stood dazed, gripping each other by the shoulders in shock. No one seemed to see us. Artira began to cry, and I consoled her, kissing her hair which was my father's gold spun finer, though I felt like crying myself. All I could know was that what Mama had feared must have happened.

My shadow-father Esora-e came staggering through the gate, unarmored, but armed. He had dirt in his black hair, and more caked in a crust on his face and moustache, except where tears had washed clean trails through it. *"The die has no mercy!"* he howled, and flung his sword down on the flagstones with a clash. That started most of the people in the courtyard exclaiming, and Artira clung harder to me. Then he saw us, and weeping to the God-In-Him to give him guidance, he pushed through the crowd.

He had the footman Sichera-e take Artira, but carried me up to my room in trembling arms. We sat by the window which overlooks the first gentle slope of Hetharin. I can see now why he told me then, if I imagine myself him looking into them, Karani's eyes, Tennunga's too, and yet with that part that is from none of us. So resolute; I must tell him. I was always one to know everything that happened around me, as soon as I could.

That morning I had filled my vase with a fistful of yellow lupines, and the room was full of their fragrance. To this day I never have lupines in a vase near me. Smelling them indoors brings that day back to me, unfailingly, in full.

He said, "Your father is dead."

There is a moment of numbness that comes right after. One might think "Oh," and nothing else, as I did; or else see the outward significances of the happening without emotion; it occurred to me, for instance, that now I would become demarch as soon as I was twenty. I am bearing up very well, I thought, and felt suddenly older and more grown-up, a proud feeling such as the steel man of the legends must have had when he first saw the missiles of his enemies bounce off his naked chest, but cold, like donning armor without ever having seen a battle.

Yet while Esora-e was telling me the story, I wondered such things as why Daddy himself wasn't, since, having been there, he could tell it best. Knowledge is not simply a matter of chalk and charcoal, but levels, like lake water, differing in warmth at different depths. I knew what a butterfly cut was from seeing it done on the ground; I could imitate the motion using a stick for a sword. But I did not know how to do it. In the same sense, I knew my father was dead, and yet he was a great warrior, and young: immortal, in other words. He would always be with me, strong and wise and golden-haired. Such things are eternal to children; they can imagine nothing else.

"A heart-stab," he said, "the quickest, easiest way. He'd hardly have had time to feel anything. One stroke will do it if you're bare-chested, the aiming's easy, from behind you can take your time. With one of those little Enchian blades, made just for that; they make them by the thousands there. Experts, they are, masters! They knew they couldn't kill him any other way."

My shadow-father raised his hands and cursed all dark work, calling on Saint Mother, All-spirit, my father's soul and Shininao, in whose beak he was now clutched, to loose their ill-wish on every murderer, until words failed him and he laid his head down on the window-ledge and howled as I had never seen an adult do. They had been friends from birth, like Mana and me. Though I was weeping myself I put my arms around him and kissed his soiled hair, to comfort him; I remember I got grit in my teeth. Panting, he sprang up and grasped my hand, and led me down to the courtyard. "I wish we could spare you this," he said hoarsely as we went. "But an Enchian backstabber chose otherwise." By the yard's south wall there was a linden tree, in whose shade we would lay in state our dead.

The silence reminded me of when he'd been underwater, last year. But this did not end. Servants just out of session and staff who had been working late still wore their white-bordered kerchiefs; the masons who had been repairing the portico rail stood with their hands empty, tools strewn at their feet. The warriors returned one by one, empty-handed, clasping forelocks. All the scullions of the kitchen stood in a row, their hands spotted with bits of vegetable. No one wept; this was still shock, not yet sunk into belief. Life stood still as death.

He looked as if he had spread out his robe to take a nap in the shade, except that his long limbs all lay straight, which they never did when he slept. On his chest in the center of the older demarchic scar was a nick from which trickled a single drop of blood, such as one might get playing with a kitchen knife.

"He's not dead," I thought. "I thought he was dead the last time, and he wasn't. He's asleep. I know him best, I'll wake him." Expert I was at slipping out of elder fingers; now I twisted out of Esora-e's, ran and knelt beside my father. He was pale; but I had seen him paler before, sick. In the breeze the flecks of sunlight from between the leaves of the tree played on his face, and the bright curls on his forehead stirred. I would wake him, and he would blink and smile and say "Chevenga," and ruffle my hair. I took his shoulders, kissed his cheek and said "Daddy, wake up," then watched for his eyelids to flutter open.

Several people gasped, and I felt eyes burning on my back; someone called me. That angered me. He may be your demarch, I thought, but he's *my* father. Then I felt myself snatched up by Esora-e. A rage as quick and blinding as lightning made me curl my fist to strike him; but I felt a wetness on my fingers. I looked. My hand wore a glove of scarlet.

His back was cloaked with it. I saw when the funerary

apprentices arrived with the bier, and lifted him onto it. They bent him forward to show the people; between his spine and his shoulder blade was a slit which opened slightly, loosing a last red gush, as he was lifted. The scratch on his chest had come from within, made by the tip of the blade running through him from behind.

When fresh game is brought in for the stew-pot, one may notice how the movements of the carcass, while following those of the hands that carry it, are reminiscent of the way the animal moved when it was alive; the bones and sinews retain in the same form after all. So my father moved in the hands of the apprentices, his shining head lolling on the arm that cradled it, his arms seeming to flex as they were crossed on his chest. By his blank face one would have said he did not care what was done to him; there was nothing within, I saw now, to care, like a puppet without a hand.

I wonder if death would be less cruel if it transformed us in some obvious way, such as turning us brown like plants, so that no child could ever mistake a corpse for a sleeper and then be struck by the truth while the lost one seemed so near. This thing that bore such a striking resemblance to my father was not him, I understood now, but only that which rots if it is not burnt, the leaf fallen from the tree. *He* was gone, never to be seen again; *he* had been taken away by Shininao, his soul dissolved to return its energy to the pool of the life-force, finished with this form; *he* was no more.

I went light-headed then. It seemed to me that all I saw around me was unreal, only a design painted on a great round curtain, behind which lay I knew not what. I heard the crashing thud of my shadow-father flinging himself to the ground, and his harsh scraping cries; I saw, vaguely, my mother's white tunic with orange, turquoise, green and now scarlet as well, browning on the edges. Her touch on my head was feathery. I looked again at the corpse of Tennunga, and saw it change.

My eyes had drawn it nearer and clearer, as a sphere of crystal lying on the palm magnifies one portion of skin to the exclusion of the rest. Doubting my eyes I tried to rub them, and found the back of my mother's hand. Yet the sight did not alter.

The face was similar, but different, the nose smaller; it

had shades of my mother, as if I had again become her, and saw something of myself in the husband I had loved. The features looked less jovial, and more careworn. Strangest of all, his hair, everywhere—on his arms, between his legs, in the brows and lashes and fine soft curls—was pure black, the color of a moonless and starless night, setting off even more the death-pallor of his skin.

He was not my father. I had never seen his face before. But I pitied him, and loved him, and felt somehow that if I saw him ever again, even as little as his hand brushing by me in the marketplace, I would know him. And though there was horror in the sight of his corpse, as with any, there was a grace too, brought by some kind of peace about him, which there was not in my father's.

Then he was gone into blackness, leaving only the memory like the after-image of the sun in closed eyes. I found myself being carried in Sichera-e's arms, my face buried in his shoulder. He took me to my parents' room.

I remember how it was full of Tennunga's presence, his arm rings and ivory comb and kerchief on the table, two of his linen shirts strewn over the bed. What had been permanent had become transient, though; tomorrow Sichera-e would store it all away. Now he watched over me. He says I was dry-eyed, but my small brows knit, as if puzzling over something, though this ended after I picked up my mother's mirror, which being made of Arkan glass threw perfect reflections. One could say, I think, I chose to find that black-haired man.

IV

The people feel the demarch as a part of themselves living; if he dies they feel a part of themselves die.

The couriers were gone even before I saw his corpse, and Assembly went back into session at once, with my Aunt Tyeraha taking up the Crystal. In Tiryina there was almost war; some of the Demarchic Guard were posted there, and a number went berserk, held only from sacking the nearest Tor Enchian village by others.

In the cities the people wrapped their heads in black, closed the markets and workfasts, wept in the streets, did the spirit-dances of anger and of grief. And everyone, at first, clamored for war, saying that this if anything was an attack. We are not used to assassinations, unlike Lakans, say, who hardly look up from their fields, not feeling struck at themselves.

His funeral was held the next evening. For the day he had lain in flowers for the people to see, one by one as he had liked to do in life. It took the whole day for all who came, to pass. It was my grandmother who touched the torch to his pyre, seeing him out of this world as she had seen him into it. The ashes were gone in half a day, to farmers for scattering over their fields; he'd had a name, for a strong life-force.

My family went the next three days being entirely cared

for, as per custom. Then came my aunt's Kiss of the Lake; I had the rare fortune to see it done twice one year.

Enjaliansi, King of Tor Ench, swore the highest oaths that the murderer had acted alone and unknown. There were no answers to be got out of the man; after using his one surprise stroke on my father he'd had to do what assassins are not used to, look into a warrior's face instead of her back. My mother had killed him with her knife. I remembered the blood on her shirt. Sure enough, being armed had saved her; just not my father.

The assassin had wanted to avenge an elder brother my father had killed in the war, and lacking the courage for open challenge, had nursed his anger over years into peacetime; I suppose he blamed my father for his own cowardice, too, in the backwards logic of the truly small-minded. I have sustained only one anger over a long time, of which the killing of a brother was only part. This anger, lasting over so many years of peace, for something any warrior would do, is the worst madness: chosen.

I suspect also he might have wanted to make a name for himself. I have met that kind. To burn himself a fiery place in our memory forever, just so his life left a mark (though that killed him); if so, he certainly succeeded with me. He twists his knife in my heart whenever there is something I should have done for or shown my father. This is why I do not give his name. I will have no part in granting his wish.

To show goodwill, Enjaliansi had the man's wife, children and remaining brothers all beheaded; goodwill, he said in answer to my aunt's remonstrations, cannot be conveyed in half measures. Those with power, I have noticed, like to remind everyone of it. But at least it meant he still wished peace. After many bitter debates, that hurt to hear, the war vote went a strong charcoal.

Three of my father's wisdom teeth went to my remaining parents, and one to me. That was his known wish, though he had not expected to die so soon. That he had never written a will was no matter, since being demarch he had nothing to bequeath. His ivory comb was my mother's, in name; now she gave it to me.

I started to know life would never be the same. Grief aged, darkening like meat; I began to wish back the day he had died, when life had been recently enough disturbed to resemble the innocent time before. In the morning when I should have seen him kiss my other parents at dawn, in Hall where he should be holding the crystal, just before sundown when he and I should be chasing the last edge of the day up the mountain together, I felt him killed again, killed and killed, the truth of it ground into me like the sword-stroke practiced a thousand times.

As well I had my own reason for wanting time to slow: I was measuring it. I had made an estimate for myself of thirty, the number I have always gone by. Thirty years, to a seven-year-old, is a long time; I'd hate to have learned at twenty-five. But I was suddenly aware that days added up to moons, and moons to years, something I had never given a thought before. I was never again scolded for dawdling. People say it is my nature to hurry; I suppose it is now, again like swordwork.

None of the thought-out reasons for keeping my fore-knowledge to myself entered my head then; I said nothing, and it would be common knowledge if not for this, only because I felt everyone had enough to bear. I remember thinking, "It will just make Mama sadder. Let it wait. It's not going to go away."

On the training ground, Esora-e and Urakaila sword-sparred to inspire us. This usually gave me joy; now I found myself asking, "What are they doing?" Then wrestling with Mana I thought, "What am *I* doing?" and found my heart not in this either. He kept beating me, miming breaking my neck or crushing my throat with the usual glee; yet it did not even anger me, and I couldn't find it in me to serve him the like. Each time I had him at my mercy he would somehow squirm loose, as if my hands somehow lost their strength when I must finish him. It was the same with Sachara. I felt Esora-e's eyes on me.

Afterwards I tried to slip away. The thought that filled me was that I might be a coward. My ethics came all from the heart, in those days, and were very simple. I would climb Haranin and walk along the edge of the cliff, I decided, and if I found it to be true I would throw myself off. As it was Esora-e caught me at the gate, having waited there. Dismissing my friends, he led me into the ante-chamber, where the Sword hangs.

He, of course, feared the same, but had an idea why it

might be. What children witness can shake them to the bones. So close to death, even one who has showed great promise might lose all heart for getting near it again. To his mind, it was his fault, if this were so with me, for letting me near the corpse.

There was no one in the room now. I remembered the feel of the Sword from a year before, the sound of the chains like a brook's trickle. Yet now it had a stain on it; I felt a flash that I know now to have been enlightenment, filling in the other half of an understanding that I had not known was only half. What I was learning to do was what had been done to my father.

I thought of my bright promise, the fame I would win, the polished wristlets I would get on my graduation, Chirel, forged in the perfect curve which extended forms the Circle; my skin went hot and cold, and didn't seem my own. All lies, I thought; masks worn by death. My own body, being shaped into a killer's; to see that tore me from my very self, the joy of training a betrayal. Even my name was a thing of war, and I had no other. I wanted to cry for Mama, as warriors do not do, or flee into some warm cave, like the one I had crept out of not so long ago.

Esora-e put his hand on my shoulder. "What is it, lad?"

"I never want to be a warrior," I said. With my eyes buried in my hands I could not see his face. I heard his long deep breath, though, a readying one like before a hard fight. "Well," he said at last. "That took courage at least. You could have told me you were having a bad day. Look at me, lad, and tell me why."

"I never want to kill anyone."

His moustache twitched; this he had not expected. His eyes were light grey-blue, fierce and weathered, though he was still young then. I thought of how he liked to show off his scars, told his war stories grinning, spoke of "full-splitting the Enkil" and blood fountaining, while my mother pursed her lips. I thought of my father. I'd picked a flower on the mountain; he said, "You have killed it. Up here where the season is so short, it takes a long time for them to grow back . . . . Well, there are more. But never forget what you're doing. That's the hardest thing, in war: never forgetting what you are doing." He understands best, I thought, he always does. Did; now he is picked.

"Anyone?" Esora-e said. "Even if he plans to kill you?"

He spoke my father's name, "What he did was twice wrong. Murder, and for unworthy hate. But we kill for the same reason Saint Mother gave us the Sword: life, and only in fair fight within our borders. Play that out, lad. You have before."

I did as he said, imagining, as a child will, a giant of an enemy. I parried the blows as always, but when the time came to strike him down, my hand in my imagination went weak, as it had in reality with Mana. "I'd be useless," I said. "I couldn't win."

He said, "Play it properly. He will kill you, if you don't him. You know that."

This time I made the enemy truly dangerous. Then it went as it always had before; feeling for him washed out of my heart, while his sword looked for a way to cut off my life. But afterward as he lay dead, I saw him on a pyre like my father's, heard his spouses and his small children weeping, and felt remorse to my bones. Yet then would come the next, and the next after that, and each would be the same. I would never tire, for that would be choosing death, but keep going, kill, regret, kill, regret, all my life. Never let it be said children can see nothing of their future.

In this tangle there had to be a thread of pure rightness somewhere; so I had been taught. For a long time I thought furiously, my hands curled into fists, until I found it, shining with truth's magnificence. "There shouldn't be any wars."

I thought his face would light up with inspiration, as my heart had. Instead he laughed, a bitter sound, and pulled a lock of my hair. "Nothing truer!" he said. "Yet those pesky foreigners keep attacking us! You'd think they'd never heard the wisdom of the great sage Chevenga."

I'd thought it was brilliant; certainly undeserving of mockery. As always, anger made me stubborn. "When I'm demarch," I said, "I'll end it. That's what Saint Mother really wanted."

His dark brows went up under his fore-curls. "Will you? By not being a warrior?" He smiled again. "Ah, I think I understand. You'll go visit Astyardk in Laka, and charm him into stopping his thugs from raiding our farmfasts.

When Enjaliansi lays claim to Miniya or Asinanai because it was inside the old empire a thousand years ago, you'll say, 'You can't have it, but I don't like killing people, so let's not have a war, shall we?' You'll go find the herd-raiders and sweet-talk them: 'I've given up the sword, so will you good fellows kindly stop absconding with our sheep?' "

He was still mocking me. "I'll make them listen," I said, stabbing three fingers of my sword-hand into the stone floor as I had seen Servants do on their desks when making a strong point. "Like when two of us quarrel and Mama makes us be the other: I'll say 'Be me, and I'll be you.' "

"So that you will gain understanding of why they abscond with our sheep, and they, why we don't like it." He laughed again. "Don't look at me like that. It's not you I'm making fun of, but your age. Well, you've spoken and I've listened; now I will speak and you will listen." He took my face between his hands, callused from the grips of weapons, his eyes turning the grey of storms.

"You think there is always a parent standing over people who dispute. But with you and some greedy tyrant, there will be none. This is foreigners we speak of, 'those who will not listen to your words of justice and sense.' She was right; they came.

"While you were showing off your naivete you also insulted your ancestors. Do you think you were the first to think of making peace?" I felt myself turn red, thinking of the stone demarchs, grave and beautiful, in the shrine. "But it cannot be done without a sheathed sword at one's side, to show the other he has something to gain by being reasonable. Otherwise the terms he will demand, in the end, are all our land and all of us as slaves. All-spirit, why do I argue? You know your history better than that. No: you just said *you* didn't want to kill.

"Well, all right, no one has to do everything; we serve each other best by each doing what he is suited for, right? So if you know your best talent, shouldn't you use it?"

Knowing what he was leading up to, I did not answer. "Of course you should. And what are you better at, than fighting?" He was right. I was good enough at my book-studies, but not spectacular, not even showing singular brilliance in one subject; I was competent enough in the harp and flute and making things with my hands; I had no other uncommon gift to give. Then something came to me. "Making friends," I said. It was true; I had succeeded in befriending everyone I had ever wanted to, as long as I could remember.

He waved that away. "That's a trait, not a skill. And you can't make friends with foreigners who want your land. Oh, they might fake it; then when you are fooled, thinking how kind and understanding they are, they'll stab Yeola-e in the back. Of the skills, from which come callings, you are best at fighting. Do you deny that?"

I signed charcoal, but said, "I have a calling. I will be demarch."

"Ah, yes, well," he said, smiling, "I was coming to that. Tell me, lad, will you send out others to do what you yourself will not?"

It fell to us to command; thus we became warriors. I remembered whose words those were, and felt weak and sick again.

Plenty of demarchs have not been warriors, including my aunt. The old age of the warrior-demarchs ended with Notyere; it became legal again only a century and a half ago, and will likely never again be compulsory. But my grandmother and father had chosen to live by the old ethic. So, from further back than I could remember, had I.

"Imagine the Enchians invade, and you send out an army, to die on the furrows while you sit easily in the safe Palace. The numbers are even and it could go either way, but we lose and ten thousand die. Those who are left bind up their wounds, and wonder what went wrong. 'I know one thing,' one will say. 'Fourth Chevenga would have been a great warrior had he not quit his training; everyone who saw him as a child knew it. Another leader good as Tennunga—he can make friends with anyone, you know—think how today would have gone differently, if we'd had one.' Another will say, 'My father got killed by an Enchian, and *I* didn't quit *my* training.' All down the line they will curse you; and why not? You will have denied them your best service.

"Think of those who should envy you! 'I wish I'd had the strength and quickness and cleverness *he* was born with,' they will say. 'I'd have a better chance of living, and all of us a better chance of winning, if I did. And he—the demarch!—who can be expected to do his best, if *he* won't?' " I threw my hand up between his to clutch my brow, tears burning my eyes.

"You were bred to be a warrior. Your blood-parents— too gentle, she is, and he was, they wouldn't tell you . . . He, and Naingini before him, married warriors so that their children would have it easier as warriors. Why do you think we still keep the stream-trial? Not by chance, will you win the tournaments and gain the promotions and be loved by all who fight under you. Now you refuse your ancestors' gift. Tell me, what would Tennunga think, if he saw this?"

I wanted to feel wind in my hair, in a fall from some great height. But he held me so I could not even turn my eyes away.

"We are all bound to duty. Should you turn from it, you shall have been proven a coward, for all you are fearless of death; a coward is, after all, one ruled by fear of what he must do. In the end, my son and Tennunga's, I do not think you are; grief will turn anyone's head for a time. But in the end, it lies with you to prove it. Whatever hinders you, you have to conquer, or fail entirely." With that he let go and walked away, leaving me alone with the Sword, which swung slightly on its chains.

As I climbed Haranin, his words lingered in my ears, but it was the words of the dead that rang truest through my heart. "As always, you choose."

I had thought them harsh words: now I knew they were tender. All who reared me loved me; but only he had understood me. Now I knew fully how I was alone.

The wind sang through the crags, growing cool; clouds covered the sun and the many-hued striations of the rocks turned dull. Past the tall pines and then the stunted ones I picked my way up following an old worn footpath. On the cliff's edge I sat, dangling my legs, the scythe of the Lake and the anthill Terera lying below, paled by distance.

I felt my limbs whose strength showed when I wrestled, my hands that were cleverer than anyone else's at hot hands and fivestones; tightening my arms beside me I took my weight onto them, while a hawk flying far above the green talus below hung tiny as a dust-speck between my feet. I flexed my muscles, which I had always thought were mine. No; Esora-e was right, he had only followed what I had been taught before. But my father was right, too. Even in the time of my greatest helplessness, my path always has one last fork.

As always, I would choose: take the Sword, or leap. My life was bound to the demarchy, and the demarchy to the Sword; but I was not necessarily bound to life, less so now than most. Leaning, I pushed myself forward a little, so that my haunches were just on the edge. Had the right wind blown then, my story would have been this short. As it was none did, but for a moment I leaned that way, and thought I was gone.

My heart came up to my throat and there was a rushing like a waterfall through my ears; half unaware I scrabbled back from the edge with all the speed bred and trained into me. The ground seemed tenuous beneath my feet, as if the nothingness beyond its edge somehow made all solids near it dubious, so I clung to a rock, clenching my eyes shut.

The wind filled with song: the notes of the Senaheri singer, one the dark and steady tone like a stone flute's, the other soaring high and bitter like the wind itself. Bound to one core like those of a jewel, facets of my life flashed in my mind: my turquoise, blue and purple chlamys, the height of the mountain racing in my legs after the climb, the oyster of the chicken in honey sauce, Assembly Hall, the marketplace, wrestling on the sweet warm ground with Mana, the swelling of pride as I mastered one more hard move. From the green land near me all the things and people I knew called me to return to them; from the blue land beyond the hook of the Lake reaching to the sky, all those I did not know yet called me to discover them, their voice the breath of All-spirit; all called, that as one is named Yeola-e. "Do we defend it grimly, like a miser his gold? No; stiffness is the way of death. We choose, always we choose. Do we subsist and grasp? No; for goods are not happiness. We celebrate life, and live a celebration." Life sang to me, and though I covered my ears with my hands I could not shut it out of my heart. There it roared like flame and went silvery, and my tears came entirely from outside myself, like those we weep hearing music too beautiful to bear.

When the wind's voice was a whisper again I lay my head back against the rock and wept. For Tennunga, who had lost all this, the first tears that I shed mourning him were for his loss, not my own. For myself, fated to lose it too soon. For all people who ever died, whom for the first time I imagined in their terrible number, more multifarious than any living crowd could be: people dressed in fabrics no longer weavable, making livings incomprehensible to us who lived now; a thousand peoples that died as one with their devices and arts and treasure beyond counting of knowledge, who were never mourned properly because too few were left to mourn them. I put my forehead to my knees and wept for all who must die: all who lived.

In the story of the Fire as my grandmother had told me, power had been in the hands of kings so that the people could do little; but all had known it was coming. I asked her what they did. "No one knows it all," she answered, "but the books say something, and one can imagine, if one plays them out. Some put it out of mind, excised any thought of it from their lives and lived as if it were not. Some began to live like warriors, fast and reckless and without thought for tomorrow; and in those days there were many more fast and reckless things to do, many more diversions and entertainments to help one forget. Some went insane, world-riven, turning frozen or berserk; some withered inwardly and died. Some prepared for it, building strongholds deep in the land, and feared it so much they yearned for it, just to end their fear. Some debated and protested bravely to stop it. Some prayed, and trusted in gods to prevent it. Some resigned themselves to it, and some just hoped it wouldn't come, not knowing that it was certain."

"But they all died," I said, "so in the end what they did didn't matter."

"No," she said. "But while they lived, it did."

Though in my life I have sometimes strayed from it, doing virtually all of these things one time or another, I made the first of my personal laws then. I had, as far as I could tell, perhaps half the time others did; so in that time I must do two times as many things and love people two times as hard, to make up for it. I can think of it in no words but these, childish as they sound, because they are the ones in which I thought it first.

I went down to the School. The Sword hung black, between walls of plain white, unadorned, unfurnished, ungraven. We do not surround our sigil with scenes of glorious battle, of splendid triumphs with treasure and captives, of the nobility of war nor even the drama. The Sword hangs plain, neither celebrated nor despised, neither reproaching nor praising, neither dark nor light, but equal parts of both, each entwined with and containing the other. The pain is there, and the loss; likewise the victory, and the gain. "Never forget what you are doing," my father had said. Never had he said, "Don't do it," or "Do it." I had not known one half; then when I'd learned it I had forgotten the other. Now I saw both.

I curled my fingers around the grip, thinking, "Esora-e wants me to fight because he can't think of any other path for me, and because he wants to see me famous, not because he sees this. He doesn't. Well, I've seen it, so I'll fight for it, and nothing else; if he doesn't like it, too bad, but I bet he doesn't even notice. All-spirit, I *am* going to be a great warrior: he's one of the best in Yeola-e and I understand more than he does. I'd better renew my oath." Once again it lifted with my hand, more easily; I felt my heart purged and still like clear air after a storm.

Some days later in training we got wooden sticks an arm long. I was swinging mine absently, waiting for the lesson to begin, when I aimed it at Nyera's head, the closest at hand, for a joke. To my horror she did not duck, but stood dead-still like one blind. I was not quick enough then to check its flight, and so for an instant had to helplessly watch what my hands did, the knobbed end streaking in, an arm, then a hand, then a finger away from her blond ringlets. It struck with a whack that hummed through my fingers.

She was knocked forward one stumbling step; then she turned around, her face first pop-eyed with astonishment, and then black with rage. To her credit, she dropped her stick and had at me with her hands. Being angry while I was bewildered, she was on top in no time and all but grinding my face in the dirt when Esora-e pulled us apart.

He got an earful of truth without asking. "He hit me with his stick!" "I didn't mean to hit her, she didn't duck!" "I was looking the other way!" "So you should have ducked anyway!" "How could I? You sneaked up behind me!" "I wasn't sneaking, you knew I was there, you're just trying to get me in trouble!" "Sir, he's *lying*, I wasn't looking and he knows it!" "You still should have ducked!" And so on.

To my surprise, Esora-e was looking darkest at me. I looked darkly right back; these last days had hardened me. By this time all the children in the ground had gathered around, standing on tiptoe to see over each other's heads. "Lad," he said to me, "if it came from where she couldn't see, how could she know to duck?"

As I opened my mouth I found I had no words for it, and groped for the closest I could think of. "By feel, sir."

The angry knit of his brows turned to a puzzled knit. "What do you mean?"

"By the feel without touch . . . you know! Like when you watch a fight with your eyes shut."

I looked all around, and saw every face gazing at me as mystified as if I had spoken Lakan, Esora-e's most of all. Even Mana; I wanted to kick him. It made me feel like a foreigner, or a lunatic. Presently Esora-e said, "Will you demonstrate this for us?"

He blindfolded me with a black sweat-rag, making sure to leave no cracks of light, and took up his stick. First he made me point at it, and follow the path of its end with my finger as he moved it. Then he tried blows, the slowest that have ever come at me in my life, which I parried with my own stick just as I had been trained. Spitting, he checked my blindfold, then tied another on top of the first, tight enough that it almost hurt, and tried again: in front, behind, faster when he understood he could. Finally he drew his sword, and though he never brought the cut through fully, checking it just before it touched my stick, the proof was made. By then I was enjoying myself, and daring him to try harder, while the children all laughed and yelled in delight.

Instead his sword went into its scabbard and he was

gone, his running footfalls thumping towards the door of the School.

He brought out all the Teachers, even the senior of that time, Azaila Shae-Chila, and made me show them. Blinking in the light afterwards I saw the sweaty-chested older students who seemed grown-up to us, gazing at me no less astonished than the children had.

After the class I was sent to Azaila, who then began to teach me how to use what I had. He said little, mostly teaching by doing, from then on, his nimble crack-skinned arms guiding my small, smooth, clumsy ones. It was Esora-e who spoke, that same day, taking me into the shrine.

We went through the standing stones, the old with their worn words, the new still shining. In the grove was a sculptor with a half-cut statue of my father, being carved where it would stand, to match the spirit of the place. Here and there were abstainers, with their white robes and rough-hewn stone cups, walking slowly or sitting in trance in the branches of the ancient trees, the only sign of them visible to those below, a crystal hung on an eye-high bough.

"You thought everyone had weapon-sense, didn't you?" he asked me, when we had found a tree for us and climbed it. I signed chalk. His eyes were bright as if he had just been fighting, his cheeks flushed. "Azaila has it, as do other old Teachers. But they have to train fifty years for it. You were born with it. Do you understand what that means?"

I thought vaguely that I might be posted at the door of Hall when an envoy came, to spot knives in sleeves, and saw no cause in that for all his excitement.

"No blind spots," he said. "Better judgment than anyone, two senses for their every one, knowing always if someone's hiding a weapon, never blind even in the dark . . . And everything else you'd need, you have." He took my face between his hands, and dropped his voice to a whisper. "You will be the greatest warrior in the world."

I don't believe such a claim could ever be proven; the world is too big. Nevertheless, Esora-e set himself to the task of making me it. Azaila was never party to this, nor any of the other Teachers I had; but if he took me off for extra work, that was his business.

It was hard. I was sick and dizzy all the time at first, feeling sometimes that all my sinews would tear, one by one, like the threads of a rag ripped across. Sometimes he would make me eat too little food for a time—he watched me serve myself from the pot one day, then reached over and took away half—or fast entirely, or go without water, to teach me to disregard the body's wants, and thus be free of them. Several times he locked me in a cellar chamber of the Hearthstone that was pitch-dark and soundless, with only a blanket and a cup of water, sometimes for several days.

Yet never did he purposely injure me, humiliate me before others, or do anything without a reason that inspired me. He taught me pride in these things, not shame, and never let me forget he loved me; nor did he ever let up and make it too easy, and by my honor, never did I. It should be understood, my shadow-father was one of those people who speak gravely of the hardship of war, how we only do it out of necessity, how it is sacred, and so forth, but one can tell enjoys both the act and the thought of being a warrior, whether he admits it or not. To this day I question his choosing an ambition for me, and have resented it. But I cannot say, had he asked my consent, that I would not have agreed at least to aspire to be the best in Yeola-e; and in the end more good has come out of it than bad. I'd be dead several times over if not for that training.

When I was eight, I told my mother of my foreknowledge. She did not disbelieve for a moment, understanding I had inherited her gift.

She didn't weep, and her embrace stayed gentle. I can guess what she thought: I am only going to witness it: I can't melt to tears in front of the one who will live it. That is not what I should teach him. That is strength. People often outlive their spouses. But to outlive one's grown children, as most likely she would do me, is to see the order of life inverted.

Then she asked me, "This was a year ago. Why didn't you tell me then?"

"You were grieving for Daddy. I thought I should wait."

Her eyes gazed, widening. "You did not come for help today. You came only because you thought I should know."

The thought of help had not crossed my mind; I could not see how any was possible. "*I* can bear it," I said. It occurs to me now that in my piping eight-year-old voice these words must have had the tone of "*I* can reach the door-handle," or "*I* can fasten my own clasps."

She took my face in her hands, and her cheeks were suddenly bright in the firelight, with tears. I reached to wipe them away, which made them come harder, stabbing my heart. I had a horrible thought: I had done wrong telling her. Not knowing what else to do, I wrapped my arms around her neck and said, "Before I die I'll do many, many things, I swear. I'll do everything two times as fast and love everyone two times as much and be the best Ascendant and the best demarch except for Daddy and a great warrior and leader so no one will forget me and on top of all that I'll marry in a six and have twenty children, and a hundred grandchildren. . . ." She drew me into her arms, pressing her lips to my brow. "My steel child—yes. You will. I believe you. You are worthy, even with that, even only for a decade."

I know now what she must have considered, when she heard, for the good of the people. Yeola-e would suffer a death like my father's again, inevitably, if I became demarch. One word to the right people, and I would never be approved.

But instead she said, "Just remember: once out, it cannot be called back. If you become inclined to tell, think first of everything it will touch—the demarchy, your loves, your training, all people who touch you and how all the world regards you—and consider carefully whether you ought to, for others' sakes or your own. If you're at a loss, you can come to me. Do you understand?"

I signed chalk, and swore to do as she said. That night I lingered in her room, lying under the wicker chair—I no longer fit kneeling—and played with the fire as in the old days. Now and then she reached down to touch my hair. Never in my life have I felt more treasured.

That night I first had the dream which is my favorite of all, and recurs to this day. I was full-grown, and very tall: 634 years old, in truth. I stood on the long balcony of Assembly Palace, the high stone buildings of the town standing black against the silver-dappled Lake and the bowl of mountains spread out before me; in fact I was the king-pilaster, made of wood so ancient one cannot see its growth rings for its blackness, its girth too great to encircle with one's arms. I felt the thousand tiny paws of the ivy climbing my legs and chest and head, and the primeval grain within. How else could I have lasted so long? I had seen time crash and ebb at my feet, but the Hearthstone would never fall, and the people would still say, in whatever new language Yeoli became, "There stands Chevenga."

V

My mother always let us come and go freely in her bed-chamber. But one day, going there with an armful of fresh cedar branches for her, I found myself rebuffed. I under-stood when I heard whispers. There was a man inside.

I told myself there was nothing wrong, being old enough to understand. She was not yet thirty, and had no hus-band. What could I want, but for her loneliness to end? Yet a deep rage filled me. My father had died. I had known there would be grief, walked through its long dark passage with her, felt its purity. I could not conceive that it would be sullied this way: that she considered him replaceable.

Esora-e and Denaina had agreed to accept her choice, as long as the man was not objectionable to them. Like a teenager beginning, she took many lovers at first. I noticed only one thing they had in common: none were blond.

She would call in one of us to send for all the rest who were old enough to be introduced to him, and it was always, "First the eldest, Fourth Chevenga." I remember their big hands clasping mine, some steely, some fishy, some callus-crusted, some sending spines of pain through my hand-bones as their owners chose to show me their strength, as if I needed to know. I was civil, but always washed my hands afterward.

She never openly asked me what I thought of whom. But I was too perceptive not to see her gazing at my face as I met them; she had to think of us. I soon learned that if I put certain look in my eyes during the pleasantries, he would not get past the ivy-carven lintel. That gave me the chill of hardness, the same I'd felt hearing the news of my father's death. Too much power, too soon; a child feels the weight. Yet it awoke a pleasure in me too. Though I banished none of them without good reason, I could laugh to myself that I ruled their fates. Not a true cure to my pain—there could be none, but time—but a balm of a kind.

Then one day I thought, "I am not alone in this." My sibs and I had whispered, sometimes arguing. I thought of the class of Athyel children, ancestors of all Yeola-e: a society, few as they were. We were free Yeolis, entitled to gather, and to vote.

All my sibs who were six or better, I had sneak into my room at night. That was Artira, Senala-e, Naiga, Lanai, and Handaotha. I sat them all in a proper circle, unfastened my crystal and said, "A very serious matter has arisen, that touches every one of us." I had heard some Servant of Assembly say this in Hall, and liked its ring; it made them all quiet and gravely attentive, as I'd intended.

Once the question had been framed, they all began talking at once. It took much naked-handed use of authority to get them using the speaker's crystal properly. "Shadow-mama is lonely since Daddy got 'sassinated; she needs another daddy." "I don't want another shadow-daddy; blood-daddy combs me enough." "They need a fourth to take care of all us, 'cause all us are so many." "But what if he's mean?" "I didn't like the last one, his smile was like the taste of the throw-up you make when you've eaten too many raisins." "Shewenga, do we have to take whoever she wants?"

I grabbed the crystal. "No," I said. Satisfaction rang through me. "Remember the saying? *The people wills.* If we take a vote, she has to listen."

Thoughts and doubts filled their small features, that echoed in so many different mixes the familiar ones of our four parents. "Can we vote out all the rules?" said Sena, eagerly.

I grabbed the crystal again. This required walking a fine

line. "No. They were made for everyone. If you could steal other people's things they could steal yours; if we could kill each other there'd soon be none of us left; if no one said please and thank you we'd all be mad at each other all the time for being rude. Grown-ups do have *some* sense, you know.

"But this is about love, and even grown-ups aren't sensible about *that*." (I'd heard this from a grown-up.) "Besides, she's choosing *our* parent. She *has* to listen to us."

Then little Handaotha burst out, "Shadow-mama shouldn't marry *anybody*! It's not fair, Daddy losing his wife to someone else just because he's dead!" So expert children are, at speaking bluntly the unspoken thoughts of adults, or older children. We all fell silent.

Were I to write that I had no correct answer to this, I would be lying. We could not rekindle his life. Should she be alone for the rest of hers because of it? Probably I was the only one old enough to say this. But it stayed frozen behind the wall of my teeth.

Words were spoken that I regret hearing, let alone not rebutting, and I am sure my sibs do not wish their childhood folly laid out in ink. It lost order, for I forgot my duties as chairman, and we somehow fell into squabbling over who had made off with the best stone in whose collection, with Handa off in a corner crying and Artira comforting her while sending me vicious looks, Lanai and Naiga close to blows, and Sena waving the crystal and trying loudly to take my place as the voice of reason.

Still I kept my silence. I felt not that I was in darkness, but that I *was* darkness, and was not ashamed. "Why should I call order?" I was thinking. "This chaos suits me; it suits the world, that burned in the Fire; it suits children who have no sense, mothers who let strangers lie where fathers should, dead fathers. What does he care whether I call order, when he is nothing, like the smoke from a candle blown out, flowing up for a moment then gone?"

Sena whipped my crystal into my hands, crying, "*You* make them shut up! *You're* supposed to!" I didn't hear her words, only felt the pain, and an anger fast and formless as lightning. I struck her backhanded across the face; her eyes, Esora-e's grey, turned murderous; we flew together, fell over and milled on the floor like two dogs. That started Lanai and Naiga. My desk got heaved over, ink spilling over a sheepskin, century-old books flung like refuse. In time the room went strangely silent, and I felt adult fingers curl in my hair. Esora-e held me dangling in one hand and Sena in the other; Lanai and Naiga were likewise gripped by Denaina.

"I am sorry, shadow-father and -mother," I said. I had to think fast. "We all are. We were role-playing *The Deliverance of the Tinga-enil*, see, and it got somewhat out of hand." My shadow-mother tended to stand back in such matters, so it was Esora-e's eyes I looked into; they narrowed, suspicious. "It's not a real scene out of the play, but one we made up. See, the champion meets up with these two Enchian travelers, a warrior and a healer. The champion is wounded so he needs the healer, and the warrior falls in love with the champion, and the champion is in a hurry and wants to get up but the healer is trying to keep him down, and we all started taking our parts too seriously and Handa got upset because we hadn't given her one yet and we started arguing and—"

Esora-e cut me off with a chop of his hand. "Enough. Do you know you woke up the little ones? And ruined a sheepskin, the gift of the Hearthstone?" I made the sign of shame, and the others did likewise. "I started it," I said, holding out my hand. "Comb me." I was still enough myself to do that. Yet I felt a dark smugness as well, for succeeding at lying.

"You are the one who should be most aware of what you do and where you are," he said. "But you others are not much less to blame. Think on Chevenga's pain and your part in it: next time it will be all of you." He gripped my wrist, and said, "Your comb, Fourth Chevenga."

We stared at one another, unmoving as standing stones. I had only one comb.

"Wouldn't he have done this, lad?" he said. "Wouldn't he?" A whisper of dark unfurling wings seemed to touch the air in the room, as I drew my father's ivory comb slowly from my belt. Five, or even three years later, I would have the faculty of mind to shape words to make him understand what he touched. I offered it to him handle-first, like a weapon.

He always combed me hard, even for defying by a look. I heard wind whistle through the tines as it came down, and felt the fiery blow right to my bones. But the true pain came as he laid the comb in my stricken hand to return it to me, crowning his point. I think Handa saw, as children feel drama without understanding it, for she began crying.

All would have been very different, I think, had my mother been there. She would have caught me in my lie by reading my face, got the whole truth out of us, and settled it with her quiet warm sense, hurting no one in the end. I knew that, even as I lay scheming, the poison in me distilled bitterer still. She was not there. She was in Terera, visiting some man.

I gathered my sibs in a cedar stand on Hetharin the next day. It was winter, the snow up to our middles off the paths; good for keeping the debate short. When she chose a man, we decided, we would line up before her, and show her our vote on him. Subtle, yes, the question of whether she should marry at all nested hidden within the question of whom. Not honest, as I knew. Yet I conceived it.

As winter eased, softening the valley snow, one man lingered longer than the rest. He was Veraha Shae-Aniya, a stone-carver from Thara-e who'd found good work in Terera, and was about her age. I was softer on him than most: on meeting me, he had traced the line of my cheek with a flat wide finger and said, "I see Tennunga, there." My eyes must have said, "How would you know?", for he grinned awkwardly at me, then her, and said, "Well, I never got a commission to carve him, that's true. But I wanted to, so I did many sketches, and one low relief, just for myself. I still have them. . . ."

Now he was in her chambers constantly. Once I walked in and found them resting, her head on his shoulder, the coal-black hair that was on my own head as well spread in a fan across his muscular chest; he was a well-formed man, though more rounded than my father, with red-brown hair and beard.

Once when it was warm enough for the walk to be pleasant, he invited me to go to the Tereran market with him. Me alone, none of my sibs. I didn't need a day of meditation to guess why. I dressed as I would any day; why any special adornments, I was thinking, for him? As we turned from my door, he offered me his hand as is civil. I took it as is also civil, my small fingers buried in his big ones. He smelled of stone-dust and polishing oil and morning sweat. On the Terera road, it was all small-talk. He was well-versed in my childish accomplishments, so I guessed my mother had coached him. Trepidation sprang from his every pore.

So I answered sparingly, looked mostly away, even let him keep calling me "Ascendant," though the fact of my position probably worsened his nervousness. Let *him* do the courting, I was thinking; besides, who is a child to put an adult at ease? I felt him struggle between speaking to me as to a child and as to an adult on whose arbitration his fate depended, and basked in the chill glow of my power. He should have dunked my head in the falls.

He took me to the stone-sellers, and named all the different kinds for me. "My favorite is a silken white marble, pure as milk, that comes from a place called Krera, which is now in the empire of Arko. There's a whole mountain made of it there, and none anywhere else in the world, and it works like the Hermaphrodite's hair in your hands. Which do you think is the most beautiful?"

I knew nothing of carving, but a warm green stone with a grain that reminded me of the curving lines waves leave on a sandy lake-shore caught my eye, and I pointed it out to him.

"Malachite," he said. "The sea of the Earthsphere's tears, frozen to bear witness." Only an artist would speak like that, I thought snottily. He picked up the stone, turned it over in his fingers; then counted coins in his pouch.

So he means to buy me with a gift, I thought. Anger warmed through my cold. But he did not give it to me with a gushing smile as I expected, tucking it away in his satchel instead in a businesslike fashion. I soon forgot.

As we made the climb back up beside the falls, he sucked in his cheek, which was ruddy in faint spots, and bit its inside, which I'd come to know meant he was searching for words. I wasn't about to help him. "Well, it's been a good day, hasn't it, Ascendant?" he said finally. I signed chalk. "I have enjoyed myself, and you have too, I think, so I hope we are friends. Are we that? May we be that?" A clever start, however awkwardly delivered; for all I felt the urge, I could hardly say no.

"I suppose so," I answered; but as this came out it sounded uncivilly reluctant to my own ears, so I quickly added, "Yes. We are." He took my hands smiling, with a touch I liked in spite of myself, and said, "May we always be." I hope I never have a child like myself to contend with. That night, I called council.

"All-spirit be witness to this vote of free Yeolis," I invoked, and stabbed out my hand. I wish I could say none of them waited to see my hand before they put out their own.

What excuse could I make? The evil in me was formless, as such evils are, rising from a chaos of emotions not thought out. But it had form enough to direct my hand in a simple motion. As monarchy has its danger, so does demarchy, the danger of any power: that poorly conceived as the opinions of its wielder may be, he wields it.

So I signed charcoal, as did everyone else, and we marched into her chamber; it was only by luck he wasn't there. I shiver, imagining myself her, facing a phalanx of my own precious children standing still and straight as warriors, their snub-nosed faces grave as news of death, their six tiny hands turned irrevocably down.

The two points of red I knew from having felt them on my own cheeks rose on hers. My mother is a woman of few words, fewer still when she is moved. Now she said only, "Why?"

They all looked to me. I looked back at them, suddenly thinking, for one of the few times in my life, that I had done my share of the speaking and leading, and now someone else should take a turn. "I don't like him," Naiga blurted. "He doesn't belong here." "His hands smell of stone-dust," said Artira. "He's fat," said Handa. "He's mean." "He's pom . . . pous." "He's not as nice as Daddy."

Clear as air excuses these all were, most of them out and out lies. Yet though shame had begun to wake in me it was not enough to quench my anger, so like a coward I stood, content to let others voice the darkness in my heart without sullying my own tongue with it.

At first, I guess, this slander was too small a thing for her to be angry at, in the face of the emotion beneath it. Bad enough that she had lost her beloved; but to see her children's grief come out so—I know it would have shaken me. Yet maybe I would have learned to be as wise, had I got to her age. I can hope so. She asked us to be silent, sat down, and looked into the fire until the warmth in her cheeks faded. Then she said, "Yes, it is unfair. Why should I be able to get myself another husband, when you will never be able to get another father?"

We all stood startled, to hear what we felt put in words so much clearer than ours; it was like pushing against an opponent with all your might, only to have him give backwards, relaxed, so your own strength throws you over his head. So the greatest warriors and the greatest sages fight.

Her dark eyes gazed clear and open at me, sincere in this as in her love. Suddenly I was her, through the channel of her eyes and mine, and felt her loneliness, my loneliness. The light of my life extinguished. The marching of days regardless, the turning of months, the changing of seasons; the wound in my soul scarring, crimson easing to pink and black fading to grey; food regaining taste, and company pleasure. He is long dead, long gone. I still live, and need a living love.

With a tearing, I felt my soul washed clean; I saw the anger that had seemed as large as myself in its true size, the senseless tantrum of a child, delicious in its purity and release, but just a tantrum, after all. I took a breath, wiped my eyes and turned to my siblings. To my astonishment, their faces were still hard, unchanged as stone. Natural it was for me to assume they had just seen what I had, just as natural, they had not. They looked at me, their eyes saying, "We voted; speak our decision. You are demarch."

They were right. As my aunt argued the will of the people to foreign powers whether she agreed or not, I must argue my sibs' to my mother, for all the heart had gone out of me.

"We voted as we felt," I said. My mother looked into my eyes. Perhaps she can tell I no longer speak for myself, I thought; perhaps not. By law, it doesn't matter. I felt like a traitor twice over.

Later I found she did sense my change. Were she a politician of craft, she might have used me to turn the others. But she was too honest for that.

She talked sense into us: that nothing could bring Daddy back, that she should have love. The one thing that surprised her was when Artira said, "You used to let us come into your room. Now we have to tap, and you always send us away." That she admitted was unjust. Then she made us go off apart, and imagine ourselves her. There was no need for her to reciprocate; her mother had died when she was eight, and her father remarried. I turned quickly, wanting after all I had done to be the most willing. But she called me back. "You," she said, "play *him*. His ghost, or himself before, as if he had known somehow what was going to happen." With our eyes we shared my secret. "Imagine what you would want for your wife, afterwards."

I am married now, and love her like my lifeblood. How can I not want her to find a new love, once I am gone? I did not play Tennunga, not needing to; I would live the same. That showed me the full depth of my wrong, as she had intended.

If every parent had her strength, this would be a happier world. She didn't even make us take the vote again in her presence, just let us go. I led the others into my room again, took off my crystal and made them all lay their hands upon it with mine. "This vote is final," I said. "No one's allowed to go back on it; if it goes chalk for him we've approved him, die cast gates fast no words and all go home. No one will ever be mean to him again. Swear." They did, and we voted. It went chalk, unanimously.

The wedding took place on the solstice, a lucky day for a widow to remarry. A good crowd came to bless us. I remember how everything seemed charged with life: my mother's face beneath her crown of ivy and star-flower, flushed like a girl's for all the widow's black ribbon was twined with the others about her neck; the embroidered borders of his tunic, which men of his family had worn only for their weddings for three hundred years; the vows and the kissing of crystals; the four standing with their arms entwined in the circle of blue braid, as wheat kernels showered on them; then the wild of night and love-feasting, the drum weaving its sacred madness through ears and feet, body and soul, binding together those two parts that as in the Hermaphrodite are one, like the heartbeat of the world itself pulsing through its branching veins, us who live. As I danced on the mountain with my sibs, rancor and jealousy were as distant from me as death.

Life went on, and laughter smoothed off the first slivers of Veraha's awkwardness, and began bringing out his quiet form of strength. One thing he had to resign himself to: our free passage, into their room. Thinking now, I would call it more kind than just, but never again did my mother make us tap on the door. I don't know what she told him; perhaps that we had been here first. At the beginning we tested it, to make sure of our rights, at all hours; we kept catching them making love, until Sichera-e suggested to me that perhaps this was impolite.

We tested, as children will, to see how firm a hand he had. He soon learned the old step-parent's trick of, "Would your mother allow you to do that, if she were here? Tell the truth, now." With me, he was afraid of making some subtle but crucial mistake for which all of Yeola-e would suffer some day and, since my education was entirely out of his hands, wondered whether I had any use for him at all. He was frightened by me too. I remember overhearing him saying, "Was that child ever a child, Karani? One gets the feeling he understands things no one his age should." She just answered, "He's just like that." Most who raised me knew nothing of what, to a great extent, shaped me. I had chosen that.

So there he was, a new stepfather, too conscious of his position, stuck with one child who was inherently difficult to know how to befriend, yet who was leader of all the others. I don't envy him at all. One day, I suspect when he had been thinking about it too much, he said, "Fourth Chevenga, comb your hair. It looks a mess." He'd said it for no other reason than to show he was my stepfather; so, hardly raising my voice, I said, "It's no messier than yours," the truth, and went on without a break in stride. He must have thought before deciding to come after; in a little time, he opened my door, his cheeks flushed red, and said in a strained soft voice, "Your mother married me; I'm your father, in spirit. You must listen to me, and not answer rudely."

I had learned how to make quiet words cut from Esora-e,

and my store of pat phrases from Assembly. "Don't play
pretend, Veraha," I said. "You're not my father, never
were, and never will be; you are here only because you
were accepted. Never forget that, and don't presume on
your rights." He gave back a pace, stunned. I went back to
my waxboard-work, in the way the Assembly Palace
Workfast people did to hint I had haunted their offices too
long. For a time he stood staring, then he was gone.

I found out later to whom he spoke and what was said.
My mother was out on some business then; he would have
been too ashamed to go to her anyway, admitting a child
of nine had faced him down. But Esora-e, coming in
sweaty from training, noticed his look, and badgered the
story out of him. "Later we will laugh," he said, astonished but not surprised, "now, we must be angry. If he
runs roughshod over us now he'll grow up to do the same
to the people; he's got a strong sense of justice, but none
of power—other people's, that is. Here's what to do, Veraha.
Go back to his room. Don't talk or listen to him. Just pick
him up, tuck him under your arm and carry him outside.
If he hits you, hit him back, a little harder; make him feel
who's stronger. Behind the Hearthstone there's a flat place
where the stream pools deep. Take him there, and toss
him in. Then walk away without a word."

Veraha took the suggestion to the letter. Though I didn't
hit him, credit me for that, I squirmed with all my strength,
yelling all manner of things. But stone-cutting is good for
the arms. The water was scalding crisp on my skin.

Now it was my turn to be too ashamed to admit something to my mother. I slunk into my room by the window
like a half-drowned rat. At dinner I combed my hair with
great deliberation right in front of him; but not knowing
who had given me my comb, he missed the full significance, and merely gave me a satisfied nod, thinking he
had corrected me. That night I lay awake conceiving evil
plots. All futile; we had sworn.

My mother found out when my shadow-father mentioned my drenching to her in passing. I don't know what
she said to Veraha, but he never upbraided me without
good reason again. That night just before my bedtime he
and I made peace. He had a bear's embrace, that a child
could lose himself in, though I was not quite ready to
enjoy it. When we let go he looked about to do something,

but not sure; then just bid me good night, choosing not to. I forgot about it.

It was almost fall, my tenth birthday coming round. Late at night at the new moon, a faint sound on my dresser half woke me, but I fell asleep again. In the morning I remembered, and began to look there excited, in the hope of finding some magical gift that the sprites of sleep had brought. Then as I woke more fully, sober knowledge checked me; I was old enough now to have learned, albeit recently, how slim the chances of this were. Being grown-up, I thought, means no longer looking for that sort of thing, in fact not needing to any more. Putting aside my sadness, I rose, and opened the top drawer to take out a kilt. Green caught my eye: the magical thing was there. It was the malachite piece I'd picked out in the market in spring, carven into a hexagon smooth as mirror-glass, with the profile in low relief of my father.

I felt many things, as I gazed at it, and weighed it in my hand. But they were muted now, and mostly I felt its beauty. Now nearly everyone in the family has at least one such portrait, of someone they love; it's lucky he makes them small, so that when the war came they could be taken to safety. My mother has the best, of course. But I got one of the first. I went to him and kissed his hand, though he pulled it away.

Years later, when I was a man and we knew each other entirely except for my foreknowledge, we spoke of it. "I finished carving your Tennunga a few days after we bought the stone. But I couldn't give it to you then. I suspected you would have felt I was trying to buy into the household, like a worker buying a share. In the crassest of ways, too: with the image of your father, whose place I was taking, as if I could worm my way in by pretending to give him back to you."

"And now," I said smiling, "it comes clear you were entirely right." No one understands the power of art more, I suppose, than an artist. We laughed together, and he went on. "When we made peace after I threw you in the stream, I almost gave it to you. I wanted to badly, then, to win your forgiveness. But I saw that would be as much as saying your forgiveness could be bought, and you would have been offended, the stone cheapened in your eyes. Was I right then too?"

"Of course," I said, and we laughed again. Then he went serious once more, his red-gold brows knitting. "I . . . I did not carve it for such a small thing as to gain your love for myself. Though I should say, that is not a small thing—but it would have been for myself. I carved it for you, not to remember my currying favor, but to remember him. Only when I had made peace with all of you, could it mean all to you that I carved. Before that, we both would have lost out, wouldn't we?"

I signed chalk, and kissed his hand again. He tried to pull it away, but I was stronger now, and yanked him into a hug. The cold knowledge is always there: that, had he not insinuated his way into our household, he never would have had the chance to do all that made me love him, so I never would have. I remind myself that I chose my shadow-parents no more than I chose him, only the time of my birth making it different. In the winds of chance blow the seeds of families, and the cast of the die of proximity is everything. Veraha was here, so we got him. My mother eventually had three children by him: Makaina in 1537, Ilachesa in '39 and Masarao in '41.

When my grandmother found out the full story, she took me aside and asked what the greatest lesson for me in this was. Flushed with the joy of having made peace, I floundered. "That you can't bring back people who've died? That you shouldn't be mean no matter what? That children are just children?"

She kept signing charcoal and pursing her lips and saying, "Obvious, obvious, if you haven't learned that already you're an idiot, you've got good eyes, boy, open them," and so forth. "One would think you'd forgotten what you are," she said finally, making me begin to see.

My father had spoken of it, once when he'd taken me up on the mountain. "Know the written law, and the law unwritten. One can find oneself holding power that comes not of position, but of others' love, or fear, or ignorance. You will come into a lot of this, Chevenga. Its lure is very strong in your soul."

As always he was right; I had come into it already. It had brought me to grief, I saw, because in my anger I had abused it. No more important lesson can there be, for an Ascendant.

VI

I laid into growing up like a starving child into a meal.

Children play at it first: House, Workfast, War, and the best, Healer. We played Trust Me Trust You, the game where one dangles over the edge of a cliff from the hands of another, each one letting go in turn, even when our Teachers hadn't ordered it. Once when I was eight or nine we got hold of a skin of nakiti, the strong Enchian stuff. The honor and peril of the first draught fell to me, and I made sure to keep my face entirely impassive as it scorched a trail down my throat. Not a sip, either: wanting not to be outdone I gulped a mouthful like water. Commending its quality sagely I passed it on to Nyera, and next thing I knew the rocky ground leapt up and struck me in the face. I was sick for two days.

Nakiti enslaves, as they say, but no substances so enthrall the mind as chalk and charcoal. Our second favorite game was Assembly. No one over twelve could vote, in our perfect Yeola-e; wine was never watered down for children and combing was illegal.

I remember the day they impeached me. "Chevenga's always demarch," Krero said. "We should let someone else be for once. Like me." I agreed, intrigued as we are intrigued to see an old part played by a new actor, and play a new one ourselves; I had always wanted to try my hand at farming. The next in the succession, Artira, who had begun to avoid me by this age, had gone off with Naiga, who was a little young for statecraft, to torment crawdads in the stream with a stick; so I named Krero my little brother.

I argued my way out of accusations of throwing dirt at servants, picking my nose and peeing myself, which led to something of a scuffle; finally Sachara said, "We're the people, we don't need a crime, we can toss him anytime we feel like it. Everyone who wants to get rid of Chevenga, sign here." Seeing them all do this with relish, giving me the most severe looks of judgment and condemnation, I knew I was doomed. The vote was unanimous. With all the gravity it requires I said, "The people wills," and gave the rock we used as the Crystal of the Speaker to Krero.

"Now you have to kill yourself," said Nyera, at which everyone pricked their ears and gazed at me. "*What?*" I gasped; I had never heard of such a thing. She said, "My mother told me that demarchs who get impeached kill themselves."

I was sure this wasn't law, else I would have known; this I told her. "I know it's not law," she said. "It's because it's so sad. Aren't you sad, Cheng?"

In truth, I was already eagerly drawing straight furrows in the green meadow in my mind; it came to me that perhaps I was not playing this properly. Trying again, I found I would be sad, but not enough to kill myself; I remembered the cliff of Haranin, and doubted I had sadness that great in me for anything. But Krero said, "I hereby forbid Chevenga to kill himself, and anyone else to suggest it." This should have been a sign. He turned into a small Notyere; after a number of fights, though there was no precedent for bringing a demarch back then, they reinstated me. When I asked Krero in his trial to explain himself, he laughed and said, "I had to find out how far I could lead you all."

Me he led further. One day in the summer of my eleventh year he said, "You're always demarch. But you've never done the Kiss of the Lake."

Blood roared in my temples. At heart I had known, ever since I had seen my father do it: I would be challenged, or challenge myself. In the daytime I could tell myself that all my forebears had succeeded; but before dawn, when one lies alone, and one's secrets all rise and open their dark petals in one's mind, I knew I had no proof I could do it.

I had been forbidden to try by every adult to whom I had ever said a word about it. I could have told my friends that, and been right. But even to my own inward ears, this rang of excuse; at that age we had little respect for rules made for our own safety. The children were all nudging each other and trading glances that said, "Will he?"

I said nothing, only turned and strode toward the swimming-hole. Bursting into thrilled babbling they followed. There had been seven or eight; by the time we were at the water's edge, there were at least twenty, giggling and jumping with excitement. Everyone swore silence, of course. I felt as my father had looked, the blood-song turned to stillness all through me; it came more easily than I had thought. As the adults had stood back from him, the children stood back from me.

We had to make do with a pretend fire-dish and torch, and a stick for the spear. Mana and Krero both wanted to be the Ritual Monk, which they settled by sharing her duty. We skipped the oration but they called me out, putting the thunder of command into their small voices. Remembering my father's grace, and trying to put it into every cell of my body, I made the sign, kneeling, stripped and stepped into the water. Just as he had, I lowered my head.

The water's cold burned my eyes; the pebbled bottom shimmered with ripples of sun and minnows darted, long brown specks among the stones. It was like diving; I had without thinking taken a deep breath in before I went down. My lungs began to strain, but no matter; I had felt that before in breath-holding contests. Mana forgot he was not supposed to touch me; I had to shake his hand off my shoulder.

Then came the moment in which one must rise out and take a breath; it almost caught me unprepared. I pulled myself lower by the stick as my father had. My chest suddenly felt as if it were being torn apart and crushed at once, and my legs screamed to leap up; just above my head was air and life, and all I needed to give up for it was my honor, and what was that? I thought of the children, how they would forgive me; I was only a child, after all, making a game of an adult's act. But then I thought, What am I worrying about? It's only death, which is going to come anyway. My ears roared as they had on the cliff, and I heard the voice of the harmonic singer enwrapping me, making my body's death-struggle fall away from me. A hand lay flat between my shoulder blades, not pressing me, but holding me; that was the gentleness I would show to myself, even taking blood-red lava down into my lungs which like a sun spreading out its spikes splits one into shreds. The pain ceased, and like a king on his divan I lay back to watch the colors flow like oil on water and hear the music of my death.

A kerchief lying across the hand of an adult: how must it feel, lying limp with its silken corners trailing from her fingers, treasured but forever carried and used? I felt so. Or like a bellows, with air being blown into me by some stronger force, some elder strength that held me utterly in its grasp. I tore my face away when I could, and light and din came shrieking back into my head. Arms tightened around me; only by that did I know I was thrashing. I vomited for a long time. Looking I saw it was water, flowing away into the ground; I remember wondering why it felt like fire. There were adults all around with piercing faces, gripping hands; it was my mother's arms I had felt. All-spirit, I thought—we've been caught.

Just as the demarch is in the struggling stage, well before he loses consciousness, the Ritual Monk places her hand across his mouth and nose, so that when he ceases to control his body he will draw no water into his lungs. Of this subtlety my friends and I had been ignorant. They had pulled me out, then run for help when I did not wake, pulling all my parents out of work; my lungs had taken in water and I'd come within a hair's width of dying.

My parents carried me back to the Hearthstone in a blanket. I remember the sickening swing of their stride, being passed from one to another, and trying to bury my face in the corner of the rough wool while the sun beat on my throbbing head. They let me yank at my forelock with my fist, but when I began rasping, "It was all my doing, no one's but mine, punish me and no one else," Esora-e said, "Shut up. You'll be punished well enough."

Bethera the healer came, wrapped me in sheepskins

and fed me a draught of warm milk; she was going to give me more, but my mother said, "No medicines, yet." That and the looks on their faces made me afraid. I called for one of them to come hold me but none would; only Larala the mongrel, who had adopted me, came and pushed his wet nose into my hand. They were taking a vote, wordlessly; I saw my mother turn up her hand for chalk.

It was she who spoke to me, putting one hand on my shoulder while inwardly I begged for both her arms, for the praise of a past day to drive away this shame. "There was a reason we forbade you," she said. "We did not tell you what it was because we did not think you would understand. Now you will have to.

"You may lose the demarchy. Not in punishment for disobedience, but by teaching yourself fear. Do you see, my child? Because it was done wrongly you hurt yourself, and when your proper time comes it is this you will remember. That will make it much harder. Perhaps impossible.

"Better not to let the years pass, and grave in the fear. What do you do, when a horse throws you?"

There is a state one arrives at in training when fatigue stops thought but the limbs keep moving, driven only by the voice of the Teacher; then all seems unreal, the lock-step-lock the turning of an endless wheel, and one knows only movement, one is nothing but movement, the mind dead of all thought.

Thus I felt now, as they led me back to the swimming-hole by my hands; my eyes saw the mountains above me and the grass at my feet, but the sights held no meaning for my mind; my legs planted and pushed my weight forward of a will not mine. My shadow-mother told the First Story, to inspire me, I think, but I heard only snatches of it.

When I stepped into the water, with Esora-e behind me this time, I threw up again, polluting its clarity. The woman I had overheard at my father's Renewal had spoken true: the second time is the worst. I was not afraid of death in itself, for I'd lived; it was feeling myself dying, a feeling I now knew. Looking down I saw only that terrible helplessness in the shining water, as a fighting-novice learns to see pain written upon the landscape on which he drills before he learns to see pride. Forgetting that I was anything but a frightened child, I ceased to be, and the rippling surface congealed into a mountain-wall I could not pass. I stood clutching myself with tears streaming down my face, inwardly pleading to my parents to have mercy on me. Veraha was looking at me with the most pity, being unused to such things, and I almost reached out my arms to him. But the three faces that my own more truly reflected were marble-cool, waiting, and the one I reflected truest, now dead, I knew would be the same. I was a child, but had done an adult thing. Esora-e lifted his hands from my shoulders.

I cannot recall whether I took in a deep breath or not, though I would guess I did. I remember the water's cold burning my face again, and that I did not open my eyes this time. In the peace beneath the surface I suddenly found the panic cleared enough to let me think; one will often find that the doing is less terrible than the dreading, for one witnesses oneself continuing to live during it. Besides, it was familiar; I had been here before, and lived to come again. I put all my soul into my shield-hand, locked around the bottom of the stick, making of my fingers the steel rings that fasten a banner to the pole, and remembered the thought that had held me last time. This time it came in the form of a memory: It's only dying sooner. As I felt pain and desperation work deep into me, Esora-e's hand clamped around my mouth and pinched my nose. Had I struggled upwards he could not have held me by that grip; now I understood the act of the Ritual Monk, in my body and my soul. The greater hand of the God-In-Myself lay upon my back again, with the sound of the singing wind. I gave myself, and ceased to know. When I awoke they were all grinning. Esora-e carried me down the mountain on his shoulders.

Many years later, when my eyes were level with his, I would ask him, "Where did you learn to be the Ritual Monk?"

"I've been wondering when you'd ask me that," he would say, and smile, scratching his moustache. "Do you really think you were the first demarch to try it before his time?" I would come away laughing, with a glow in my heart. I should have known.

*   *   *

I turned twelve, and outsparred fifteen-year-olds tall as grown-ups, with hair under their arms. My friend Kamina Shae-Buraina, who'd always had trouble with fear, was required to jump off the cliff of Akaturin. It is forbidden, when it is not required, because it is truly dangerous, claiming a life every now and then; in spite of that, when his nerve failed him at the top, I leapt myself, commanding him to follow. He managed it. For that, I got from him his best shirt, from my parents a combing to peel my hand, and from Azaila three moons cleaning the School latrines: justice entire.

One day my little sister made a curse on me so close to that of ostracism it left me breathless. Telling myself she was too young to know its full meaning I mastered myself, and asked her why. Her delicate face under her shock of brilliant curls, Tennunga's curls, wrinkled up ugly in rage and she said, "I hate you!" When I asked her why, she said, "Everyone loves you and no one loves me. *You* always do everything so well and everyone's always talking about *you* and it's always Chevenga this and Chevenga that and it makes me *sick!*"

I made her play me, which made her cry, and repent, and make up. But as I walked away I still felt as if my stomach were an anthill that had just been stirred with a stick.

I knew precisely where I stood, as children of the training ground do, in strength, quickness, aim, courage, fivestones, hot hands, finger-wrestling, unsword, killsparring or any other measure that children have contrived. Everyone knew what Esora-e thought I had the design in me for. And certain girls, who had eyes on me long before I had eyes on them, praised my looks. I am not in my rights to be angry at her envy, I thought; what is it?

Shame, I thought; in ignorance of the nature of the shadow I cast upon others, I've caused harm. I made the rounds of my family and friends and the Assembly Palace staff, making each one swear truth on my father's wisdom tooth, and asked what impression they had of me. Yes, that story is true.

Mostly they said things like, "You're a fine lad and you'll be a fine demarch, now go away. It is also the truth that I'm busy." Finally my mother called me to her hearth.

Nowadays my eyes were higher than the back of the chair. In my survey I'd skipped her, my stepfather, my shadow-parents and my grandmother, since they furnished such knowledge unasked, and at first I thought she was angry at me for this. But she only asked me what I was about. "It's my shadow I want to understand," I said. "How it falls."

"Ah," she said, and laid her hand on my shoulder. On her forearm was the long scar that she'd got by treachery in a parley; the Enchian had struck at our negotiator with a knife he had hidden, and having nothing else she had fended off the blow with her arm. The scar's end moved under the fringe of her half-poncho as she gestured. "That is something a demarch ought to know. How to forget about one's shadow.

"Grandma'am explains this best, but she's busy with Aunt; I suppose I can try. How it falls upon others is as much their choice as your own. As in the sky, for you there is only one guide-star that will stay steady: what you are to yourself. Don't think of what the shadow is: think of what you are. Tennunga said it well too: be what you want people to think you are. Then the shadow will be the best you can make it."

I had been taught that, by tutor and Teacher alike. It's just Artira, full of child's envy, I thought; no one else said much bad. On my bed I sat twisting my leather bracelet with my fingers, my heart smouldering. The world burned because of wrongful anger, I thought. Why shouldn't Artira envy me? People *do* think more of me than her, I *am* favored, the die has given me gifts, gifts that will always benefit me, gifts of a worth beyond any number of *ankaryel*, gifts which cannot be lost as long as one lives.

Thus I was answered.

The lintels had seemed to stop shrinking next to me those days, while time flew past all the faster. I'll never make it to man-size if I don't hurry up, I would think, exhorting myself in front of mirrors, "Grow!" Everyone else would have their blessings longer. That night I took a new blackness into myself, my own envy, called out by Artira's.

First it was only people older than thirty. For the number of snowballs I threw and led others to throw, I should have been combed till my hand-bones showed; but I knew by then how not to get us caught. I learned to read the age of a face quickly. I sneered behind my tutors' backs at their wrinkles or paunches or sagging breasts, such childishness as might be taken for any child's ignorant contempt of age. Not that I could do this to my grandmother; instead, when I found by asking exactly how old she was, I avoided her for a sennight. All I could think of, imagining her ancient cracked face was: all those years.

Then a few days later Sachara, who was the eldest of us in spirit, played his own fatherhood, making us all roll on the ground laughing to see his children chase through all the same games and trials and scrapes as we did. That false dawn I woke up sweating. Using my fingers so as to be entirely sure, I counted. To see a child my age I would have to be married at eighteen. No, seventeen—I was forgetting gestation. I would never see my Ascendent become demarch or even warrior, unless I married within the year.

I could not sleep until I had planned action, a habit that has stayed with me. Nyera would do this for me, I thought, if she knew. I cannot tell her; but seeing the fervency of my courting, she will understand without knowing. I imagined her hazel eyes softening, the slow approach of her hand, slender hard fingers closing around mine; "Cheng. You need me," and the warm embers of friendship sparking into passion, whatever that was.

Then I thought, Am I mad? I'm boy-sized. What do I have for her? I should say, my friends and I were at the age to notice how people older than us all went through the same sudden dark and baffling turn, that made them give up fivestones and House, preen their hair every spare moment, talk awkwardly, and become obsessed for some incomprehensible reason with forming into pairs; watching them succumb one by one, we knew with a sinking feeling that this would be our fate too. As well as traitors, they seemed to us less free.

Now I had reason that was not at all incomprehensible. I fingered between my legs, as if groping would make it big for good, and grow more black hairs than the seventeen I'd counted. She would laugh. At the thought of that my testicles felt as if they were burrowing up into my belly; but on me was the sweat too, for my child. It is a dare that must be done, I thought.

No one else came into my head, naturally enough, I suppose, since Nyera was my closest female friend. Also, the change had happened to her; sometime when none of us had been looking she'd sprouted breasts, and a thatch of curls between her legs like my mother's, but red-blonde. Crucial for my cause, her month-bleeding had started, a good half-year before; it had been she who let us boys in on this mystery. Though formally it is for the woman to ask, everyone knows that marriages are made by two at the very least; every man knows how to place the right word or look. We'd make a two now, I planned, and become a four as soon as Mana, who had already sworn to join with me, found his girl. That settled, I slept.

Next day I got Sichera-e to cut my hair in the warrior-cut; that was the end of my child's ringlets, forever. I tucked my father's ivory comb in my belt, so it would show. Now, looking in my mother's Arkan mirror, I felt I cut a very fine figure; if I sucked in my cheeks, held their insides between my teeth and turned my head to get the shadow from the right angle, I had a man's cheekbones. There was a man named Iri-kai in second rank (actually he was only fifteen, but a fast grower) whose sigil was a necklace of bright smooth-polished stones, set in just enough metal to be daring. I needed something like that.

In those days I was permitted to have money, though I never got an allowance as other children did, since once I was demarch I'd be forbidden it. But once Mana had taken pity on me, and slipped me a copper bit. I bet Sachara the coin that he could not beat me at naughts and crosses in ten tries, even if he went first every try; I had found an old book that showed how one can always draw, if one makes no mistakes. Having been given bad odds, I tripled my fortune this way. Now I ran down to the market-square of Terera, and found the jeweller who had made Iri-kai's necklace.

Odd and beautiful it is to see things one has never seen before that because of their style are familiar, and to understand more deeply the spirit of a work by seeing its precedents and antecedents on the table. She let me feel the stones, which were smooth as one imagines a drop of water would be if one could feel its surface, and showed me the tumbling-drum in which they were polished. I chose a necklace whose stones were mostly of red hues, and put it on halfway up the path. With the flash and weight of the stones on my neck I felt ready, for when Nyera came out of training.

She was as tall as Krero then, four fingerwidths taller

than I, with a woman's face to match her body: lengthened, filled out, the eyebrows grown into a curve of adult
grace. As I greeted her she took off her training-tunic and
wiped between her breasts; she sweated and smelled like
an adult, too. No matter, I thought, kicking myself out of
the spell, she's still just Nyera; or else if she is something
greater than she used to be, then so am I.

She admired the necklace, touching the stones, and
praised my boldness; I had done right. I would always
wear it, I decided, like a crystal. I touched her hand, and
gave the hint that every woman knows how to hear.

Those mature brows flew up under her fringe of fore-
curls, and she laughed in her way, that had in this last
year become rippling. "Why laugh?" I said. "We are people of more sincerity, surely."

She was not, being too astonished. "You're *serious*! . . .
are you?"

"It is not for me to say more."

"Well, I . . . !" She burst out laughing again. "Cheng,
you turkey-mind! We can't get married!" She wiped laughter from her face, and said, not we are only children, no.
She said, "You are only a child."

She was three months older than me, and girls are more
mature at that age; still. I suppose if one needs proof of my
immaturity, it was what I did next. "Am I?" I cried, my
blood rising. "And you're grown up? We'll see!" She usually gave me a good fight finger-wrestling, but I had her
down in an instant, making her swear she would never
again call me child. Thus my first attempt to marry ended
in sweat and dust.

Esora-e saw the necklace for the first time that day. His
brow darkened, but all he said was, "That's too much, lad;
frippery." I ignored it. Among the children, I was a good
month putting an end to the mock proposals with my fists.

Again I lay awake, fingering the red stones. There are
many fish in the sea, as the saying goes, but one cannot
send one's second hook out so soon after without insulting
the biters both first and next. I'll wait a month, I thought,
and then go after Checharao. She was a rank higher than
me and a year older, but a boarding student, from Tinga-e.
Since she had never seen me as a drooling toddler but
only as a student of the Sword, I reasoned, she would be
less likely to consider me a child.

Events caught me up before the month ended. The Harvest love-feast came, and as usual people came from Terera and from further up the valley. After the feasting was done, I wandered beside the bonfires, avoiding snaking lines of dancers, my feet following the drums without thought as one's feet will. It was late, my friends sent to bed by their parents, mine looking for me, and a good many of the other adults gone into the bushes. Suddenly I felt myself seized and lifted by several pairs of strong hands.

At first I thought my friends must have come back, and struggled with all my might, nearly squirming free. But the laughing grunts and the remarks, "Shhh, for the love of Saint Mother, sparrow-brain, you're plenty ripe enough!", "We want you, you're pretty!", "You'd think the little wrestler didn't know where we were taking him!", were in voices strange to me. I looked. All five were girls.

In the moonlight their skin shone pale, the curves of their hips like the moon's with its ivory glow. Their breasts were high and young and pointed, except for those of the one who gripped my sword-arm; seen from below they were round as my mother's, the nipples big around as my thumb is long. The end of a red ringlet bobbed above them; a tuft of the same red below. In firelight it had been the hue of paprika; in daylight, I thought, it would be fire. She was not a day under sixteen. I remember her look, and her laugh, the sound of a mountain stream. "Put him down," she said. "He can walk. You can see he's not going to run anywhere."

We went into the woods and drank wine; then all but the red-haired girl went away with the skin, saying, "Well, the God-In-Ourselves calls, we must go pick flowers." She pulled me down beside her onto a soft patch of moss. "You are young," she said, clearing away the needles. "You must be started gently."

At first it was nothing more than I had felt before from my mother, to ease me, a stroke through the hair, a tender cheek-kiss. It being the thing to do, I put my arms around her. Her scent filled my nose, a sweetness that was not perfume, but her innate fragrance, rising from her skin and hair. I kissed her ear as I had seen my parents do each other, but what exactly I should be doing with my hands I hadn't a clue; that I had not seen. Well, I thought, she is

the teacher, let her teach. Just when I had begun to feel
too much to think and be shy, her tongue, wet and warm
and delicate between the two dry cool pads of her lips,
slipped into my mouth, and her hand, that had got under
my kilt without my knowing it, slowly closed.

Healer is a giggling warmth, like a hug; an adventure,
shyly and carefully and slowly tried, in which everyone is
a novice; a tickling in the loins that brings a smile. That I
felt again, but then it grew into a streak of fire in me such
as I had not imagined was possible, and I understood then
the truth of which Healer is a weak reflection. I had
thought people could only touch each other outside, for
even her inside was bounded by an outside, the smooth
surface, warm as the inside of a heart must be, between
her flesh and mine; yet by a magic of which I had been
ignorant she did touch my inside; with each thrust and
gripping it was the cords of my innards she struck. Each
moment I thought it could not possibly become better; but
then it would; and as well I knew I wanted, and therefore
there must be, more.

At the final rise just before the peak's summit, my skin
wherever she touched it sent colors in streams and flow-
erets into my inward eyes; then it seemed to me that we
ran and swam and soared, and that when I climaxed my
head reached the sky and my body spread out to touch the
bounds of the earth. I felt a presence I knew, but laughing
instead of grave; sex, too, is a face of the God-In-Ourselves.

I learned long ago how a sword's stroke touches the
deepest inside, bringing death, I thought, as I clung to her
after. Now I have learned the stroke that touches the
deepest inside to bring life. Yes, I see why adults so
cherish this. It is something to die for—no. To live for.
And I wept with joy.

One of her hands lifted from my skin; she was waving
away the others, who hearing us finish crying out had
impatiently come back. She threw her thick ringlets over
my back, and traced lines that seemed etched of fire and
silver along my hip with her fingers. "My salamander,"
she whispered, her lips beside my ear. "You know you
belong in fire; because fire is in you."

On the heels of joy chased fear. That I should never feel
this again, for surely such pleasure could be only be had
once in a lifetime; I should never find another woman so

good, as if she were a goddess, though I now knew all women had this in them, and indeed all men. I clung harder, wanting to bury myself in her warmth and softness, in the scent of her musk that mixed warm and deep with the cool tang of pine. As if she could read my thoughts, she said, "Don't worry, sweetling, it's always like this, or better. I'm just a love-feaster playing teacher, and plain; think of what it will be like with a woman you love and think is beautiful." I wanted to say, "I love you, you are more beautiful than the sun on the mountain, ask me to marry you." But she loosed her arms and untangled her legs from mine. "Be as good with them as you were with me," she whispered, and kissed my forelock. It was sex between friends she had given me, not sex between lovers, something delicate that my clumsy grasp to hold her would shatter. As well I could not bring myself to say, "I love you—who? I didn't quite hear your name. . . ." Somehow we had forgotten formalities. To not know would be insult to one such as her, it seemed to me, so I asked, hand on forelock. She was Kagratora-e Shae-Itana, of Chegra. I will remember forever. Then, without thinking, I told them my name.

For a moment I could not tell the girls from the pines, as they were all frozen. Then the one with the wineskin let out a high peal of laughter and fell over, her legs kicking in the air. "The Ascendant!" she shrieked. "We carried off the Ascendant!"

I had forgotten they were from up valley, born and raised in a clutch of farmfasts, not used to Servants and envoys and Ascendants wandering about the place, brushing shoulders with real folk. Now I heard receding giggling, breathless, as if they were fleeing the scene of a prank, as the other three dashed away. "And Kagra initiated him! Ah-ha-haaa!"

She sat with one hand clenching her two foremost ringlets and the other flat over her mouth. "*Babies!*" The cry flared abrupt in the dark, harsh in her voice after its tenderness. "Brats, running off like bugs! Ascendant, I don't know these children!" She was in her rights, I think, to be angry at them, deserting her like cowardly soldiers a brave commander. "Well," I said. "We adults seem to have been left alone."

She turned and stared at me for a moment; I could just

see the point of moonlight shining in one eye. Then she smiled, moonshadow pooling in her dimples, as only a woman can at a man she has had, her stance straightening and softening. "The Ascendant. Salamander . . . Well, sheep-turds, I haven't done anything wrong."

"Ascendant is so cold, for one who knows me so well," I said when we had found our moss-patch again. "Just call me Chevenga."

"Chevenga." Her chalk-sign was her last gesture; from then on she spoke without using her hands. "And when you're grown up and come to Chegra to speak," she whispered, "I will call 'Psst, Chevenga!' and wink at you from the edge of the dais when you look, and we'll remember."

Now I understood the change. That facet of it in me was begun and finished in one night. Though I was young, I sought loves from then on, anywhere I imagined I might find them, except, of course, in the arms of others. I have ever since except when I was unable, or with a steady one.

After Kagratora-e I began my rounds of the unattached girls of Vae Arahi. Soon I had my lines set. I would give the marriage hint first, and if she was uninterested then I would ask her if she would like to go up the mountain with me anyway, as friends. At least then if I didn't get a wife, I would get to make love. Very soon I learned to take it as a lesson as well as a joy.

Checharao said I was too young, but I found out later she had her eye on one of the students in her rank, so I took it as a white lie. She taught me many new tricks, being older. Avorcha, my half-cousin, said, "Are you mad? We're too little to have children!"; on the mountain it was I who taught her, though she had kissed and fondled before. Terini of Checharao's rank said, "My father told me never to marry a politician"; she was delicate as a moth's wing for all she was one of the best fighters in the class.

In the shrine among the standing stones, I hinted to Komona, who had lived down the corridor from us in the Hearthstone but now was apprenticed to the Senaheral. She had black hair and eyes like my mother. "I can't marry you," she said, drawing a black tendril across her cheek. "My egg's just falling, this time of the month; it wouldn't be safe."

I should have known this would happen. Who would

take a twelve-year-old's looking to marry seriously? Though
in my anguish I had liked to forget, I had never heard of
anyone marrying under sixteen, least of all an Ascendant.
It was not possible.

The next few days I cried on my mother's shoulder, and
then my pillow when I thought I had troubled her enough.
In the cold dry time afterwards, I thought, I'll never see
my children's wristlets, die cast, gates fast, no words and
all go home. From then on I had the young to envy as
well; they might yet die early, but they might not; they
did not have the iron wall of certainty set in their path to
cut short their dreams. If someone asked me to play my
fatherhood, I would have to feign, to lie.

For a time, I answered with anger. I made the dares
harder, and anyone who would not follow me I would
shame or hurt. I got us all stung by wasps, and Krero's
arm broken; it's lucky I got no one killed. They turned
cold; I called them all cowards. I remember Mana laying
his hand on my shoulder and asking, "What has come over
you?" But I could only curse him. I hated him, then,
utterly unjustly, for being my best friend and not knowing. Luckily I remembered my old oath, to love twice as
much, before all my friendships were broken. To my
affliction there is no other remedy. I had to contemplate it
again and again, to make a discipline of it, as of the sword.

This while Handaotha asked me one day what our father
had looked like; sometime in the spinning days, she who
was too young to remember had become old enough to
ask. I called them all together and pulled them in close in
front of my mother's Arkan mirror. "Daddy had Artira's
hair, just the same color that shines really bright in the
sun, Naiga's eyes, pale and fast and smart, Handaotha's
nose, except because he was a man it was very long and
strong and beautiful, and his face was shaped like mine.
Close your eyes and stick all these things together and
you'll know what he looked like." I was a war-student
when he died, I thought, and already I must be his
historian.

Our custom of the month away, in case you do not
know, sends a child, Ascendant or Senahera apprentice, to
live with a family or a workfast other than his own in a

place other than home, to learn in a small way at least the lives of others.

All told I was sent twenty times over five years, starting when I was ten, to serve as the apprentices' apprentice in one form or another. The joys and the drudgery are to be shared by all, as the saying goes, and Ascendants, since their adulthood is spent in office, have all their drudgery in childhood. No one knew that most of my life would be childhood. But there were wonders, too.

Esora-e wanted my first month away to be on the border, preferably a border where there might be raids. My aunt felt otherwise, and sent me to a blacksmith's in Thara-e. The apprentice's lot is having to do all the work too simple for his parents; I being his apprentice, he gave me all the work which was too simple for him.

People in the Hearthstone who, having never done such work in their lives, glorify it, had scared me into worrying that I might not be strong enough. But the bellows-pole moved when I pushed it, like the sword of Saint Mother. I carried metal and water and wood until I steamed, and began to learn pride in this sort of endurance, which feels different from that of a warrior. The dark shop with its tools and scraps and nameless objects hung on the walls or strewn on the floor was full of the secrets of how things were made.

I went once to a money-bank in Tinga-e, where my arithmetic was tested all day and forever found too slow. I herded sheep in the foothills of the New Mountains, crossing the limestone-flagged ground barefoot until my feet were hard as horn. I served in a shrine once every year, mostly sweeping the precincts, sometimes copying the books which needed less skill, or standing all afternoon to watch the carving of a stele.

I was a month on a warship patrolling the coast near the Enchian border, doing all the same drills as the warriors, and rowing with them too. My father had gone on a month run on a merchant ship as well, but it was decided between my parents, my aunt and my grandmother that the times were too dangerous now. There have always been, and always will be, pirates; but these days one heard stories also of the ships of Arko, which long kept the seas mostly clear of such, seizing ships themselves for no reason. "They are old for an empire now, and leaning toward

the dust, for all they are young for a people," I remember
my grandmother saying, "and they always believed right
lay with the sword. Now they think it their due to be rich
as they can get, no matter how. Well, they can only do
this sort of thing so long; it rots a people from the inside
like a tree, and weakens them, and one of these decades a
woodcutter will come along, angry and strong."

Best of all, I was given what every child must think
about one time or another; a month travelling with the
Sinere Circus.

There is an old rumor in parts of southern Yeola-e that
All-Seeing Rao, the Boy With Eyes in the Back of His
Head, was actually me. It is entirely true. I would rather
have gone by my real name, and without the wig; but the
circus elders, fearing the reproach of the strict-minded,
would not let me. To perform I did choose to compromise
myself such, which I admit now was a wrong. Now I
complete my atonement; as you read this the lie is slain.

In my act I wore a waist-length fire-red wig, my eyebrows painted red to match, a kilt painted with dragons
and flames, and wristlets, Esora-e forgive me, with gold
sequins. One of the circus hands would blindfold me, and
lead me to the edge of the stands, for the people to test his
work. While the ringmaster pattered on about my ability,
the circus hand would produce a knife, and have me point
where it was, follow it with my arm and so forth. Just
as the ringmaster was exclaiming how great a warrior
All-seeing Rao would be when he grew up, a savage warcry would come from under the stands, and a man charge
out: one of the acrobats who had some war training,
costumed in full gear, Enchian, Lakan or Arkan, whomever was hated most where we were playing. Shouting
that I must be slain before I could grow into the scourge of
Tor Ench, Laka or Arko, he'd first throw his spear, which
I would dodge by a hair's width, then chase me around
the ring with his swords. I would trip and sprawl in the
ring-dust (as often as not, that drew screams from the
crowds); I must then avoid his strokes, ducking, dodging,
twisting, leaping, all the while yelling for a sword. Finally
they'd throw me one, I'd catch it, and turn, and he and I
would go at it, wide-open furious stage-style with all the
flash we could muster, clashing our swords together hard
to make the crowd know they were real, (though neither

had a good edge) until he tripped, and I held mine to his throat. Only then would I pull off my blindfold, to a roar of hailing from the crowd. They ate it up; but it got me into my first bad trouble with my shadow-father.

At one town there had been a general in the crowd, who sent a letter commending him for the fine training of "the boy some eleven or twelve years of age with long flame-red hair, who as a member of the Sinere Circus demonstrated an extraordinary weapon-sense."

Esora-e called me into his room. "Tell me the person who wrote this letter has her schools mixed up and speaks of some other boy," he said, "and I will believe you, without another word."

The one strand of his peaked forelock that shook when he was angry was doing so now; but I said, "I cannot lie," and drew myself straight.

He sprang up, and seized my hair, almost knocking over the desk. "Is this Fourth Chevenga Shae-Arano-e?" he cried. "Is this the child we chose to so name, our first, our Ascendant, my heart's brother's seed—did *this* come from him, and us? This creature of wood, who feels nothing given him, but whose imagination for new ways to spit on it has no bounds?"

Esora-e believed the path to something great was long and therefore must necessarily be narrow. That was, after all, how he had been formed, and he was trying to form me into something even greater: hence it must be narrower. As well, he felt any mockery of warriorhood was a questioning of it. At any rate, I suppose it was a rite of passage of a sort. Part of me wanted to cry, "Who have I hurt? Who have I harmed?", and make amends; but more of me was angry, remembering a morning five years before, and other times. Always, I thought, he wants to put his hand to my life. From somewhere came a courage I had grown into without knowing it; perhaps it was from being Rao, who was carefree, who had no duties, no lessons, no foreknowledge. I fixed my glare on him like a fighter, and said, "Let go."

He did, and stepped back, drawing breath to speak. I drew my father's ivory comb out of my belt to comb my hair where he had mussed it, thinking "Answer enough, whose child I am. Why should I share even words with him?" I finished combing, then turned to go. There was a heartbeat's length of stillness, in which I saw his brows crease in amazement, then blank rage.

In one stride he was on me, the itch in my legs to run come too late. Next thing I knew I was down, the stone of the hearth pressing into my cheekbone and eyebrow, and his fingers, long and hard like talons, clamping the back of my neck and pinning my wrist to my back. I squirmed, and he gave the wrist a twist, sending pain in streaks through my shoulder. "Lie still and make no sound, Fourth Chevenga," he whispered. "I am afraid what I might do, if you make me angrier." I tried to break free twice again anyway, but it gained me nothing but pain, worse each time.

Then to my surprise, my anger snuffed as quickly as it had flamed; for it came to me what had happened. He was my shadow-father and war teacher, and I was all of twelve; yet when I had spoken, he had obeyed. For one unthinking moment I had had him in my hand as a commander has a warrior who has relinquished his will.

No wonder he is so angry, I thought. I was afraid, then; but only half of him.

There was silence, but for his ragged breathing, and the fire's hiss. "Someone else should train you for a while," he said almost absently. "We have got too close." He took a long slow breath, and shifted his hands without loosening them. For a time there were only the fire-sounds again, and I watched the flame dance over the coals sideways, and wondered vaguely where my mother was. She might take my side; but that no longer seemed to matter. Suddenly he let go.

On the floor near where he'd held me down lay the comb. I took it up and slipped it in my belt again. "I hope I did not hurt you," he said. "No, shadow-father," I answered; I wouldn't have admitted it if he had. "Good, then," he said briskly. Then he began the harangue.

My anger came roaring back, driving all else from my mind, and drawing me into the debate I had not intended to have with him. I called him a tyrant; he said my father would have been angry; then we were arguing over who had known him better. I haven't the stomach to record all we said, railing over that. There is yet another disadvantage of being dead: anyone can make what they like of one's opinion, since one is not there to set it straight. I can imagine what will be done with mine.

Finally he said, "Enough words," and seized my wrist. I

said, "You don't need to hold me." Let him see that, at least. I found it easier than I had expected, to keep my hand steady, even though the tips of the tines on the third stroke drew blood. He held out his hand for me to kiss in gratitude, and sent me out.

There was a niche between the bed and the corner of my room which was always my place of contemplation. I went there and drew the shutters.

It is like when we voted on Veraha, I thought: the power of the law unwritten in me. I shouldn't be afraid of it. More words of my father's on the mountain came back. "Never seek it," he'd said, "for that way you will become either a puppy begging for affection, or Notyere. Ends in themselves, being without purpose, are corrupting. Yet don't fear it, for there is no good in that either. Don't think how to use it before it comes, however good your cause, for that would be seeking it. Only see it, and if it comes, use it justly." At the time, I had understood perhaps one word in ten. Now I understood it all.

Yet if this is power, I thought, it is not absolute; had I not felt such injustice in his words, I could not have called on it at all, for it would have had no sound foundation to stand on.

Yet in time anger came creeping back, aided by the pain of my bandaged hand. I thought, and still think, that my blood father would have combed me lightly, if at all, but mostly laughed. A few days later I dallied with a girl on the mountain, though I knew it was the time of training. I'll miss a day, I thought; what of it? Why should I worry about catching up to the others when I am ahead of them? Provoking Esora-e, I admit, was in the back of my mind.

What I forgot to think of was him worrying that I might be lying with a broken leg in some gorge. The girl and I looked up absently from our business, to see a search-fan of people threaded across the valley below, small as ants. We watched bemused for a time, wondering which child had gone missing, until I heard a snatch of their calling on the wind: "Che-ven-gaaaaah!"

For a while I considered lying down, pulling a rock or two on top of me and faking it; I could say I'd thought it was broken and I had not dared move. I considered fleeing over the pass and joining the Sinere Circus for good. In the end I kissed the girl good-bye, and walked down to face them, without preparing a lie. My mother would see through it, and if I ran everyone would think I was dead.

Esora-e never shamed me in front of others. He gave the class to one of the senior students, and took me into the inner chamber. I had never been here before. The walls were bare white but for the circle, the sigil of the void.

"It was a girl, wasn't it?" he said. I signed chalk. "I thought so." He knelt thinking for a time, his grey eyes under the thick dark brows turned to the floor, much less angry than I had thought I could hope for, which put me in more fear. His hand reached, and played with my necklace, rolling the stones over his fingers. "Do you know how you look in this?" he said.

"Well enough, I am told," I answered, honestly.

"By children, who are easily amused. To us, you look ridiculous." My father's ivory comb was tucked in my belt as usual; he ran his finger along the grip. "And this. Can you name me one other person, lad, who wears his comb showing?" I could think of no one, so said nothing. "And now you take it on yourself to decide when you need to train or not. All these things say one thing. You are reaching beyond your grasp, seeking to be something you cannot be, trying to be greater than you are."

"That's strange, shadow-father," I said. "I seem to recall it was someone other than me who chose that I should be the world's greatest warrior."

"So you will be, if you are a warrior at all, which I recall you chose; else you will have done less than your best. When you are grown; not now. That's it, Fourth Chevenga: you are trying to be older than you are. That is why it looks ridiculous; a child trying to pass himself off as an adult always does."

Esora-e, my shadow-father, if you read this: I know, I never gave you the chance to understand. I considered telling you, and decided to err on the side of caution. You thought good had to be beaten into me; I did not believe you would leave my choices to me. If I was wrong, I am sorry, and beg forgiveness.

The Teachers' chamber darkened for a moment and I saw only his grey eyes; then I felt my nails pressing into my palms, and all my muscles twitching and bristling. "Do you think you are an adult?" he said softly. "Show me. No, not here." I followed him trembling to the anteroom. Before the sword of Saint Mother he held out his hands, fingers spread.

So it was my shadow-father played the stone wall set before me in my mind, though he did not know it. I would smash it down, I decided; I would crush him, throw him to his knees and grind his face on the floor; I, who would be the greatest warrior in the world, who if I chose to do something always did it, here in sight of the sigil that told the people my destiny, would crumble his hands to dust in mine. I would make my fingers steel, like the claws of Shininao, that nothing can withstand; I would be tireless as the waterfall, for all his hands seemed stone; I would break them if they would not bend, for all they seemed bronze-cast, for all it hurt, for all my fingers became fire, for all my tendons tore and my wrists strained to near breaking, for all I might weep with the pain of it. . . .

I looked. He was holding, our hands locked between us, unmoved from when we had started. Though his knuckles were white and forearms hard-ridged, his eyes showed no effort.

That was all he did, while I kindled my anger again for another such surge, and another, giving all my strength. When I began to feel truly spent, his chin rose almost too slightly to see, his eyes narrowed, and he began.

He knew a thousand finger-wrestling tricks. He used none of them on me, to show he did not need to, save one: the lifting of the hands, used when one is the taller. All else was main strength. I need not detail the struggle. I fought him so hard the pain made me cry out, but it made no difference to his motion, as if my strength were nothing at all. When he said, "Yield; I do not want to hurt you," I cried out, "Never! Even if you break both my wrists!" He ended it by taking me to my knees with a down and forward jerk. I was so spent that when he let go I fell on my face.

So a doll, broken and cast aside in the heart of its maker's home, must feel. I kept my silence, but the tears came, and I heard the faint creak of the chains of the sword of Saint Mother. Someone else had happened in; lying at Esora-e's feet I saw him wave them away. He knelt beside me, felt my arms over, and gently massaged them in his great callused hands. He could afford to be gentle now. When I had the strength I tore the necklace from around

my neck and hurled it across the room, and did likewise
with the comb.

He stroked my hair with his fingers. "One day you will
be able to beat me. Time always takes care of that, for those
who are patient." I would have poured it all out to him
then, and called him out to role-play, except for my oath.

"Up," he said in time, "and into the ground." There he
trained with me alone, for as long as usual, so that I was at
my other lessons late into the night.

My mother had waited up. I meant to kiss her goodnight
without telling her, but she noticed the necklace missing.

"My child," she said, when I explained. "Little Warm-
Arms. It's just a few bright stones, a chain of cheap metal."
She took my face between her hands. "You are you. Do
you really think you are not handsome enough without it?
Do you really think no one would notice you?" No one had
put it that way. When Esora-e gave me back the things,
the necklace had changed overnight, looking overblown
with all those stones and links and whorls; I soon gave it
away.

When I saw the comb, it was as if a sword went through
my heart. It lay in two pieces in his hand, one of the end
tines broken off.

In my place of contemplation I clutched it to my forehead, and swore a thousand times I would never again in
my life throw any precious thing in anger, an oath I have
kept. I planned to repair it, though I had no idea how;
then thought again. I would carry it the way it was, I
decided, so that each time I saw it I would be reminded;
so my father's comb remains, to this day.

VII

In the winter of 1539 Enjaliansi's heart seized up, killing
him on his throne. His son Kranaj replaced him without
the troubles one often sees in a monarchy, whose contend-
ers often consider themselves above law. A good name
among the warriors stands one in better stead than birth,
and he had that.

When he and Tyeraha met at Nefra they made friends.
Finished meeting, they hunted deer together in the great
forest, with their heirs.

I had been taught only so that I might join such hunts
with foreign guests once I took office. This was the first
test of it; my aunt had finally judged me old enough. As
we rode to the forest she said to Kranaj, "My friend, why
don't we exchange squires for the chase? That'll keep the
boys' eyes sharp. It's this one you'll be dealing with instead of me, give us eight years." I kept my face serious
though I wanted to caper in the trees; never had I been
entrusted with anything so important.

Kranaj's son Reknarja was fourteen, two years my elder.
His freckled cheeks darkened between two brown sheets
of straight hair, and he blurted, "What, that slip of a boy?
Father, his head hardly comes to my shoulder—" upon
which the king kicked him.

He swallowed a yelp and his jewels tinkled; then a

silence fell in which everyone cast their eyes at everyone
else's. His flashed angrily from me to his father and back,
full of words he dared not say. My aunt, knowing it was
my custom to challenge older children who insulted me to
unsword duels, gave me a look that hissed, "Don't even
think of it." Kranaj's eyes, wide-set and blue-grey under
straight forelocks, flicked between mine and hers, trying
to judge how we had taken it. All the fragile goodwill that
had been built up so painstakingly over these past years
could be destroyed at a move.

What I must do came clear to me just quick enough. I
smiled eagerly at Kranaj and said, "I'd be honoured to be
your squire, *Amaesti*," as if I had not heard. Everything
fell back into the procedure it should follow; Reknarja and
I traded places. When the king and I were alone I said, "I
hope my smallness does not displease you, sir," to show
him I had heard. His eyes blinked a little. "Not at all,
Ascendant," he said. "A lad with wits is as good as one
with size. You forgive Reknarja, then?"

"Yes, *Amaesti*. I know how it is, yearning to be older."
One might as well use what one has. Across his broad face
a smile flashed.

A foreign monarch doesn't necessarily reflect his people
as a demarch reflects Yeola-e; even so, I began to learn
tolerance for Enchians from Kranaj. They had attacked us
and an Enchian had killed my father; but here was another
Enchian who would explain to me the old stag's trick of
running over his own trail to mislead his trackers, instead
of commanding me to follow, all he was required to do.
Even if he resembled only himself, it still taught me that
they varied, like us, for all my shadow-father said they
were all the same. It sowed in me the seed of the question
that is so needful for peace: who am I to hate a whole
people for what one has done?

At any rate, our worst enemy became Astyardk of Laka,
who was trying to push his borders through ours. The
raids came more often, the gifts ceased, it was the Lakan
delegation for whose hidden knives I must feel. In Esora-e's
drills, it became a Lakan instead of a Tor Enchian whose
imagined heart we struck.

It first seemed to me, seeing the Lakan envoy's party in
Hall, that they had stained their skin brown, pulled their
hair straight and dipped it in ink. Even after I had seen

their hands stay brown through many dippings in finger bowls, it still defied credence. Of course in the village near where the Shac-Tyucheral lived I saw people who had hair in waves instead of true curls, and dark skin, having Lakan blood.

Likely you do not know the name Shae-Tyuchera. It is borne by the border family on whose farm I stayed for a month-away in the summer I was thirteen. I have found that few know it, though many, mostly novices of the sword, can recount the story stroke by stroke.

So I shall give all their names to you. Their surname Shae-Tyuchera as I have written: the member first, Binchera, her daughter Rigratora-e and her husband Osilaha Shae-Chini, and their four children: Bukini who was nineteen and Nainano-e who was fifteen, both blooded, Kicharesa who was eleven and Inllai who was ten. They lived near the village Krisae.

As I say, the story is well-known, so I must warn you that I am bound by the Oath of the Scrivener; meaning, since like snowballs such accounts tend to grow with travel, it will almost certainly be a lesser tale than the one you have heard. But truth is truth.

They lived almost in the shadow of the circle-stone that is our border-sigil. As always I was one of the children, no more, no less, in all but two things: my accent was inland, and Nainano-e took it upon herself to further my learning in things sexual, in the part of the month in which it was safe. I was a head smaller than she, but my face was lengthening, my shoulders beginning to lose their boyish sharpness for a man's curve.

The first time, I wanted to go up on the mountain, but she took me to the vegetable patch instead. "We shouldn't go too far from the house, in case the Lakans come," she said, and we lay down together between the grapes and the tomatoes. There was no fear in her voice, only a caution that was a matter of course, as against drinking suspect water or eating meat that has stood too long. I took it just as calmly as it was given; but the thought was as distant as a dream to me. Once I asked her about her blooding; I expected a grand telling, but all she said was, "There was a raid at the Raseyel's that we knew was coming, so a gang of us hid behind the sheep-house, and took them from behind. I stuck him beside the codpiece,

and put him out of his pain after. Then we got in trouble
for not fetching enough grown-ups. Oh, stop asking questions; you unblooded talk about nothing else; don't you
think we have better things to do?"

In the third quarter of the month, in the dead of night,
the dog woke me, barking as if he had gone mad. Then
Bukini, who slept almost as light as I, roused the others
with a yell. Through the stone walls came the second
sound, one such as men might have made in the pits of the
time before thought: a long furious deep howl, like a
wolf-pack baying all together. It froze everyone but me,
who understood less than they; I had not believed such a
sound possible, and thought it was the echo in my mind of
some terrible dream. I had not yet learned to wake up
fighting.

Osilaha, Bukini and Naina had all leapt to don their
armor; they knew where it was even in the dark. But
now my month-father said, "That's too many. We'll run."

The cracked voice of Binchera rose above the din: "The
Ascendant! He goes first!" Rigra pulled me in her two
strong hands to the window of the children's chamber,
furthest from the door. But we saw the shutter with its
carven wheat-ear sigil struck so hard it shook, and a man's
voice outside shouted chopped harsh words I could not
understand. Lakan, I thought dully. He had a spear; I
sensed its point, aimed where no true steel had ever been
aimed in my life; at my heart. They had ringed the house;
their yelling was coming from all around. Through the
chamber door I saw Osilaha looking at us, his strong face
full of despair.

Then his eyes thought, and took on resolve. "Buk, Naina,"
he said, his voice quiet. "The God-In-Ourselves speaks.
Weapons ready, follow me." I saw her pale fierce eyes,
angry, but more resolute, sharpening the resemblance to
her fathers; she tightened her hand on the long shaft of her
spear, whitening her fingers, and set stance with a hard
deep fighting-breath, just as I would in training. Her father
unshot the thick worn wooden bar with a bang and threw
open the door, opening us to the full clamor of the Lakans'
yells, and they sprang out together with a long war cry.

The part of me that was sensible thought, "No! Stand in
the door, and then they will only be able to come at you
one or two at a time!" For the first time in my life I felt

the stab in the heart of seeing a move ill-made that will cost dearly, and could not believe what it would mean even as I knew. But there was no time to think it out; as the true clash-clang-clash started, and I wondered at its sound, the spear at my window was gone, the Lakans running around to the door to fight. I saw why the three had done as they had.

Naina must have understood as he said it. I know now what that pale anger was, so fleeting: that she would never finish the sweater she was knitting, never lie with a boy in the garden again, that so much would remain undone, unseen, unlived.

Rigra threw the shutters open. "Run to the village and call the warriors, go!" She held back her two youngest, and the grand-ma'am waited for me to leave first. I threw my leg over the sill. Outside the stars danced on the mountain, and in the embrace of its shadow was a thousand man-lengths of safety, that my legs itched to run to. But then I thought, "They are dying, for me."

"Go, boy! What's taking you?" Rigra's voice was hoarse; she pushed, and I clung. Kicharesa cursed; said, "I'll get them, Mama," squeezed by me on the sill and was gone, her small legs flashing away; border children are well-taught. A scream came from the door, with more outpouring of life in its frenzied length than I had ever heard before; because, I saw slowly, it was a life's last expression, its farewell to itself. The voice was Osilaha's; a moment later Bukini screamed likewise from closer, inside. Naina I heard nothing of, though the clutch of swords no longer seemed to be striking. They were in the hearthroom. I swung my leg back over and said, "I'll go last." That was some measure of gratitude, at least.

Something stinging struck my ear, hard enough that I reeled; Binchera's hard-tendoned hand. "You little ingrate! They've given their lives, all three, to make you this chance—go!" She kicked me just as Rigra freed whimpering Inilai to slip past me into the night. Then I flew. My month-mother had picked me up by the hair and leg, and flung me headlong out the window.

Through the black sky flowed hails of yellow sparks; not in my eyes, but in the air, coming wreathed in thatch-smoke from the roof of the sheep-house. They had set it on fire; but the terror-stricken bleating came from closer.

Someone, Kicharesa I would imagine, had unlatched the gate; the spirit to save what one can is in border peoples' bones. I pulled myself up and looked back; Rigra's leg swung over the sill. I would have expected Binchera, since she was member first; but it is customary among border people for the elderly to wait till last, since they have only a short time left to them anyway; this I learned later. My month-mother fixed her eyes on me, readying herself to kick me all the way to the village if she must, as she began to swing her other leg over. Then torchlight filled the room, and her head jerked back and was gone.

What I remember, I remember as in a dream. There was the feel of the grass on my palms, and the dog still barking furiously; he was the kind to make noise from out of reach instead of fight, and so lived. There was the smell of thatch-smoke, the sound of the sheep's hooves tamping the packed earth; bleating, more calm and distant now. Yet it seems to me that I perceived all these things from the skin outward, like daylight from the bottom of a well, against what happened above.

I knew it all by sounds. Her first yells, war-yells, pure and tearless, the rustling and grunt of struggle, the Lakans' laughter; then when they saw they could not wrestle her down, blows, some sharp and cracking, some thumping bone-deep, and her cries breaking into sobs. Teeth-set silence, and more laughter; the tearing of cloth, the creaking of the bed; hoarse deep breaths, quickening, mingled with higher strangled panting, a choking cough.

What would they want of me now? I thought. To be safe; but I am. I felt so, crouching here free while she was raped. To see, and learn their lives, as an Ascendant on a month-away is supposed to. I raised my head so that my eyes were just higher than the sill.

They had hung their lights on the wall-hooks and laid down their weapons to free their hands, which were spattered with blood. Like the Lakan delegates they were earth-brown, their straight hair never cut, oiled slick and tied back with long leather thongs; but lean, the smaller one's muscles like rope on the outside of his arms, their wide breeches stained and leathern cuirasses worn; two forest brigands with bad teeth who carried the eternal shame of themselves Laka requires its poor to feel in their very souls, and who therefore, as the rich Enchians hold themselves above the law, held themselves beneath honor.

But men, with faces that wore expressions, where I had thought to see monsters, one could read them as one read Yeoli faces. There was the fire of exertion, ruddy on brown cheeks; hidden fear, rage unleashed, joy at what they had found here. For the smaller, hunger sated. They were young men, sons of pioneers whose crops looked to be weak this year perhaps. But their humanity made what they did now all the more terrible. It would have been different, I think, had I been raised on the border. As it was, for all the veracity of the role-play, for all the training and dares and boasting that had been my childhood, I had never in my life seen true violence done.

I watched, and thought sluggishly, "So this is what it is. Now I have seen." She lay half-stunned; I understand it takes much beating of a strong woman to force her legs apart. One had taken a turn; now the other pulled down his breeches. What my eyes least believed was his member, brown as the rest of him, standing high and hard; I had never thought much about this and had childishly imagined that men who did it must somehow force themselves to feel pleasure before, perhaps by use of their own hands in the way of children. But he took pleasure in Rigra's very pain; throwing himself on her with the roughness of an attack, thrusting as hard as he could, making of that part of himself a weapon as an unarmed warrior makes of his hands, but in hate against one helpless, as no warrior would do. When she closed her eyes and set her teeth to will herself away in mind, he struck her or closed his fingers around her throat until her attention was drawn back and she suffered enough for his pleasure once more. In the way of a child naming the things of the world, I thought, "This is love-making killed and come back rotten."

My shock turned to rage. I wanted to stifle those panting lungs, make him scream and thrash naked before her eyes as she did, strike off that brown part he so joyously stabbed her with, kill him, see him dead.

But it is for children to rely on adults to act. I was three years away from my wristlets, seven from my full coming of age. My helplessness twisted like a blade in my heart;

as before a mirror I screamed to myself, "*Grow!*" But in tears there was no relief; they did not end her pain.

I thought, why are the warriors from Krisae taking so long? Where are they, who are sworn to save us from such things, to fight so that we may sow quiet fields? I am three years away! I remembered feeling my hands move a wooden blade with their first skill, flexing my forearm and finding a new ridge there, my arrow striking the eye dead center, my ceremonies of promotion. Through my tears as through crystal I saw the sword of Saint Mother, rising with my hand; Esora-e, the finger-wrestling, the darkness of the cellar seeping into my soul, all the things that had tempered me. Where were the warriors—would they ever come? Three years! Rigra couldn't wait that long.

In my eyes and hands the world changed, becoming weightless; then rising through me sang the wind, and the harmonic singer. I ceased feeling my childhood, my smallness; I felt nothing of myself at all, but only moved. The large Lakan's sword was propped against the bed; I felt it before I saw it, amber with his groundless hate. The other had his back to me. I crept over the sill; with neither looking there was time. Once both my feet were steady on the floor I sprang across and snatched it up.

It was a straight thick longsword, slightly wider near the end in the Lakan style but tipped sharp for thrusting, a one-hander for him but for me a two. I wrapped my shield-hand around the pommel and shouldered it.

That was a mistake; I should have struck immediately. As it was, in the moment's stillness they both cried "Ahai!" and I lost the benefit of surprise. When they saw my size they broke into laughter, and the man on the bed made of his position an insult by staying in it, still thrusting with his head turned to watch his friend deal with me. The other grinned a sinewy grin, teeth white against brown skin, and drew his sword. He was guessing my worth in the slave-market, his round black eyes stripping away my name and my freedom: *a black-haired boy, healthy-looking, bright-eyed, without marks or deformation, so many gold pieces*. He stepped toward me, blade centered.

The voice of the God-In-Myself wavered. It spurs one to do; it does not always tell one how. I realized lamely I should have struck him before his sword was out. "Now what?" I wondered; I should do something. But to my horror I found that every move I had ever learned in my life was gone from my head, as if it had never been.

All my will and strength drained out like water down a hole. He was coming, his sword and hands bloody already, so much closer now, close enough to smell, still fresh like at the butchers'. I wanted only to throw up. There was no escape to the window; he had blocked it off. Nor to the door; more Lakans were that way. There was nothing I could do; presently this nut-brown man with great wiry arms would strike me down. The urge suddenly seized me to throw myself into his embrace, bury my head in his neck and let him do what he would; it was the child, I suppose, who had never met an adult who did not wish him well. The other guffawed again, behind me. Then, as he raised his blade, there was a pricking and a tightening all through me, and the world went still as a held breath, my thoughts freezing like flies in ice.

His stroke began. I remember being admonished, at its slowness. Instead of readying my parry I turned and cut the other Lakan, aiming between his leather-clad shoulder and the tip of his beard. Not expecting it, he did not move except his eyes' widening. From his neck-vein blood spurted, splashing a red crescent on the wall; a part of me absently marvelled, "So that is what it looks like." He made no sound; I had cut his windpipe. Now the sword behind was coming at my head from shield-side—the flat, for he had begun the stun-stroke, wanting his gold—so I ducked as I turned, just as I had done a thousand times with Azaila, felt it fly over whistling, and whipping from the turn, cut side-height, which my hands guessed would be his thigh-height. It went in to the bone; I felt the grinding in my hands, and remembering Esora-e's warning that an edge can get stuck, jerked it free fast. He kept his feet, but flatly, with a gape of surprise and then a teeth-clenched moan as the pain reached him. While his attention was on that I stabbed into the thigh-artery of his other leg; it was just where my teacher had said it was. But my wrist and fingers were too weak to make the correct finishing twist. In the Lakan style the sword had a long narrow guard with curving ends; I grasped them with both hands like levers, and did it that way.

He fell, shooting up blood, and lay staring amazed at me, trying to stanch the bleeding with his hand. I saw him consider calling to his comrades in the hearthroom, but they were making too much din themselves for him to think it worth the effort, which would have been very great for him then; such a wound drains one's strength fast. The blood kept pumping out; he yawned, then whispered something to me in Lakan, and lay still.

Silence rang. I heard panting—my own. Suddenly I was so tired I thought I would break. Esora-e had said one tires very fast in a real fight, especially the first. All-spirit, I thought, I've just been in a real fight. I'm blooded.

Once I had pretended to know what to expect: the singing wind guiding my limbs, or Esora-e's voice, calling "Strike!" as in training, when I ought to. I saw now I had known nothing, that indeed I never could have, until I had done it. The land of the training ground and the land of the fight are as different as two continents, and before he has been to the latter the student can never know, but only hope, that what he learned at home will work here. He will invariably find that it does, having been taught by those who have visited before him, and is free from doubt from then on. But until then, he must just trust.

My hands were slippery as if with oil; without thinking I wiped them and the sword-hilt off one by one on the skirt of my sleeping-tunic, then saw the color of the oil: scarlet. The iron taste in my mouth I knew from having bitten my lip in the past. There was more blood on the floor and walls and ceiling—the ceiling, how?—than I had believed could come out of two people.

Rigra lay staring at me wordlessly, the Lakan still lying across her, the bruises on her face coming up red under the spattering of his blood. I pushed him off her with my foot, the naked thighs limp and grey-brown now, and knelt beside her. I tried to say "Mama, are you all right?" but it came out a croaking like a frog's; my mouth and throat were dust-dry.

She had been preparing herself to die, or become a slave; now to know herself free as before she needed pause. She had seen her mother slain too; now I could see a long clothed bundle lying beside the bed: Binchera. Rigra drew in a long trembling breath, and squeezed my hand. "We must save ourselves before we grieve," she said, as much to herself as me. We linked arms to rise; then came the twinge of another straight Lakan blade, swinging toward the door.

Not trusting my voice I said nothing, let go her arm and crept back beside the door. All I knew was that I must not let him make any sound to warn the rest. The wall left me room only for a half-swing, but I steadied my arms, ready this time; I was experienced in this now, and so knew I could hit his throat as I could hit the throat of a practice-dummy.

His face appeared a little lower than I had expected, his thin black brows flying up at the sight before him, and I made the throat-stroke true, a little too fast so that the door-frame and not his spine stopped the blade, but good enough that when his mouth opened no sound came out. I grabbed his shoulder to pull his fall into the room where the others would not see.

"Listen for them for a moment, while I get clothes," my month-mother whispered. "Then we'll go." She opened Naina's trunk. I still wore my sleeping-tunic but hers had been torn, and one wants to be dressed after such. She threw on the first thing at hand: Naina's half-poncho, crocheted proudly in the colors of Krisae. Naina had done it herself, and wore it often. I remembered its warmth, which I had so many times put my arms around, then under. A thought cut through my giddiness.

I should have heard a scuffle, or her cries, as they served her like her mother, or a moan if she was just wounded. But I only heard men's laughter, and the sounds of things being broken. It was a mercy, I suppose, for Rigra.

Naina, I counted inwardly; Osilaha, Bukini and Binchera too. Half the faces that had shone around this hearth, sharing warmth and food, gone as in one stroke; half the hands, strong and graceful with skill learned over years, turned to nothing like leaves in fire. So much easier it is to destroy than create. Rigra a widow now; the two little ones, fatherless.

I thought of what they must go through now, the years they would suffer by this one night's work. I knew it too keenly. But my father's assassin had not been close, in the next room, while I held a sword in my hand, and the knowledge of what I could do with it.

Most would say, I think, that what I set out to do was not evil, given the circumstances. It was not even purely vengeance, but thought for the future too; the worst it cost the Lakans, the less likely they'd be to come back. Yet whether the cause is just or unjust, I think, the feeling is the same, dark and half-numb, always seeming just. I just wanted them dead, as if they were sheep to eat or child-killing bears, not men with homes and children; I wanted to see more of their blood spill, hear more pain in their voices. They had not paid enough, for what they had done.

Rigra was going, pausing only to spit on the dead face three times quick as a snake, and grind it into the floor with her foot. Instead of following, my legs took me to the corridor, winged. The story is that I charged pell-mell, but in truth I peeped first; I had not lost all sense. They might be looking, wondering after their three comrades or want-ing a turn at Rigra; I did hear three words called that had the tone of names.

They milled about, ready to go, carrying two wounded: more brigands with crumbs of Rigra's bread in their black beards, laughing, clapping each other on the back for their brave victory, the leader carrying our money box tucked under his arm. When none were looking my way I ran out cougar-footed, gave my war cry when I was close, and struck.

The first I cut on the side of the neck; he fell like a stone into the arms of two others, who dropped him to seize their weapons, crying "Ahai!" The leader had been the first out the door, something I would never do; for now as those still within leapt to face me and those outside yelled back asking what was happening, I imagine, he must push his way through to see. Meanwhile one with a long beard and a red ribbon around his head said something that made the others stand back, gave his torch away, and set his gaze on me. I was in a duel.

He was whip-cord built and looked over thirty, which didn't endear him to me. I would have done better to turn away from him and attack others who were not ready; but his motion had taken me back to the sparring-ground, to measuring, to setting my mind to read his intentions. Close to his body he held a short spear, its blade red-ribboned like his oil-drenched hair, and wet with blood. "Very well," I remember thinking, "if you want me to come in, I will." And I did, like the stupidest of novices. Just as he'd planned, he turned my thrust on his spear-shaft and brought one long dark shin up quick as a wolf's bite between my legs.

I was lucky, for my smallness made the aiming harder, and it did not land where it would have hurt worst; still, I went blind to all things but his spear. Dimly I heard them all laughing, above; I was on the floor. A great weight pressed my ribs; his knee, pinning me. Wiry hard fingers closed on my shield-wrist; opening my eyes I saw him reaching for the other, and above him another Lakan bringing a coil of rope.

So I formed the steel fork with my fingers, and drove it with all my might into his eyes. Lakan bandits don't learn much unarmed fighting, so don't know to expect that sort of thing. He screamed, and threw his hands over his face, freeing my other wrist. The only weapon in reach was a dagger on his belt, so I snatched that, and jammed it into the inside of his leg.

I squirmed free as he staggered off spurting blood, grabbed the sword and dragged myself up, wiping it out of my eyes; warm at first, it always soon turns cold. I must have been a dreadful sight, dripping from head to foot. They all stood still, amazed. Checked, while I felt my exhaustion; it was the time for bravado.

"Who's next?" I said, flicking my eyes from one to another; my voice, to my joy, was there. "Come on, who'll face me? I've only got five of you; I want all." I'd forgotten: they could not understand Yeoli. But they got the gist of it from my tone and my stance, and the five spread fingers of my free hand.

All it would have taken was one to say, "All in at once!" Then I would have run like a rabbit, or they would have got me. But no one did; they all stood frozen, torn, their faces showing the truth of what they were: farmer's sons bearing swords, who had expected easy hunting. Probably I'd downed some of their better fighters: the first in, whom they couldn't know I'd got by surprise, then this last one.

Finally the leader came back in, the box still in his arm. He read the story from me, the corpses and the faces of his men, with old flat eyes unchanging; they had seen such many times before, I saw. He was still chewing something, like a cow her cud; only that moved his heavy face, even as I fight-stared him, while he thought. Then without raising his voice he gave the word and the sign to leave.

I know his thought now. Everything valuable they had, since I was likely too spirited to be worth anything as a slave. Of some fifteen, they had lost nearly half their number, for gain not worth these strong young hands, needed on pioneer farms; I might take one or two more with me. They must have felt shame to run from a boy, but, as I have said, honor did not concern them. And the warriors of Krisne would come soon. They filed out, the last stepping backwards in stance to keep an eye on me, and ran off, throwing a torch or two onto the roof.

I found myself in darkness faintly reddened with the coals of the broken hearth-fire, and quiet as their voices faded. The slowing beat of my heart filled my ears; there was breathing full of death-bubbling too, from near the door. As I tried to light a candle, the tinderbox trembled madly in my hands. It was over; fight-frenzy faded and I went sick and weak with fear.

I realized I was smelling a smell like that of an abattoir, but with vomit and excrement on top, and burning. The candle-flame lengthened and brightened, and I looked around me. All was chaos, cupboards open, chairs smashed, ashes from the hearth strewn across the floor. The bodies lay where they had fallen, each with its seeping blackness: four Lakans, and Bukini. He was alive, lying on the threshold. I took the candle to his side, and knelt, laying my hand on his shoulder. His shield-hand was tucked into his sword-armpit, and blood welled up around it; I knew from my lessons in medicine that his lung must have been pierced. Still I said, "They'll be here soon, Buk, with a healer," again thanking my luck that my voice was there. Likely he knew he was dying; but I did not know what else to say.

His hand gripped mine, weak as a baby's. "You mad boy," he mouthed. "We would have saved you. Even if you can fight; why risk? Ascendant . . . Why for all the spirits did you come back?" I answered, "I thought I should"; I wasn't about to say, "Your mother was being raped." The words exhausted him, and he had faded enough that it made him wander, though his eyes, green like Rigra's, were full of some concern he could not speak. Finally he whispered, "The others?"

I heard myself say, "Safe," my voice hoarse now. It was one-quarter a lie, but a good one, I think. Then I heard a step from behind; Rigra came, still in Naina's Krisaeni half-poncho, knelt beside him and lifted his head onto her arm. They whispered to each other, things I heard but will not write, it being their business, her hand pressed over his right ear. Once he looked at me, made a brave smile, and breathed, "I wish I could have seen you being demarch. Good luck." After a few more words the rattle ceased, and she drew her hand away; his hazel eyes went still, like glass, and he began to look like my father had. She rose, and went out the door, not even looking to see what the flicker on the roof was. The other two corpses must have been there; I heard her screams begin.

I got up, and was suddenly dizzy almost to fainting; staggering sideways I stepped on a Lakan and nearly fell. I shook my sodden head, and, as I had been taught to do in training, seized myself, slowing my breathing, setting in a straight stance, fighting off the rushing in my ears. Presently, it seemed to me, I should hear the command of Shari the third-rank Teacher and we should go on to another lesson, perhaps archery on the long green field, bright with star-flowers in the sun; then it would be finished and I should find a girl and go up Hetharin, or chase trout in the sparkling stream with the gang.

The whirring in my head I suddenly understood: it was the wings of Shininao, as he had his fill here. Two of these corpses I had put there, three more in the back room. I had been numb, but now it came back: dark eyes mad with pain and shock, dark lips biting for air, choking, brown limbs in death-spasm; the crunch of bone on my blade, running up through my own bone, the warm splashing on my face; the death-rattle, and weakening grip; the black joy that Esora-e had told me I would feel, that to myself I had sworn I would never feel, that I had felt.

My stomach heaved up to my throat, but I held it down; I had been taught that gore does not make a warrior vomit. The end of the Lakan sword that I held throat-height wavered; I tightened my grip, then loosened it, to no avail. All of me was trembling, worse now; not fading as it should, but increasing. The room began to spin and quake; I felt I would fall. But warriors stand steady. "I never want to kill anyone," I had once said. Now I thought, "I didn't even know what it was like then."

We live our first nine moons in a warm enwrapping cave, fed all we wish, sheltered by our innocence, embraced without end by our mother's flesh. Then, for all it hurts, for all it dooms us, we are thrust out naked into blinding winter, to face the world with only our hands and mind; to feel the pain, to dare the trials, to work for what we once had free; to open our eyes, and know.

Thus I felt now, again. I may be forgiven, I hope, for doing what a baby does. It has its comforts: the memory of the freedom of the crib, where one may yell and thrash unfettered by thought of danger or face; the sense that gentle arms will soon enwrap one and a tender breast press to one's lips; the pure pleasure of hurling emotion into the air and out of one's heart, like a singer, to begin its healing. I clenched my eyes shut, and so thrust the house and the blood and the wings of Shininao away; I threw back my head and poured out my soul into the night.

Thus, standing in fighting stance in a burning house, sword in hands, blood-covered from head to toe except where my tears carved out clear streaks on my cheeks, and bawling for my Mama, the warriors of Krisae found me.

I stayed the rest of the month on another farm just as close to the border, that the verdict of a heated Assembly debate and vote. The news was soon all over Yeola-e, and people were saying I would be a warrior as great as my father. The story grew wings of gossamer within a month; I had wept in remorse, I heard, for not killing them all. I avoided accolades, hating to hear joy while I was in mourning.

When I got home, Azaila called me into the inner chamber of the School of the Sword. We knelt facing each other; as always when I was alone with him I felt honored to the point of ill-ease, wondering what I could possibly have done to merit such notice. "Fourth Chevenga, tell me," he said. "From your new knowledge, what do the wristlets signify?"

As always with his questions, I had no easy answer. His pale old green-gold eyes were cool and silent as lakes, no clues to be found there. "Don't answer what you think I would approve," he said, as if reading my mind. "Answer what is in your heart."

I didn't answer what I wanted to: the wristlets signify those who didn't come from Krisae fast enough. The answers I thought he would approve came to mind, the repetitions of what he'd said himself, the quotes from Saint Mother. What, I thought, is in my heart? I'm in mourning. I said, "Those who have to use the sword, for the sake of those who can't."

"Yes," he said. "But is that all that's in your heart?" What *is* in my heart, I thought, not what should be. All-spirit, must I say that? Azaila never accepted less. "Those who must do terrible things," I answered. "Things that should never be."

Saint Mother, I thought then, let me die, let the wind fling me off the cliff, let anything be but this. For with the memories my words raised in me, tears had come to my eyes, faster than I could stop; I who was three years away from being a warrior, who had had my face ground into the dirt, who'd driven my body near to breaking, all of it dry-eyed, was weeping, in front of Azaila.

"Good," he said. "Put out your arms."

The whole world froze. While I watched, my heart and skin gone dead and numb as a wooden doll's, he spoke the litany, drew the wristlets out from his tunic.

They were wrought of layered steel ridged in the pattern of the School, gleaming-new, sized slender, their leather linings gripping my skin like hands, becoming part of me as he clasped them on my wrists in the way of all things we wear. Yet in all their beauty, which part of me saw too large and vivid as through water, they mattered nothing; this day that I'd thought all through my training would be the day of my dreams was a day like any other. None of it mattered, the insignia, the rites, the symbols; only the knowledge, which they showed to others I carried. Many new warriors wonder why they feel no different, first wearing wristlets; I knew, I was no different. We all have the seeds in us; a warrior is one chained to sow and reap them. For the first time I thought then what I would many more times in my life: a wristlet is a manacle with an invisible chain.

In the corridor Esora-e hoisted me up like a child and swung me in his arms, laughing and whooping. "Ha-hah!

Didn't I tell you, didn't I tell everyone? Look, everyone, see my son, the warrior!" You don't care if people die, as long as I'm the greatest at killing, I thought. This wasn't entirely just—he hadn't invited the Lakans—but I could not forget he had hoped for a raid. "Many years ago you chose this," he said, when I tried to squirm out of his grip. "Now you are what you chose. No more, no less. Accept yourself as you are."

When he put me down I dashed away. In my room, my breath caught. Such things are done without fuss in the Hearthstone; it was mine now, and ought to be here, and so someone had brought it. Lying on its stand on my plain wood dresser, its immeasurable curve as familiar and close as my hand but strange and ancient as the moon, lay Chirel.

So long I yearned for you, I thought; so long I remembered your brightness in my father's hand, and ached to be in his place in the flower-petals and rain of wine. How small a child I was then! They said I could not wear these and bear you until I knew the price of it; sure enough, now I know it, here they and you are. The price is using you.

Clarity like that of being blown through and through by wind, and the voice of the harmonic singer, came then. I was not the boy who went up Haranin; I had taken the stance of receiving a weapon, without thinking. As Esora-e said, I thought, I am what I chose, for when I chose, I finished choosing. I stood pellucid, in the breath of centuries; in chambers like this, I saw, perhaps some of them in this very one, my father and his mother and warriors before them for fifteen centuries stood feeling this too, then kept it our workfast secret, just as I would.

The dark hide of the scabbard shone faintly in the light of my lamp, the curve like muscle beneath skin. I curled my two hands around the grip as I had practiced a thousand times with wooden swords, and it rose cool in my fingers. I wondered childishly if it accepted me, then remembered Yeola's words: this is nothing but a piece of steel, without a living hand wielding it. I turned it to sling it on, and felt a faint clang; its tip had struck the floor.

I flinched to the bones. Telling myself it had come to no harm, I tried again, and found once I had it on that the tip rested on the floor. I was too short to wear it.

My hand reached to my forelock, wanting to tear it out; my mind thought, will my suffering never end? Tomorrow I must train, and full warriors always bring their family's own true steel. All these things came lockstep, by habit, like hide-bound soldiers on the march.

But from somewhere in me too deep to deny rose a giggle, and then laughter so hard I felt I would fall over. Had anyone peeked in at that point they would have found a thirteen-year-old Ascendant wearing brand new wristlets and a five-century-old sword longer than his legs, flopped out on his bed raining tears yet again, but this time in mirth. Though I'm not sure whether I am the author or the butt, I thought, life is one wide-as-the-sky joke.

I put in an order to Aigra Workfast Military for a proper shoulder-scabbard. It meant I must forget the hip-draw I had learned since eight and start anew, practicing the shoulder-draw more times than I cared to think about; but such is life. Eventually, of course, I did grow tall enough to change back; I just never bothered, having got used to this way, and have worn my sword on my shoulder ever since.

VIII

My training got harder again. Esora-e sent me into a cave with only a trickle of water, having the entrance blocked off with rocks; I had to move them away faster than the other students could place them to escape, else, he assured me, I would die. Not wanting to find out whether he meant it, I worked unceasingly. It took three days.

The high beam at the School is the height of a tall man and wide as his foot; my feet soon knew it like hands, and my body knew the ground underneath like feet. By my fourteenth birthday, I was sparring with Esora-e on it, and had to learn to fall without letting the sword touch the ground or cut me. The whip of winter was in the air when they first made me spar Esora-e and role-play tactics at the same time. Azaila would conceive some battle, sometimes one of the many he had been in which I had never studied, and we'd play it out, I commanding the Yeolis and he inventing the counter-moves of the enemy. He was brilliant at plausible hitches. Nor did it end if I fell off; I learned to land springing back up.

One day after winter solstice I fell wrongly, landing full on my sword-arm. There was a crack, then a gushing as if all my blood were pouring out, though I saw none. I began the usual leap, lifting the sword, and pain the like of which I had never known in my life threw me back to my knees.

I laid the sword across my thighs and tried to feel my wrist through my sleeve; when I touched it the falling snow went black and then grey. Bones were broken. All the while I was expecting warm strong arms across my back, leading me to hearth, and a healer. Instead Azaila was shouting the same things as usual when I fell: "Chevenga! Chevenga! Where's the demarch?"

The sense of it came cold to me, ground in by training. In battle one might fall from a wall, be thrown by one's horse, or break one's arm a thousand other ways; yet that does not end it. I was not playing a child. War-training is all, or nothing.

I looked up. The beam seemed high as a mountain. But one must not waste time wondering whether one will succeed; better just to try, in which way one is sure to find out. I pulled my sword out of the fingers of the one hand with the other, sheathed it and stood, jumped, hooked my one good arm around the beam and swung my legs up, trying to remember through the hammering of pain what had been happening in the battle. For a moment I must cling with my legs while I got the good arm wrapped over the beam, trying not to jar the bad; then I drew myself up, sword in shield-hand, just in time to parry.

Fighting entails a thousand jolts. I had never noticed before. As well, my wristlet seemed to tighten on my arm as it swelled, like a torturer's vice. Yet I must keep my voice steady as I called the orders, tears straining in my throat along with the sourness and watering that heralds vomiting. *Do not think of pain*, I commanded my mind. *Think of the tactic, of the strokes, not of nausea, of dizziness.* . . . My sight, full of Esora-e and his fight-stare, misted around the edges as if seen through a window frosted with ice. *Think not of training, but of battle.* . . . I would be of steel, of rock, no pain would touch me; thus I drove it out, while the voices and crackings of swords came to me muffled one moment and clear beyond bearing the next. When my shadow-father's sword quavered in my weapon-sense, burning and smudging in turns, I knew I couldn't keep going.

Yet I could not fall again; nor could I stop, for that would be breaking play. I had gained, for the first time in my life, the impossible crossroads. But there is always a way; thus I was taught. If the road is east-west, the warrior jumps north; if it is on the ground, he jumps up; he takes the path unconceived. When I remembered this it showed itself to me.

"Second!" My call sounded like a frog's croak, but was heard. "Here, sir," Azaila answered, close beneath; I know now he would have caught me. "Take command, from now. I am too hurt to do more." He said, "Yes, demarch, sir. They fight." It was in his own voice, not his playing one. "For you, it is over." I felt a hand grip my good forearm, then an arm my waist, and Esora-e's voice close to my ear said, "Lean on me, my son." But I said no, and got down myself; I'd got up that way.

The outer bone of my forearm was broken, in two places. It was set by Ensahis, the Haian healer of Terera. Instead of splinting my arm as we would, she wrapped it in strips of gauze dipped in plaster and water, which hardened into a solid sheath that gripped it all round; when it was hardened she signed and dated it. This is the standard Haian practice, and ensures the bone will heal true.

For all I could fight as well as them, I was too boyish for the girls in my war-class. I was never a fast grower; at fourteen I looked fourteen, short, rawboned, and not even thinking of beard, though the hair between my legs was coming in thicker, and, being black, showed up well.

I didn't play only with girls; Krero and I had something of a tryst until we both saw it was all pretense. My wristlets were necessary to it, which should have been the first warning. All the while Mana, to whom I was sworn already, stood patiently by.

Nyera stood apart from all the games and secrets and matchmaking. At first I thought it was because we'd had an argument; she'd said something about me no longer being a child after my promotion, and my head still being too much an upturned anthill to think sense, I had answered something about killing being her only measure of adulthood. Now she was almost shy of me, which seemed ridiculous. I'm still amazed I was so much a child as not to see. She came to visit me after I'd broken my arm, and wrote on my cast that she loved me.

I needn't dwell on it. Everyone knows teenage love: the weeping for having to part each night, the solemn oaths, the silly jokes made into treasures, the endless clinging. During lessons I daydreamed, of our hearts thundering together, of her hair and her soft breasts, until my tutors combed me.

It lasted about a year. My shadow-father gave me grief for being too young, but less than I expected; he knew her, from the training ground, as a warrior student, suitable for me to breed with to his mind. I shot up, so that I could look Krero in the eyes, and my voice changed, cracking sometimes in the middle of words, to Nyera's rippling and clear laugh. "At ten one is a boy, and at twenty a man," she would say, her cheek on my shoulder. "You are fifteen, half-and-half."

I had not made a marriage hint, age had brought wisdom. But it seemed inevitable, and I began planning. There were the parents to be informed—well, asked, at this age—Senahera services to be requested, invitations made, the announcement; it must all be done demarchically. I wondered happily how many children we could get before I died. Then, in the warmth of my room, the husk of the fire still red on my grate, I felt my body turn cold, and my heart ashen, as I saw what I must do. How could I say I loved her, and not warn her?

I had never thought of it. I saw myself deceiving her all through our life, every plan we made, every child we had, worst when I was twenty-nine and we spoke of next year. I doubted I could do it if I tried.

Yet just imagining opening my mouth to tell put me in a cold sweat. For eight years I had been training myself in secrecy: to bite back my thoughts whenever someone said something that awakened it, to see the fatal slip of the tongue before it came, until I knew all the possible ones as naturally and unthinkingly as the alphabet. Now I found my lips truly sealed, like a sliding window left closed for eight years.

And her; I imagined her, my beautiful Nyera-cha, her face shocked, then horror slowly sinking as the future played out in her mind. Would she be happier not knowing, I thought, like my mother? Perhaps it is only selfishness that makes me want to tell, my integrity truly conceit; I've lied to everyone else so far. If I cease lying to her, why not to them? I meant the question as rhetorical, but it was a heady thought, never again feeling riddled with dark secrets, like a criminal. Remembering my mother's caution to consider before I told anyone, I played out the results, in the light of new experience.

Their faces: Mana, Krero, Sachara, with narrow half-childish brows peaked. Artira, faced instead of with the chance of succeeding to the demarchy, the certainty. Naiga, who calls me "biggest brother." The people: my people, all knowing when they will lose me. Naingini, possibly outliving me.

For a time they'll pity me; then someone will say, "Wait! Why are we all weeping—who says this is inevitable?" Probably Esora-e. People think augury is as good for prevention as for prediction, so everyone will try to protect me. I will end up fortressed in some tower, or at the very least, constantly watched. Despite all the tales in which people try to defy death prophecy and fail by some slip impossible to foresee, I will never convince those who love me it cannot be done; they are too brave and cheery, and think I'm too young to truly understand. They will just try to foster my hopes, and if I argue long enough they'll think I've gone mad and bind me to a bed. One way or the other, a prisoner.

Then there was demarchy; that small matter. I might never be approved; Yeola-e wouldn't want two short-lived demarchs and regencies in a row. I had never thought of this before either, lacking the understanding; now like a worm the full meaning crawled out into sight. I would be concealing knowledge that might touch the vote, serving under false pretenses. By the law, I should declare myself, and renounce my succession.

All the cliffs of Hetharin called me, then. I'd never been anything but Fourth Chevenga; I would be nothing otherwise. Standing on a dolomite edge, the land below distant enough to be turquoise, I thought, I'm fifteen, it's half over; why do I cling so hard to another miserable fifteen? I will feel only the wind of the fall, and then this little scrap of life everyone sets such store by will be shown at its true worth. I suppose adolescence is the worst time for death-wish.

As it was, I remembered my wristlets, reminders that a purpose can be accomplished even in a moment of life;

then my older oath, to love twice as much; finally, how absurd it would be, dying to save the world from my death.

I went out onto the mountain and prayed about it. No voice came from the sky, only from within: that of the harmonic singer, and the wind. The world knows what it sang to me: "Keep your secret, and the demarchy." Call me selfish or conceited, for wanting a life with more purpose than waiting for its end; my name is yours to judge now. It also sang, "Make it worthwhile."

After training the next day I swore Nyera to silence on the sword of Saint Mother. Then we went up the mountain, and I told her.

Not that it went as smoothly as these words make it seem. Seeing me troubled she reached to touch my cheek with her fingertips, comfort I ached for in every trembling sinew; but I drew back. I was afraid of her letting go when I told her; better she not touch me at all. After eight years of silence, the words came out rusty and broken.

It was seeing so many oddities of mine explained all at once, I think, that made her believe me. *That's why you hurry, why you want to marry so soon, why you would go quiet sometimes when we played House, why when we threw snowballs you'd aim for older people, why you're getting Chinisa to teach you shorthand* . . . I told her why I had told her: in case she meant to propose. While she sat silent I looked at the grass between my crossed legs, the stunted mountain stuff with tiny blades like claws, brown with the cold of coming winter, a twisted white stem like waxed string with a dead floweret. I can see it clear as yesterday. She leapt up and ran away down the slope.

Everyone who has just revealed such a thing must for a time wish their listener tongueless; I saw her throwing herself into the arms of the first friend she saw in the Hearthstone, and spilling it all. But I reminded myself she was no oathbreaker.

I did not dog her. She had wanted to think about it alone; when she was done she would seek me. That night I slept a little, exhausted from the night before, in which I had not slept for a moment. My father was insomniac; in that way too, I follow him.

She met me after training. When I saw her face, I truly

regretted telling her, wished it all back and buried, wished indeed that I had never courted her, never touched her life at all. I knew for certain what she would say when she clasped me in greeting, for her touch was like that of someone clutching that which is wrong to clutch, being impossible to keep. She had wished marriage, it turned out; but no more.

So this is what it is, I thought, to be a broken lover. I wanted to scream at her, "Am I not worth it?"; to hear my ruin justified in detail, as if it mattered, to make her apologize and beg forgiveness even more times than she did, as if that would form some sort of mythic half- or spirit-marriage, so I need not feel flung from the world. As it was I just consented, forgave her everything and told her to stop apologizing, for I understood why better than anyone. I am lucky, to have a mouth that can still speak sense while my heart raves. We embraced goodbye, and went down the mountain apart.

Some have called her a coward. They should try being her, at her age too. I am stuck with foreknowledge; if I could be free of it, I'm not sure I wouldn't leap at the chance. For a time I lived a blackness; everyone knows losing teenage love, too, and with me it had its special pangs; I wept at night seeing myself a childless bachelor at twenty-nine. But it passed.

It is customary for an Ascendant's first foreign month away to come after he turns sixteen. But the next spring, fifteen and a half, I pestered my aunt to send me now, since I had my wristlets. My first idea was Laka. I could make friends with anyone, as all agreed. Maybe I could prevent the war; who knew, until it was tried?

Without glance or expression my aunt answered, "Are you completely out of your mind, boy?" When I asked her what Astyardk had against me she said, "Well, you can start with the five of his people you killed two years ago. Of even more interest is your position as future king, as they put it, of the patch of land he is most interested in seizing. You, a hostage—it might start the war. I know, lad, you want to be the hero, and likely you feel its buds in you. Heroes have heads as well as thews. Out of my office, until you use yours."

The next day I returned, having thought and seen her

point, and asked to go to Tor Ench instead. "There's an alliance to be made there," I said. "If we go to war, they'll get so much less Yeoli grain, which they've just admitted to us again they need."

"Where have you been?" she said. "That's been in the wind around the Palace for two months; you insult us all, to act as if only you have thought of it." On the mountain with Nyera was where I had been. I apologized quickly and said, "But I'll bet you didn't think of sending *me*." She admitted she had not. "I get along well with Kranaj; remember when we went hunting? And there won't be any incidents this time; Reknarja wouldn't call me a slip of a boy now. *If he did . . .*"

She sent me to Brahvniki.

The ship I went on was fully soldiered and armed. Better safe than sorry, I suppose. A year before a Yeoli merchant ship carrying weapons had been boarded by Arkans, searched, its captain tortured and its full cargo confiscated, all on suspicion that she intended to sell them to the Srians, with whom Arko was at war. In answer to my aunt's protest, the Marble Palace had been very polite and proper: it had been a mistake, but we were best to avoid the risk of such a thing happening again by refraining from shipping weapons through Kurkas's waters. Whether it was his waters or ours, I hardly need say, was a matter of dispute. "It's the way Imperators are raised," I remember my grandmother saying. "Spoiled as year-old meat, so they grow up thinking they're gods. If you behaved so, Tennunga, I'd comb you."

I always said the same thing, whenever she made that mistake. "The hair, Grandma'am. Look at the color of the hair."

"Oh," she would answer, "did I call you Tennunga again? I'm sorry, Chevenga." Always I would say, "No matter, Nainginin. There are worse people you could mistake me for." It had become a ritual.

As we sailed away from Yeola-e, the design of the ships, with their nameplates in several languages or devices for the illiterate, grew stranger. As we came to the city, the strangenesses compounded, until I felt as if I were in a story. The Benai Saekrberk, where I would stay for half my time, was as big as I'd imagined a king's palace must be, the walls a glistening blue that glowed almost purple in the russet light of sunset, the many onion-shaped white domes of its towers burning orange like fires. The customs clerk openly wore riches that could only have been the fruit of bribes; they peace-bonded Chirel with wire and a lead seal that I saw a good pull would break. Thus are protocol and practicality melded, in Brahvniki.

The corridors of the Benai smelled sweet like flowers, because scent had been mixed into the mortar. Yet despite all this grandeur, which I understood foreign leaders were given to, I thought the Benaiat Ivahn was an artist when I first saw him, for he was painting an onion-arched mandala in the office I'd been shown to.

He was healthy then, for all his age. His step down from the stool had spring in it, and the grip of his hands an old hardness as if he had once trained with staff or spear. I already knew several people who struck awe merely by their presence; here was another. One could not find the source of it in any one thing; his brown eyes were plain, pinched narrow over a long nose like a beak, his lips a touch severe; all in all, he was vaguely birdlike. But the bird was an eagle, such as sees the peaks of mountains from above; those eyes apprised themselves of all things, and could see one's soul in a glance. He hated formality; it wasn't long before we'd shared the salt, Brahvnikian-style, which signs the end of form and the start of frankness.

We liked each other right off; perhaps we both knew what would be. He was one who could find truth in a dust-speck, and accepted all things, good or terrible, with grace.

We spoke of the Benai and its affairs in the city, its creed, which is more one of question and contemplation than of law and prayer; they hold no one god or gods. Brahvniki is not a demarchy by any means, the people having no vote; nor is it a monarchy, with one person holding all or even most power. The Benaiat shares power with the Praetanu, the council of guild-clan leaders, and Brahvniki does not worship him so much as respect him, as a wise grandparent or an elder in a village. It is best called a benevolent oligarchy, delicately balanced; the Clawprinces, as they are called, are wealthier, which is everything in a city worked by guilds and wage-slaves, but they forever weaken themselves by jostling for position or feuding, and the Benaiat is more loved by the people. Yet, as in most foreign places, one will see in the street a jewelled carriage passing a beggar in rags.

Besides serving as a bank and agent for a number of concerns (I tried to imagine the Senaheral doing that), the Benai makes the famous distillate Saekrberk, which he gave me my first sacred sample of. First came the scent, sweet and strong as musk; then the liquid itself, which seemed to burst into flame as it struck my tongue, a fire dark and deathly and more naked than any nakiti, like lava, or the juices of a woman's loins. Foreigners have the strangest sacraments.

When we each had had three, he talked me into going into the city with him in disguise, to hear about ourselves, something he'd been doing for forty years. He went as a ragged old man, and I, in plain voluminous-sleeved Brahvnikian shirt, his grandson, Vik, mute, of course, to hide my accent. We went to a tavern called, as I can best describe it, a "K," a clearing of the throat, then *Nota Voorm*; best for news, but somewhat rough, and full of people of races I had never even heard of. In the way of foreigners, none gestured properly, but twitched and waved their hands unintelligibly, some still gripping mugs. Any Yeoli who travels should know to expect this, and not misconstrue it if a stranger fails to put down what his hands are doing to speak. For the first time I saw Arkans: a clutch of marines, heads high and long golden hair tossing, one with a full steel breastplate lacquered red; they hid their hands under the table, as if ashamed of deeds they had done. It was there I first heard my name dropped; one of the sailors from my ship was telling someone I'd killed ten Lakans at Krisae, and ate rocks for breakfast. I also heard someone say, my first time for that too: "I wonder how much Astyardk would pay for Fourth Whatsisname's head?" All part of my learning.

By the month-away customs of my people, I became a novice of the Benai for the first half of my time, and then I was to stay with certain Clawprinces. Being foreigners, though, they never ceased to see me as an honored guest, and treated me to all manner of Brahvnikian entertainments; not to mention the deference, which constantly scraped my skin. I was always wanting to say to obsequious servants, "Why do you act less than human? Do you think you're fooling me?"

Of all of it, I remember best the concert Ivahn took me to, composed and conducted by Ilesias Janisen. I met

Ilesias, a bejewelled Arkan, with a sheet of golden hair down to his waist, who had been born into the *okas* caste, higher only than slaves, so that he'd had to flee Arko to pursue his calling. Even more, I remember the conversation Ivahn and I had on the ferry returning; quite casually he said, "No one will ever own you."

I stared; he was the sort of person one could easily expect augury from, and this had the sound ring of it. But I thought again, and answered, "That cannot be. My people will own me." Own me; such a foreign turn of phrase. Even conversation here was exotic, like smoky spices.

"Oh, I don't mean you'll turn into a tyrant," he said. "Not you. It's just the more your people know you, the more they'll command you to do what you choose."

The law unwritten, I thought. The harbor wind, licking up from the black water, was suddenly chill. "I won't allow that," I said.

"Oh?" He smiled. "You'll impose your will on them?" Ilesias's music was still soaring and thundering in my head; its echoes and these words have become inextricable in my memory. "No, no. You misunderstand me, lad. They will love you, and being in awe of your judgment they will command you to do as you advise." Then he changed the subject. It came to me this was the same thing my father had told me; but from a foreigner it somehow struck as deep again.

Komona Shae-Ranga-e, the dark-haired girl who three years before had said she would not marry me because her egg was falling, was also in Brahvniki then, on a Senaheri month-away. Between our monk's tasks, something began between us.

She was the first woman to whom I cried in bed, "I give myself to you!", and "Your touch is my life!", quite to my own surprise; she had a manner that inspired—no, obliged—trust. Of course, boys of that age will yell that the Earthsphere is moving in their throes of ecstasy; but never have I uttered any such thing that I did not feel just as wholeheartedly afterward.

Then my month away was cut off; we were at war.

My guards woke me at midnight, and we set sail right then. They knew only that Lakans had taken the pass at Kamis and had laid siege to Nikyana, the closest way into our plains, and to Leyere, far to the south. Astyardk wanted more, it seemed, than one fertile valley. The ship bearing the news had just come in; our ambassador was left to make my farewells and apologies for me. I remember the sea in the first paling of dawn, smooth as an Arkan mirror reflecting the flowering hues of the sky, except where our oar-blades cut through its skin to show the deep turquoise of its flesh hidden underneath. I stood by the rail stunned, for Yeola-e, and grieving, for myself. Komona was not a warrior. I would be sent straight to my posting, I thought; until the war ended, years perhaps, I would not see her again.

That was not, after all, how it went. When we got to the Hearthstone, and I trotted into Tyeraha's office all geared up and glittering, she said, "You'll cut a fine figure, when your time comes to go." By custom I should go on the first tour, then stay for my general's apprenticeship; but there is another custom, whereby, if an Ascendant or demarch is greatly gifted or has some uncommon ability, he must marry and produce an heir before going into battle, to pass it down. It had never crossed my mind that I qualified. "Whatever's in your blood," I remember her saying, "is good soup-base for the next." It is not done if it will keep us away too long; it is only hedging a bet, after all. But she had her spies, and knew I stood a chance of marrying Komona.

I argued passionately, of course, as one will as a matter of duty when one's secret inclinations are opposed. Nearly three years in wristlets had not changed me; I was a swordworker who could cut the wings off a fly in midair, and would have given anything never to fight in my life, but my people's lives. Still, imagine seeing myself as others must see me, cooling my heels in the Hearthstone while people died in Nikyana, I feared being called a coward, as anyone will, especially at that age. But, as my aunt said, "A warrior's pride doesn't always suit a demarch; only a demarch's does."

The signs of war were everywhere, the gate-guards old, no one playing Unsword in the courtyard. My sibs kept saying, "Cheng, aren't you going? When are you going? Will you come back?" I got more news. The wall across Kamis had been taken by surprise; they'd sent mountaineers (how should we have known they had them?) to climb around behind and open the gate. "There is a name you should know," my mother told me: "Inkrajen." That was

the Lakan general who had conceived it; he had the name
of a brilliant tactician.

In Leyere it had been planting when the sentinels had
lit the fire of warning; so no crops would come in this year.
Yet the city, having been sacked before, has a vegetable
patch and a cistern on every roof. Likely they could hold
out alone until winter, when the Lakans—twenty-thousand,
apparently—would have to retreat or ease off, so we could
send most of our strength against Inkrajen.

The first tour of Vae Arahi had left for Nikyana seven
days before I got home. Esora-e and Denaina were not yet
posted, being older than thirty-five, nor were my friends,
being younger than or barely sixteen. Tyeraha was war-
trained, but no general, and so had appointed Hurai Kadari
to command on the border; she would stay to do demarchic
business here unless war came far inland, which a certain
young augurer of excellent promise who had just joined
the Assembly Palace Workfast, one Jinai Oru, had said it
would not.

Azaila, missing a good half of his Teachers, set me to
instructing. Some of my students were taller than I. I was
still child enough to be troubled by this, until he drew me
aside after class, and stood close, saying no words, only
smiling. I was looking down at him, by a good three
fingerwidths. With him it didn't matter; nor did it, I saw,
with me.

Komona came home. She was astonished to see me,
having resigned herself to forgetting me, too, till the end
of the war. Now we picked up where we had left off.

It was her philosophical bent that drew me to her,
I suppose; it was certainly not the camaraderie of the
ground, as with Nyera. We couldn't wrestle; the one time
I tried, she cried afterwards, "You *bruised* me!" I remember shortly after I'd introduced her to my clutch (of
which Nyera was no longer part), we went climbing; seeing the first crag, she looked at me with dark eyes full
of terror. Marvelous, I thought; they'll despise her for
a coward, and never hear her talk philosophy or sing.
Afterwards I started a water-fight in the stream, so we'd
all have to go in to dry off; then I invited them all
into my chamber where we lit a fire and lay naked drinking tea. I brought out my harp, so she had to sing; in
between songs the conversation got pulled round some-

how to philosophy. Soon the others were giving me the chalk sign behind her back.

Leyere held, the twenty thousand Lakans dwindling to ten thousand. It was Emao-e Lazaila, called Steel-eyes, commanding the relief force; she was able to drive the besiegers off to bring in supplies. But Nikyana fell. Once again Inkrajen was our curse. Laka always has its cavalry, made up of those great black warhorses and the slave-owning lords that breed them, riding with their hench-men. Our watchers had spied only a few in his army. But near the town is a small plain, that had been harvested already, and Inkrajen lured us (under Korotora Shae- Serao) there, then attacked just before dawn on a moonless night. From nowhere came a thousand horsemen, to cut us to pieces. He'd sneaked them over the pass with covered lanterns and muffled hooves in the night. We lost three thousand, including Tyirao Krai, who had taught me the shoulder-draw, and Checharao Sachil, whom I had sought for love once at twelve. Our army was scattered, the town walls stormed, and everyone within chained and marched away to Lakan slave-blocks. On Nikyana's burgeoning stores, so carefully laid in in case of siege, Inkrajen's army could winter on our land. For a day I could bear no tenderness, not even from Komona.

We sent reinforcements; Esora-e rankled that he was not called. The war held still for a time. Hurai had gone himself to Nikyana, and made sure he fought on talus and hill, harassing, raiding baggage trains, the style of war that suited. My aunt made her second Renewal. Afterwards my fingers were bruised, from Komona's squeezing them through the rite; she'd been thinking of me.

Summer ripened; the crops looked to be the best in ten years, as even we Athyel will thank the Hermaphrodite for, in times of war. Krero turned sixteen and got his wristlets, then Sachara, with the rest of us following hard on their heels. Komona and I lay together in the mead-ows, twining flowers in each other's hair, and playing debating games.

I remember how the moment came. She had got the better of me; losing sorely, I said, "Politics is built on dialectic, philosophy defies it. So there." She kissed my nose, and said, "Concession accepted, beautiful man. You know, love, my mother always told me to marry someone I could out-argue."

There is little more to say. I remember drawing my hands out of hers to tell her, a custom of mine, now. She too, found my mysteries explained. She took it calmly, and did a seven-day abstinence in the Shrine to decide. I remember kissing her crystal, as it hung from the branch. It wasn't enough.

A Senahera wants peace of mind in life, not haunting. That would have been hard enough, married to a demarch; this was too much. Later, I found she had sworn the oath of celibacy, for life. I knew it was not by natural inclination; no one knew better than I. But though I told her she was punishing herself too much, she never revoked it.

The morning after she left me, I lay in bed past dawn, following the running patterns on my ceiling. My body saw no reason in the world to rise. Two of two have refused, I was thinking; no one will ever marry me. Sooner or later I will have to confess why; I should anyway, to live honestly; there goes the demarchy, and so I have no reason to live. None but the running patterns anyway; they are fascinating.

In time my door sprang open, and my shadow-father came in, dressed for training, his face full of worry. "Saint Mother!" he said when he looked into my face. "You don't look sick. Are you?" I just told him to go away.

Were a child of mine to do this, I think I would say, "Very well, it is your own training you are losing," give his and my students to another Teacher, and not leave him alone until I knew the reason. But I have lived what I have lived. Esora-e had not.

"If you aren't dressed in a count of ten," he said, "you'll have the combing—no, the thrashing—of your life. One . . ." I said, "I didn't invite you into my room. Get out." He stared disbelieving for the length of a heartbeat; then he leaned down to throw my covers off, intending to yank me up by the hair, I think. Before he could I hurled myself at him.

The dead anger in me was great, but not enough; he was in the right. We crashed backward over my desk, sending my waxboard and my amethyst paperweight flying, and bringing down a rain of papers. I threw him, but he wrapped his legs around me and twisted our fall so that he landed on top; on my sheepskin he kept his weight on me, then when I was fighting hardest to turn onto my front he let me, twisted my arm behind my back in its moment of laxness, and turned me prone again with my both arms pinned, and one of his free.

We locked eyes. His were vapid with rage; mine must have shown no fear, for I felt none. He drew his arm back, and struck me full in the temple, using less than his full strength but hitting with the edge of his wristlet. I saw flowers of purple and black for a moment on that side, and my ears rang. But I kept my eyes on his.

He struck me seven such strokes, all with the same force, his intention to drive the defiance out of my eyes. It worked, for at the last I was semi-conscious, the walls loosing themselves from their moorings in the floor, and spinning all around my head. But it was only through harm to my body, not pain to my soul, as he intended; my soul barely noticed.

The floor heaved; bile rushed to my throat and I vomited until I was empty. "When you are recovered," he said, standing over me, "I shall see you on the training ground." While we fought his hands had been steady as stone; it was now they trembled, as he knelt to kiss my brow. Somehow, that was the worst cruelty. He only loves me, I thought, when I am defeated. Death seemed preferable again, and I knew where. Close enough to the place of testing is a place wide enough in the stream to cover a youth. A little late, I thought, but my pyre will still be andirons, since I am still a child.

Put it down to adolescence, when strain between childhood and adulthood pulls us to all manner of excesses, worse for one who tries to hurry it. Put it down to those seven days of waiting, that had stretched me thin, or Esora-e addling my brain. Or put it down to nothing, and Shininao take the excuses. On that day, I, Fourth Chevenga Shae-Arano-e, was an idiot. I have been on other days too, to my recorded and remembered shame. Who can say they have not?

Though standing made me dizzy, I dragged myself up the mountain to the stream. In a bath of rushing ice-water I lay still, watching a hawk wheel in the steel sky; my skin scalded, silvery, like in the swimming hole in spring. Cold reminds one of one's fragility, as anyone who has leapt into a glacial lake will know; it crept deeper than my skin, burning the fire out of my heart. A headache beyond description came; I began shivering, and knew I would not die until after it stopped.

But my mind, being alive still, must think thoughts; there being no reason to think about anything to do with life, since I was done with it, I could think nothing but "Well, then. I'm about to die." Soon I noticed I must turn my mind from everything which was anything to me. Then it was only a matter of time before I thought, "This is insane!", got up, and staggered back down the mountain to my mother's room, where the fire always burned, fearing I'd caught my death.

I don't know what the Haian said to her, nor she to my shadow-father, once she'd got the story out of me, but the next day he apologized, with the sign of deepest shame. We forgave each other; in explanation I said only, "It was madness." For him that would answer questions, not raise them.

The headache took two days to end, and the cold four more. When I was recovered, I geared up again. I would get a breastplate when I was demarch, my father's if it fit me; now I had a long chain mail shirt, belted above the hips, that could be widened as I filled out, and his steel helm. I said farewell to my room, in which I had lived all my life. On the long tapestry that hangs in the stairwell are woven the Twin Hawks, whom foreigners call gods, and warriors call the Oldest Lovers, (since how can two face each other for so long and not fight, except that they are lovers?) a sign of war left over from before the Fire. They stare, never fight; though they stood locked in threat for a century, the fight lasted only a moment, and then the world was ashes, so great was the power of their weapons.

The armor felt steely around my heart as well as my shoulders. "No reason now," I said to my aunt, "why I should not go. Send me."

IX

Mana, Nyera and Ramiha Ketariha, Krero's new girlfriend, were, like me, not yet sixteen; but they had been judged worthy to receive their wristlets, and so we were all posted together on the next tour.

Our Ten was them, myself, Krero, Sachara, Kamina, who still glowed whenever he caught sight of his own wristlets, Alaecha Nikari, whom I hardly knew, and Kunarda Nung-Shae-Zen, who had joined the School of the Sword in spring. He was a dark bristling boy with long black locks that hung nearly as straight as an Enchian's; his first training was fighting off taunts about his hair, I should think. Those who think I was the strongest man in all Yeola-e or the world should know, he could finger-wrestle me to the ground all my life.

Our decurion was Kesariga Asenga, a man old enough to have patrolled on the border but not to have fought in the Enchian wars. I felt sorry for him, stuck with both me with my position and Krero with his nature. "You know, he's not even blooded," the grumbles were, on the march. "The moment we get there, let's impeach him, and elect you." I just ignored him.

It was midmorning when we came to Shairao.

It is not walled—no foreigners had ever won so deep into these parts before—and commands a pass above a wide valley. We were camped near the top of the pass road, beside the town; the Lakans were camped on the valley floor, too far away to see as more than a dark motley mass that drew our eyes irresistibly.

We were saluted by the sentries, and led in to the quarters of the others from Vae Arahi and Terera. Thus I got my first taste of the life I would live so much: the guy-ropes and trampled grass, fire-pits and latrine-pots; smells of sweat, canvas, smoke, potatoes, mutton stew; the rasp of sharpening stones on steel and the ring of axes in wood; the horseplay, training yells, comings, goings, messages, errands, swear-words; the sense in the air of multitude, full of a single purpose.

A town is placid, going about its business unconcerned with its existence, since it is a thing that should be. A war camp, being a thing that should not be and hence ever full of concern, breathes its news, good or bad, into the air, showing it in every stance and voice, the bearing of every shoulder and the sheen of every wristlet. Here, it was: "We are defeated." Every face but those of newcomers had a grim set, and one could hear people curse each other; everywhere were bandages and crutches, too, and faces pale with injury.

I reported to Hurai, to begin my general's apprenticeship. I remember the squire who showed me to his quarters, a girl of fourteen or so, silent as stone. Thinking we both needed some laughter I teased her for conversation. She stayed dour, and mentioned losing all her family. I must have looked an idiot, staring. Innocence always dies in silence. She just said, "I'm from Nikyana."

Hurai was in front of his tent with a scrivener, a runner and two hovering squires. I had never met him, and knew him only by the signs of the circle on his collar and arm rings. He was a big man, just past forty, tall and thick and spear-straight, with a short brush of tight red-brown curls, thinning on the crown.

"Yes," he was saying to the scrivener, who worked, I saw by the quill tattoo on her arm, with the Workfast Proclamatory; a western stringer, no one I knew. "It was necessary to retreat. The piss-drinker would have cut us to shreds! And when was your wisdom requested anyway? I thought you were requesting my information." When she was done, I stepped forward. "Samo, get me some water,"

Hurai snapped. "Perha, go count tent-pegs. Everyone else go away unless it's important; I have to *think* before a war counsel, curse it! What in the Garden Orbicular do you want, boy?"

I saluted, and introduced myself. "Ah," he said, saluting in return, then gave me the once-over, his eyes lingering only on my swordhilt. "Black hair and Chirel on shoulder, sure enough; you even look a bit like your father, if I squint. Too slight to be impersonating such a dreaded warrior. The famous Fourth Chevenga, killer of five Lakans at thirteen, born possessor of weapon-sense, combat genius and master of the principles of strategy: just the person we need." I was foolish enough to smile at this, which made him laugh.

"Well then, famous Fourth Chevenga, I have your first assignment. Come." I followed him past the tents, onto a path that led up the mountain. Here the view was broad, our camp and the town laid out below us, and the Lakans, far more distant, beyond the saddle of the green valley. "We are here, as you see. They are there, as you also see. We have so many swords, so many spears, so many horses, so many archers;" (I cannot remember the exact numbers) "they have so many swords, so many spears, so many horses, so many archers. The land over the rise is talus here, fields there; the stream runs along there to there, and over there is forest. We've lined from there to there with dung-sticks. Their larder is full, and so is ours. We fought them yesterday, had to fall back fighting and lost a thousand." It had been the strength of the Lakan cavalry; he told me in detail how they had broken our spear-line. "They have a general who is as tricky as a snake both planning and in the field, curse his brown guts. You can hear, probably better than I, how our morale is. Anything else you want to know, you can ask.

"I want one brilliant battle plan, as comprehensive and detailed as you should have to give if you were me, practicable and inspired in all its aspects, overlooking nothing, sure beyond a doubt to bring us a massive victory at negligible cost—in short, an example of perfection in the strategic art—and I want it by the time the sun is one fist over that crag tomorrow. Go."

A reputation has its hazards, I thought. Then: I shall live up to it. But this sounded hollow, even to myself. I had less time even than I expected, for one thing: wood must be cut and water drawn, and Kesariga drilled us long and hard. I must greet my shadow-parents. There were more details I needed, and since I could not summon the people I must ask, I must track them down and then meet them formally. This isn't traditional, I thought, as yet another officer said to me, "Well I suppose you look a little like Tennunga. . . . The General First sent you? I heard nothing of it. Why aren't you with him?"

The only place to plan was our tent, where my Ten, our tasks all finished, played knife games. I entreated everyone to shut up so I could think. They asked what call I had, as a mere common-ranker, to think, so I told them; then of course they peered over my shoulders at my waxboard, and generously donated an avalanche of suggestions. "You could link all the horses with chains, then charge through their footmen, like that eastern tribe does."

"You could start a forest fire."

"You could give every warrior a sling-shot, and have them all shoot their hardtack into the Lakan camp instead of eating it; that'd defeat them for sure."

"Cheng . . . Hurai's not actually going to *use* this plan, is he?" This had not crossed my mind; in theory I must imagine it being the true plan. If it were good enough, it occurred to me, bringing vague notions of both grandeur and terror, he might; why not? I told them so, which turned them green and, to my relief, shut them up.

Then it was the thousand dead that hindered me. History, and the news of this war, was full of such numbers; but here, among the people who had shared fires and eaten and joked with the dead, their deaths hummed about my head, too many to consider at once, crying to be counted, understood, mourned. Hurai had spoken to me as easily as any of my tutors would, his voice unchanging when it shaped the word "thousand"; and he had led them to their deaths. That was what it is to be First General First, I thought: to conceive the stratagem that saves the people while seeing them cut down all around. The thought froze my mind.

Every idea seemed to have some fatal flaw, or an easy counter that anyone clever as Inkrajen would easily see. I met a wall at every path; my thoughts tripped over each other, fought themselves; the stylus in my hand stood idle. Despair tempted me: it was late afternoon, in no time it would be dinner, then night, then morning and the sun a fist above the crag. Maybe if I sleep on it something will come to me, I thought; but there'll be too little time to refine it in the morning. When Krero joked, I wanted to rail at him, "I'm only fifteen! What do they expect?" To live up to my name, that was all.

A line from a strategy text came to me: *High on the mountain the general takes his vantage point, away from the noise and warmth of camp life which will fill his heart and empty his mind.* Now I'm on a good path, I thought, put waxboard and stylus in my pack, armed up and set off, finding a sentry who would not recognize me or Chirel and so would let me pass.

I climbed higher than Hurai had brought me, to where the plants were like those near my window in the Hearthstone, at home. Here in these low southern peaks that was a fair climb; they do not even keep snow all year, wearing only a dusting of it now. On a ridge I found a place where the air was a mixture of rising breezes from the sun-heated talus below and the icy breath of the sky, hot and cold by turns. The peace that brings inspiration came easier.

Just then, from a rock some three arm-lengths away from me, I heard a "Hsst!" I sprang up, drawing Chirel, all ready for my part in the war to begin. Out stepped a tiny ragged girl, not more than ten years old, with grazed knees, straw-colored snarls of hair and a fierce begrimed smile. "Sib warrior," she said, in an accent like the Nikyanani squire's, but even broader. "You want to see them Lakans up close? For a piece of tack, I'll show you my secret way."

I felt my brows harden, thinking of traitors, and Lakans waiting behind nearby rocks. Not that I would not know they waited; the range of weapon-sense, which grew as I did, was some thirty marching paces then. Still, better safe than sorry; I asked her for a certain tongue twister only those born and raised in Yeola-e can speak. She rattled it off perfectly, with a hint of reproach. I knew no one had shared with me our spies' newest intelligence; so why not do some spying of my own? Nothing need stop me from thinking as we went. She held out her little hand for the tack first, her face all business, like a merchant's; I was obviously not her first client. But as we went, she devoured it like a dog fed for the first time in days. I thought of us, complaining of its hardness. We knew less than nothing, of war.

She led me along a winding goat track on the side of the mountain, then down through forest. It was longer than I had expected; I glanced at the lowering sun, but decided I had come too far to turn back. Near where the trees dropped we crawled on knees and elbows to the edge of a cliff. Some three longbow shots away, engulfing the black ruins of a village, close enough that I could see spear-shafts, lay the Lakan camp.

The books speak of how Lakans look on the field, not encamped, so this was a surprise to me. The tents were not placed in rows, as in a Yeoli camp, nor even in circles, but higgledy-piggledy. Unlike our plain brown ones, they were in as many colors as in the rainbow, bright as jewels, of all shapes and sizes; here and there were ones as big as houses, decorated with bright trim, stripes, flags and giant tassels.

My guide explained in her piping voice. "Those big tents are the big rich Lakanil's. They keep all their horses near them, see? Sometimes you can catch the sentries asleep, if you know when; me and my little brother Sech, one night they almost caught us. I want to be a spy when I grow up. My parents are dead. You're a nice man; can I have some more tack?"

I gave her my last piece—I'd get more—and asked her what pattern they placed their sentries in. She shrugged with utter authority, as only a child can. "They call around though; that's how you know where they are. I know all the lords' tents. See, that there is So-and-so's . . ." She listed off eight, less than all but still impressive; then with a flourish she pointed out a huge golden tent in the shape of a cross with a turret at its center, not unlike a miniature castle. "And *that*," she said grandly, "is The White Fox's." His use-name here was that, for his long mane of white hair. "In-kra-chen's."

I stared. "He makes where he sleeps so plain?"

"It's 'cause he's their General First," she said. "You know Lakans, it's all who's richest and famousest so he has to have the biggest, fanciest tent. The roof is real gold."

I suppose she thought I believed that, seeing my face;

my soul filled with fire. I tore my waxboard out of my pack, erased everything on it, and drew as fast as I could a map of the camp. There was the great victory at negligible cost, the perfect stratagem.

I said farewell and ran back to camp, the plan composing itself in my mind as I went. *Dark clothes, wristlets, knives, blacken my face with soot . . .* Should anyone wonder at my madness, I would remind them of my wonder-sense. Darkness is no constraint to me, but freedom greater than daylight, for at the same time I am hidden, I can see what I need to, where warriors are, even which way they are looking, by the angle of their weapons, as clearly as in sun. What I had felt today spurred me, perhaps beyond reason; so you see I was not completely mad, only fairly.

Then I realized: those who do not have the gift have no feel for what it can do until they see it, sometimes not even then. Hurai would never allow it. With the fire turning to vitriol in my heart, I heard his answer in my inward ears. "What? Are you out of your mind, boy? You're Ascendant! You're not even sixteen!" What it always comes down to, I thought: age.

No, I thought. This is a thing which must be done. It's easier to get forgiveness than permission; and if I am punished for it, I'll bear it. I felt a breath of the harmonic singer and the wind; that made it certain.

I spent what was left of the day memorizing what I had drawn. The sun fell behind the mountains, we ate, and the night turned dark as black wool, with a new moon and patchy clouds which thickened to solid. When Kesariga ordered us to bed, it was so dark one could barely see one's hand in front of one's face, away from torches; perfect.

He took the first sentry-duty, with Ramiha. I took off my greaves and boots, put on soft leathern shoes, my dark sweater and trousers, and armed myself with my two daggers. We'd voted Krero Kesariga second, though they'd wanted me; I didn't feel I could be said to have started common rank unless I fought there. "Curse it," he said now. "I knew this would happen, the moment anyone put me in any power over you. You know I'm supposed to not let *anyone* leave, Fourth Chevenga."

"So you didn't see me," I answered. "You were asleep, it was hardly your fault." After a moment, he said, "So I was. As a matter of fact, we all were. Weren't we?"

"Where are you going?" That was Mana.

"Into the Lakan camp, to kill Inkrajen." Sometimes the best lie is truth.

"Ah, I see." His voice was sage. "Well, be sure it's his safe time of the month." They all began snoring loudly, and Krero buried his head under the covers.

I was seen but not noticed, assumed to be on some errand. I put in my pack two small torches and a tinderbox, darkened my face and hands with grease and soot, slicked my hair back straight with oil. At the edges of our camp, I saw the torch-hooks of the sentries, held dead still; the moment one moves, a check is made. As I crept in the grass through the first line, I found myself sweating. It occurred to me they would almost certainly strike before they challenged, seeing a dark figure crawling along the ground. Far worse than being killed by Lakans: for one thing, no one would ever know why the Ascendant had been stealing out of the Yeoli camp in the dark of night. But I can shout before he strikes, I thought; then it will be merely an extreme embarrassment. Why didn't I just ask clearance? But they would check, since I'm so young, and catch me out. Since I'm so young. I prefer sneaking to lying anyway.

I took the mountain-girl's goat-track, slipped around two guards where a stream crossed it—they had a signal fire the camp could see, ready to light—foot-groping over fallen trees and rocks. Now I was in their territory. One is best not to think of that as a wall, but as a sieve; this was still Yeola-e, in scent and feel and spirit; I told myself the land would be kinder to me than to them.

I came to the streamside path going down, a faint ribbon of slate black against velvet black. A thought came to me: should I stumble into someone in the camp and hope to be mistaken for a Lakan, I should smell like one, and they wear scent. Coming to a meadow I felt for flowers, smeared a few on me. Through branches of feathery black, the lights of the Lakan camp came into sight below. There were two more sentries where the path joined the cleared land; I cut around them, and hopped a stone fence into a pasture. This had not been burned off, but the crops beyond had; I smelled lingering smoke, and ash raised by my own tread.

It was now I began to wonder whether I was in my right

mind. As I had learned before, the singing wind will set me to a deed, but not necessarily tell me how to do it. I only got to the front this morning, I thought, and here I am a stone's throw from twenty thousand of the enemy, planning to be in their midst. What in the bounds of All-spirit induced me to do this?

Sweat broke out cold on me again; my whole body trembled; I tasted the taste that precedes vomiting. I could still go back, and nothing lost, as I had determined to if it appeared too dangerous; I crouched in the corner of two stone fences to reconsider, and almost chose that.

But I saw I was thinking the wrong thoughts for a warrior, fear pretending to be sense. Nothing has happened that should make me change my plan, I reminded myself; the night is just as dark, no alarm has been sounded, and as far as I know I haven't mislaid any of my skills along the path. I took the deep slow breath Azaila had taught me, into my stomach, from which fear and strength both come. The vomit-taste faded, and I saw sense: terror is a child's feeling, not ineffable truth. When my thoughts were clear again, I went on.

They had knocked down all the near fences to be rid of hiding places, but had built no wall, intending, I guessed, to attack soon. The sentries had no lights, and did indeed call each other, in sequence around the ring; I'd be given away in a moment if I knifed one. The signal word I practiced a few times in a whisper. But to pass them I must creep across scorched ground, every movement raising ash-dust, and they were nowhere more than fifteen paces apart. They might not see or hear me; but if they were sentries of any ability, they would smell my passing on the wind.

Well, so much for that, reasoned one part of my mind, time to go back to bed. Then I thought of the stream: dark, trickling loudly, containing no twigs to snap or dust to raise, the channel it cut in the earth just deep and wide enough to hide a youth. I knew where it ran from my map; doubling back, I hitched my pack high, set my teeth against the cold and lion-crawled in.

Careful not to tumble the slippery rocks, I worked my way past the first line of sentries, passing almost within spear's reach of one; I heard him clear his throat. The second line did not call, being the secret sentries; the first

I knew of them was their spear-heads. Just as I was past
them I sensed a moving spear, being carried precisely
towards me.

I can't have been seen, I told myself, freezing; they'd all
be calling and running. The man was moving at a walk,
meaning to cross the stream. If he uses his spear to vault
over, I thought, I'm done. Or he'll hear my teeth chattering; I set my lip between them. If a man pisses on you,
how do you make the sound it should make in a stream?
His footsteps drummed the earth beside my ear; I clenched
my jaw, and turned my head down lest the whites of my
eyes show. He leaped right over my back.

It was the changing of the guard; midnight, perhaps. It
seemed ten years since I'd left our camp. I crawled on,
aching to the bones, now, with the cold, until I was among
the tents; there I lifted myself out, careful not to let the
dripping from my clothes make noise.

The Lakan camp smelled of horses, and spicy food.
There was silence but for snoring. I foot-groped; in our
camp I had known by heart where the guy-ropes were,
from having pitched such tents; here every one was different, and closer together than ours, so that I almost did trip
a few times.

Inkrajen's quarters loomed against the sky. It had two
stories, the ground level a cross, each arm wide and high
as a small house, the upper level square-built with a
turret-roof, glowing faintly with a light from within which
I could see by the softness of the shadows shining through
two walls of cloth. Along its corners were the silhouettes of
what seemed to be pillars until I perceived they were
giant tassels. On the ground, one guard stood at each of
the eight points of the cross.

I got down again and aimed for a crook of the cross
twenty paces of open ground away, telling myself not to be
afraid lest they smell my fear. It took me the time it takes
to walk from Vae Arahi to Terera, my muscles screaming
all the way to leap up and run; I dared not even open my
eyes when the wind was not making some sound, nor
when the guards were looking my way.

Then, sheltered in the shadows of the corner, I gained
bitter intelligence by my gift. Two armed people stood
awake in the upper chamber. I understood. He slept with
two bodyguards in his room, and a light.

My heart seemed to fall from my chest. I should have known before I came it would be impossible, I thought; why would Inkrajen be any more of a fool at night than day? What commander makes an attack on such slight reconnaissance as a glance from a cliff? Having come all that deadly way to no purpose, it almost seemed too much trouble to creep all the way back, having failed. I remembered a war story my mother had told: they'd found in the morning a young Enchian assassin sitting stone-still in a hiding place in camp, who gave himself up without resistance. Now I understood.

But I was thinking with fear again. I imagined my friends waking up to find me vanished, the faces of my parents as they heard the news, Hurai, cursing my idiocy while he and a smug Inkrajen haggled over the ransom price of one Ascendant, slightly used. Back, or onward; all, or nothing. Seizing myself, I thought, I have time before dawn. The two guards are human; sooner or later one of them must visit the latrine.

I cut a slit along the edge between floor and wall of the ground story of the great tent, and crawled through it into darkness like a wall of coal before one's eyes, that makes them scream for light and in desperation see non-existent dancing shapes. I lay still, just to listen; how many could be sleeping in such a huge tent I could not know. The air was thick with scent. I felt canvas floor, a quilt, a hard shape beneath it; that stirred, with a man's low grunt, turning me to ice. I think it was his foot.

Groping towards the center I found a canvas wall, with a door-flap edged with small tassels, which I opened just enough to fit through. It followed that in a tent big as a building there should be corridors; sure enough, I was in one now, which formed a square around the central chamber. At one corner of the square was the one doorway to the outside, from which a ladder of painted wood led upward; but knowing that a Lakan on guard holds his spear in his right hand and wears his sword on his left hip, I could tell the two guards above both faced it.

Somewhere there had to be tent-poles. Feeling at the corners of the central room I found through the satin the hardness of wood. The upper chamber was supported on four posts at each corner. Delicately I cut my way in; here was enough light leaking through chinks in the floor of the upper chamber to see shapes and light-catching things. Before me lay a wooden cage, centered in the room; in it on satin bedding slept a Lakan boy who by the line of his shoulder was about my age, wearing a golden arm-ring a finger-width thick. Some favored slave, I guessed, and had no more thought for him but that he must not wake. He could not attack me, nor I him, but he could call help.

So, fast and silently I climbed halfway up the pole and felt about its top. This wall was attached to the edge of the platform planks with knotted ropes, and the canvas ceiling of the corridor likewise joined. I felt the outer wall of cloth; it had two layers, canvas and netting, fixed at the base only by silken cords tied in bows. Around the sleeping chamber was a promenade, to be opened in fine weather. No doubt he ran battles from it.

The boy tossed; around his neck he wore a collar that was either counterfeit or worth an Ascendant's ransom. I untied knots, quickly. On the balcony, it struck me, my silhouette might be visible from outside. Not that the guards would think to look up here; that would require admitting to themselves that an intruder had crossed the ground in front of their eyes, a lapse warranting death. Still, I kept flat on the planks. Inside someone shifted his weight, making the floor creak. So often in life one finds oneself blessing the same thing one has cursed some other time; now I was thankful I was young, and light.

I lion-crawled to behind the shadow of what I guessed was a tall and grand headboard—the bed centered between the two guards—and turned my dagger over to use its unused edge. A blade must be sharp, to cut through silk both fast and quietly. I knelt, careful not to creak the floor, and waited.

Time passed, and my senses went sharper still. I counted how many times they shifted, how many times they raised cups, swallowed, then quietly put them down, blessing each draught; what goes in must come out. A breeze flopped the canvas and the flags, creaked the ropes; then it stilled, letting the calls of the guards sound clear from all around, even the distant ones. Somewhere a baby bawled; satin swished, a different sound than canvas. Time passed. Cold found me again, tonguing me through my mail-shirt from my sodden sweater; I drove calm and warmth outward into my skin. Time passed, and my legs and ankles went stiff; fearing they would lock too tightly to move when the moment came, I gingerly shifted. Time passed; I counted my breaths, had to shift again. Time passed, and I imagined myself sitting here all night and through into the day, so silent no one would find me, and indeed all through the war; when they dismantled the tent they'd just roll me up with the poles, and when it was pitched anew I would be sitting here still, waiting for one guard to piss. Time passed, in utter stillness. Just when my bones had started to whisper that it was growing short, one guard whispered, and went away across the floor, and down the ladder.

While a breeze was making sound, I stood and made a hand-span long slit at eye height behind the remaining guard. The fabric was like oil on the palm. I made the full cut, quietly enough, sheathed the blade and unsheathed my pin-dagger, fast; he might sense my presence just by feel, as people do. I stepped through to his back, choosing the ring of his mail I would put the needle-blade through just as in training, put my hand over his mouth and nose and did it. He gave a great jerk, but though I felt the bristles of a moustache on my palm I had sealed off his breath so he could make no sound. I made ready for his weight, and let him down quietly when he went lax. He never saw me; his black eyes were frozen, in the shock of knowing. The first person I ever murdered; such is war, and why there should be peace.

I turned to the bed, seeing the room only from the corners of my eyes and taking no more impression than gold and a sense of richness; it was long white hair I looked for. There it was, almost too real to be true, like the surprise gift a child finds after wanting it for years, creamy silver peppered with the odd strand of black, unoiled, the straight tendrils disheveled with sleep. Inkrajen did not move; he had not awakened. The body beneath the gold satin covers was small and slight; the face, its brown startling against bright hair, was some forty years old, clean-shaven and delicate in a Lakan way, its wrinkles of sun and strain smoothed in sleep.

In such an innocuous scabbard, I thought, comes the deadliest steel. Presently I would pin him with my knee, lay my hand on his forehead and draw my dagger across his throat, and it would be done. Yet watching him sleep, I felt my hand weaken.

It might have been that he was asleep, I suppose. Or that I knew him, in a sense, by what I knew of his record: so many victories, the career of any apprentice-general's dreams. Now seeing his face, standing in his presence, I wanted not to kill him, but to greet him, hear his stories, learn from him.

Thus I stood on the knife-edge of half-action, teetering. Any moment then he could have awakened and called guards, and I would have done worse than failed. But sense spoke to me in Azaila's voice. *Why did you come here, then? It's too late to regret. All or nothing.*

I pinned his chest with my knee, clamping his mouth and nose with my hand. He woke as I did it, and his eyes, like two oiled jets framed wide all around with white, flickered with each catching of the knife-edge on sinew in his throat, looking at me but seeming to see only pain. When the stroke was finished and his life-blood pouring out, they stared, full of shock, disbelief, sorrow, anger at the guards who had failed him: but no rancor for me. When his eyes fixed on me, they went puzzled.

I saw: all or nothing went without saying for him. I was Yeoli; what else would I do if I could, but kill him? His was the perfect acceptance of the aggressor: I chose; I paid. Though he would have stopped me with steel through my heart if he could, I don't think it even entered his mind to hate me.

Only one mercy could I give him. I took his head in my hands and lowered my lips to his ear; having no time for all I wished to say, apology for his pain, praise of his generalship, blessings for the next life that Lakans believe in, I whispered one thing. "My name is Fourth Chevenga Shae-Arano-e, Tennunga's son. I got here by my"—translating as best I could into Enchian—"weapon-sense." It was what he would want to know. He understood, for he looked me over, though his sight was fading; I found myself wishing my face was clean of grease, and my hair combed. When next I looked, the life in his eyes was gone.

I got up from the bed slowly. My intention was to kill the other guard secretly as well when he came back, so no one could sound the alarm as I crept off; I must wait here.

I wiped the blood off my hands on the sheet, and looked around me. He'd had little furniture, just desk, night table, shelf, one chair and the bed, whose headboard was a three-tiered shelf full of books; but it was all ebony carven more ornately and smoothly than I had thought wood could be carved. Everywhere were prizes of war, jewelry, carvings, tableware, statuettes, all gold or crusted with gems, in our style or Enchian or Hyerni.

Jewels always help; into my pack I quickly put the smallest ones, few enough not to burden me. On his night table lay a sand-timer and several large maps. Even with him dead his plans could still be used, if I left them, so I folded them all into my pack. Inside the carven doors of the bookshelf were personal things I would rather not have seen at all: a letter in childish Lakan script, a child's play-sword, three busts, fashioned from real Lakan hair and mahogany to depict their dark skin, of a woman and two children. I presumed the books would all be Lakan, but an Enchian title caught my eye, being familiar. Cold stabbed up my spine. He had Enchian translations of every major Yeoli work on warcraft.

I remembered one of the oldest teachings given me: "Know the enemy." All-spirit, I thought, no wonder he beat us! Yet no one in Yeola-e goes this deep with *them*— why not? The lesson seared into my soul, never to be forgotten. To show Hurai, I took the most concise classic, Naishana Krai's *Warcraft*.

One thing more caught my eye. Set apart from all else upon a cushion of red satin under a petaled arch of gold-inlaid ebony, lay a miniature spear, bound with tassels, its head wrought of gold polished smooth as glass. A sacred talisman, I saw, and being in the chamber of the general, one of significance to all the army, if not all the nation, like the sword of Saint Mother. That would be a loss to cause them anguish; then it struck me as petty malice, like a child's prank. I laid it straight on his chest, instead, curling his hands around it, as weapons to be cremated with their owners are laid. Let them take what they would from that.

For proof, I cut one lock of his hair. Just as I was knotting it to put in my pack, I heard a gasp at the door.

I had expected the warning of weapon-sense, or at least a polite hail from the foot of the ladder if someone else came. I did not know Lakan servants are considered no one, their comings and goings expected to go unnoticed. A round-shouldered brown man, half up the ladder, and I stared at each other, both freezing. He knew better what to do, though, and so acted first: throwing back his head he let out a scream of anguish that seemed to last a day, and ended with "Ahai! Ahai! Ahai!"

I threw what was nearest my sword-hand—a sand-timer—which made him jump down. The thought came with an unreal slowness like the movement of a glacier: *The alarm's been sounded.* I remembered the word from the raid on the Shae-Tyucheral. "Ahai! Ahai! Ahai! Ahai!" Many voices took it up; the floor shook with guards climbing the ladder.

My hands thought for me, snatching off the helmet of the fallen guard, a peaked cone in the Lakan style. I scrambled out the slit, hacked through the outer wall with my dagger and dived onto the canvas roof, taking its slope in a roll, tumbled off the edge and landed running. The cry sounded all over the camp now; torchlight spread fast as flame catches. Now thousands of Lakans staggered out of tents or ran by with spears, every way I turned.

Now when I had true reason for terror, it vanished somehow, leaving my mind clear as water, perhaps by the knowledge that what I had feared longest I need fear no more, since it had happened. The plan I thought of, had I considered it beforehand, I would have spurned as too dangerous to try; now, as there was no other choice, I did it unthinkingly. Between two tents I buckled on the helmet, and ran out shouting, "Ahai! Ahai!" It was the thing to do.

Perhaps it was then that I learned that the flamboyantly unexpected can work, for it did. In the confusion and the madly flickering torchlight, I suppose, my darkened face and straightened hair aided them in seeing, as people will, what they expected to see. I certainly never stayed still long enough to give anyone a good look, and for all panic was gone from my mind there was plenty enough left in my body to give my cry sincerity. Thus, pretending to be running in a daze of panic, uncaring where I went, I worked my way towards the edge of the camp.

When I had got within twenty strides of it, a man with a torch seized my arm and rattled off something to me in

Lakan, pausing after; I imagine it was something like "Calm yourself, boy, and tell me what's going on!" Not knowing what else to do, I shrugged, shook him off and dashed on, shouting, "Ahai!"

I know now what gave me away. We Yeolis, as I didn't know until a foreigner told me, have a unique shrug, a double motion: first the hands and forearms turn up, then, distinctly separate, the shoulders rise. As I cleared the edge of the tents he bellowed to his comrades, and next thing I knew fifty Lakans were chasing me.

Though I could not see the ground I ran flat out. Carrying no light, I soon lost them in the dark, and heard what I knew by their tone were curses. The sentries closed in to where they thought I would come, so I dashed wide around them; then a command must have been given to spread out, for the bobbing knife-point of lights behind me widened into a comb. Suddenly one of my feet found air instead of earth and I flew headlong, into a ditch; the lie was kind, not to break my ankle, or neck. I would come to grief running across fields and fences in this darkness without a flame, I saw; so I trotted gingerly with my hands out before me until I found a fence, crouched behind it and groped for my tinderbox. It lit, Saint Mother bless it, on the first try. When the line of Lakans came even with me I joined their number again, pretending to give death-chase to myself.

We all headed for the foot of the stream-path, *for even if that demon wool-head assassin fled through the woods, we can head him off that way.* . . . I pulled ahead; like those of the rabbit that outruns the wolf, my legs had more compelling reason. The pair waited in stance with spears levelled, searching in the dark for pale skin and curly hair. Beckoning grandly, I ran right between them. It was only some way up the slope that it dawned on them that the most enthusiastic runner had been strangely taciturn, and spearless. Their cries sharpened with rage, and several spears were cast; but by then I was far enough ahead to dodge them.

It was a plain race now, on a long, steep ascent. They were scores to my one; but I had run up the side of Haranin every day in training for nine years, breathing air too cold and thin for trees; in the Breaker of Hearts, as our long obstacle race is called, I had scrambled up steep Hetharin for the last stretch, after all the other ordeals.

Beneath its mantle of forest the slope seemed to laugh, and say, "You know whose side I am on, lad." There is not much of such training ground in Laka.

Where the path resorted to switchbacks, I climbed straight, pulling myself up on trees and rocks with my free hand. Two sentries stood at the junction, I remembered, their legs fresh; I veered into the forest to my sword-side again. It slowed me and strained my luck, but did the same to them; I heard one crash down yelling behind me. On the mountain-girl's path and its gentler incline, I increased my speed; my legs were jelly with streaking pains now, my lungs and heart wanting to tear loose from my chest, my body to fly to bits. I knew from experience they lied, though, and I had strength left if I willed it. Soon I was staggering, barely making a fast walk; rested legs could have caught me easily as a baby. But the Lakans were all the same. As often as not in the Breaker of Hearts the racers come to the finish on hands and knees; but the first there still wins.

Where precisely they gave up I do not know, but I did not stop using all my strength until I was in sight of Yeoli torch-hooks. I had never thought flames could seem to have embracing arms. I had planned to creep back through our sentries, but now I could not find it in me; so I called out the tongue twister, wiped my face as best I could, and tried to make my curls curl again with my fingers. One sentry knew the shape of my face, having seen me with Hurai. "Ascendant! What in the name of—" he began to say. "Secret assignment," I gasped. "No questions." They let me in.

X

When the sun was a fist west of the crag, I went to Hurai. "I have it in my head, sir," I said. "Out with it, then," he said. I took a breath. "Assassinate Inkrajen."

For a time he lambasted me, for gaining intelligence for a field plan, not an assassination—he must have checked my contacts—and mostly not asking whether it had been tried before. It's probably best I hadn't, else I'd never have done it; it had been tried three times, costing two veteran assassins. No wonder Inkrajen slept with guards in his room. At this point I thought it best to draw the knotted lock out of my pack.

His stare widened. "You got this from some straight-haired oldster," he said, "or a horse's tail." I brought out the sand-timer, the gems, the sheaf of maps covered with Lakan characters. He gazed at it all, gaping.

I was not ready, for, expecting different, I did not understand why he should be drawing back his arm. He could ring one's skull as hard as Esora-e; I cannot even remember falling.

The pressing of the tent-floor into my chin and chest came to me slowly; then words, in a haze. The voice was familiar, one I'd come to know recently; absently I remembered, Hurai Kadari. "No stripling not even sixteen

141

comes fresh to a fighting army, and puts himself in the general's place, no matter *who* he is."

I tried to lift my head, felt and saw the tent turn end over end around me, and lay back down again. His voice turned crisp, giving orders. "Samo, get a courier, Ina, take a letter. Saint Mother shit on me! You tell me, boy, how to word this, to the demarch, your mother, your shadow-father, your Teachers, to all Yeola-e . . ." It was then I remembered the story of General Maha outcasting her son for acting without orders. I had relinquished my will; if he cut off a fistful of my hair, it would be done.

Struggling to keep from getting vomit on his tent-floor, I said the only thing I could think of: "Sir, I knew I might be punished and chose to accept it." There was a long silence; I felt his eyes on me. Then he said, his voice quieter, "You'd better tell me everything. Start with who you sent."

That made me understand his anger. To give orders for such was indeed usurpation of his authority. I told him the truth.

"You know," he said thoughtfully, once he'd canceled all his orders, "your shadow-father told me to expect surprises from you. I resolved to be surprised by nothing. Now you've laid waste to that in one day. A follower worth shit you make, Fourth Chevenga; but one day you'll be a great leader."

I'd broken the assassin's law of secrecy, mentioning it to Mana, joke or not. "Well," Hurai said, "we'll just make it another brick in the Chevenga legend, Assembly tomorrow and . . . Perha, get the news-scribe!" Outcast to legend in an eye-blink, I thought; never has anyone lived a life less dull than mine.

Before I was finished recounting it to the scribe—a spry bookish woman by the name of Ankarye Chermena—a Lakan parley delegation was spied. Hurai took me with him, to meet them.

"Black hair under the pegasus and tassel," said Hurai, "sure enough." A Lakan General First's helmet is plumed with a stiff tassel extending from a gold silken rope an arm thick coiling around his head, somewhat silly to my eyes; the banner he carries is the black pegasus of Laka, his wings, mane and tail made of golden flame, on a field of scarlet. "It's Inkrajen's second, Orbukjen."

Looking at his squire, I suddenly knew where I had seen those golden arm-rings and collar before. "I guess they think foxiness runs in the blood," Hurai said, when I asked, "and want to keep what they have. That's Inkrajen's son."

Some things in the heart the mind has no answer for. But before I could feel much, the Lakan herald began to call, in Enchian with the odd Lakan lilt, beginning with ponderous formalities. It must surely be beneath Hurai's honor to murder his honorable counterpart, he said in effect, so the assassin must have been "a renegade, a coward and a criminal, who acted without your authority." To prove his honor intact, Hurai need only deliver said person into their hands.

Looking into the face of Inkrajen's son—now I saw the resemblance—I thought, "I murdered your father." The army had come out to watch, behind us; I saw his eyes scan the line, wondering which of that host was the one. His father chose, I thought; he was brought along. If we ever meet on the field, I will tell him, and let him fight me knowing. Meanwhile, Hurai was chuckling. "Without my authority; they hit dead on there. Maybe I should give them your head as they're asking, eh, boy?" Through the herald he made our reply.

"Inkrajen, called the White Fox, was indeed honorable enough never to send one man creeping in the dark, but only a thousand horses; the world has less ingenuity in it, for his loss. It is a great shame, therefore, that he contrived to take land beneath the sigil of the circle. It is a matter of honor to us to defend ourselves with every advantage to hand when invaders come to kill and enslave, however much that might offend their delicate morals; we do not fear the same treatment because we do not do the same to you. If, O illustrious Orbukjen, you find this disagreeable, you have my wholehearted permission to turn around and march home." Behind us the army had come out to watch; there was a roar like sea-surf of laughter and cheering, and a thousand hands shaped obscene gestures.

Orbukjen cursed us with his own voice; though I could not hear I could see his waving fist. Most of the knights stood steady, but two or three had dropped their banners to one hand and whipped out their straight swords; one spurred his poor horse against the reigning of his own squire. No surprise, they'd loved him. Thus the parley ended.

"You shall tell the story," Hurai said the next day, when the army was assembled. "Don't look so green, you've only got four years until you're demarch. . . . Just think of it as saying hello to eighteen thousand friends." Such a knack for reassurance, he had. "They probably have spies watching," he said as he gave me the speaking-crystal, "so incriminate all the sentries you can so they execute plenty."

He was right; the army was all friends, having suffered at Inkrajen's hands. Once I remembered to project my voice as I'd been taught, they clung to every word, roared with laughter where I least expected, adored me with their eyes at every pause. There was nothing I could say, even admitting fear, that displeased them. Love-drunk, I suddenly yearned to tell them all that was in my heart, and had to restrain myself. When I finished they cheered me standing, the clashing of wristlets ringing like a gong's hissing thunder.

It was the Serpent Incarnadine he gave me, the highest award for stealth. I was the only one of eighteen thousand who was taken aback, I think; I remember my shadow-father standing at the edge of the speaking-circle, looking not surprised at all, as Hurai fastened it to my collar. But a flogging-post was set up too, and a whip-worker warming up his arm. I had acted without orders. The reward and punishment in one; it was just.

Hurai Kadari was always a brilliant general; he was not so good a politician. He had not bargained for how much they would warm to me. When he announced it—flogging to falling, the punishment that is pure punishment—someone shouted, "He did good! Spare him!" In a moment, the whole army had taken up the cry.

For once, he stood frozen; in the sun I saw sweat on his head, where his hair was thin. They didn't love him as much as he truly deserved; they had at best held fast under him, recently lost, never won. I had given them victory with my two hands. I saw my power, by the law unwritten: I could draw myself up, say to him, "The people wills. You can't flog me," and walk away unscathed.

I had never been flogged to falling before, let alone in front of eighteen thousand people; I didn't want it. But I saw us tomorrow; his authority defied successfully, thus weakened, the warriors divided over who had been right, factions forming, disunity weakening us from van to rear. If I turn against him I have turned against them, I thought, whatever they think. Then, if life is just, I will have the same done to me four years from now, when I am demarch.

I stripped to the waist, and the yells of "No!" redoubled, a hint of anger in them now. I held up my hands for silence. It was almost instant; they were still in my hands. "You are kindhearted," I said, "and I thank you for your mercy. But mercy doesn't always serve; in war, justice is better. The General First is right; I did act without orders, as no warrior should do. I have accepted his reward; I will accept his punishment." They stayed silent as I went to the post. The guard came with the rope, to bind me, thinking of my age, I guess; in front of the army, I thought, she must be joking. I waved her off, and took a good grip on the post with my arms, to a ripple of acclaim.

I can remember every grain-line and crack in the spot of greyed wood before my eyes to this day, though the memory of pain has been effaced somehow, as it usually is with me. I remember the temptation to fall before my legs gave out, and staying up, almost more from ground-in habit than will; I remember thinking, as my senses began to surge and ebb by turns, "It's probably a good thing I never got flogged to falling before; if I'd known it would hurt this much maybe I wouldn't have done what I did." Soon after that it was over. When I woke I saw the shine of tears on faces, something I hadn't expected; "Tell them I'm all right," I must have croaked ten times, as they lifted me onto the litter.

Two days later we celebrated; the morning after, Hurai called me to his tent. It was only by leaning on a spear that I got there, my body still in pain from the flogging, my head from hangover. I'd been offered enough wine to swim in; it was only civility to accept as much as I could. "Next assignment," he said. "What you don't know, you can find out. Everyone knows you now. I want one brilliant battle plan, perfect in every aspect, overlooking nothing, certain to bring us great victory at negligible cost, in short, a perfect example of the strategic art . . . *and I don't want anything like last time!*"

*   *   *

So began my part in the Lakan War. It was all much more ordinary after that

I won't detail it. In battle we faced a thousand strangers, four in every five of them levied serfs, there only because they were required to be. To fight such people one must forget they didn't choose, though that's easy enough, in the fury of battle. If I could persuade every nation in the world to become a demarchy, I would; until then, we must fight conscripts.

So I've forgotten their faces, having never seen them truly, but only their blows coming at me, the spear-thrusts, the arc of a black axe, already bloodied, aimed for my head. These things are the same in any battle. If you've fought, you know what it's like; if you haven't, you're better off not knowing, and my thin words cannot truly make you know anyway.

My prescription now was not to attack but to hold ground and harass them, destroying their food. Winter would favor us. To my delight Hurai agreed, and we did it.

We built a rough but serviceable wall across the pass first, then all the way around the town. Inkrajen, we found by deciphering his maps, had planned to lead his army around our defenses by night, before we'd had time to build the full circle; Orbukjen waited, then flung his forces straight on against the wall. We shot down scores of them while they were clearing the dung-sticks alone, the poor serfs shoved ahead to do this work, armored only with shields and leather coats, while the plate-armored knights waited out of bowshot. When they came close, our orders were to shoot horses before men; they were the Lakans' strength. I felt sorry for those beautiful coal-black beasts, strong as draft-horses but swift as racers, who had less choice than the people to be here.

In Orbukjen's boots I think I would have just gone around Shairao by another pass, leaving us behind; he might have had time to do it before it was all walled, had he moved fast enough, and no matter that his supply line was cut, when so much lay defenseless before him to forage. Then to stop or follow him we would have had to come out. Instead he called for reinforcements, settling another five thousand Lakans in Nikyana (at this rate they'd have half the forest cleared by spring) and threw them against us. We were holding off siege-towers with poles; I remember when Renaina Chaer, who was a centurion then, had her people heave instead of hold, the tower being on a steep slope. It toppled slowly backwards, landing softly, with not one thud but a score of crackings; there was a press of Lakans behind it. I will never forget those screams, first a few in terror as they saw death fall toward them, then the entire mass in agony, all starting in unison as if commanded by a choirmaster, and fading raggedly to a few that did not stop.

We were the sort of Ten that fought full of fierce cheer, trading grins and jests; we didn't understood people whose faces curled in carven hate when the Lakans came, as if they held a grudge against every one. In one of the Shairao battles we learned; Ramiha took an arrow in the stomach.

I remember how she lay at first, her head hanging over the inner edge of the wall-walk, as if thrown back in ecstasy, and the arrow standing in her. In the University Hospital on Haiu Menshir, there were the people and things to save her, but not here. Krero had to put her out of her pain; they'd sworn an oath. I remember how she put her arms around his neck, and swallowed her cries. I did not need to see his arm move; weapon-sense has no eyelids, to close against such a thing.

For a long time after, I kept hearing her voice in the cacophony of talk at night before Kesariga shut us up, seeing her eyes shining in firelight. She had always won all the archery prizes; now that uncanny skill, gained over so many years by such toil, was gone, extinguished in a moment like a mosquito happening into flame. I remembered what I had said to Hurai, as we'd cut the plan; "We'll lose a few." When he saw my shorn hair, he was very kind about it; of course he knew that pain.

It drove Krero a little mad; for a time he didn't comb or eat, and seemed alive only in battle. The scars her nails made on his hands as she died he bears to this day, having worried at them to keep them from healing, so they would never fade.

The moon of my sixteenth birthday came. Fall turned the hills to gold, Orbukjen moved his army back into Nikyana, and the news came that Leyere had fallen. Crowded and hungry, it had been struck with a plague of fever, leaving too few people well enough to defend the walls; the Lakans had stormed over with sheer numbers,

thirty thousand in total. Some half of the prople had got
away, and the city had not been sacked, but everyone who
had fought to the last was dead or in chains, and the
Lakans were on the march up the valley, while Emao-e
scrambled to reform her army. My aunt went there, with
Jinai Oru, who had won further renown by predicting
Inkrajen's death (I wish I'd heard); she called reinforcements from everywhere, including the whole Demarchic
Guard, to march before winter closed the passes. That
thinned us by almost a third. But Hurai had them march
out quietly at night, commanded us to light just as many
fires, shipped in an equal number of tents and had us
pitch them and hang about them, spread evenly. If Orbukjen
ever saw through this, I do not know it; he was content to
wait, and before the first snow fell some half of his army
and most of his horse were called away too.

I wanted to go; I imagined myself asking Emao-e, "Do
they have a general they can't do without?" But Tyeraha
kept me where I was. She expected one pitched battle in
the valley of Leyere, into which we would throw all our
strength, do or die in one toss. If we lost, she might even
come to grief herself; best I didn't as well. Doing raids
under Renaina and others took my mind off it.

I became decurion the hard way, on our first raid on
woodcutters. Being young fools, we went expecting it all
to go precisely as planned; whether it did, I hardly need say.
We spread all around to wait in ambush; twelve Lakans
came, axes on shoulders. The one standing watch, in the
center, wore a long mantle, under which he had hidden at
his side a bow slung for quick draw, and on his hip a full
quiver. I knew only by weapon-sense. And I'd hid across
from Kesariga; I couldn't tell him.

I frantically made the call a blackbird does for "danger,"
hoping he'd take the warning, and he might have, for
there was a longer delay than he had planned after the
axes began to ring. But a twig must have snapped or a
movement been seen, for one of them shouted, "Ahai!" and
they flung down tools for weapons. A bad time to call
charge, but Kesa had no choice, really; they'd have checked
whatever they'd noticed. By manner or insignia, the archer
guessed he was leader, and aimed without hesitation. The
arrow came high, and I hoped it might glance off his
helmet, but he stopped dead, as if he'd meant to, and fell.

Our charge faltered, the war cry breaking in the middle; I kept running, knowing only that I was in a race with his hand reaching for another arrow, and he had cursed good aim. I won it, with a stroke at his hand gripping the bow that cut both in half; but then I found myself in a circle of Lakans, with my friends I knew not where, all yelling "*Shit, Cheng!*" A death cry tore out of a Lakan about to spear me from behind; there, bless his grinning soul, was Mana.

In the end we won, at the cost of a deep cut on my leg that I hadn't noticed myself getting (my first proper wound, stitched by the camp Haian, no less), shallow ones on others, and Kesariga. The arrow was through his eye.

We had to break the shaft off, before we carried him back to camp; Isatenga, who'd been closest to him, was sure he would not have wanted, to be seen so. I could understand; I had always believed that one's appointment with Shininao ought to be private, perhaps because I had been secretive about my own for so long, or perhaps because it is, like making love, such a deep and personal thing. Being decurion now, I was the one who did it. I remember how the other eye, staring emptily as blue glass as I wrapped my hands around the shaft, shifted slightly as it broke, and Sachara ran into the woods to throw up.

Winter came, hard, but no curse to us in a friendly town. We went on growing up; war doesn't stop that. When I became demarch and First General First, by custom I would visit a different campfire every time, and deny no Yeoli who wanted me, to bind the army as one. An Ascendant need not feel so obliged, but I always felt I should practice.

Some two moons after the solstice, when the hope of spring had just begun to whisper, three hundreds under Lurai Roranyel seized a Lakan caravan carrying a moon's supply of food to Nikyana, whole, by sweeping down on skis.

In twenty days one could see Lakan sentries leaning on their spears, weak for want of food. Then plague struck them. It was the disease of thirst, for which one must be given great amounts of water. All day one could see them scraping snow from the earth around the town to melt; when they had to come further out we raided them. The last of our spies to leave their camp brought the news that without enough healthy arms to cut the needed wood the corpses could not be cremated; so the living had had to heap them in alleyways until spring thawed the ground enough to bury them. Spring came slow that year. Their number was halved, leaving six or seven thousand to our twelve, which for all they knew was eighteen; as well they were weak, despairing and facing starvation, and had little hope of relief, their king having turned his attention south.

We need do no more than surround them, demand their surrender, and if they refused, wait. Hurai made me think of this in my lesson. Stuck in thoughts of siege and battle, I took a while to come to it, while he led me all over the Garden Orbicular by the nose with deceptions. "An enemy general will do the same, and crush you as fast as he can," I remember him saying as I stood yearning to bend my head with my wristlets in the hope of making it work. "When you're demarch I won't be there to give you hints." Oh yes, you will, I thought; you'll be in my command council, or I'm an idiot. We broke camp, and closed our ring around Nikyana.

After six days, a herald waved an ivy branch without leaves, and a delegation rode out. They were different now than in autumn: gaunt beneath their bright panoply, both horses and men, their steps slow and weak, their proud bearing straining; grief, that had been fresh and spiced with anger in fall, was now worn deep into their brown faces. I noticed Inkrajen's son was not there; later I heard the plague took him. We would never have our fair fight.

The glow of triumph faded from my heart. We were finished fighting; they were enemies no longer, but fellow humans, starved, sick, bereaved, broken, with no choice but to give themselves into our hands, and accept what that brought them.

Some say we Yeolis are barbarians, for thumbing. But we have reason, fighting against slave-holding countries. If they capture us, they sell us into slavery, thus ensuring we do not fight again. If we capture them, we have no such means; so we let them go, but first make sure in our way. Sometimes there are mercy agreements; but there were none in this war.

I felt most for Orbukjen, whose face wore the shadow of illness. What his fate would be in Laka, I did not know. Here we impeach failing generals; there, all is subject to the king's whim. He could make a defense of circumstance, and bad luck; yet one knew, had Inkrajen lived, everything would have been very different. I remember the reins trembling in his satin-gloved hands, as his herald went through the ubiquitous formalities, whose pomposity rang so discordant now; but he was steady, as he handed Hurai his sword, and cut off a thick lock of his hair.

The plague had mostly run its course, but many Lakans still lay sick. We took the walls, but Hurai forbade us to enter the town, lest we catch it. One could see them when they came out into the streets, the faces of the camp-followers and servants, who in the way of Lakans had gone hungriest, looking like brown death's heads, their clothes hanging like sacks on their bodies. We waited until all the sick had recovered or died, a half-moon, sharing our rations.

When the sun was well up, meltwater dripping silver from the dark eaves of the houses—how the Lakans must have cursed to see spring come, a bare moon too late—we gathered them in the square, where the two blocks and the brazier for the irons were set up. The trained warriors were separated from the serfs; even now when one would think they'd want to hide it, all but a few still wore their insignia of warriorhood, the spear-head shaped earrings. Now I learned the old trick for catching the rest, of having someone strike a Yeoli war gong at their backs; it is easy to pick out those who spin around into stance unthinking.

Orbukjen we could ransom, and therefore we did not intend to thumb him; but when all was ready, he left Hurai's side to go to the head of the line. The murmurs among the Lakans sank to silence. He bore it with grace, too, his chin high and steady all though. In the throng of brown faces many cheeks glistened in the sun with tears. Then the line began to move, and soon the air was thick with the smells of blood and burned flesh.

Though I had got used to battle, I felt sick: I think it was that it was done in such an orderly way, like in an infirmary, or that there was no fight in it, like in a slaughterhouse. My stomach was most turned, somehow, by the way the hatchet-worker would clear the block with his hatchet after each blow like a cook discarding rind, as if what he added to the brown heap beside it had never been part of a person. Of course I did the same, in my own turn. I had to take a turn in every position in the thumbing-crew. The hands come fast, and you think only of the ten lashes you will get if you don't bring the blade down hard enough, that being the standard punishment for taking more than one cut. It was seeing them tear their spear-earrings from their ears afterwards, equivalent to Yeolis flinging away their wristlets, that most struck my heart.

Using the hot iron, at least you can tell yourself you are a healer, stanching their bleeding even as they flinch. Asking their choice, thumbing or death, is worse than it looks; you must see their faces. And look for tricks; a left-handed man, we caught out by the wear-mark of his scabbard-strap. He wept like a child, unlike the others; unlike the others, he had nursed a hope.

Then came a middle-aged man with long hair-earrings, who answered my question by drawing a finger across his throat. I tried to dissuade him, first with gestures and then in Enchian. He stared at me astonished; then he drew himself up. I had never seen such a look, immutable as a cliff-face and pure as diamond in its contempt, knowing as much of humility or uncertainty as gold knows tarnish; the disdain, through this one man's black eyes, of a hundred generations of Lakan nobles.

I understood. That pride required him to die rather than return home thumbless, dishonored. I had tried to take it from him, who had nothing else left, and who had made peace with death. It occurred to me I saw the God-In-Him. While I tried to find words to apologize, he turned away and strode to the death-block. The guards moved to take his arms; before I knew it, my hands were on their shoulders. I ordered them off him, and he looked at me as if to say, "Perhaps I underestimated you." Then Hurai called me. I must have a turn at every position, and there might not be another who chose death today; he beckoned me to the block.

Bile crawled in my stomach and throat. "No one does it more than once," he said, "so this will be it for the rest of your life. One stroke; it won't make much difference to him, but it will to the rest, and to you." I shall say no more, but that the Lakan lord laid his head down without hesitation, and I did it in one stroke. I could never be an executioner. I still feel it, hefting that lethal weight, feeling the edge catch for the shade of an instant on a nub of bone before it thumped into the block, in my nightmares.

We sent all but those we ransomed over Kamis, and

claimed, as is our custom, a Lakan valley large enough to feed all those lost on this front in this war. Foreign scholars ask us how, if we were never the aggressors, Yeola-e acquired land from other nations. It was all gained this way, every fingerwidth the payment for life, which once taken can never be returned. We take no more than has been taken from us, nor do we always win, but we've had one and a half millennia, a long time.

Tyeraha summoned Hurai to Leyere, and me with him, my Ten among his guard. He brought along most of the centurions, about a hundred. In the winter we'd obtained some Lakan strategy works, and in one found a counter-tactic for the deadly Lakan cavalry: some two hundred years ago the Lakans had made war against hill-tribes in what was now northern Laka, and suffered great losses, because the tribes would hold a solid line, some ten ranks deep and packed elbow to elbow, armed with three-man-height-long pikes set in the ground. We had drilled in this over the winter, but never used it; in Leyere we could.

The great battle expected there had not come after all. The Lakans had stopped marching upriver at Kantila once the snows became heavy, but left a garrison in Leyere. Plague does not distinguish the color of one's skin. They caught it, and then through a messenger or supplies, I imagine, it spread to their army in Kantila.

So at the same time thirst-sickness had been plaguing our Lakans through the winter, fever had been plaguing Tyeraha's, likewise halving their number. With those left of Emao-e's army gathering together, and the reinforcements, our force matched theirs by spring. We fought a series of battles against them, using the long pike to great effect on the plains. I remember horsemen coming like thunder, and impaling themselves on our points, and the screams of horses, louder, longer, much more terrible than those of the people, being uncomprehending. When we advanced, one did not look down to see what moved beneath one's feet.

I sat on the command council, and was even permitted to speak, or work out details, in front of the flower of Yeoli military leadership, some carrying fame from my father's time whose names, suffused with an aura of legend, I remembered from childhood. I remember Emao-e, whose nickname Steel-eyes anyone who has seen her would agree fits, saying, "Let's see what this boy's made of, who's going to be leading us all in three and a half years." I would take comfort from the familiar glare of Hurai.

Sachara got wounded, and almost killed by fever; one of the Shairaonil in my ten died of an arrow in the throat. In the third battle my century, then under the command of Elera Shae-Tyeba of Terera, a young man of whom I knew little, was at the center of the Yeoli line, fighting infantry on infantry. Suddenly the Lakans before us fell back fighting, but quickly; Elera sprang after them, beckoning us to follow.

I cursed my shortness, which kept me from seeing where we were in the forest of warriors. The oldest trick in history was in my mind, the horseshoe, in which one falls back at his center to draw in the other's center, and then sweeps in the flanks to surround them. Somehow I felt, more than saw or heard, that the Lakan flanks were not retreating.

"Mana! Lift me on your shoulders!" He looked at me as if I were mad. "That's an order!" Sure enough, our line was curving, like the edge of a glacier. As if to support the evidence of my eyes, the gong boomed, in the rhythm that means "Keep the line straight," and all the other centurions shouted it. I called back my nine, who turned as one. Elera, to my disbelief, charged on as if he were deaf, and the rest of the century, torn two ways, scattered themselves all out in a halfhearted advance. In a moment we were all in the open. Like a nightmare clearer than waking, I saw what would happen.

There was hardly time to curse. "Stay here!" I told my Ten, and dashed out again. The nightmare began playing itself out, with a volley of Lakan arrows falling unanswered; Oteka, our commander of archers, was holding back arrows to avoid shooting the one hundred that had not fallen back. Any moment now she would change her mind or be overridden, sacrificing us for the cursed fools Elera was making us. I could just hear Hurai's voice: "We're all dead if we don't shoot! The Ascendant be damned!"

I found Elera advancing a bare spear-length from the Lakans, who kept up their orderly retreat; perhaps he thinks he is forcing them back with his stare, I thought. They were beckoning us to fight them with smiles on their faces, as if it weren't obvious enough. In truth, I wouldn't have risked a Yeoli arrow in the back to save his brainless head; it was to save those who would.

"Centurion! I am compelled to advise you, don't you hear the child-raping *gong*?" Perhaps he'd misunderstood the rhythm; I don't know. What he claimed afterward was the root of his misjudgment defies my understanding. Without even a pause, he said, "I knew I'd have to say this. Shut your cocky brat's mouth, Fourth Chevenga."

I was so stunned, no action even came to mind, not even anger. He said it with satisfaction, I thought. All-spirit, is this envy? Here? *Now?*

Several Lakans called out a word at which all ducked behind their shields. Oteka had changed her mind; the crossfire began. Preferring to be killed by a Lakan arrow I ducked with my shield behind me, and heard a shaft thump into it. "All those who don't want to get their own people's arrows in the back," I bellowed, "follow me; I'll take the whip!" Almost as one, they did; they'd only needed someone, no matter who, to command it.

The day ended in stalemate. Afterwards we helped Kamina, who had taken an arrow in the shoulder; he was leaning on my arm when I felt a hand seize my hair. Elera would not even wait until we'd got to the infirmary.

I had already announced that I would take whatever he gave me. But now as he dragged me along like a child, an old rage like fire sparked in me; I came within a hair's width of fighting him. But there was too much rage here already; remembering whose actions on the field had brought bad results, and whose good, for all to see, I went along. His harshness would add only to his shame, not to mine.

He wore a grin, as he struck me the stroke of shame, and had me bound to the flogging-post, though eighteen thousand in Shairao had seen it was not necessary. The warriors, who had been heaving off their armor, salving their scratches and getting the cookfires going, now gathered around, leaning on each other's shoulders, anger on their faces. For a moment I thought they'd taken his side; but someone said, "Elera, he was right."

To my astonishment he answered, "I know he was," though I suppose it would have been more astonishing had he not. "He was right with Inkrajen too, but got flogged.

Insubordination is insubordination. Is that not so, Fourth Chevenga?" I answered as I must, from where I stood bound, "Yes, Centurion." They fell to muttering, and he took up the whip in his own hand.

I knew the envy of children, of overshadowed siblings, the grudging admiration of friends wishing themselves in my place, of older warriors imagining what I would someday be. But what I felt on my skin now, I was naked too, having never dreamed it. There before all his warriors, as if it were right, he laid into me as if his mistake had somehow been my fault, as if he could erase it by purging his anger on me, as if he could make himself greater by causing me pain. I did not see his face, but my friends did, alight with satisfaction, in the guise of discipline.

I woke hanging by my arms; Mana and Krero untied me, their hands, even as they tried to be tender, trembling with rage. As Elera turned to walk away, a score of voices called him back, the loudest his second, Karili Senchara. There had been whispering all through the flogging. "The people request a vote; our wills as one are our own until it is done," she said, formally, then: "Your balls are ash, Elera." He froze, his features stone-grim. I cannot see how he could not have expected it.

All who had survived were present: seventy-five. A good half of the dead, as we would never mention aloud in camp, had fallen to Yeoli arrows. Seventy-one voted chalk to impeach him; even his friends did not vote charcoal, but abstained. Without a word he surrendered the insignia to Karili, and strode away.

Mana and Krero carried me back to the tent, and on the way I began throwing up; after I was empty it was dry heaves. It was a cursed hot day, I remember. They laid me naked in cool shade, and put wet cloths on my skin, and in time my head and stomach settled. Kunarda meanwhile followed the news for us. The high command had sent for Elera, and witnesses. I was excused, and Mana to be with me, but the rest went. They came back laughing.

"You know how it was," Krero said. "He disregarded orders no less than you did, ignoring the gong! Of course he didn't deny it, since so many saw, but you know what he said? You won't believe this. 'With someone like Fourth

Chevenga Shae-Arano-e under your command,' he said, 'it gets hard to think clearly sometimes.' Yes! On my crystal, I swear!"

I slowly saw: he really *was* blaming me for his mistake. Bitter loud laughter cut the air. "Oh yes," said Mana, "and Cheng's to blame for the plague, the flies, and last century's poor harvests too, I suppose!"

"And the heat!" snapped Kunarda.

"And the hardtack!" added Sachara. The fast give-and-take of jest suddenly cast me back to the past, nine moons ago, when it had had no hard edges, when we'd known nothing and had no scars; when we had been children. The times of peace before seemed like a distant dream.

"Well," Krero went on, "Steel-eyes gave him the stroke of humility and ordered twenty-five lashes. I spoke then. 'To air a fact, if I may,' I said, 'he flogged Chevenga to falling.' Everyone signed chalk. 'Well, if you see such severity as fit, Elera, certainly,' Steel-eyes said. 'To falling, then.' " My friends all cackled, until I said that flogging to falling was nothing to laugh at, whoever got it.

The evening coolness was a blessing; I could walk a little, with help. We assembled on the training ground; it seemed Karili didn't want promotion, so we must elect a centurion. Krero nominated me; the vote went chalk. Karili stayed second. There was no celebration; we had more cause for mourning. When I excused myself early, the sky still purple, I saw Elera's eyes shining in the firelight.

The next few days as I was healing, I thought of him far too much. It made my insides curl black like burning paper, tasted of poison, chafed worse than I could understand. If skill and fame and position are what he aspires to, I thought, he has every reason to envy me. It isn't that he'll outlive me; I've outgrown that. Why does it send me so? My flogging-pain told me just to hate him, that it was as simple as an honest soul's distaste for a petty, vicious one; for a time I indulged myself in contempt. But I am adult enough, I told myself, to see he is human and Yeoli, not so different from me.

I tried being him, and found so much pain I cringed away. Then my heart went out to him. But it left me where I had started. I could not fight him: that would help nothing. I could not comfort him in his shame: my comfort would be scalding oil to him. Yet I could not forget him; I could never forget him. An ancient thought twinged: how many other people do I so touch? There was nothing I could do to make peace with him, but one. Realizing, I understood my heart.

He hated me for my capability. To end that I would have to diminish it. Envy sends the knife I carry to cut out the imperfections in me twisting into the good, asks me to blacken my heart, dull my mind, slow my hand. It turns one against oneself.

I sprang up. By the woodpile was an axe; I snatched it up and went to look for him among the tents. "Elera?" said some warrior gleefully when I asked her where he was. "Good, you've found something to punish him for already! His face needs rubbing in it." I went the way she pointed.

It was evening. He was at a small fire, surrounded by his friends. Through a field-hedge I heard some of their conversation. "We'll elect you decurion, at least. In a while, when this is all forgotten. One foul-up doesn't cancel two years of good command, to my mind." The reply was in Elera's voice. "No. I couldn't stand it either way, serving under *him*, after this. I'm transferring, and if he doesn't approve it, I'll go over his shit-eating head. . . . Of course he's *their* little darling too. He goes to command councils, did you know that? At *fifteen*." I backtracked silently, then approached again, rustling grass, snapping twigs. They went quiet, looking to see who came; then quieter still when they saw.

Never before had I been fixed by so many eyes with a glare meant to freeze the spine. Most thought I'd come to rub salt in his wounds; but two faces bore the same cold shape, alien as a moonscape, that I knew from his. Whether he had infected them with envy, or they him, or it was a matter of like to like, I suppose does not matter. For a moment, again, I wondered if I was in the wrong. But I said what I'd intended, "Elera. I wish to speak with you, alone."

He could not refuse, lest I command it, nor plead flogging-pain, while I stood before him. Slowly he rose. I saw his eyes flick puzzled, to the axe in my hand.

I brought him to a copse by the edge of the camp that had been left standing to serve as a small shrine, and the clearing hidden by trees. I gave the axe to him handle-first, unclasped my sword-wristlet and laid my forearm across a fallen tree.

"Go ahead," I said. "We can say we were here chopping wood, and it was an accident." He stared at me, his eyes hidden in shadow, the stare apparent only by the stillness of his body. "Isn't this what you want? One chop, and you need never be bothered by my skill again." I offered him my dagger. "Or is it my judgment? Take out my eyes then. My courage? Take a slice from my stomach. My weapon-sense? I'm not sure where that is in me, but if you dig around you're bound to get it sooner or later. Well? You want to be free of whatever you envy in me, don't you, so you can think clearly?"

He whirled, and flung the axe into the ground, where it stuck. "You overrated stripling! Don't play Teacher with me! You could never understand, in a thousand years."

"That's a call to be the other," I said, "if ever I heard one." I rose and stood where he had, unfastening the centurion's collar from my neck. To imagine I had got my stroke and flogging from a general instead of him was not hard, for me.

Yet the act was difficult in itself. I was out of practice; like a clam's shell grown around me were the hard habits of war. Fighting, one clings to oneself with all one's might; it goes against the grain, to dissolve oneself the way one must for this. I was too young yet for the warrior's lesson in that.

What I feel you could never understand, in a thousand years. How could you? Look at you, a warrior at thirteen, Tennunga's son, carrying Chirel—how could you know what it is to be ordinary? Everything was made easy for you; how could you know what it is to have to work for anything, to strain every moment against the bounds within you, knowing the ones you yearn to cross most you only will in your dreams, because the die fashioned you medio-cre? Then to see some slight-built boy dance across them with ease . . . and know it will be him who lives your dreams, not you. He will command the army, not you; he will do the great deeds, not you; he will get carried through the streets of Terera, showered with wine and flowers—not you! It is his name the women will sigh and the warriors chant in love, never yours; I can hear it now, 'Chevenga, Chevenga!' where once I heard 'Elera, Elera!' Of him the songs will be sung and the tomes written long after his death, never of you! You will just be an arrow in his quiver, forgotten the moment you die.

"And now Fourth Chevenga is under me. He says nothing; he doesn't have to; his presence is enough. The general's apprentice, watching my every move for flaws, waiting for his chance to catch me off-guard and make his name correcting me. . . . Is it any surprise it happened, when it was always on my mind, and he wished it so dearly? How could I think?

"So I am flung into the dust: caught, corrected, struck the stroke of shame and flogged by the General First, impeached, a common footsoldier when I was a centurion . . . what am I? What am I now?" I touched the plain collar of my mail-shirt, and felt tears on my cheeks. This was the pain I had turned from, toying with playing him at the fire. The last cruel cut came to me, full of bitter symmetry. "And who, who in the great Earthsphere, have they elected to take my place?"

I looked, and saw I had touched him too. He was gazing at me stunned, tears bright on his cheeks. He sank to the log then, burying his face in his hands.

For a long time I sat beside him, not knowing whether he would want my hand on his shoulder or not; in the end I chose to err on the side of comradeship, and put it there. He did not move, nor show any sign of feeling it. "Who could you ever have envied?" he said. Not about to say, "Everyone over thirty," I did not answer, and he said, "It's none of my business, never mind. I suppose I must be you now. So many times I have imagined I were Fourth Chevenga Shae-Arano-e. Always wrongly."

"It's all right," I said. "I said it all when I gave you the axe. May I tell you a story, instead?"

He signed chalk, drying his eyes, and I sat down next to him, both of us starting to lean our backs against the log and deciding not to almost as one, which made us share a shy laugh. I wished I had a wine-skin to pass him. Like a warrior recounting old battles, I told him of how I had not wanted to be one at all at first, of Esora-e choosing to make me the greatest in the world without asking my choice, of my fights with him, of the worst trials of my training, of all the tribulations the things for which he envied me had brought me. Soon he began recalling his own training, and a tyrannical Teacher he had had, and we ended up laughing.

Of course I could not tell him the worst; no matter. We were friends; though he doubted he would cease envying me he swore not to hold it against me, we forgave each other for everything and gingerly embraced, and he invited me to his fire. I remember the looks on the faces of his friends, when he introduced them to me with his arm over my shoulders.

XI

The Lakans locked themselves in Kantila, which is walled, and we settled in for a siege. It struck me that the gate should be opened from within at midnight; I had been practicing the stealthy arts all the harder, these days. I went to Emao-e and volunteered. She thought I was mad, of course. I made her a bet, that she must at least agree to send to my aunt for permission if I could sneak into her tent even if she doubled her guard and gave them torches. Driving spring rainstorms are a boon; they obscure sight and sound but not weapon-sense. "Fourth Chevenga reporting for duty, General!" I barked from beside her bed. Muttering sleepily, she reached for a pen.

Requesting leave from my various commanders (I alone was blessed with more than one), I went to Tenningao to visit Tyeraha, whom I hadn't seen since marching. Like any ability, weapon-sense should be used where it served best, I argued.

It was a harder choice for her than for me, as it is harder to watch a loved one climb a cliff than to do it oneself; one cannot feel the other's strength of grip and steadiness of balance, watching. If I got killed on this escapade, she would be remembered for having permitted it. Yet, she'd watched me grow up, trusted me to know myself, and wanted to see me become the sort of demarch whose

162

name alone is enough to discourage aggressors. In the end she called for Jinai Oru.

We were standing in her borrowed office as she said this. I remember the silvery tongue of fear shooting up my spine. What might an augurer of such skill feel, probing me? There was no good reason I could give my aunt for refusing. A springing step came in the corridor. Somehow I had imagined a ghost-slender man, grave of face, piercing of eye and wearing a long black robe; in truth he had a bear's build, wide with short thick limbs, and a cheery round face, now flushed with exertion, and wore nothing but a loincloth and a towel, having been power-dancing in the courtyard. He looked for all the world like one who would talk boisterously at drinking parties. My aunt spoke to him as if he were a touch slow.

He pulled me into a room with its window shuttered and curtained, a candle and a sitting mat on the floor the only furnishings, flung the towel into a corner and knelt on the mat. "A little time," he said, "to shut up the words in my head." Soon he got up, gazing at the blank wall, which was of smooth plain stucco, and signed me to stand before him. I did, facing him. "No, no," he said, and turned me around by my shoulders brusquely. "What's behind you, anyone can know, just by remembering. It's what's ahead of you that's interesting." He pressed close, his chest warm on my back, set his chin on my shoulder, and laid his large hands on my arm and my brow. To my surprise, they had turned cool. I told myself he probably always felt some nervousness in his subjects.

"Is it worth the risk?" he said, half to himself. "If she lets him do all the crazy things he says he can, will he learn to be a great demarch, or do himself in?" For a while he was silent, every now and then shifting me slightly, as if setting a mirror for the best angle. I wondered whether I should feel a tingle from his hands or some such thing, then dismissed that as silly, reminding myself I knew something of augury. In time I found myself straining my own eyes on the candle-yellowed wall.

"Well," he said. "It's balance; if he's careful enough he'll live, if he isn't, he won't." Almost before I thought it, he said, "Oh come on, anyone could figure that, with figuring. Where's what they don't know?" He looked hard again, muttering. "Maybe if I shut up . . ." My aunt

spoke, and in her tone I heard experience in guiding him.
"Jinai, should I let him open the gate of Kantila?"

"Yes," he said, without hesitation. My skin prickled, as
if a ghost were in the room. It was the ease of his certainty, like a child's in a truth he is not yet old enough to
see might be wrong. I knew that feeling. "I see that
working. Unless he gets too . . . cocky, you know, from
me telling him it . . . it's for sure but if he *thinks* it's for
sure, that's foreknowledge interfering, and then for sure
he's dead." My aunt looked hard at me; I said, "I
understand."

"What of the other deeds he'll want to try, Jinai?" she
asked him. He set himself again, his hands pressing my
skin as if to get a closer feel. "I see things. But I don't
know whether they're about this question. No, they must
be, for you asked, and I'm seeing them. What they are I
can't explain but some are bad and some are good."

"Bad in what way?" my aunt said.

"Bad . . ." he answered, "in way of trouble. I feel the
feel of fear, of helplessness. But in the end, better good."
A shiver ran through me, not from fear, but from a sudden
sense of the vast shape of fate, a feeling like looking over
the edge of a cliff to see a distance one never has before.

"The end good," my aunt asked, "is greater than the
initial bad? And therefore worth it?"

"Yes," he answered, a grin like a child's pressing his
cheek against mine. "So I advise, let him do it. Anything
else, demarch?" He gave my shoulder a proprietary pat.

"Why don't you tell his fortune in general? You two will
be working together in three and a half years."

I felt sweat break out everywhere on my skin. Jinai's
hands were still on me; I must force calm without taking a
deep breath, without setting my teeth, without tensing; I
took up an inner chant. She left, a great relief; but I was
still not alone.

Jinai's hands leapt off me as if I were red-hot iron. "Do
you want this?" he said, breathless.

"Yes," I said. "I'm not afraid."

"Yes you are," he said, with such matter-of-fact honesty
that I didn't even think to be insulted, only felt my own
foolishness for denying it. "The thing, the secret you've
got, do you know about it?"

"Yes," I said, swallowing. "Jinai, tell me nothing we speak of will go beyond this door."

"I see so many secrets, I forget them all," he said. "I'm a scatterbrain. On my crystal, I'll remember nothing. Don't worry. Shall I tell your fortune? You aren't like anyone else. I didn't say that while the demarch was here because I thought it was only your business. These things, they are not even my business, how can I tell? The shape, the look, is all very . . . not *clear*—I can't see any better than with anyone else—but what is clear is very . . . bright, like leaves just fallen into a pool in the fall, the lines, the edges, sharp, you know. That doesn't say it all. I'm sorry if I'm hard to understand; the die didn't give me a gift with words.

"I see a thousand things. Amazing things. But they're all too little to say what they mean. If I told you, you'd ask what they meant and I wouldn't be able to tell you, and they'd just torment you. Don't interrupt me, and I'll just say what I can stick together, all right?" I signed chalk.

"Fourth Chevenga Shae-Arano-e, Ascendant to the Demarchy of Yeola-e. Fourth Chevenga Shae-Arano-e, Demarch of Yeola-e . . . That's planned. The die has six faces, but can only land with one up. The path has a thousand forks but Fourth Chevenga Shae-Arano-e can only walk one. God-In-Myself, show me that face, point me that fork . . .

"I see: Lakans. Oh, come on, Jinai, how obvious can you get? Plans and expectations. The ground beneath the ground, further down than the one we're standing on; I'm seeing it from your full-grown height. I see a dark-skinned woman. Not Lakan: short hair. Don't know who she is. I said just patterns, didn't I? Here's one: many lovers. I've seen seven, just now. A child with bright blond hair, like Tennunga's, and eyes the spitting image of yours. Terrible trouble you will have, I can't see what, but you . . . now you have come through it. You'll get through it, and things get better, remember that. I see a war-map, your hands spreading it. You must be demarch, yes, there's the ring. Oh oh, another fight; better keep up your training. . . .

"So many weird things. What does a green ribbon around your wrist mean? Or a huge orange jewel? I'm seeing your dreams: the ground wheeling far below as if you were a

bird flying, or you being a pillar in the Hearthstone Dependent, with ivy growing up you—"

I couldn't help interrupting. "I've had that dream before!"

"Yes," he said with utter authority, "and you will have it
again. There's a strong one, a death-duel against a man
with black skin and blue hair, with a yelling crowd all
around you, whose edge goes up to the sky. A whole city
of straight-haired blond people. Must be a dream; let me
tell you the things that make sense. Lots of war things.
But peace too. I'm starting to lose them, I'm getting tired.
You will get wounded, right there"—he poked me in the
side—"and a Haian will take care of you. He's close to
you. It's going . . . patterns. A blind woman you are
helping. You'll be very famous . . . obvious, obvious, Jinai,
everyone says that . . . I've had it, I think . . . yes, I can't
see more, much as I want to. Your life will be very
crowded, you'll do and get done all sorts of things, it's a
wonder to see, and I've strained myself looking at it." He
sat down with a thump.

I ran out into my aunt's office, begged paper and pen
from her, ran back and scrawled down all that both of us
could remember. I remembered much more than he. He
had spoken true of himself: he had a mind like rapids,
through which much flowed, given out almost as fast as it
was taken in, not like a vessel which retains. But his
prophecy I have carried with me ever since, to watch it all
spin out.

We were finished, but I had one question more. "Jinai,
have you ever looked into your own future?"

"Oh, no," he answered with an awkward smile. "Never."

"Why not?"

The smile grew, becoming more awkward, and he picked
and pinched at one of his fingers. Finally he said, "Because I might see it." No doubt whatsoever, he was a true
augurer.

I went back to Emao-e with my aunt's authorization.
Opening the gates of Kantila was much easier than killing
Inkrajen, in truth. I went in rain again; the sentries were
too busy cursing their luck to have drawn wall duty on
such a night to notice anything, and no one was in the
streets. The hardest part was throwing the bolt, which was
thicker than one could hug and had three cross-grips for
the three large people by which it was meant to be moved.

One small one could, but only a fingerwidth at a time and only because it was either this or climb back over the wall and tell Emao-e I could not do it. When it was open, I thought for a moment that the waiting army had all decided it wasn't worthwhile and gone back to bed, leaving me alone; then they came swarming dark out of the rain, roaring "Ai-yae-oh!", and the gates were thrown wide.

The Lakans never got in order or even properly armed; we cut down men in nightshirts, or naked, their brown skin shining wet in the rain. It was a slaughter from the start; before it could go far, they surrendered.

With the command the next day, I watched the sorting of those who would be ransomed and the thumbing. When the rest, some ten thousand, were about to be set free, Emao-e called a command council. Astyardk, it seemed, was sending in reinforcements, among them many peasants, reequipped, whom we had driven from Nikyana. It seemed he was made of money, at least when it came to this war. Now Emao-e was considering thumbing every prisoner, war-trained or not, to keep them from rejoining the Leyere force.

It should be explained, perhaps, why we don't hold prisoners of war, at least in any numbers for any long time, even when it would give an advantage. We are not a monarchy. If their keep is more than the war treasury can afford, it must go to a tax vote, and most Yeolis take a dim view to feeding invaders, so they end up starving. Why then, foreigners always ask, don't you make them work for their food? It is only a short step from that, we answer, to slavery.

Ten thousand was far too many. I remember that command council, as if I'd lived it a thousand times. Voices rose, and Emao-e's eyes were truly steel; this had never happened in the Enchian Wars.

I remember the arguments. "He is trying to outmatch us in ruthlessness. He can force those peasants. While we've got ten thousand more in Kantila—doesn't he care a dust-speck for them? We could put them all to the sword, for all he knows! Maybe we should; we've been too kind."

"But these people are farmers. You can't swing an axe with one thumb, or plow a straight furrow. They might as well be slaves, for what choice they had to be here."

Then, when it had become fairly heated, Hurai turned to me, in his way of doing things unexpected to break such impasses, and asked my opinion.

I was divided in myself. The argument for thumbing was compelling; but I imagined the square in Nikyana, the smoke, the pile of severed thumbs, tenfold. I sat torn, and Hurai said, drumming his fingers on his belt, "When you're demarch you'll have to settle these things in the wink of an eye."

I thought, almost absently, "I have not looked for the path unconceived." It flashed, and then I could barely believe no one else had thought it.

"If it is a contest of ruthlessness Astyardk wants," I said, "why don't we tell him we *will* put them to the sword if he doesn't retreat? That way we will win without fighting, we may free them whole and still have won." It fleshed itself out on my tongue, as I spoke. "We could ask for all the occupied land, then let him bargain us back to whatever he'll give us for ten thousand lives. Declare it publicly, in front of all their army, so he'll have to agree, or be blamed for it himself; then no one will have lost, but him."

In the silence that fell, I felt naked; of course there must be some plain reason why it could not work, too obvious even to mention, which was why no one had proposed it. I remembered the first plan I had thought up in council, and the empty moment just after I'd spoken it. The first heady instant, I saw them overwhelmed by my brilliance; the next I suddenly saw a thousand rents in my conception, enough to reduce it to tatters, and thought they only refrained from laughing out of civility. As it was, they casually took up refining it. The truth was somewhere between, that it was a serviceable plan, needing some polishing as they all do, and we'd use it.

Now I told myself, *be sensible. It'll be the same this time*. Emao-e slapped her head. "My mind's going to stone," she said. "What's that old saying? 'The children shall lead . . .' " All-spirit, I thought: I overwhelmed her at least a *bit* with my brilliance. But two or three others were looking at me with the thought clear in their eyes: "What is going to be leading us, in three and a half years?" Hurai looked at me suddenly in his unnerving way, and said, "You understand, lad, that if there is no agreement, we *will* have to kill them. Else no one will ever trust our word again." I said, "Of course."

We made the threat in parley. The Lakan general, Arzaktaj, said we must give him ten days to consult, to which Emao-e agreed; it meant he was sending a courier to the King. In the meantime, we let go the nobles in return for ransom, set free all those not armsbearers (whom I did not count among the ten thousand), and took the food-store, to serve them day to day. On the tenth day, a Lakan delegation came out.

I was not in the parley, and we were upwind, so did not hear even the declarations. It was short; while I wondered what to make of that, Perha came running, breathless. "Ascendant. Command council's called, immediately. Hurai orders you there." I asked him the news. "The Lakan King said he wouldn't give up a fingerwidth of land, for any number of lives."

The fastest learning, say the sages, comes with the truth that shatters the mind; one is changed forever after, for one can only live after a rebuilding. But like skin tightening before it splits, the mind resists. So I had to run the news through my head a few more times, before its meaning came clear. Hurai's words came back, clear as if he were standing at my shoulder. Ten thousand—suddenly I could no longer see in my head how many that was.

A jabber like in a market debate erupted. I had almost forgotten my friends were there. Sachara fumed at the madness; Krero shrugged and reminded us we'd killed so many in the war already, then wondered how we would do it. Mana laid his hand on my shoulder. "Cheng, you look sick, what's the matter? It's hardly *your* fault!"

You know me so well, I thought, very cold and clearly; but not well enough, who I am. "It was my idea," I said.

His face froze, and he stepped back, his hand lifting off my shoulder. I heard our fire crackle, and the camp noises all around, while their faces all stared silent, eyes white-ringed. I followed Perha, without looking back.

In the command council, they made me devise the method. It was either that, I saw, or renounce warriorhood and the demarchy, which I almost did. We would march them to a plateau a half-day east, we decided, have them dig a trench and a mound-wall in a circle around their camp, telling them it would be the bounds of their prison, while in truth it would be their grave. It touched slavery; but one could argue that it was something they did for their own sakes. Then we would poison the common pot.

They had a Haian, who had insisted on staying with them. Of course we must not kill him; but he would no doubt warn them, if we told him. I saw a way. Like all Haians, he was a vegetarian; already we had supplied meals just for him when the common fare had meat. We need only put the poison in a meat stew.

That night I slept at the command-post, telling myself I slept away from my friends to save time in the morning; we would march the Lakans the next day. In truth, I feared my friends' questions, in the dark.

Their host was a strange sight to see, warriors with bedrolls and tents but no arms or armor, their hundreds of brown faces drawn but with expressions varying: endurance, shame, fear, anger, hope, even the odd youthful laugh or defiant stare as we passed. To see them formed up, a line that stretched out of sight into the heat-haze, even in ranks of ten, was to see how many they were. Hurai had said, "You showed emotion in council. Don't in their sight; think what would happen if they guessed." So I closed my face tight, though I felt unreal almost to dizziness.

Bearing the shame of defeat, and leaderless, they came docilely enough. They were serfs, half-enslaved to their landlords at home, brought to this war by levy in the first place. Those who chose, I thought, we've let get away, because it brought us money, because Astyardk cared whether they lived or died, unlike these.

On the march, a few did make runs for it; but orders were strict, and we shot them down. One man near the front of the column, the guards did not finish, but left screaming in pain beside the road as an example to the rest, until someone further down gave him mercy.

On the plateau we set them to work digging the trench. They knew how to work, pacing themselves with songs. Starting the next day we dropped them to half-days, letting them off when the sun was highest and hottest; finding and bringing the poison took whoever did it four days. It was arsenic, bought from the copper-works in Arahameno, simple to add to a garlic stew.

On the morning of the fifth day, Hurai sent Perha down with orders to the cooks: feed them half-portions for breakfast and nothing again until evening, so they will be hungry.

I must be hard with my heart, I thought. "Who are they?" I asked myself, looking down on their camp. "Warriors, levied or not, who would have cut us down without a thought. I've seen that many and more die in this war, without a blink. Why should I care any more for these now? It is not even by us their lives are thrown away, but their own king."

We raised the command-post on the mountain above the plateau, but camped our warriors in a bowl on the other side of the ridge behind. After training I tried to sleep, but my eyes would not close. I told myself stories, studied, read; but even so, it pressed heavy on my skin and body, a mass too vast to bear looking at, nameless, inexorable, growing worse as the sun crossed the sky. It didn't matter whose fault it was; ten thousand people would die tonight.

The end of the afternoon came, as it must, and the head cook reported. Now as I stood beside Hurai he explained to her all that had happened, and what she must do. She went pale, but saluted; war-cooks are still warriors, and she could tell herself, "I have been commanded." The poison would be brought in like a delivery from Kantila. All the cooks must be told, since they must add it, but the scullions would be commanded only not to taste the stew; and as soon as they had served all, the whole kitchen-staff was to march straight to Kantila, nighttime though it would be. He wanted them out of earshot, a mercy, for those who had done, but not willed. I remember the head-cook was shaken enough to want to sit for a time before she went back down; but Hurai had allowed for that. That was a lesson I learned from him: a good general will think of such things.

Evening came clear and bright, the sun's descent bringing a gentle coolness that chilled away the haze, while above us cream peaks turned to flame against purple sky. So many strange peaks I had slept below since fall; I wondered what the names of these ones were, then thought of Hetharin, and home. Perhaps I can be forgiven, for wishing I were there, now. Below us, the trench and mound-wall were a clean circle, around a ragged quilt of motley tents. Now and then the valley breeze carried up to us, mixed with the scents of pine and meadow hearts'-ease, the homey smell of garlic-mutton stew. In the same pattern as always, the food-lines formed.

Hurai wrote out something on a waxboard, and showed it to me: an order signed and sealed, to pull the sentries as soon as the Lakans were finished eating; they would no longer be needed. It was an order the commander wouldn't take just on a messenger's word. "And the Haian," he told Ina, who was to take it. "You know what to say to him." That was, one of our people was deadly ill, we had no Haian here, and could we beg him to come up. We had to get him away; when the Lakans found out he couldn't save them, they might do him harm. "You also know what to do if he refuses," Hurai added. If he was anything like our Haian, I saw, they were his companions, his helpers in the infirmary, his friends; he must have healed hundreds in this war, and to a Haian patients are sacred. In one stroke we would undo his work of months, perhaps years. He might have to be brought away by force.

The sun reddened and the wind died. A great height is not so great a distance, so sound comes from further than one would think. I heard the quiet buzz of a thousand conversations, someone hammering a tent-stake, and from here and there, mixed together, their strange songs. Somehow one had kept a stringed instrument, for on the barely-moving air I heard faint plucking. Most were finished eating; it was done.

I saw the speck that was Ina begin up the path, with the Haian, black in his robe with the two broad white stripes; he'd believed the story. Haians tend to be trusting. When they were most of the way up, our sentries moved off the mound-wall, formed up and began running the path to their camp. "Pack up, and to camp," Hurai ordered the command-post staff. I was helping with that when he barked, "Ascendant."

I saw the Haian, his face in the typical mold, flat and chip-eyed and copper-hued; his hair hung long, straight-cut as usual at the ends. He was in a sweat from climbing in a hurry, his bag in hand; I could read the thought on his face, "Someone is dying; why have I been brought before this general?"

"Do you speak Yeoli?" Hurai asked him in Enchian. He

answered "No," on which Hurai called two guards away from the packing. "If he runs for it, restrain him. Without hurting him, on pain of flogging." He told the Haian our names and offered him water, which he took with growing puzzlement on his brows. His name he gave as Imenat of Oiroru.

"Haian, we lied to you," said Hurai. "No one is dying, not here. I am sorry, but it was necessary; you will understand why as I tell you what has happened, and what will."

I don't think Imenat believed it at first. His honest brown face seemed to be straining, as if to hear clearly. Finally he said, in a calm voice, "That's impossible."

"No," said Hurai. "It's done." The Haian sprang to his feet then, making the guards tense, and gazed down at the Lakan camp, which looked no different from before. "No," he said. "No. It's a lie. It's madness. You couldn't do this. They are more than ten thousand!" Of course, he had an accurate count.

"Who have been your patients," said Hurai. "For that, I am sorry. But it is done. You may stay with us, if you wish; you may go anywhere but down there, where you would be no use anyway. I recommend strongly that you go with these people here to our camp; there you'll see and hear nothing."

Somehow that was what made it strike him; and it looked like a death-stroke. For a moment he stood frozen, all the blood draining from his face, to leave it yellow; his bag dropped from his fingers and crashed to the ground, sending glass vials flying out to shatter on the stones and bleed their various herbal tangs into the air. His body jolted all through; the guards seized him by the arms, and he began screaming.

He intended no effect; the words that came out were those that came to his mind. I don't remember all he called us: inhuman mainlanders, mind-sick brutes, barbarians with no notion of civilization, evil madmen who should all be in restraints. I opened my mouth to answer back that it was Astyardk who had chosen this, but Hurai put his hand on my shoulder, and said, "What does what he says matter? We know what is true, don't we?"

Then from fury he went without a pause to abasement; falling to his knees in the guards' arms, and beating his head against their greaves, he begged us to be merciful, as if we could now. Next he took to shrieking in their direction in Lakan, trying hopelessly to warn them, I guess, or saying farewell as best he could; I heard words which I knew by their tone to be names, and tears poured from his eyes. He vowed we would pay for this, that once Dinerer in Haiuroru heard, there would not be a single Haian left in all Yeola-e in a month; that we should learn what death was, if we gave it out so freely.

One of the guards angrily drew a hand back, and looked at Hurai for permission; Hurai chopped charcoal. "Just hold him. Chevenga, go help with the packing." I could not look away from the Haian, though, even as I worked. After a time, he weakened, and lay spent on the ground, clawing with his delicate hands, and now and then hitting his head against the ground, at which the guards would put their hands under to soften the blows.

"To camp," Hurai ordered, when all was packed. "Him too; go on, healer, you've done all you can; call this a battle, that you can have no part in." Imenat answered that these people had been his patients, and he would watch them die; so he stayed, and Hurai commanded the two guards to stay also. He himself went to the slope's edge, and knelt in the warrior's kneel, facing the valley.

He had not ordered me to stay. As I tightened packstraps on Samo's shoulders, I glanced past his head to the mountain's spine. Beyond that, safe from sight, safe from sound, lay the camp; and it was being left to me to choose. I saw them off, and went to kneel beside him. He said only, "Good."

Thus it began, to end only, as it began, in silence, with only five witnesses. I will try as best I can to describe the indescribable.

We had forbidden them fires or lamps, but allowed them candles; now a thousand tiny flecks of flame sprouted among the tents, pinpricks in the dying sun. Presently some of the people, on the outer edges, noticed they were unguarded, and a few crept out and into the woods, dark shapes against the dried earth; others called friends to join them, and a whispered debate half-quieted the camp. Then came the first cut-off cry.

It did not strike all at once, but started with those, I suppose, who had been first in the food-lines. Exclamations rose from here and there, all over, and all conversa

tion died. Sometimes I imagine what it must have been for
them, to see one of their number fall convulsing, then ten,
then a hundred, until it became clear none would be
spared, and they understood. When a din of cries, strange
to hear in none but men's deep voices, spread across the
camp, I knew it had come.

One needed no Lakan to understand it, the curses against
us, the calls to their gods. The camp burst into madness; a
gout of flame spouted, where a candle knocked over had
set a tent on fire; then another. A few, then a crowd,
swarmed across the trench and down the slope towards
Laka, as if escape lay there, or anywhere on earth; others
knelt, as Lakans sometimes do to pray, lay down and beat
their heads against the earth, or ran aimlessly. Some took
out their rage on each other with their fists; others clung
together.

Still others seized up shovels, tent-poles, whatever they
could find, and set off up this path, which they knew led
to us. It was a good fifty at first, that soon swelled to two
or three hundred, all giving the Lakan warcry. We all
looked to Hurai. He shrugged, and did not move. "They
won't make it," he said. "It's a long way, and the exertion
speeds up the poison." So we sat still, and watched his
words play out true.

More than half were down before they'd got a quarter of
the way to us; we saw the bushes beside the path shake
with their throes. But many got close enough for their
dark faces to became visible, twisted as if with madness,
streaked with tears and sweat. Their chests heaved, the
waryells now broken between sobbing breaths, full of
pain and fatigue; fingers clawed at rocks and grass. One
would crumple gasping, clutching at his heart, and let out
a cry of frustration and grief while the others left him
behind, or crawl a little further, his eyes still burning on
us, until they rolled up into his head and the throes took
him. The last were the best, the strongest; one could see
how it spurred them, to see us kneeling calmly. But their
fight was hopeless, being against that which cannot be
fought; the death-blow had been slipped into them without their knowing long before, and their spirit earned
them nothing but the bitterer grief of failing by a lesser
margin. I remember one who must have been a champion,
built like an oaken statue of the athlete's ideal, who pulled

himself to within thirty paces of us; with his last strength he threw his tent-pole like a spear. When he saw it fall short, the poison seized him, as if he'd let it.

The Haian was crying again, his close wail loud against the distant ones; when one of the guards with him offered him a drink, he threw out the water and thrust the cup back, spitting. As the sun sank behind the mountains, darkness fell deep enough to hide the plateau from our sight, but for the tent-fires that were many now, spreading, and the black silhouettes that dashed before them. The noise changed, the thousandfold cries growing louder and losing words, fear and anger fading into the pure outpouring of life that any sentient thing gives as life is torn from it. It was nothing like a battle; there, one hears war cries as well, victory shouts, the clash of weapons which mean at least that everyone has a chance. This was like the death-howl of a single great animal with ten thousand mouths, that has eaten poison bait and now dies by parts. Though I have gone through so much else, sometimes in the dark of night when my thoughts are not entirely mine to direct, I still hear it.

Now I heard gasping sobs mixed in, and wondered how they could be so close when Imenat was ten paces away, and Hurai never cried. I knew them, having heard them many times before: my own.

Hurai saw me bury my face in my hand. "Why feel so?" he said. "Why cry? What fault is it of yours? If it is true what you said, their fate is in Astyardk's hands, not ours. It is he who has killed them, if you were right. What are these tears then?"

That was the foundation-stone of the dam, I guess, and he worked it loose. All I had held in broke out of me. "For them! For their deaths! How could he? How can he call himself their leader, and allow such? For his cursed greed, he sent them here and threw their lives away! *Ten thousand*! How can he sleep at night? *I* won't! Why isn't he crying for them, when *I* am? He won't, so Saint Mother accept me, I will!"

"Why?" he cut in, loud over their noise, and mine. "They aren't your people to cry for; they're his. And he's no demarch, we all know that. How many Yeolis do you think they've killed, between their ten thousand? Saint

Mother, this is *war*, lad. You never shed a tear striking them down in battle."

"But they aren't fighting! They're defeated, they're weaponless, helpless! Hurai, should I have no heart? Should I feel nothing? Isn't that the way to barbarity? To the Second Fire? They have families, homes, children! Now this, and we did it! I did it! I thought of it!" Tears leached the strength from me, so I bent over burying my face in my arms.

He said, "Are you asking yourself 'what has Astyardk made me?' "

I unclenched my hands from my hair. Their familiar shape shone black against the flame below, where what we could not see, but only hear, went on. The wet warmth that slicked them seemed to be blood; the plateau was between my hands, as if I held it. There was no answer, but to hold down my gorge, and weep harder.

"He has made you nothing, Chevenga. You are no different from what you were; the lad who conceived a plan, one of whose branches we are now enacting. If it was only he who decreed that it should turn out this way, how is it your fault? Do you plan to carry these deaths on your shoulders—if so, why not all the others you've killed? This is war; our hands are all red. We didn't attack. We only did what Saint Mother permitted us, when she gave us the sword, and what we consented to do, when we lifted it. You conceived, and you conceived well, else we wouldn't be doing it. We stood to gain, either way; it's ten thousand less Lakans to plague us, after all, and Astyardk's bound to catch *some* trouble for it, at home. We did what we chose, carried it through, and now it is done. Why regret?"

I could not answer, except with tears. He had to use his commander's voice to be heard; Imenat was screaming again, from the ground where the guards wrestled him. "Because you are gentle-hearted, Chevenga? Is that it, do you call yourself that? More so than I, who watch this with dry eyes? Yet you were ruthless enough to suggest it. Which are you? Which is the truth inside you? One day, these hands will hold all the power, these hands will make every choice for Yeola-e in time of war. You will have to learn, or decide."

I found myself trembling from head to foot, as if I were fevered. "Or is it just that you are young," he said, "and didn't understand what it would mean?" He was kneeling before me now; his face leaned close, and in the starlight I saw it was neither gentle, nor hard; only calm. "That's the one sickness whose cure comes without effort: youth. Not your fault; you can be forgiven for it." He poked a finger under my chin, and lifted it. *"Once."* Into the screaming fire-pit below, he pointed. "Weep, then; you're right to, after all. Weep for them, and know what war means. Weep for them, and grow up."

So I did, and now and then heard Imenat wail, until the death-howl of the Lakans, which sustained loud and steady for a long time, faded into silence.

That night seemed years. I did not sleep; my thoughts were waking nightmares.

Reveille came at the first paling of sky, not dawn; the sooner in the day we got them buried, the better. We marched over the ridge, into sight. A brown mottled mass lay spread over the plateau, lying in and over the trenches like a liquid spill half-congealed, here and there charred black. We found the first bits of it on the path.

Though they were fresh, it was hard not to be sick. They lay tangled in the tents and each other, limbs twisted and faces contorted; where there had been fire, some were burned to raw red flesh, some blackened. We scared the birds off them, but there was nothing to do against the flies, or the stink of open latrine that was everywhere, from their throes. We were a thousand; each pair need carry twenty to the trench, Hurai ordered, and no more. With a little thought, I saw how his order would get it done quicker than a plain command of double-time. Some of them had gone far afield, before they had died. Whoever moved fastest bringing near ones would not be stuck searching for those in the woods.

I had the luck to be paired with a woman from Leyere who was all jokes. "Let every dirt-brown army come to us this way!" she said cheerily as we worked. "They're easier to deal with, don't you think, Ascendant?" Not for her, to lower a corpse respectfully into the grave by climbing down; everyone else was tossing them, she reasoned, so we'd end up rooting through the forest if we didn't do likewise. Or else she'd pretend to pick wax out of their ears and eat it (switching fingers, of course), and ask me enviously, since I'd seen, what their deaths had looked like. I suppose that was her way of bearing it.

Then, in a moment that my hands were not full, I heard my name in a voice and a lilting Enchian I knew. It was Imenat; he threw himself down in front of me, clasping my knees, and begged me weeping for something I could not at first make out. "Spare them, don't kill them, I beg you, for mercy's sake, for All-Sprite's sake, or whatever you believe in, I beg you . . ."

"Spare whom?" I said; I hadn't thought there was any-one left. "The infirmary," he gasped. "Some are still alive there. They had no appetite . . . Prince, King's Heir, please, I beg you!" By proper procedure, I should have told him, "You are begging the wrong man; I am only a general's apprentice," and kept working. Instead I ran to the infirmary with him.

It was like seeing a man return to the burned ruins of his home; he knew his way through the devastation. Then as we entered the large tent that was the bed-quarters, it was as if he found a new flame licking at the last sound beam. He ran screaming to where a Yeoli had raised a sword, and fearlessly grabbed his arm, at which they be-gan wrestling. There were several people with blades drawn, seeing a quick way to complete their twenty. Even those patients who looked capable of doing something lay still, as if they had no argument with death; in the bed beside me lay a round-faced Lakan who could not have been more than seventeen, his eyes alive but staring sightlessly upward, as if the soul behind them were turned to stone. The words tore out of me. "*Chen! Stop!*"

I could think of nothing, when all the Yeolis straight-ened and looked at me, but, "By whose permission do you do this?", thinking only after I'd said that it might well be Hurai's.

It turned out it was no one's. "Wasn't it the plan, to kill them all?" a man answered. "We're just finishing off." "Nine-thousand nine-hundred and seventy dead Lakans out there," said someone else, "what's another thirty in here?"

"You cannot do this without consent of the General First," I said, though not without a quick glance around to see if any were higher-ranked than I. "I will check with him. Not a drop of blood is to be shed until I get back, and perhaps not even then. So go somewhere else and find some bodies that are deader." Dragging Imenat along, I ran to find Hurai, who was carrying corpses like everyone else, and directing at the same time.

While the Haian pleaded, Hurai looked over his head straight at me, his eyes narrowing. "He came right to you, didn't he? No fools, these Haians." He spat into the dust, always a sign, with him, that he was persuaded. "Let them go home and tell the story, then, it will make it worse for Astyardk. But *you* are in charge of it. Now get lost." By the time we got back they were only twenty-two, the stone-eyed youth gone; people had been taking those who looked like corpses. I hope at least they gave them the grace-stroke, so none were left to smother among the dead.

We spread quicklime over them, then earth. In the sun, the shovel I held still seemed warm, from their hands. There was not enough time for us to entirely fill and mound the tomb; that work Emao-e later contracted to the villages nearby. We finished by early afternoon, bathed in the river and then marched back to Kantila. I had the twenty-two carried, and found an empty house in Kantila for Imenat to use as an infirmary. When they healed I secretly freed them one by one.

A stone stele was raised on the ring-mound. Whenever I visit Kantila, I go there, so I remember the epitaph:

"In this circle lie ten thousand Lakans, their names too many to know, captured in Kantila by Yeolis under the command of Emao-e Lazaila in the Equinox Moon of Summer, 1544, slain by Yeolis under the command of Hurai Kadari in the same moon, by reason of the will of their king, Astyardk, who would return no amount of Yeoli land for all their lives. May reason bring peace to the living as death has brought peace to the dead."

XII

A runner came to command council in midsession with news: twenty thousand more Lakans were coming. It made us wonder whether Astyardk would send every male in Laka, and starve his country feeding them; in the meantime, until we could get reinforcements, we were severely outnumbered.

This would be a new lesson for me, who'd seen things go so well; how to retreat, though it means giving up hard-won gains, when necessary. We barricaded ourselves in Kantila, Tyeraha promising to send relief to us in a moon; she ordered Michera and Hurai back, to command them, and the Demarchic Guard, trusting Emao-e to hold Kantila long enough. I do not know whether the Lakans knew or guessed aid would soon come to us; at any rate, they wasted no time. That very night they surrounded us, and came at midnight, driving at the gate with a great shielded ram.

Kantila gate was built solid, of iron-bound oak half an arm's length thick, and a bolt whose stoutness I knew myself. But in the morning we found it cracked. We did not have another such piece of wood, carved whole from the bole of a great tree; from the houses of the town we took beams and rafters and heaped them before the gate; then those skilled in carpentry took up hammers wrapped in cloth to muffle their ringing, and on Emao-e's signal all began at once to nail them to the bolt and the gate-planks themselves.

The alarm was sounded; the Lakans had heard, and moved faster than Lakans should; Arzaktaj was one who knew the worth of speed. They began ramming before we had the first set of beams nailed on and, scenting blood, put all their spirit into the heaves. I could not see, but I remember the chorus of hammers desperately striking, then the thundering boom that shook the ground beneath us, sharpened with the creak of loosening nails and the cracking of boards, and the curses of the carpenters as they found their work undone. They did not give up even then, but worked on, for all our lives. In vain: in three more charges, the ram smashed through and the gates burst open, and Lakans flooded in.

Emao-e had set up a pike-hedge across the thoroughfare behind the gate, but whether because of failing courage, the pikes slipping on the cobbles or the sheer weight of the Lakan numbers, it broke soon. Fighting spread like a pool, and flowed ragged down the streets.

Before it reached us, Mana seized my shoulders. "You should flee." I saw agreement in the faces of the others. "We're done for, Cheng, it's just a matter of how many of them we take with us. Go, save yourself, become our demarch."

"If I should not be here," I answered, "I should never have held the sword of Saint Mother." They could not argue with that; faces turned grim. So I added, "If it's any comfort, Jinai foresaw a lot more future for me than this day. Hey, they've won nothing yet, but entrance into the wolf's jaws! Are we the soft palate or the teeth?"

I split my Hundred in half to hold the two nearest streets, hedging our spears. We were beset by footmen; I ordered a jagged line, ten across in the narrow street, taking the center myself, while the rest watched our backs and sides. On the roofs were our own archers. We held them, but Lakans charged our flank across a backyard; elsewhere Yeolis were being driven back.

I ordered a fighting retreat; then a cry of alarm came from behind, and the banging of hooves on cobbles. Somehow horsemen had got behind us, and now charged our rear, a good score of them. We were beside a tall stone building, some large workfast's home barred on all windows by the Lakans to use as a jail, with an iron door. It opened to my hand.

I saw they would reach us before we were all inside, for all we hurried; someone must slow them down long enough, and knowing it would probably be death, I froze trying to choose whom. Then Kamina Shae-Boraina, who had once cowered in sparring, and knelt weeping on the spur of Akaturin crying that he was unworthy to be a warrior, ran out and took up stance, steady as in the School of the Sword, full in their face.

But he needed someone else with him. It was the moment of hair'swidth timing, the instant, when a flame blows out, between light and dark, and I missed it. I ran for his side, Mana with me, too late; a great-shouldered horseman whirling a morning-star over his head, got to him first. He pulled up, then his horse reared, and he must wait to come down again before he struck; and that was Kamina's victory, whole and perfect, for by it everyone got inside. Knowing that by weapon-sense I cried to him, "Fall back!"; but he was already fighting.

The star came whistling down; Kamina turned it on his shield and struck at the horse's chest. I think he would have made a standing leap backwards then; but in those thick shoulders was the strength to bring the star around again fast as a scythe's stroke, faster than Kamina expected. He saw it in time to begin raising his shield, but the black thing curled blurring around the edge, into his head. For an instant I thought it had somehow not harmed him, but that was the effect of slowing time, and the wish of my heart. That pure-lined stance sagged and toppled; the sword he had struggled with himself so long to bear slipped from loose fingers. He landed with his face to the cobbles, twitched, and lay still.

I still had the shirt he'd given me, for leaping from Akaturin. Close enough, I felt myself turn into flame, that knew no direction but one; it seemed I floated to the apex of my leap rather than jumped. The stab-kick I aimed between the Lakan's brown eyes, that were half-fight-frenzied, half-startled; I heard his nose and neck snap almost as one. Then we ran for the door, Mana beside me, the other horsemen barely a spear-length back. We flew through; Krero shot the bolt.

I had them jam that door with furniture; they'd already started shuttering all the windows and barricading those without bars. I had them do all three stories; then we ran to the roof. It had a parapet with arrow-slits that the Lakans had added.

We were thickly surrounded; we wouldn't have had much of a chance to rejoin other Yeolis, had we tried; I'd done right in that. Now we nocked arrows, and watched them try to shoulder through our door, then take a beam to it, then send for the ram and find it was much too long even to turn in that street, then try all the windows and find that their own prison made a solid stronghold. They flung torches onto the roof, which was made of slate; we flung them back. They tried to shoot us from other roofs, but all they had for cover were chimneys, while we could use the arrow-slits. They called for grappling-hooks; but in the meantime I sent people through the building to find anything useful, and they came back carrying sacks of quicklime. The Lakans threw up ropes and climbed in a mass on all four walls. When they were a bare man-height below us, we poured lime into their sweat-filmed faces, their upward-turned eyes, until all had fallen or slid screaming to the ground. I saw their commander, a middle-aged noble with long hair-earrings and the helmet-device of a ferret, cursing us.

Now he sat down to think, and they waited in silent anger, like a wolf pack around a treed cat. That gave us pause, too; and it was then we learned the truth of the old saying, "Action is carefree; in pause comes grief."

The sounds of full battle were distant now, the Yeolis driven across the city; if they did not have their backs to the inside of the wall, they would soon. I found myself hearing Hurai's voice: "Where was our fault?" Entrusting ourselves to the gate, I thought. Yet we had been caught weak anyway, by this new force. Underestimating Astyardk's will to fight, then; insufficient spying within Laka itself. And what now? It all lay with how many had got away, how fast our reinforcements came and so forth, things I could not know. I was far away from the place of information, of command. It sank in dully. So this, I, who had known nothing but victory, thought, is defeat.

In pause comes bewilderment. Here we stood, thirty-five in the midst of numberless Lakans, strongheld yet still trapped; doomed, whatever we did, to one fate or the other. I imagined Tyeraha, wondering where I was, cursing Jinai for having been wrong. If I ever became demarch, it seemed, it would be by my people paying ransom. From the roof I could see Kamina's corpse, shoved aside like a broken weapon into the opposite gutter; like fear catching up with one's body when danger is past, anguish caught up with my heart.

I should just have thought, as I was always reminding others, the stroke of the past is in the past. Instead I thought, *I killed him. If I'd moved quicker, done something else* . . . Mana put his arm around my shoulders. "Cheng, he went beautifully, he knew, he chose, it was how he wanted to . . ." Too kind, I thought, pretending I have reason only for mourning, not shame; so I spoke it. He shook me. "Fourth Chevenga, don't be an idiot! You didn't swing that star!" "Someone had to give his life," said Krero. "It couldn't be you. He knew that."

I squirm, thinking of it. One would expect I'd have woken up when a voice from one of the other Tens said, "Shit. Who's second?", or when Isatenga said, "What in the child-raping Garden are we going to do?" Just as it came to them how deep in they were, they got to see their commander, and Ascendant, in tears. Sachara saw, though, fetched me a backhand across the face and said, "Cheng, we're in the shit. Isn't that what you're for—First General First? Demarch?"

I'd learned to recover mindlessly on the high beam. "The stroke of the past is done." My tongue was thick, but worked. "All right. I'm back. Next one to look at me worried does a hundred push-ups." They all stiffened, but their heads lifted.

I peeked through an arrow-slit. The Lakan commander was still thinking, pacing now. I gathered them, and took off my crystal to pass round. "Our options are two," I said. "Surrender, or fight. What does everyone say?"

Some say it is a mistake, even cowardly, for a leader not to decide this himself. I will admit, I was not good at sacrificing someone else for the good of all, as witness Kamina; that has always been the most difficult thing for me. But to this day, I would call the same vote. If one does not permit one's people to choose for themselves when there is time, then one might as well take the name

Notyere. I never took my trust lightly, even now, when it seemed I might not live to shoulder it.

Kunarda beckoned for the crystal. "A girl from Leyere told me that if they catch you and you're a woman, they'll rape you, and if you're a man, they'll castrate you. That's worse than crippled. I say fight to the death." The sounds of battle from the town's north edge had ceased, I noticed in the silence. "Better my parents know I died for Yeola-e," Nyera said, "than I'm a slave in Laka somewhere, suffering Saint Mother knows what." "I know what Kamina would have voted," said Isatenga. Sachara took the crystal. "Sibs, we're thinking we're just citizen warriors, and forgetting we have an Ascendant with us. What do we do about that?"

I reached for the crystal, but Sach passed it to Mana. "I'd say fight, except for that. There are cracks in the walls for captives, chances for ransom, for escape, that you'd be good at. To fight to the death—well, death ends all hope."

Now, finally, they gave me the crystal. I remember the circle of eyes, each pair fixing me in its own way.

"It's our duty," I said, "to make as much trouble for the Lakans as we can, to take plenty of them with us. As for me, well . . . You saw how that commander down there cursed, when we did them with the lime. He will blame me. They have known since last fall who killed Inkrajen. I suspect they have a good idea who opened the gate when we took this town too, since I was the only youth all in black in the vanguard. They might even know I was behind the deaths of the ten thousand. Lakans are vengeful. I'd be dead or worse, I think, if I fell into their hands."

There was a silence so terrible I found myself wishing I'd said nothing. I saw: I had just declared myself dead, either way. Why, I wondered, doesn't it feel like that? Why don't my eyes doubt they will see the sun rise tomorrow? It is the fearlessness of the young, I thought, who think they are immortal. Then: but *I* never thought that.

I remembered Jinai's prophecy: bad for a time, leading to good. "*Chen!*" I barked, and heard the wind and the voice in my ears. They all jolted straight. "Enough looking at me as if I'm a ghost, the next who does does fifty. . . . Look, it may be that if we stand firm, they'll give a little, propose some deal to keep from losing more. Of course they may not. But if Shininao's pecking, I don't want to see such miserable faces all around. Why look at my death with any less courage than your own?"

The silence turned surprised; no one had thought of it that way. I made one of our in-jokes, and they broke out laughing. I thought of myself when I had turned sixteen, stumbling over answers to Hurai, and felt the familiar exhilaration of finding I had grown. Something of a joke on myself, though, now: one of the greatest joys of growth is the promise of more.

The vote went chalk. I knew what Mana was thinking of by his look: his urging me to save myself, which I had ignored. For a time we sat together, clasping each other's shoulders; some wept hard as rain, though silently. I remembered, from the ancient work of strategy: if a general sees his warriors weeping while standing still, he should know they weep not in fear, but in the sorrow of having chosen to give their lives. Now I saw. And us, all but a handful under twenty.

Then a call came from one of the wall watch. The Lakan commander had raised the ivy branch, for a parley.

He had a herald, a border man, I imagine, who spoke Lakan-clipped Yeoli. "My commander, the illustrious Klajen, says you should surrender. You are but a few in the midst of a host. We will starve you out, if there is no other way. Surrender, or we will kill you all."

"While your commander was lazing," I shouted back, "we chose to let you kill us—but taking ten or twenty of you each!"

The lord's brown face clearly showed his thought: "So much for *that* idea." He struck me as a little slow. I mimicked it in words to my warriors, with the Lakan accent, and smiles cracked; next thing I knew my clutch had let loose a volley of jests. Having given ourselves, we were lifted out of ourselves; the burden was on them now, and we were free.

He sat thinking, frowning; I sent people downstairs to seek supplies, now that he had spoken of starving. They found a courtyard well, and food enough to last us for several days. Then Klajen had his warriors empty the street before the door, and the herald hailed.

"My honored commander wishes to settle this matter quickly, and so will be generous. Though he suspects you,

O barbarian centurion, are far too cowardly to agree, he offers this: that you yourself face a champion of ours, Sakrent, his name, in single combat. If you are victorious, we shall grant you and all your men safe conduct out of our position and to freedom, sworn upon our highest oath. But if he wins, your men are all our prisoners. Do you agree?"

I leaned back from the parapet, and said to my warriors, "Well, there it is, just like the saying. Seek something and it flees, relinquish hope and it comes. If we'd surrendered, they'd be castrating and raping us right now." Kunarda looked as if he wanted to kick me. Mana said, "There might be a trick in this."

I called down asking for the oath. " 'By my honor,' my commander says," the herald called. The lord stepped forward. " 'May the King of Death and Lord of the World Beneath Worlds whose name is Parshahask strike off my head, my arms and my testicles and consign my heart to the everlasting fire, should I lie or try treachery.' " Touching both his hair-earring and his helmet with his shield-hand, Klajen mimed the strokes on his own body with his short sword.

I could imagine no one breaking such an oath, who believed in gods as Lakans do, and I had seen Lakan honor at Nikyana. Nyera wondered aloud whether Parshahask was truly a Lakan god, or just a made-up word; but someone else knew it. A Lakan shouldered through the brown crowd to the open space, having little trouble, since his shoulders were level with their heads. They were the broadest I had ever seen on a man; his arms were like a lion's legs, thick and with the veins standing out under brown skin. He bore a hand-and-a-half sword a good two hand-spans longer than Chirel; he began swinging it at blurring speed with the ease of the wind, and with such integrity that I knew he had not only strength. I went down, leaving the order not to use my real name while they cheered for me, but All-seeing Rao. Parshahask might excuse Klajen breaking his oath to capture Fourth Chevenga.

Good-byes at such a time are, of course, very bad luck, so I let them give me their blessings, and went downstairs, with five others to clear the furniture from the door; they refused to let me help, in case I strained a muscle. As they slapped my shoulders, I said, "I will be back in a moment."

It was past high noon, the sky cloudless. The month was that in which summer comes to seem weary, the green of the leaves worn and tattered and soon to be killed by fall; yet the air carries no hint of crispness yet, still making flame-shapes over town cobbles at high noon. Blood spilled on them turns rank in no time. On a roof one is above that feel, that smell; now I was in it. Three times now, Kantila had been bathed in it. Today's dead had been carried away, the Lakans to their burying-ground, the Yeolis to the fields outside for the birds—perhaps we would find Kamina, if we looked there, after this—but scraps of their valueless things—a comb, a darkened rag, a broken wooden arm-ring—lay scattered. Here and there on the stones was a white sprinkling of our own lime; I must not fall, in this fight.

I stepped out, while Mana slid the door-bolt of the prison home behind me. The Lakans, so small from above, now seemed a head taller than me to a man, chewing aromatic leaves as is their habit, their faces a brown as uniform as mahogany. Sakrent was a tower to me; his great hands at the center of his arcing strokes were at my eye-height. I was afraid, but no more than I should be; I'd learned to fight bigger people.

I think the Lakans thought I was a squire; Sakrent took no notice of me at first, and an impatient buzz rose, full of the clips and rasps of their tongue. I drew Chirel. They went silent for a moment, then broke out laughing, while Sakrent stared at me amazed. "Laugh, you fool Lakans!" my warriors bellowed from above. "You've never met our Ch—Rao!" "Take off his leg instead of his head, Rao! He's just as dead!"

Sakrent said something to Klajen, which I suspect from his face was, "Should I really kill this child?" I answered that myself by calling, and advancing on him. He faced me, and I saw his wide-set black eyes change into a pure cold battle-stare, with just the touch of a sneer as is Lakan custom.

With a short grunting "*Hai!*" he began his sword whirling, the circles alternating sword-side and shield-side, at hissing speed. The blade was a silver mist in the air, making a sword-shaped flash in the sun once on each pass. No doubt he always fought this way, could do any stroke he wished from this start, and could keep it up all day if he wanted, so that I shouldn't think to outstay him.

This is the story I tell my war-students, when I want to show that size, strength, skill, speed and form all matter nothing, if timing is correct. By sight his blade seemed everywhere at once, forming a shield of steel; weapon-sense saw it for what it was, a single shaft which was in each spot along its path one moment of every hundred, and, because of its pattern, predictable. My eyes only confused and disheartened me; so I closed them. He had fixed me with a terrifying gaze and opened his mouth to give a great cry; but now he stopped in startlement, the sword continuing to turn by habit, its speed slightly checked. When it was on the bottom of its arc on his sword-side I sprang close and down-struck his shield-arm from that side, cutting off his forearm just below the elbow.

The great sword whirled wavering in his remaining hand, and its tip smashed ringing into the cobbles. He stood still, looking stunned from me to his sheered arm, which spurted blood; I could kill him at my leisure now, but guessed Klajen would acknowledge this as victory enough. Sakrent would not be back to fight us, worse than thumbed; with his bleeding stanched, he'd live.

There was a silence so deep it seemed every Lakan in sight had died. It had been a moment; they'd just been drawing breath from laughing at me. Then a high whooping laugh came from Mana, and the others. "Hah! What did we tell you brown shit-eaters, eh?" "We've rubbed your faces in it all day, and now you have to let us go, ha ha ha!"

Sakrent lifted his sword slightly, fixing me with a fight-stare that was desperate, expecting me to come in for the kill. I stepped back; his gaze turned dull, and he fell senseless, his armor creaking beneath his weight. Klajen's cheeks were dark with rage; he expected a sure victory, I thought. "Interpreter," I said. "Tell your commander I claim my victory and my comrades' freedom, but not his champion's life."

He set his teeth, and through the herald, agreed, then gave orders. Three Lakans came out to Sakrent, one seizing his arm-stump to stanch the bleeding. I beckoned the

Yeolis to come down, wiped Chirel with a rag and sheathed it.

The stroke of the past is in the past, but for a long time after this, I ran over all the other paths I could have taken. If I'd sensed, if I'd seen, if I'd kept Chirel in my hand or left someone by the door to let me in, if I'd known how Lakans herd cattle. . . Yet, in hindsight, my life would have been less.

My body tingled, but did not know what to evade. Something fell on my shoulders like a necklace—I had a moment to see it was a rope—then snapped tight around my throat and yanked me to the ground. What a lasso was, and could do, or that the skill is common in Laka, I had not known.

I went down choking, and two of Sakrent's healers leapt on me; I could not even yell warning to my warriors. I felt my thighs pinned, my arms seized; I saw a coil of rope, got a wisp of breath, fought and shouted like a madman. Their bodies, stinking of sweat and Lakan spices, blocked out the light of the sky; enemy fingers touched me all over, tore off my helmet. Fists flew at my head, making lightning bolts behind my eyes, and day spun into night. Distantly I felt my wrists bound, and Chirel unslung from my shoulder. A faraway voice screamed *Cheng*! In the gathering darkness I felt one last thing, that seemed to linger long as a night: my hair being hacked off.

Sometimes senselessness is peace, and waking the nightmare.

At first I knew only pain and nausea; I turned my head, and threw up. I thought—I wished—I was in the Hearth-stone, sick with some childhood ailment, and imagined my mother near, and Bethera with some soothing extract. What I remembered was too terrible a thing to have happened except in a nightmare, I decided: a gentle illusion to cling to, against truth.

But daylight clawed at my eyes, and neither the throbbing of my head nor the soreness where the rope had bruised my throat faded. I saw my wrists, bound, and at each motion, no matter how slight, felt the cords. A thousand implications lay in this. I felt I would rather die than think them, but my heart knew, and tears ran down my temples. Death, I had accepted; not this.

A man's voice spoke, in Lakan. He smiled, a young warrior, toyed with my cheek with one sandaled toe. In defiance, I found strength and seized calm.

Klajen broke his oath, I thought. *Why? Does he know who I am, knowing my face up close? Or is he just a poor loser?* Not knowing, I must give away nothing. Whether my warriors were dead or alive or captive, how many and who we had lost in the battle, I could not know. I could only hope that the knowledge would somehow slip my way. So it is, for captives, I learned then. But for my guard I was alone, on the floor of a bed-chamber.

He poured water over my face, and hauled me up. Just raising my head set it to spinning and pounding with pain, but it was stand or strangle. My ankles were roped with just enough slack between them to allow short walking steps; I was naked, plundered of everything but my father's wisdom tooth. *Someone is wearing my crystal as a trophy,* I thought. The only reason the tooth was left came to me later: it was worthless to them.

Where Chirel was, I could not know. The thought nearly made me cry again. Worse that Chirel had been captured than I, far worse; I thought of my father, of my grandmother, of my forebears before them. Then I turned the thought away. Another lesson of slavery: one must stifle most of one's thoughts, at least at first, for they are unbearable.

I was led to the hearth-chamber, where Klajen sat with his attendants. The guard thrust me forward, catching my foot-bonds with his toe, so I fell on my face at the lord's feet; a sandaled foot held my head pinned to the dirt. The interpreter spoke. "My illustrious commander says, 'Welcome, quicklime boy.'" *He doesn't know who I am,* I thought, else he'd have called my name to show me. Barked orders sound the same in every tongue: these were to stake me to the floor, for that is what they did, face up, my arms stretched over my head. I caught sight of what was leaned against his chair: a sack of quicklime, taken from our own store.

Be afraid, I told myself. *Be afraid, but do not lose your wits.* I felt sweat break out all over me, no help if he did it. My fear must have shown on my face, for I saw his retinue, guards and squires and servants in an upside-down circle, grin at me in amusement, their teeth bright in dark faces. Klajen knelt beside me; I remember his scent, which was patchouli, against the sharp tang of the lime. He dipped a cup into the sack, and spoke.

"The illustrious lord Klajen," said the interpreter, "asks whether you barbarians who have no god are aware of the concept that what a man subjects others to he shall be subjected to himself."

I used it as a weapon of war, I thought, not of torture; his warriors were not helpless, as I am now, but came of their own will. I opened my mouth to say this, and then thought better of it. He would hear it as defiance, not reason. There was no answer I could make to help myself, if he intended to do it. So I set my teeth and held my silence.

He seized me by what was left of my hair, and brought the cup near my face. Terror has a taste and a scent, as well as a feel, so like illness. "My commander asks why should he not do this." He took a pinch between his gauntletted fingers, brought it near my eyes; then over my sword-side nipple, and let fall just a dusting.

I have kept quiet through two floggings to falling, I thought as it began burning; this can't get worse than that. Why am I so afraid? Simple: those floggings came from friends. I had never been in enemy hands before. Now I learned how different they felt. I scraped my tongue along my lips. He looked close into my eyes, grinning, and moved his hand again. It stopped above the tip of my penis.

Always, in such times, I split into two, some part of me staying cool and sensible even if the other is gibbering. "I'm being tortured," that part thought casually. "So this is what it's like."

"My commander wishes to kill you with the lime," said the interpreter, "but he requests that you try and talk him out of it by speaking of ransom, of your value to the woolheads, and such things."

Woolheads, I thought: that's what they call us. Some part of me laughed. I understood: it was profit as well as revenge; he was trying to find out from me the most I could be worth, by putting me where I would dearly want to tell him. I know, for that was my inclination. "Are you a noble's son, so that you might sell for more than the pleasure of killing you is worth?"

Don't be a fool, I told myself; I'd be in far worse trouble if I told, and my people too. He might be lying; what I'd earn in the slave market might be more than the pleasure of killing me was worth, too, and, as Mana had said, "There are cracks in the walls, for captives." I need but lie one better.

"Ran . . .s-s-som . . ." My voice came out rasping, my mouth being desert-dry. A young centurion, of good promise; how much? No one I'd met who'd been through this had ever wanted to speak of it at all, let alone tell me his price. "I don't know, how much. I don't know the standard rate. I am—" To make myself sound as valuable as I could was what he must be expecting me to do. "A champion, I do have that name, that's how I got to be a centurion so young—I'm going on eighteen, I'm just filling out slowly,"—that in case he'd heard Fourth Chevenga's age—"I won all the contests in my village, Unsword, wrestling, sparring, Breaker of Hearts, everything. . . ."

Then the sweet light flashed, along the path unconceived. "My name is Rao Kyavinara," I said: Rao All-seeing. "Tell the generals that. They know that name." It was true: in an easy moment I had told Hurai the story; Tyeraha had known it long before. They would guess exactly who I was, and get me for the price of a centurion; for that I was willing to be sold. I forced a defiant grin, as one trying to prove himself would.

Klajen absently dropped the pinch of quicklime, brushing off his fingers on my middle. Thinking of my father branding himself, I kept my silence as it consumed my skin. I have the scar still. Then they dragged me back to the room I had awakened in, staked me there so I could not move, and left me.

This will not be long, I told myself; tomorrow, or the next day, or soon after that, the ransom will be paid and they'll let me go. I cheered myself imagining the joy on my warriors' faces, when I sauntered into camp. I thought of Kamina, and wept again. After a time a servant came in; one can tell them easily even by their bearing, subservient in every motion. He gave me water, then washed, salved and bandaged my lime-burn, then led me to the midden, watching me all through. Then he took me into the hearth-chamber again, where two of Klajen's warriors pinned me down face-first in the dust, clamped my head between their knees and pierced and ringed my ears, as Lakans do with slaves.

I underplayed my worth too much, I thought. I was in the dark, as anyone is, haggling for something he has never haggled for before. Have I been sold? Or are these Klajen's tags? I could not know. I remembered the Benaiat Ivahn's words, "No one will ever own you," and bit back a bitter laugh.

Then I thought, though they have my hands bound and I must go where they lead, he is still right; no one truly owns me until I choose to be owned. I'd find my crack, and Tyeraha would save the ransom money.

They kept me in that house for the night, giving me a blanket, and a little stew, no worse fare than a warrior's, though it was full of *kri*, the spice Lakans put in every dish, turning it golden brown and tear-wrenching hot. They all ate without a blink, while I thought my tongue would burn away.

In the morning I was brought out to the hearth-chamber again, where two men I knew as underlings of Klajen were. They examined me as one would examine a horse at market, though perhaps less gently: pinched and felt my muscles all over, peered into my eyes and my ears, forced my mouth open with a switch-butt and poked about my teeth with their dirty hands. They pored longest over my privates. I knew better than to struggle or speak, but soon I was quivering with anger. This they ignored, as if they had seen it a thousand times. Then they led me out.

In the street outside the gate, which still hung splintered, other Yeolis, naked and chained, stood in the bright sunlight. It struck me with grief first, then fear. Someone I knew might see me and blurt my name, or show an expression that would tell the Lakans. But once among them I saw I was safer than I had thought. No one spoke, and we avoided each other's gaze, each ashamed in the sight of the others, or lost in his own pain. Many wept, which made raking pains through my own heart. They too were plundered of crystals, and ringed in the earlobes.

They were being linked into coffles, each bound to the line by his neck, close enough together that they'd have to march in step. I remember thinking it strange that they should happen to be in such even numbers, until it occurred to me, the slavers had come to buy twenty, or fifty, or a hundred. They must cling to Lakan armies, like ravens, or lice, I thought. My guards bound me onto the end of one, and I saw no good chances to slip away would come. All twenty of us could not flee in such perfect unison that we could be as fast as unbound runners. I must have patience, I told myself, until the crack opens.

The three mounted up, the head hitching the end of our line to his saddle; and snapping our backs with switches, they started us, on a journey no one of us knew how long. So it starts, and for some never ends.

We found, if we kept to a whisper and did not look at one another, that we could talk among ourselves without getting whipped. I said little, frightened that someone might know my voice; no one asked names anyway. When one does not want one's own known, it is rude to ask others'.

That way I learned that Emao-e, and a number of the other higher commanders, had been thumbed. "Most got away, but she was trapped under the wall, and surrendered. They did it in revenge for their commoners *we* thumbed. . . ." The speaker, who'd given his name as Kraiya, laughed faintly. "She did the lefty trick, though—did you know, Steel-eyes is left-handed? Well, this Lakan general is finickety, wanted the surrender in writing. Smooth as water, she signed it with her right hand. And so thick she laid it on, at the head of the line, as if it were a terrible choice for her; I swear, she sweated."

There was a silent chuckle, more felt than heard. One soon learns to be thankful, in defeat, for small victories. He seemed to know precisely who had been thumbed, and so was asked after many. Casually, as if they were just my Teachers, I said, "Did it happen to Esora-e Mangu? Or his wife?"

"Yes," Kraiya said. "Not a grimace, from either."

I thought of my day of reckoning with Esora-e, agreed upon without words; of having yearned all my childhood to know what age I would be when it came, when I proved better at Unsword, if I ever did. I thought of his great iron fingers enwrapping my small weak ones, sinking me to my knees, and his words, "One day you will be able to beat me." Like any student of the School, he was trained to do one-hand swordwork with either hand; but his left hand had been his weaker. When I defeated him, if I lived to get home, he would acknowledge me his better and never breathe a whisper that it might have been otherwise, were he whole; but in my heart, I would never know.

At home would be sympathy, which would hurt him worse than anything. She will bear it better than he, I thought. I resolved, when I returned, to speak of it little and only with curiosity, hiding my pity. Then we would go on as before.

"I didn't see Chevenga, though," Kraiya added. "Let's hope he got away." Sickness filled me; from then on I barely raised my head, lest they see. Chevenga, without the Fourth, he called me, I thought, as if he knew me; do they all do that?

Then someone asked Kraiya how he knew all this. There was a long silence, and the questioner suddenly said, "Never mind. I didn't ask." Kraiya answered softly, "No, no. I was always taught, there is no harm in truth. Lakans don't know how to thumb, and we were prisoners. . . ." His voice thinned almost to a whisper. "I was in the crew."

A day into Laka, they cut me from the coffle, at a farm gate. What became of Kraiya and the others, I will probably never know. The handlers did some business with papers, and gave my rope-end to a tall ill-natured looking Lakan with a switch in his belt, who, to my amazement, spoke Enchian, bad, but understandable. "*Akdan!*" he snapped, bringing the whip out of his belt and across my shoulders in one expert move, when I asked him to whom I belonged. "To me, for now. You will always call me that." He pulled me past cornfields, in which slaves were working: Yeolis to a person, without a link of chain on them, just like free farmfast members. I stopped myself from gaping. Perhaps from hearing the expression "in chains," I had thought all slaves wore chains always. So close to the border, I thought, why are they still here? *I* won't be. When do these ropes come off?

But the overseer, for that was what he was, left them on as he took me to a rough tiny hut, and gave me to a Yeoli slave-boy there, whom he introduced by some Lakan slave name. Those names are always short, and chosen for a diminutive, charming sound. He did not free me either, and spoke to me in Lakan, as if I had no native tongue; there was something in the way he moved that set my teeth on edge, too. "Don't they like it if we speak in our own language?" I said, in Yeoli. "Unless you know Enchian we have to, because I don't know *that*."

He stared at me, and I felt horror with a thousand tendrils creep through me and onto my skin, the horror of seeing a lamb born headless, or finding an apple that looked good on the outside filled with rot. His stare was uncomprehending; his brows, pale on his tanned face, drew down in anger, and he snapped something at me in Lakan, waving his hands senselessly in the Lakan style. Several times, his hand chopped the sign for charcoal at me. But he had to think for it, and it was awkward, unfamiliar. He did not know his own language.

Slowly understanding came to me. They bred slaves, like horses. He had been born and raised in Laka. All things Yeoli had been taken from him; no, he had never had them; he could not even know what he missed. He had no name, but the Lakan.

Just then his brows knit harder. He barked something, turned and stamped away. I know why now; I was looking at him with pity, and he did not see how he deserved it, so took it as contempt. If I ever needed proof that blood is nothing and breeding all, I thought, this is it. Yet no matter how many generations his blood has been here, somewhere in Yeola-e he has kin, who can be traced somehow and would welcome him, make him a whole Yeoli instead of the husk of one, a person without a nation. Then I wondered whether all the others were so; and understood why they wore no chains. They didn't know what freedom was, to want it.

At dusk the overseer came, grabbed up my rope. "Any boy your age knows how to do what you're going to now," he said, then guffawing at his own fine wit, "especially a Yeoli." In another hut waited a woman. "She's proven, catches quickly; it's *you* who are not. If she isn't big in good time, your balls come off." Right in front of her, he said this, and left me.

I stood numb, as understanding came. They breed slaves.

She could have been from Erealanai or Selina, with long pale red hair of a tight curl, so that it hung in two woollen clouds in the light of the lamp; she was not beautiful, and I would have guessed her age as twice mine. She drew off her slave-shift, showing a body worn with childbirth, and beckoned me to her, as if to say, "Let's get it over with."

I stood stunned, thinking of Nyera, Komona, marrying, my Ascendant; tears burned in my eyes. One could not think of this as a roll in the woods with some soldier-girl in her safe time; a child would come of it, must come of it. It must be worse for women, who have to bear the child, too. But she rose and pulled me down on the pallet beside her by my rope; with my hands bound behind me I could do nothing. Into my loin-cloth she slipped her hand, chuckling. My Ascendant, I thought, then imagined the blade coming down, to cut off what her fingers were now cradling. She somehow knew to turn gentle, motherly, caressing, so I would not feel forced; and I was young.

Long I have begged forgiveness of myself. Yet whatever my body thought, I was forced; if I'd refused they'd have beaten me, flogged me, put me on the treadmill, All-spirit knows what, before they got around to gelding me. Perhaps it is my body I despise, for not resisting harder, for thinking too soon, "Why need this be unpleasant?" I ended up making love with her as I would with a friend, making sure she had pleasure as good as mine, as best I could, tied. I was thinking we could both forget, for one soaring moment at least, our chains.

We were coupled three times, every other night, as is the custom in Laka. After the third, she clung to me; we would never see each other again, we both knew. By signs, though, I got her to tell me her name and her owner's. I knew the time of year. When there is peace, and I am free and demarch, I thought, I will find my children here, and buy, shame, or carve them free. What the precedents were for this, I had no idea; I was the only Ascendant in recorded history who'd been a slave, though that might only be because such a tale was deemed unfit for recording.

In the same way, I was set to stud—yes, they use the same word as with horses—with two other Yeoli women. In between, the overseer kept me carefully enough, feeding me well and making me do no work. I was earning my keep, he would say, seeming to think that was the height of wit. He unbound my hands, but kept leg-irons on me so I could not run, and had me watched always.

I learned a touch of Lakan, and the third woman knew a

smattering of Enchian, enough so we could speak in words as well as motions. I learned her name, Tanazha, and asked her if she knew who I belonged to. "I hear you new-caught," she said in her halting way. She fingered my earrings. "Look warrior-*Akdan's.*" I spoke the name Klajen. "Yes, I hear that." It seemed I still belonged to him. "Keep you for something," she said. "While wait, rent you." I thought, does he still mean to ransom me? I clung to my hope, and to hiding my name. To have one secret from the masters is to have an inward fortress against them, one thing they cannot violate.

After the third time, she said, "I miss you. Name child after you. Even if sold." She'd born and nursed five babies, to see them taken away on weaning.

It was out before I knew it. "Then call it Chevenga."

She gazed at me puzzled, and I felt sweat break out cold. "Actually my name is Rao," I said. "Kyavinara. But I always liked Chevenga, it means 'lion's heart.' There were demarchs named that . . . kings, you'd say. I know it sounds too Yeoli. How would a Lakan say it?"

"J'vengka," she said softly. "But what if it boy?"

Lakan names are strictly designated, male or female; none can be both. Mine happened to have an ending just like the common Lakan feminine, "-inka." I said, "No matter. All lions have hearts, male or female." She looked at me very strangely, but said, "I beg *Akdan* that. For you."

A half-moon passed this way; then a warrior came riding in through the gate, one of Klajen's, leading a spare horse. The overseer brought me to him and bound my hands again, some paperwork was done and money passed. "No tricks now, quicklime boy," the warrior said in Enchian, as he boosted me up onto the second mount. "You don't want to get killed, on the way to freedom, *hai?*" Saint Mother accept me, I thought. It worked.

The Yeoli camp was near Tenningao now; we held where the valley narrows. It was not even Klajen who took me to the parley, but one of his lieutenants; on the other side, strange to face them as if against them, was not even Hurai, but Perha, though my shadow-father was in his guard. "Did they mistreat you, Rao?" he called across. "No, sir," I answered dutifully. They'd already made half-payment; now the rest was delivered in a sack. The Lakans cut my bonds and sent me running by a foot-shove in the back. I kept running until I was in Esora-e's arms.

So it ended for me; I got only a taste of it, then. But as I flung myself into my friends' embrace—yes, Klajen had freed them—drank the wine and told the tale as I had played over so many times in my mind ("You were put to *stud*? That doesn't sound so bad!"), I kept remembering Kraiya, and the slaves on the farm, tongueless and nationless, into which Laka planned to change him and his children, or kill him trying.

XIII

Fall came, and the war stood mostly still, for harvest. I turned seventeen. Our millennion died of a festered wound, and his second's tour was soon coming to a close; so Hurai named me her second. When she went home a month later, he promoted me.

That meant nine other centurions, all older than me by as much as twenty years, got passed over. Of nine such, usually, three are happy to remain where they are all their warring lives, three are looking to be promoted but not yet, and three feel they are capable right now, and would be promoted if life were just. So I knew envy would come my way, as well as fear, for my youth, and they would try to trip me up, to test me. The whisper was, of course, that it hadn't been Hurai's choice, but orders from my aunt.

After we'd all sworn our oaths—ten times as heavy on my shoulders again, the oath of relinquishment—all the officers gathered at the campfire afterwards. Certain eyes shone narrow on me in the firelight, as I made my speech.

"If anyone envies me," I remember saying, "I couldn't care less; if I hear it I will pretend I didn't, but if it leads to any harm in the field, punishment will fall like a rock-slide." I'd learned, from Elera. "If you fear my inexperience . . . well, words prove nothing. You'll have to grit your teeth and wait till we're on the field to see. I listen to advice, but I hate being talked down to. If it seems strange, pretend I'm ten years older." Brows rose, those who felt hard done by taking no care to hide it.

They asked me this and that, and I made my stances clear. Then one asked, "What about the matter of discipline?"

I'd thought this out already. "Are you worried I'll be too shy at my age to keep it?" With a look on his face as if he wondered whether he should have opened his mouth, he answered chalk. "Ten lashes," I said.

He stared, blinking. Silence fell, but for the hiss and crackling of the fire; I'd said it loud enough to be heard by all. "Ten lashes? But! Me? What for?"

"Make it twenty," I said, "for asking who, when I said it perfectly clearly, and not seeing why. Tell me, Minao"—I knew all their names by now—"would you have asked this of me if I were ten years older?" To that he had to admit charcoal.

"But . . . sir, a flogging just for asking a question? Isn't that a touch . . ." I knew the thought in their minds: the shyness of youth that made one too easy might make another too severe.

"You were worried that I might be too shy to keep discipline," I said. "Are you still?"

"No, sir!" he answered, seeming amazed I should ask.

"Then you are reassured enough; I'll let you off the flogging." His brows vanished up under his forecurls, but he said nothing; best quit when the going's good. Around the circle, once they'd done blinking, smiles spread. "Question, sir," someone asked. "Are you sure you're only seventeen?" At that, of course, I laughed a seventeen-year-old laugh.

Drilling the next day, I told them no punishment awaited anyone who fell behind, except the knowledge he couldn't keep up with one not even full-grown. Of course I was tireless *because* I wasn't full-grown; I'd give my hair now for the staying-power I had then. But let them figure that out for themselves. Several days later we fought, and I did well enough to prove myself in the last test. Then, with as little warning given us as I have given you, my reader, the war was over.

There'd been a coup in the Palace of Kraj, Astyardk overthrown and executed by his eldest son Astalaz. The heir couldn't wait, I thought; it seemed he also disagreed strongly with his father's ways, thinking for one thing that this war was a waste. Their victories had been costly; one need only gather the death-counts and add them up. Astalaz sued for peace, proposing the border remain where it had been before the war.

He came to negotiate himself, being steady enough on the throne to leave it, since many in the Palace had agreed with him; those loyal to his father were well-purged, that is to say dead, as per Lakan custom. My aunt met him, and had me sit near. Of course every Yeoli was objecting to his offer; all the losses were Laka's fault, since they'd attacked, so we should be repaid in full with land. But Astalaz stood very firm on that, and Tyeraha was not in a position to hold to it; they still held Yeoli land all the way into Kantila, she could not forget, and we'd suffered our losses too. It was there I first learned that sometimes justice does not win, but position, and no matter how much the rankling, one must sometimes be happy with less than is fair because it is all one can get.

So Tyeraha agreed, and the peace was drawn up. After they'd spoken alone, she called me into her office to grill me on the negotiation and what I thought of Astalaz; reading people through brown skin and straight hair was something I should learn. He'd seemed honest to me, and sincere in wishing for peace, a touch scholarly, and sheltered, without being spoiled; a warrior in theory only, though he was trained. "Yes," she said, "that's what I thought. Lad, how'd you like to go to Laka for three moons?"

To seal the bargain, it seemed, the king had proposed a mutual fostering; me in return for his son and heir, Astazand, who was six, and by every report loved dearly by his father. We'd never arranged such a thing with Laka before, as far as history knew, but we had with Tor Ench; the precedent was set, in case it was argued I'd be exposed, at my tender years, to foreign corruption. Some said it was a bad trade, that if something went amiss, it wouldn't take Laka as long to get another six-year-old as it would Yeola-e to get another me, if that were even possible. But a Lakan loves his child as much as a Yeoli.

I thought on it, and didn't take long to agree. It was for peace; it was an adventure; it was like a very long month away. I even had notions of doing some discrete spying for my people. I would certainly learn all manner of things I'd never conceived of. (Tyeraha assured me, to my disappointment, that at least one of my tutors would be sent along to make sure I missed no lessons).

So, amidst the peace celebrations, I took off my wristlets and put on the peace-sigil, traded armor for the immaculate tunic of a diplomat, and made my farewells, knowing at least this time I had little cause to fear anyone would be dead when I came home. Once my tutor and little Astazand had made their journeys here, he and I walked our opposite ways across the border, I clasping his little brown hands in my long pale ones in the middle, and I was in Laka the second time.

Thinking slavery was a different world, I'd known nothing. Now I was treated as a noble. That defies belief.

I had learned in books of the basic Lakan ethic, that one has many lives, and is rewarded or punished in the next for what one did in this, so that the favored are considered innately better, and their iron-fisted rule of all less fortunate, just and sacred. It is quite another thing to see it in practice, to see how it permeates Lakan life down to its smallest act.

A true Lakan noble casts cloak off shoulders unthinkingly, for it never occurs to him that someone might fail to leap to catch it; he will sit trusting his weight to air, never thinking a seat will not appear under him. He need never walk anywhere; that's what carrying-chair slaves are for. I need only mention a wish, and they'd sweat or kill to see I got it; every Lakan around me, including my envoy guide who was a noble himself, by his dress and earrings—to his mind I was royal and therefore above him—bowed, deferred, called me Akdan and hinted everything instead of saying it until I wanted to scream, "What are you *really* thinking?"

When one speaks of rich in Laka, one doesn't mean just having a house on the lake or a bigger herd of goats or several fine shirts instead of one. There are houses that hold fifty in Tardengk, owned by one, clothes that we would put only on a demarch at a festival being worn by ordinary citizens every day, jewelry I would not have dreamed possible. As I learned in the Palace of Kraj, each

Lakan noble is a law unto himself, thinking himself worthy by will of the gods. Each has what power he can muster through wealth or force or friends or religious fear, to wield according to his will. Not that there are no national laws, for there are; but as the King considers himself above them, having made them, the nobles consider themselves above all but the King's will, and sometimes not even that, if they can combine against him, as with Astalaz: no wonder so many get assassinated. What binds the nation together is a common language and faith, an incredibly complex lattice-work of fealty oaths and vague but strict customs, blood and marriage-bonds, friendships and quickly-shifting alliances. When I first understood this, I thought, no wonder their armies are less well-ordered than ours; it's a wonder the country isn't always starving.

Yet it is at least half-starving, and holds a good half of the people in it in chains; these riches have to come from someone, who would have liked to keep them. Laka is a country of almost-mountains, tipped with naked rock but not snow-capped, of great hills cloaked in vines and cypress, of forest so thick its green is almost night-dark; beautiful, but cut all through, everywhere, with the mark of domination. Commanding every town is a castle, with three-faced turrets in the Lakan style; every plain person we passed made obeisance, though they could not know who I was, to be worthy of it; every village had its stocks, with someone in them as often as not. Once I came around a bend to see a pale corpse, his back in darkening shreds, being cut down hastily from a tree; out of courtesy they'd thought to get him out of my sight, but had been too slow. Someone probably got flogged for that.

In Tardengk, which is as large as Brahvniki, they gave me a scented kerchief as we went down into the city. Hovels slapped up from planks and broken tiles seemed to stretch to the horizon; through a chink one would see the wan flicker of a smoky lamp, and hear a child's weak mewling or voices raised in quarrel. The stink of rot and excrement mingled with the aroma of *kri*; across the rutted dirt street a dark creature scampered that I thought must be a dog, until I saw its naked tail, long as its body: it was a rat, big enough to steal a child. Yet every house, however poor, had a frontispiece larger than its front, even if only an unpainted board. These people, who must wonder how they would feed their children tomorrow, put on appearances. Since riches are virtue in Laka, gold is pride, so pride in some way can substitute for gold.

The houses grew larger and finer; then we came to the Palace. Passing through a gate framed with tassels thick as tree trunks that looked like solid gold, I kept my eyes forward and my face blank, as if I had always lived among such splendors, (so Lakan I was, after only seven days) my guide ushered me on without a word, thinking I had, and all was as it should be. Seeing it from the rise coming into the city, I'd thought it was built on a hill, all starred with twinkling lights; now we did not go up, but straight in, the corridor not turning to tunnel, and I saw the Palace was not on a hill, but was the hill, built up over centuries from the level. They claim the foundations predate the Fire, but I suspect they are Iyesian work; Lakans have only been here seven centuries.

One must hire a guide, as we did, to lead my chair (just because I was indoors was no reason to make me walk, you understand): the lavish gilt-wood corridors run seemingly without order or sense, not even keeping to the four directions, but running slantwise or curving. Sometimes we came to a jog in the hallway, as if its builders had started from both ends agreeing to meet in the middle, but mismeasured by a handspan or two.

I noticed the slaves, of course. Palace slaves never wear more than jewelry and codpieces, and are of every race on the Earthsphere, exotics being a mark of rank for their owner: I saw people coppery red, olive, golden like a dried corn kernel, so black they shone almost blue; one woman seemed to have no color in her at all but the red of her blood, her hair white as an ancient's, and her irises a sickly flesh-like pink beneath white lashes. They were nothing like farm slaves. While I had always thought it a moot point where one was if one was not free, they most certainly did not. People denied pride, like people denied food, will take it in whatever form they can; for these, it was that they had been the pick of the market. They even got to keep their real names. The highest irony, I think, was Astalaz's Arkan slaves, who all wore their blond hair down to their waists, that being the mark of an Arkan noble, which to a man they were. They let one know it too, noses high in the air as any Lakan lord.

I came in at dusk; yet everyone, free or slave, walked either briskly or sleepily, as if they had just got up. I'd heard stories that Lakans were nocturnal, like mice; before they had come here from their old island, I learned now from my guide, they had all lived that way, even farmers, sowing and reaping by the light of moon and stars. They say it was a decree laid down by Kazh, their High Father God, after the Earned Fire. The rest of Laka has changed since; but the Palace still lives that way. I would have to get used to it.

I was welcomed formally, in the throne room, which is as big as Assembly Hall at home. Astalaz welcomed me, saying, "My son," which rankled a little; he was only ten years my elder, I knew. But it was custom, the meaning to be taken that I was as precious to him as his own child in Vae Arahi. I was presented to the Kin, as the Palace nobles are called, clasping hands with one long-hair-earringed man after another who wore enough jewelry to buy a house and whose name I forgot instantly. Finally I got to see noblewomen: they wore more gold than the men, and long gowns cut to cling to their figures in every brilliant color one could imagine; their black hair hung to their hips or past. Though I wore satin, I felt plain; mine was black, and not embroidered. When that was done, King Astalaz sent for me, and we sat together in a parlor.

We took each other's measure, of course, more closely now since we had more time. He was a tall, broad-shouldered and thick-armed man, thoughtful of face, with the long straight square-ended hawk-nose that is classic of Lakan nobility, and thick hair. His full whiskers hung fine and straight as they do on Lakan men, scented with oil. Though he looked at me oddly when I thanked the wine-server, he was at least not harsh with servants.

He'd been well-polished, of course, and was one who liked to do things correctly, as I'd thought before; I was surprised how well he pronounced my name. Yet there was the faintest touch of awkwardness about it all that I knew was from being new, as if the king's mantle was still a little stiff on his shoulders.

We did the usual, telling each other our life stories in summary, praising each other's accomplishments, touching on politics. "Precocious," he said of what I had done in the war; it struck me he meant to remind me of my age, that being a word usually used for children. I've fought and killed a hundred your age in war, which you have never even seen, I thought. "Oh, I'm not so new to it," I said, "I've been a blooded warrior for four years." Nothing impolite, just support of his own point. "Yes," he said. "Quite." It struck me then that he was not good at retorts, nine times out of ten the mark of a loner. Then it was more agreement than friendship that gained him allies, I thought; good thing for him he made his opinions clear.

Though I was not sure he'd believe the ways of Yeola-e possible, let alone proper, he questioned me on them, showing at the most a deep puzzlement, his questions full of the keenness that shows quick understanding. I explained the vote to him, the Assembly, the tax and child-bearing laws, and, what he seemed most interested in, the position of the demarch. I told him the story of the War of the Travesty. He even wanted to learn a little Yeoli, the political words with no equivalents in Lakan or Enchian.

We went on to the war, very cautiously, as we ought to. I saw immediately he looked at it all as a hill-top general does, and so answered his questions as another general would, being vague and taking liberties with truth where necessary, of course; I omitted, for instance, that I had taken part in command councils, and when he spoke with regret of the ten-thousand, saying, "Of course I do not blame you for that," I bit my tongue. He asked me if I had indeed assassinated Inkrajen and opened the gate of Kantila, but as if it were all a game on a distant board. Now and then we touched on the act of fighting itself; and though he had trained from childhood, as he told me, and affected a manly air of experience, half-hidden was a fascination that reminded me of my wide-eyed friends at thirteen. It made me feel older than I would ever be.

By the long way round, we came to speak of his father. I'd asked him whether Astyardk had been sore-pressed in his decision, to let us kill the ten thousand. "No, as a matter of fact," he answered. "Not at all. He hardly blinked. 'Too many peasants and too little land, that's the whole trouble, isn't it?' he said. 'Now the Yeolis give us a solution, and even offer to take its execution, so to speak'—he laughed at that, he thought that was hilarious—'out of our hands. So be it, then, and thanks to them.' " I stared, wide-eyed, remembering that night. "Cynicism ruled then,

J'vengka. You see why I had to do what I did. It wasn't always that way; ten years ago he would have grieved on the steps. False tears, of course; but at least he'd have made the gesture. One glosses those acts that are unpleasant but necessary, for a king, you have been taught that, I am certain. But he stopped caring for the people, and would have brought Laka down."

It was then, I think, I truly started to like him. A Yeoli talking falsely might say that, citing a common ideal to give an impression; but in Laka it is a notion for a king to hold in private if at all, so I knew it was sincere. Perhaps it is better said thus: in me, caring for the people is only to be expected, since I was trained to. In him, it was extraordinary.

Yet, I thought, here I am, drinking with a man who barely a month ago killed his father and his two brothers. It was the only way to dethrone a king, of course; he might even have done it to save himself, since if he'd left it to someone else they'd have killed him too, fearing he'd seek revenge in the Lakan way. But, if he felt pangs for it, I saw no sign, and that spoke of a very deep hate, that could not come purely out of concern for Laka.

I settled in, to my guest-chambers: anteroom, bedchamber, parlor, study, gamesroom, midden-chute, my own courtyard, and five personal slaves of all colours (for variety), all of which I was welcomed, indeed urged, to consider my own. Quite a change, from the slave hut, and the war-camp. Not that they'd paid no mind to my aunt's letter asking that I be put up austerely; this was their idea of austere. After the first night, retiring to my bed in the morning exhausted, in the hopes that solitude would ease my spinning head, I found a woman there. No, she told me, startled, she had no designs on me; she'd been sent compliments of the king.

By the old measure, that the civilization of a country is to be judged by how it treats those who must bear its children, Laka is quite barbaric; forbidden, not trained, to fight, and held to be inferior, women are very much under the heel of men, kept as brood-slaves, having to marry or sleep with whomever they are commanded to. It is quite normal there to feed and love one's daughters less than one's sons; and then they say women are born weaker than men.

All these things I thought as she caressed me, the air all around filled with the sandalwood oil she wore; mostly that she was not here by her will. "What are you saying, *timnimuz akdan*?" she asked—barbarian master, it means —"we drew lots for the honor!" It seemed every night it would be a different woman. You must not see your own chains, I wanted to say, you are only making the best of your lot, it's force even if indirect and I would never . . . But she paid no heed to my mind and firmly set about convincing my body she wanted me, mostly by taking a firm grip. It listened, in the end. Afterwards, in the fragrance of sandalwood and Lakan beeswax and the rosewood of the carven screens, on silk satin sheets smooth as water, I drifted to sleep.

I came to know my way around, got used to and in time came to like *kri*, and learned the language. As in Brahvniki, when my work of studying was done, they treated me to lavish entertainments. I had to tell them that watching tortures was not to my taste, since they thought such fascinations quite natural; I saw a guard impaled for sleeping at his post (though I think it was more for displeasing some noble), to the cheers of a throng who I doubt knew nor cared what he'd done.

I feasted every night with the Kin in the Dinner Hall, and found it is true that they sometimes fight sword-duels inside the ring of tables; it happened four times while I was there, though only one of them was to the death. Lakan lords carry swords in the Palace as if it were besieged, counting the right as their honor; I think they looked down on me somewhat for not doing so. It came to me: even in peace they are at war, with each other, rich against poor, free against slaves, nobles against other nobles; all the aspects are there, the blood, the strict punishments, the oaths, in essence, of relinquishing will; they carry it to their very hearths. Once I asked Astalaz what I should do if someone challenged me; he said no one would, since I was under his protection, but since it would be unmannerly to give anyone just cause for challenge when that was so, I should keep a civil tongue and not cuckold anyone too often. As if I could possibly want to do that, I thought, when there's a woman in my bed every night.

Court functions, wine-parties, feasts and dances, were endless, of course. I became the rage among the unbetrothed women. I should say, everything is fashion in the Palace; the women would wear dung on their heads if they imagined it gave them an air of sophistication and newness, and the young men are not much different. I was "dear" and "darling" to everyone under twenty-five; one would think they didn't know I'd been out on a field killing their countrymen a month ago. It was said that I had a god's son's pride, which in the Palace is the highest praise, though I had no idea what I'd done to earn it.

The party I most enjoyed was one in which a new girl came flirting; she and her father were in town to present her at court tomorrow night, she said, but had not wanted to miss the fete this morning. Presently she saw him, and felt obliged to introduce us; he'd spotted her hand on my shoulder. Seeing his face, I had to set my teeth to keep from laughing. It was Klajen. When he saw mine, his greed in its shock overcame civility, at least for an instant. "*You!*" As his daughter in her sweet voice said, "And Papa, this is Fourth J'vengka, the Yeoli prince," I could see the coins flashing in his eyes, as he figured out how much he should have got for me. He threw back his head and laughed—what else to do?—then glanced worried, as he remembered he'd tortured me, who now had some position. To show him he need not fear I laughed back, and we made a toast to old acquaintances.

I made better friends with Astalaz. There was no need to draw him out about the family trouble, it turned out; it was commonly known. Both Astalaz and his sister Klaimera, who served as Laka's high priestess, had always blamed their father for killing their mother; since Az (as those close to him called him) was king, now, it was commonly accepted as truth. No slight grievance, if so.

Klaimera struck me from the start. She was nineteen, and had the family height and almondine eyes, though on her their darkness flashed with life; in her the family quickness was less scholarly, more incisive. Her hair was marvelous, falling in a shimmering black waterfall over curving crimson or leaf-green or gold, whatever color her gown was today, to her calves. I saw her do rituals; had I ever doubted that Lakans truly believed in their Hundred Gods, I ceased now. As she raised slender arms with fingers pointed to the sky like two whips of brown flame, it was a clear fire in her, infusing every motion with grace; a Yeoli would say it was the God-In-Her. Perhaps a Lakan would too; perhaps, I thought, we disagree only on the god's name and origin. She was not betrothed; but I was given to understand that her position required she remain a virgin, so I put all such thoughts out of mind.

Astalaz set out to teach me how to play *mrik*. "The board's in my true office," he said. "Well . . . you might as well come up, why not?" He led me into a great room, lit only by a tiny flame; as my eyes cleared to the dark, I saw the usual satin ceiling-drapes and tassel-fringes, gold arched screens. A curtain of thick gold-threaded ropes hung from the ceiling, all across my vision; then, pausing to speak, he reached his hands out open, in what seemed unthinking habit, as if he could lean on them. Just as I was wondering what I should do if he got hurt falling when they slid and swung away from his fingers, they took his weight, not moving a hair's width; they were solid, not ropes, but bars, gold-leafed, fashioned to look like ropes. "When I must think hard," he was saying, as he opened a gate in them that only became apparent as he did it, "I come in here, my old home . . . it's calming, it takes me back to playing the game from the side. Of course when Astazand gets old enough it will be his place."

I remembered the boy in the cage in Inkrajen's tent, who had turned out to be his son. It is a tradition for Lakan heirs. As every Lakan storyteller will tell you, people lust after the throne, and none more than the next-in-line, knowing power will be his once the king is dead, educated, prepared for it, impatient, or disagreeing with his father's ways. What more natural for the king or lord than to take precautions against his firstborn?

I thought of my father, assassinated in my childhood; how grief for his loss had been my whole world for a time, and shaped my growing. I thought of my aunt Tyeraha, after a long lesson on statecraft, touching the demarchic signet to my chin and saying, "Hurry up and grow, lad, I want all this off my hands." Wouldn't love, I thought, be a better defense? After all, *this* hardly worked, for Astyardk.

"You're a very capable one," Astalaz was saying, "surely you've had at least the urge to murder your aunt—what is it, lad? You look as if you've seen the Many-Tentacled

One; she—a woman, of all things!—must have very strong friends indeed, to make you so afraid." All I could gasp was, "She's my *aunt*!", which, of course, explained nothing.

The scent of expensive incense in this place was undercut with the mixed smells of sweated clothes, book paper, dust, mustiness; coming closer into the light I saw beyond the bars a wide desk heaped with papers, inkpots, quillpens, a wall-high column of shelves crammed full of books and curios, sculpted heads, incense burners, waxboards, pieces of stone, jewelled earrings, all layered thickly with dust; necklaces strewn on the night table, heaps of satin clothes spilling onto the floor from the bed, a collar worth five farmsteads slung carelessly over a screen. There were even swords of various length and shape foundering in the floor-clutter. No slave could get away with this; it had to be by his decree.

I said nothing; after a time he found the board under the bed, inlaid with lapis lazuli, and the stones, onyx and marble. I had known only that the game was supposedly already ancient at the time of the Fire, and a passion among Lakans, held almost sacred. The board is empty to start, and the stones once placed cannot be moved; the trick in capturing ground is all in where one places them. The rules are simple, but the choices touch the infinite; also as in real strategy, one can get a sense of where one stands by a glance at the board, as on a map, and play by feel; nor does it usually end with a decisive victory, but when the players agree they have no more to gain by going on. I began with the novice's handicap of nine of my stones placed in advance. We played about every third day, and by the end of my time I'd worked it down to one, almost his match. "You are one of those, I think," he said, "who excels at anything he turns his hand to."

Another day we were speaking of my capture, and I mentioned I might have a child in Laka. He promised to look into it. "You were plundered of the Yeoli royal sword?" he said. "At the second victory of Kantila? Blessed Kazh—was it made by Nekari, in his usual style?" He collected swords, and knew something of them, even Yeoli ones. "A square sigil on the blade, about that far down from the guard? Good Kazh!" He began delving, throwing up papers and sandals and silken underwear, cursing in the way of messy people. "Where . . . it's right around here somewhere . . ." His fingers found it, making it flare shining clear into my weapon-sense. My soul knew that curve, and my eyes that shoulder-scabbard. He lifted it with reverence; even buried in clutter, Chirel could command that.

Klajen did not know swords, and so had thought by its plainness of look it was just one of the lot; of course the sword-dealer, who knew a Yeoli smith's mark is never to be found on the blade, but hidden on the tang, among other fine points, snapped it up, thus barely saving the edge from a rough Lakan whetstone. Twice, poor Klajen got rooked, once for me, once for my sword. The dealer had given it with his compliments to the new king; in Laka such a gift makes for dividends as good as or better than the selling-price. It had got cleaned and oiled since my fight with Sakrent, but not sharpened, both the dealer and Astalaz considering it beyond their skill. "It should be done," I said. "A sword not kept sharp forgets its edge—a Yeoli saying."

Then I found myself looking at him awkwardly as I held it in my hands, feeling the swelling in the heart that always comes with that, much stronger for having been missed, go sour. Should I say, "Give it back to us, as a gesture of peace?" What if his face darkened? Was it an international incident if he refused, or if he didn't, or if I offered money?

I suppose he read my eyes. "I've never seen that sword looking to be where it belonged," he said, "until now. You know it is no trouble, if you wear it among us." I didn't even know whether to thank him. "Don't worry, my son," he said. "Giving it back to you is no loss to anyone; remember, the dealer gave it compliments to me, and of course he will still be rewarded; it's the thought that counts." So, Chirel returned, into Yeoli possession. The next evening, I considered wearing it. Then looking in the mirror, I thought, "No, I'm a Yeoli. Here more than anywhere, I should keep my ways."

The women in my bed always came and went while the sunlight was curtained out to darken my room. I never got a true look at their faces, so that if a serving woman winked at me familiarly in the corridors, I could never know for certain whether I'd made love to her or not, all part, I was assured, of the delights of royal Lakan hospitality. If my people had any idea what a seductive place this is, I thought, they'd never have sent me.

Then the women stopped changing; no complaint, for the one who stayed, Velvet Petal, as she called herself, made herself one of my favorites the first night, my lone favorite the second. Her hair was long, thick but gossamer-light, flowing between my fingers like silk, her body lithe and smooth and strong, yet softly pressing in to fit against my side, tiny curls brushing my hip.

She taught me things I'd never have conceived, in bed; it was she who first bound my wrists with a silken scarf. "Don't you trust me?" she said, when I balked; yet somehow the danger that someone would leap out from a screen and knife me while I lay tied made it all the more alluring. It was she who showed me the helplessness that releases one from all cares, and the ecstasy of consigning oneself entirely to another's hands and will.

On the sixth night, it first came into my mind to return the favor. A hundred times I had answered the ritual question, "Are you mine?"—so exotically intimate, in Lakan—with, "Yes, I am yours." Now after I'd lain basking for a while, I took a gentle grip of her wrists, then suddenly tightened it. "I am yours," I said. "Are you mine?"

She stiffened; for a moment I thought she was going to call the guards. Then she took a deep breath, laughed a quiet silvery laugh, and husked, "Yes, *timnimuz akdan.*" I knew to keep my hands from trembling while I bound her; that would ruin the whole feel. Then I served her as long and sweetly as she had me. Her body answered as it never had before, thrashing, arching, trembling to every feather-stroke; afterwards as we lay limp and sweated she clung to me, saying, "Oh, to live every day in such pleasure!"

About midday I woke, and lay thinking. She had laid her head on my shoulder like a child, and pressed her brow to my cheek, eyelashes soft on my chin like a moth's antennae. My body still smouldered with the imprint of her touch. I've never seen her standing, I thought, and stroked her ankles with my feet; she was taller than I. When I seized her, I thought, it wasn't fear, for she didn't shrink, but rather drew herself up, ever so slightly; it was affront. And why does she know so well how to bind, but this is her first time bound? She's no serving-woman.

I started to pull away; she clung tighter with a faint sound, full of the tone of "Don't displease me." When I'd worked my way free, I rose, opened the curtain a crack, and looked on her face.

All-spirit, I thought; is this an international incident? They'd call it blasphemy. Yet it was her who came here, under false pretenses. And if she's a virgin, if she was a virgin less than five years ago, I'm a Lakan's uncle. Another Lakan thing I don't understand. My head started to spin.

I closed the screen, before the brightness woke her, and slipped back in beside her. If there was any wrong, it was already done, more did not matter. As usual, she was gone before I woke. The next morning when we had been settled in snuggling for a time, I said, "Velvet Petal, I am seized with one desire: always you are in the dark, always your beauty is obscured by day's necessitating shades." (You learn to talk this way, in the Palace.) "For once, I want to truly see you, in all your lusciousness."

"But *timnimuz akdan*," she said, "you would see my flaws, then. The perfection that only imagination paints and truth always stains would be ruined for you." No hesitation; her wit and tongue had always been quick.

"Any flaws I have not felt I would never see," I said, "and I swear I found not a one; my admiration of you could only increase."

"O sweet *timnimuz akdan*, you flatter me no end; but surely the mysteries of womanhood are best not pierced to an over-great depth by manhood. . . ."

So we argued, until I couldn't stand it any more, and said, "If it's that you don't wish me to know who you are, don't worry; I already do, Klaimera."

One would think I'd bested her beyond recovery. I thought so; but she had a stroke to get the better of me that I could not foresee. Drawing herself up, as best one can lying in bed, she said, "I wondered how long it would take you, Fourth J'vengka. Men are so slow! All that time I've had to wait, to tell you: I love you."

By seventeen I knew the quick test, to divine my own feelings. I imagined how it would be if another woman and not her were there next morning. All through my chest I felt a crushing.

My first thought was, I must be mad. A Lakan princess, and priestess, brown as tea and with ideas stranger than her color; for all I knew she watched the human sacrifices they did here with sacred glee; I could see Esora-e's face. And her, raising a sixteen-armed idol, throwing curses and trying to hold the state that befitted one of her position, in the Hearthstone Dependent . . . Of course marriages were arranged, here; since her father was dead I would have to make suit to her highest-ranked male kin, that being Astalaz. (He might even have had a hand in this, I realized, wanting such a match, to ensure lasting peace.) Then Assembly would have to approve it.

Love sparks where it will; were it less fickle, there would be no need for marriage. Lacing my white fingers in her brown ones afterwards, I would see our fingernails, the same color; her tongue was, too, and other parts; her blood and mine spilled would be indistinguishable. Who can deny, that inside all races are the same? The nights, when our duties separated us, stretched achingly long; the days, ours to drown in each others' arms, heartbreakingly short. Love became our world, and its language, so much more perfect for nuances of meaning than Enchian or Lakan, second languages, became our first. I buried my hands and face in the endless black rivulets of her hair—its length whispering of limitlessness, the impossible attained, like a record harvest or the most ancient tree—and learned her brown lines as an artist does; she pulled the short curls of my forelock, then let go, the way they sprang back into shape giving her endless fascination. We made our signs and rituals, our jokes and tease-words, all the more charming for the misunderstandings of race: when she spoke of appeasing the goddess, or offhandedly of having a slave flogged, it was endearing, for it came from her; when I spoke of the God-In-Myself, or the vote, I would see in her face the same bemusement.

I came to understand a little later, the matter of her virginity. It was nothing for the high priestess to lie with slaves, as she had many, or with a Yeoli; anything but a Lakan, for only Lakans were considered men here. In name, she was a perfect virgin. And she can have all the pleasure she wants, I thought, laughing; how like this land of lattice-work. Well, who am I to object? Yet I also saw, she'd never before had someone free.

* * *

One morning as we were undressing I asked her about the family. All have their way, when a question intrudes a touch deeply into heart or memory; hers was to be high-handed and distant. She walked away; I followed her, knowing she wanted it. Like a servant I caught the satin lapels of her robe as she threw it off, and kissed her between the shoulder blades, through the blanket of hair. It would have been the nape of her neck, but I couldn't do that without going awkwardly onto tiptoes.

It came out as if it were the events of last night's soiree, or a snide remark among the ladies. "Tell me, J'vengka, do you believe a man owes love to the woman he has claimed?"

"If he wishes her to stay with him," I answered. I wanted to show her my stand on that rather than say it; but that must wait.

"Of course he gave her everything a woman could want. Jewels, perfumes, silken cushions, twenty-four-slave chairs, winged cats, the most golden of *kri*, the finest wines, but . . . tell me, J'vengka: do you believe cold eyes, a thought-less touch, a manner that weighs one only in gold can kill a woman?"

"If I were her," I said, "I would seek richer pastures."

"Married to the King?"

That stopped my retorts. Of course she could not di-vorce him, or seek lovers; not in this land where all gold and hence power was passed down from father to son, so a man must be certain his wife's children were his own, and so imprison her, in spirit, by custom. This was important to no one more than the King. The heir is caged, I thought, only because he is a man, and believed to have strength. A Lakan woman needs no cage; it being unthink-able to fight a man, she will stay where he puts her.

"He wanted four sons. But when I came, he decided three would do, and wanted nothing more to do with her. Of course she was always on his arm in public, but he would not see her alone . . . she kept up her smile at functions. She was the Queen. And kings have always enjoyed other women . . . It was the greatest mystery of the grapevine, why she became so pale and quiet.

"When she fell sick, he sequestered her even more thoroughly. He wouldn't even allow us in, saying we would catch it, though even the Haian did not know what disease it was, whether it was catching. Once Az, when the guards were taking him to the training court, broke away, and ran into her room; he was there just a moment before they caught him. Father had him thrashed, and kept him locked in the cage, forbidden to see anyone, for a month. He was thirteen.

"She had a finer funeral than you could imagine, golden bells, a hundred carrying her bier, dyed flames, all her slaves whipped to death, everything. No woman has ever gone in greater style.

"My other two brothers, like any children, thought Father was divine. But Az was too old. He had seen what none of us had. He never said what it was; but never again did he let slaves care for his chamber. They have to sneak in to do any cleaning. You may draw your own conclusions." Then she asked me not to speak of this again, and we went on to other things.

One can barely tell it is winter in Laka, and spring planting comes before the snow is even thinking of melting in Yeola-e; I would be there long enough to see the Festival of Planting, the greatest of the Lakan year. I'd loved Klaimera for a moon. In a letter home I wrote my thought, to see what answer it would get.

"This was raised in Assembly," my aunt wrote back, "and resulted in uproar. The question immediately asked, of course, were how set you are on this, that considered a fair measure of how far you've taken leave of your senses. Cool your young loins and think, Fourth Chevenga. Would you have a half-Lakan demarch succeed you? A brown-skinned person with his mother's customs instilled in him as well as his father's? You already have some name for being reckless and headstrong. People wonder whether you have succumbed to foreign corruption. You must abandon this notion or put your own approval at risk."

I'm the only person in all Yeola-e, I thought, slapping down the letter, who can be told whom to marry. I did not answer; that is to say, I wrote but mentioned nothing of this. Nor did I speak of it to Klaimera or Astalaz; they would only be offended. Family considerations they would have understood; but Lakan royalty having to be judged worthy by the riff-raff of Yeola-e? It was an affront. I put it out of mind, and went on living my dream-life.

Then it came into my knowledge, I am not quite sure

when, that the Festival of Planting is the one at which they do the human sacrifice. It was a certain sense, almost a taste, in the air and on the faces of the Palace, bright and dark at once, strengthening as the day came nearer, not entirely unlike the feeling that comes before a demarch's Lake-test, but less austere and more visceral.

I asked Klaimera how they got the victim, who, I had learned, was always a boy of my own age; only one in the flower of youth, and male, of course, is seen as a gift fit for the gods. "What do you mean, got?" she said. "If we gave all who wished to be given, the streets would run with blood, and the gods would see our life as cheap indeed." It is the highest honor, they believe, ensuring an afterlife of eternal pleasure instead of the misery of more lives on earth. The candidates must vie at all manner of contests; then the chosen one undergoes a year's training, to sufficiently purify his soul. I did learn, though, he tends to be a poor boy, noble sons being reserved for more important things such as inheriting holdings. I suppose the poor of Laka are harder driven, as well, to escape this life. How he would be killed, I did not ask.

On the seven days before, I ceased seeing Klaimera, as custom required she be genuinely as well as officially virginal then. The halls were decorated with flowers, a different color each day: pink, violet, blue, white, yellow, orange, and on the day itself, red. I waited through that night—the ceremony is done soon after dawn—with a stomach full of emptiness; it being a public function, I would have to attend. I reminded myself how much gore I'd seen on the field, one death nothing to that; our Kiss of the Lake was not so different, recalling how I'd felt seeing my father's Renewal.

First came the parade of the Chosen. He is king for a day, covered with flowers, showered in wine, kissed by women, bowed to just as they bow to the real king all other days. As Astalaz's foster son, I got to meet him: a handsome but ordinary youth, a little smaller than me, fine-boned and slender in the way of the poor, and burning hard with the glow my father had had. Near him the wings of Shininao sang their song of too-deep silence; seeing his wide smile and feeling his hands warm in mine, I thought, he and I have something in common: foreknowledge. But so much sooner for him. Just then his dark eyes caught mine. "Don't grieve for me, Honored Yeoli," he said. "I'm having a wonderful time, and it will just get better." Almost as an afterthought he added, "Far better than all you hoity-toities, for once." The nobles near just laughed; he could get away with such, now. At this price.

As dawn paled the sky from blue to purple, the square by the Palace filled with people, singing and chanting and raising scarlet flowers. Gongs clanged; the sustained metallic notes of the *zinarh*, the Lakan stringed instrument, hummed. The great idol of Kaili had been brought out, four man-lengths high and carven out of black stone, its many arms and one face oiled to shining.

There were prayers and benedictions and so forth for a time, all in old liturgical Lakan which I could not understand. The sun sent its first shafts of red light across the square, giving the thousand flowers petals of scarlet flame. The crowd's voice buzzed, then leapt to a roar; the gate of the Palace had opened, and the Chosen appeared, on a carrying-chair with red satin trains. He smiled still, his bearing the picture of perfect courage.

All through the crowd he was carried; it is considered a blessing to touch, or better still kiss him. Then the greatest of the gongs, which, as Lakans say, like a mother calls him home, sounded. One of the idol's hands lay palm up before her, big as a table; that was the altar, I saw, as they bound him to it, limbs spread, his face to the sky; whatever death they gave him, he'd see it coming. Does he ever change his mind now, I wondered; yet he lay with his head thrown back, as if awaiting the touch of love.

The gong, and then the crowd, went silent, so that I could hear only the wind, and the beating of my heart. *The Chosen awaits*, the herald cried; *his seed and his life to give life to the land*. One death, I told myself again; why am I so afraid? *The Goddess comes, to exact her price!* To a cry from the crowd, half whoops, half screams of fright, the belly of the idol opened. The first thing one saw was the knife, straight and double-edged, as the sunlight, now golden, caught it. Then the Goddess in her earthly form, as I had been told she would appear, enrobed all in scarlet, her hair hanging unbound, her face full of light and her arms of grace, stepped into sight, the knife in her two hands.

I can hardly bear to write the rest. Some sluggish,

sensible voice spoke in my mind. "They didn't tell me, assuming I knew. She's High Priestess, after all. It wouldn't bother them." That was the last thought. In my balcony seat, near Astalaz, I could not move, nor speak, nor do anything of my own will, only watch.

I learned what the Chosen had meant, when he had said it would only get better. In his year of training he is kept celibate too, a boy my age, in the flower of his passion. On the altar the Goddess strips naked and makes love to him, for his seed bursting out brings the blessing of fertility; and I knew, as I watched, what those hands, those lips, could do, as if I felt them on my own body. The crowd quieted; on each of his ecstasy-moans they joined in yelling and whooping. Then when he was close, writhing, his eyes clenched shut, she lifted the knife, and touched it to the place over his heart; he felt it, I knew, and if anything, it increased his joy, as the threat had mine while I lay bound. Then his back was arching, the muscles turning to rope all over him, his voice rising even above the crowd's; the first white spurt came shooting up, a thousand brown hands reaching to catch a drop. In that moment she drove the knife into him. Even with his heart pierced through with steel, he still came, all his life pouring out with it now; she drew the knife out again, the stream they strained to touch was red, and he fell still and limp, his face still full of ecstasy.

I stayed rooted to my seat, though Astalaz went in. The Goddess, having taken, withdraws; the husk is left for the people. Anyone who gets a scrap or a drop of him is blessed. When I could move, I put one foot before the other. "No international incidents," the stolid voice ran in my head. "She's High Priestess. It's one of her duties, natural and proper to them."

I gave my regards and excused myself; I wanted to speak to no one. "You see," I heard someone whisper as I went, "atheist or not, he has a bone of spirituality in him, look how moved he is." I staggered to my chambers, threw off my clothes in the darkness, and fell into bed; like a child I sought comfort in the covers and pillows, burying myself in them.

Slender arms I knew slid around me, and the familiar tongue flicked hot in my ear. "Ah, my love," she whispered. "It's the Chosen gets all the pleasure, in public. But we're in private now, and I can satisfy myself. Are you mine?"

How it is to be a dog with his tail between his legs, I learned now. I found myself pressed back against the inside wall; it didn't seem entirely odd that I had no notion of how I'd got from the bed to there. It's something diplomatic I should say now, my sensible part thought, but my tongue wouldn't move.

"J'vengka!" She sat up straight, her nakedness shining. "Love, what is it? Is something wrong?"

"Wrong?" I gasped. Now I found my voice, but my tongue tripped over my beginning Lakan and switched of its own will to Enchian. "Wrong? The woman's just done— what she's just done, and she asks me is something wrong! Oh, no, not at all, I see my lover eviscerate people every day, it's no trouble!"

"What?" She rose out of the bed; I put a pillar between us. "Do you take me for a fool?" she said. "You're a warrior! Don't tell me you've never had a roll with someone who's just killed many more than I have."

"They weren't bound!" I answered.

"But you yourself heard him say he went to it willingly! You saw how he felt! You fool, you're jealous of him. Of the Chosen, merciful Kazh! Come here and I'll show you who is my true love."

Fleeing I blundered into the curtains, letting a blaze of sunlight into the room for a moment; I caught sight of her hand, and the blood still clinging in the edges of her fingernails. The sense in me spoke again: *she and I could never be*. Then idiocy seized me. I won't quote my diatribe: enough to say it put Lakans in a less-than-flattering light, the kindest word I used, "mad."

When the words ran out, she was standing rigid like a doll, hands on hips, her eyes black stones, her hair dark flame. I could see Astalaz's face, when he heard it repeated, the black horses marching, and war, again. My foolish heart ran away with my tongue, I began to say, I mean no offense, forgive me. She cut me off. "Oh, yes! You and your so-superior-we-Yeolis-are, every cursed moment! What do you call it when you put your babies in those mountain streams? Can they fight back? Do they choose? And when you *do* call it sacrifice, that supposed drowning in the lake, you fake it, you hypocrites, what you pretend to offer your God-that-isn't, you take back at the last moment! What kind of sacrifice is that? How does that face the truth, that for life there must be death? And what sort of God wouldn't notice? It's true! You are atheists! You have no god! It's amazing your country isn't starving!"

No, my mind said again, she and I really can never be. That cut through my anger; slipping through the curtains onto the balcony and daylight almost too bright to bear, I sat on the rail. She slowly sat down beside me, robed now, but did not touch me. Perhaps it was having invoked the God-In-Her that brought clear-sightedness. "I know what you are thinking," she said. "And, my heart weeps, you are right."

We seized each other, of course; like all who have done this, we clung for a time, wept for how we would miss each other, vowed never to forget each other, swore eternal friendship. We reminded ourselves how one or the other would have had to give up their calling, the dearest thing to our hearts. We did not make love again, agreeing without words that would make it worse.

I wrote home, saying they need no longer worry, for which all were grateful. The women in my bed began changing again, but I didn't touch another. Of the rest of my stay, which was only a few days, there is little more to say. I crossed the field, clasping hands with little Astazand, who'd got bigger, again.

XIV

Call me a coward: I gave up on love.

My eighteenth birthday came and went, then my nineteenth. I did my schoolwork, grew taller, filled out, went on searching my chin for proper beard-hair; and love danced in its spritely way out of my fingers, a poetic way of saying nothing worked well enough to consider marriage. But I had to marry.

So, on the traditional speaking tour a demarch-soon-to-be does, I wrote ahead to each town that I was looking for a wife, of convenience.

With my heart having no say in the choosing, I could set the crassest of requirements. She had to be fertile, of course, healthy, intelligent, not necessarily a warrior but of strong physique, full-blood Yeoli (let me have no more arguments about that) and, of course, of good character. If she fell in love with another afterward, no matter; we would marry him in too, as long as she would still bear my children. I didn't want to set out in writing that she must swear not to love me—I would be asked why—but made it clear between the lines.

My friends all thought I'd got a badger bite. "But you're such a passionate man!" they said. I just answered that I must make sure I had heirs soon; love could find me another wife, later. I don't like it either, I wanted to say; but

226

what do I do? Love comes when it will, taking longer with me, who has less time. I was already inuring myself to the idea it might be never.

Mana, who was the second person I told I would do this after my mother, was angry. "So we'll be a six instead of a four," I told him. "I'm sorry, I didn't know it would be this way. But I can't make you choose yours by my rules, and bind her to conceive from me, not when our agreement was from the heart. Unless you can find one who's willing to put up with all this."

He said, "Cheng, you're always in such a damn hurry, with *everything*! Why do you always act as if you're expecting Shininao next year?" I almost told him. Luckily he was too angry to read my face.

The tour went well, except for weather which one must bless, since it helps the crops, but is a curse to travelers. It was on this trip that I began to have to truly shave every day. The people were flushed with victory, especially on the Lakan border, I saw, not inclined to worry about Arko, except on the coast, and content for seeing a good harvest coming. I got hard questions about myself, lots of advice, and all the usual complaints about bad roads, skinflint workfasts, and young people these days. But I did well enough that Esora-e, who had insisted on coming along, said, "You could charm an Arkan out of his boy, boy; better not learn to depend on it." It was Arkans he hated now.

By day I spoke and traveled; by evening I talked with women recommended to me. We would meet after sunset in some private place I'd specified in my letter to her, like conspirators. I would swear her to silence, and put the proposition to her—the first few times I was awkward as a teenager, but I got better with practice—and then she would refuse. She'd want to stay in a two, or in her hometown, or not get so close to the demarchy, or her lover didn't like it. Or—more than anything else—it was just too odd an arrangement.

In Thara-e my luck turned, with a woman named Shainano-e Anataeya. She worked in the town hall, the daughter of a long line of bureaucrats; at the cenotaph where we met, she was surprised to see me, thinking her workfast mates had been playing a prank on her with the letter. In the moon-shadow of the standing-stone, I could not even see what color her hair was. She was twenty-seven, old enough to have mastered silken bureaucratic polish, and to call me "lad." But when I'd made my suit, she said, "That's intriguing."

Crass purposes call out other crass purposes. It seemed she had ambitions, and so did her lover, of the same profession, one Etana Shae-Sai; they already had their names in as associates of the Assembly Palace Workfast. Tied to me, they'd have an easy time finding posts in Vae Arahi.

The three of us met for dinner the next night. It was at Tyara's, and I made sure Tyara tucked us well away, under the weeping willow in the courtyard. Finding my nerve stripped as I waited, I begged a jar of wine (I was close enough to being demarch that I was getting many things free already). I had thoroughly wet my lips when Shainano-e came in, brushing open the hanging branches. In the candlelight I finally saw her face well: open and practical, pleasant to look on but not breathtaking, framed in two long clouds of frizzed brown hair. The man with her was clearly Etana. I'd hoped he'd be at least close to my age, so we could joke like two boys, but no, he was at least twenty-five, lion-jawed and serious-looking. They were both in Thara-e ponchos, but with their office kerchiefs; this was business after all.

Once the introductions were done, I poured them each a deep cup, unmixed, and kept them topped up as we chose meals. That done, we must make small talk; it was too early to get to the point. I had not had enough wine to soothe my nerves; just to bring that first state of mental clarity, like a pool of still water, showing in all its sharp edges the perversity of my intentions and making me feel as conscious of my skin as if I'd suddenly put on someone else's. This didn't help in making talk. Politics was out; we'd all spent all day at that. The war was out; neither of them was trained. I ended up pouring more wine, and saying something poetically banal about the willow and how its leaves shimmered, with which they both earnestly agreed. Etana observed that the weather had got a little chill in the past day. Shainano-e remarked that the table at which we knelt was smooth, and wasn't it interesting that it had four legs.

I stared at her, feeling the flush of wine sharp on my

cheeks. Etana did likewise, face confounded. Silence stretched like an overtightened harp-string; then a tiny smirk tugged her lip. We all burst out laughing so hard the cups danced on the table; I buried my face in my hands, and she patted my shoulder. From then on I was in my own skin again, and we were friends.

They were agreeable in spirit, and going over the details they found them satisfactory too. We would marry as a three, and on my ascent move together into the demarch's chambers; we set the date for a three-quarter-moon before, the soonest it could be arranged. Our lovemaking we would time so that the first two living out of the stream were mine, the third Etana's, the fourth mine, and the rest Etana's unless one of mine died. I wondered if I even needed to have Shaina swear not to love me, by the way she looked at him; they'd been together for four years or so, and had only held off having children to save up for a place of their own. But she made the oath, Second Fire come, I think more for his sake than mine.

Negotiations need not be done, nor dinner eaten, with parched tongues; we kept the wine flowing. Another jar seemed to appear, and the contents shrink like a rain-puddle in sun, and then somehow we were out in the bushes of the river park with more wine and no light but a moon laced across with clouds. I recall some words, about trying a taste of married life now, conceiving an Ascendant perhaps, and feeling grass fronds tickling my bare side, by which I knew my shirt had been removed. Then it was all warm limbs and hands and tongues and hair. At one point as we lay mostly sated but still giggling, the night-guard came with his torch-hook, saying "Wastrel striplings—get home before you catch a chill!" He was one-third right that we were youngsters, at any rate. We clapped hands over mouths, sides splitting, as he cast about yelling, "I know you're here! Answer me honestly, are you here?" Finally I decided such a forthright question deserved a clear and civil answer: "No." As that didn't get rid of him, I stood up in plain sight and said to his face again, "No!" Being of the Hall Workfast, he had seen me speak this morning. His jaw dropped, three times. Muttering, "No, no, there's no one here, absolutely no one," he scurried away.

In the morning we published our banns on Thara-e's

paper-wall, and sent a courier to Vae Arahi. We didn't
need to have it cried; the news was all over the city like
fire in a gale, just as I was leaving. "Congratulations," my
friends all said, "but, Cheng, they're so *old*!" If I heard
that word once more, I promised them, there'd be teeth
on the ground.

From Thara-e, we went up by boat to the end of the
Ereala, then south through Shairao and Kolohisk to Kantila
and Leyere, where everyone wanted to clash wristlets
with me, remembering the war. They'd fixed the river-
lock, smashed during the war; in civic pride they built a
dais on a barge for me to speak from it. A bit much to my
mind, but the people wills. When we were done they just
poled me out through the lower gate and down river to
the inn, to keep the crowd from dogging me.

I was in my room speaking with a Leyereri news-scribe
when Mana tapped the door. I'd trained my friends not to
do that unless it were important. I hadn't, unfortunately,
trained them not to say certain things in front of news-
scribes. "There's a woman, a freedwoman from Laka," he
said. "Says she has your child. I wouldn't trouble you with
this, Cheng, except she has the kid right here, and on my
crystal he *does* look like you."

My heart began pounding. Astalaz had said nothing,
which I'd taken to mean he'd found I fathered no child.
Now it came to me: he wouldn't think I'd care what
became of offspring out of wedlock, beyond their freedom;
to a Lakan it would be nothing. Of course the scrivener
asked, quietly like a spy creeping past guards. "I have no
child that I know of," I told her, the truth; I wouldn't
know until I saw. When we were done, I invited the
freedwoman in.

It was the third, Tanazha. In good light her face looked
older, more careworn; or perhaps she had changed. She
wore a crystal and spoke Yeoli, haltingly, Lakan-accented;
but life-long slavish habits are hard to break. She went to
her knees before I could stop her.

The child peeked out from behind her, fixing me with
bright piercing eyes, unwavering as sunlight, and green
like hers. But his hair was black, and certain lines in his
nose and chin were unmistakable. His face lit in a sudden
smile. "Chevenga!" he repeated, when I asked her to call
me by it, his pronunciation better than hers; he'd heard it

from Yeolis. "S'*me!*" She'd named him as I'd asked. That was all I saw; tears blinded me.

I wondered what a woman bred in Laka would think of such emotion in a man. But I'd waited seven years for this, my hopes dashed again and again, every year heavier on my shoulders. Wherever he goes, I thought as I blinked my eyes clear to look at him, whomever he becomes, he will carry on the thread of my life.

I took him in my arms; he came willingly enough. "Your daddy," Tanazha was saying carefully, "your father. You remember I told you about him." He peered at my face, a look that seemed measuring beyond his age, then seized my crystal and thrust it all the way into his mouth. I giggled like an idiot, tears pouring fresh.

This went on, probably for much too long, before I remembered certain matters. He was her son, not mine, since we were not married, nor in love; I had just contracted to marry, and Shaina, Etana and I had just made an agreement, to get me heirs. Typical of my luck, I thought, joggling my son on my knee. I take all manner of trouble and draw up all manner of words arranging to produce an Ascendant properly, see it finally fall together, and the firstborn drops into my lap a bare moon later, already two years old and not mine to rear.

"Daddy!" he said to me in his tiny flute-voice. His mother said, "He's yours, Ascendant, if you want him."

The world seemed to freeze. They say it sometimes takes time for a father to feel his child is truly his; for me it had taken all of a glance, and was down to my bones. Now I felt it turn to ashes, as I said what I must. "It's not for me to take him from you, Tanazha. Not by the way of Yeola-e. Only in Laka is the child the father's."

"I give him," she said in her harsh Yeoli. "I know I can have no hold on you. But he can live better with you."

I imagined. The agent of the King of Laka had bought her and freed her, with no explanation; she had come to Yeola-e not even knowing who I was, and fared as a freed slave must. She must be alone with the child, in an old house left burned or at best stripped in the war, on the sliver of land a single person would be assigned, probably gone half to weeds, and no money to start with, in a land full of strangers whom she happened to look like. What she had gone through to make ends meet so far, while I had

been a guest of the Palace of Kraj and the Hearthstone
Dependent, I couldn't know. Now she would give up the
only soul she loved. Yet she said it with her head up and
eyes dry; she'd steeled herself to it, long ago, for his sake.
That, I thought, is love.

"I have more than I ever dreamed," she said. "I and my
child are free. And you have given me land." She would see
it that way. "But he'd live better with you. They say no
matter that I'm slave-stock, but still I can't teach what he
should know, to be Yeoli, the Yeoli your son should be. I
don't know enough how to be Yeoli myself. I can't even
teach him reading." She switched to Lakan; it was easier.
"Even in an heir's cage, he would live better." I recoiled
inside, seeing for a moment that tiny sweet face behind
bars. Of course she'd think that.

"We don't cage heirs," I said. "Though being Ascendant, as he would be, is not an easy life. . . . You can teach
him all any child truly needs: love. You have plenty of
that. Tanazha, I could send money to you here." How, I
had no idea, but I'd find a way. "Or you could come
to Terera, let me find you a place or a share somewhere."

She shook her head, charcoal. "I know nothing but
peach farming." Peach trees won't grow as far north as
Terera; she was bound to her land. "You can teach him
love too, Ascendant." She touched my cheek, still wet. It
hurt like a sword-cut in my heart. "I did *not* come for help
for me, I am not of your family. *Akdan* ruled you . . . you
had no choice, as Yeolis say."

My son yanked on my ear, and yelled "Ma, ma, *maaaah!*",
just for the joy of it. She tried to hush him, and he went
on louder. It seemed he took after me in more than looks.
I wanted him in my sight for the rest of my life.

"But who loves him most?" I said. "Who loves him
enough to lose him for his own sake? Who does *he* know
loves him?"

"It's not like the others." The memory of that night, in
the stinking lamplight of the stud shed, came back searing. I'd forgotten she'd had five taken away already; that
made it so much worse. "I will not lose him, giving him to
you, for I will know he is loved. And so will he." I
searched through my night-cabinet for a waxboard one-
handed, my other hand full of someone sacred. Of course

as soon as I'd managed it, he crawled off me and behind the bed. How much more of a favor Astalaz would grant me, I did not know; but I must try. "Tell me their names."

She was speechless at first, unbelieving, but told me all, and how old each must be by now. I got her to give me the names of all her other kin, too, and the man she loved, whom she almost didn't mention because he wasn't her blood. I'd forgotten how little slaves believe they deserve. Now it was her turn to weep, trying to hide it between her rough-brushed ringlets. It hurt not to be able to promise her anything certain, when she kissed my hand from her knees.

"If you wanted him," she said, "I swore I would give him to you. You want him." She took a deep breath. "You Yeolis—*we* Yeolis—hold the mother decides what will become of the child, for the best. Then I say you *must* take him."

Little Chevenga, who'd climbed back up to watch me write, stamped his tiny bare feet on my knee. She wants to free me to take him, I thought, by binding me. Yet she could accept money I sent; it's only her own pride that forbids that. She thinks he would have a better life, as Ascendant, and demarch. Perhaps, perhaps not, I thought, watching his eyes, which gazed hard at the hairs of my chest (enough to be a tuft now), his tiny silken brows furrowed in grave contemplation. Not much of a baby's character can be read on his face. Then a thought came to me.

"We could let him choose," I said. "I know how. May I take him up on the mountain?" She looked puzzled, but agreed.

I put on my cloak, then Chirel, since Krero wouldn't let me out of his sight without it. The child didn't want to come at first, until I perched him on my shoulders and twirled; then he didn't want to let go my hair. Leaving Mana to keep Tanazha company, I slipped out the inn's back door and through side streets, my hood hiding my face; running the gauntlet of my friends' questions had been bad enough.

I took him up to a meadow, from where Leyere with its circular wall was a huge cauldron, brimming with a stew of black slate roofs and green gardens. His eyes widened; Tanazha's work left her no time or strength, it seemed, to

carry him to high places. In a green cedar hollow by a
stream I hunted, looking over my shoulder now and then
to stop him from putting all the world into his mouth.
Toads were many here, this year. I caught one, found a
stick, and brought both to him.

"S'toad," he chirped, as I gave it to him. It struck me
that he was precocious; but then, I thought, every new
parent thinks that. "Careful, he'll get away," I said, and
showed him how to close his hands. "He's yours, Chevenga."
The toad shuffled, and emptied itself, making a green-
brown stain the shape of a leaf on his tiny spotless palm, as
they will. He cried out in disgust.

"What a terrible thing to do!" I said, curling my lip.
"Well, he deserves punishment for that, since he's yours."
I held out the stick to him. "Go on, Chevenga, he de-
serves it. It's all right. Hit him. Kill him."

I doubted he was one to destroy with glee, knowing his
mother. What I expected was that he would either do it
hesitantly if I kept urging him, or sit staring at me puzzled
as to why I'd ask such a thing. That would have decided
me.

As it was he cringed away, shoving the toad behind his
back, and stared at me in a way that stabbed my heart; I
saw myself being Toad-Murderer in his eyes for the rest of
my life. His tiny frown deepened, his green eyes flashed,
and with every drop of will in his body and soul, as it is
with children, he cried "*No!*"

I threw away the stick. "All right, never mind, you
forgive him." He glanced over his shoulder, to see if the
toad was safe; of course it was long gone, and I had to find
another quick, and say, "See, there, he's all right," before
he'd let me pick him up. Even on the way back down to
the city, he sat stiff in my arms and kept looking distrust-
fully at me, as if thinking, "Mama said you were good. I'm
not so sure."

"I had reason, my child." So strange, to hear those
words on my lips. "One day you'll understand. Forgive
me, Fifth Chevenga, for all you will suffer." He would
make a demarch.

Tanazha wished him farewell smiling, though I'd expected she would weep. I remembered how much practice she'd had at losing children. It was when she begged
me to let him visit her once or twice in his life, that

I saw her fight tears. "I'd die before I'd let him forget you," I said, and promised it would be every summer for a month or better, and whenever else either she or he could make the trip. A long time away from his education, for an Ascendant; I'd catch trouble for it, I knew. But I also trusted I, and he, would be forgiven, it being his only way to see his blood-mother.

I stopped her from going to her knees again by catching her in an embrace, with him in the middle. All that was left was to give me the sack of his toys and clothes; then, as he cried for her, reaching frantically with his fat little arms, she turned, square-shouldered, and was gone.

I was to dine at the mayor's that night. "I hardly dare ask," my shadow-father said drily, as we made ready. "But to whom does that child belong, and why do you have him?"

My friends all swapped smirks. "Two questions, one answer, no words needed," I said. "Look closely at his face and mine."

For once in his life he was speechless. Not, alas, for long enough. "Oh. I see. You pronged some poor Leyere girl during the war, and now you've charmed her out of her baby so you can be a father before you're really finished being a child."

Mana crept like a cat out of the room, pulling Krero and Sachara with him. But the child's presence, more than anything else, kept me from answering as I was inclined, with fury. I just told the story. When I said the child's name, I added quickly that Tanazha had chosen it, not me. "It will still be seen as the height of vanity," Esora-e said, frowning. But there was no question of changing it, when the child knew himself by it. "And I somehow doubt he was stream-tested," my shadow-father went on. I hadn't even thought of that. "Well, he'll have to prove himself other ways, then." He went on to ask if the child had weapon-sense, of all things. I just said, "*When* he's six, *if* he touches the Sword, we'll test him."

Because Fifth Chevenga was not in a state to be let off my arm, I had to take him to dinner. That ensured that the news would be all over Leyere in a day, and Yeola-e in a half-moon; I must hope my letter to Shaina and Etana got to Thara-e first. Well, I'd had to let it be known somehow. I hid nothing about his conception; to be tight-lipped would make people think even worse, as I'd learned from Esora-e. Eyebrows rose, but everyone congratulated me.

The tour went for another month, larches on the heights turning to gold and maples to crimson; and my son gave me my parent's initiation. He would scream for mama at night, sometimes all night, waking everyone; he lost his pot-training, so that after I'd paid one inn for a ruined feather mattress I had to put him back in diapers; he threw tantrums until Esora-e said, "You either comb the brat to silence or the two of you sleep in the anteroom."

I slept in the anteroom. I never gave him into anyone else's arms except while speaking to the people, I let him cling or have my notice whenever he wished no matter whom I was conversing with, played with him every spare moment, gave him bright toys and soft; I let him scream "Hate you! Hate you!" and batter my chest with his little fists without a hard word back. How many times I curled around him and said, "She loves you, she's not dead, you'll see her again soon, I love you," I cannot say. I was the only constant presence for him now, at the time when a child is most delicate for need of constancy; so it seemed to me I had better be perfectly constant.

My schedule had already been full to the eyeteeth, and I didn't get much help, Esora-e cold to him, my friends not knowing what to do; I was the lightest sleeper anyway. Soon I was feeling like the walking dead from morning to night, my arms and heart leaden; I felt nothing would change and I was a slave on a treadmill, chained to it for twenty years; I caught myself wishing him gone, no matter how, then loathed myself for the thought, and made myself sick imagining him dying. He and I would cry ourselves to sleep together. It was harder than war.

The tour ended none too soon. Though then I was busy every day in Tyeraha's office, soon to be mine, and arranging my wedding, the Hearthstone was an unchanging place for him to get used to, and my mother lent her hand. His nightmares eased, and he learned again how to use the chamber pot. One day I came in after training, and he trotted to me with his hands out. I swung him as usual; then he threw his arms around my neck and said for the

first time ever, "I love you, Daddy." My eyes rained tears;
the brush of a finger could have knocked me flat.

Shaina and Etana came early. So much had happened
since, they seemed almost like strangers. I suspect Shaina
had become somewhat fond of the notion of bearing an
Ascendant; but she said nothing, and though at first their
delight in my child was forced, he charmed as children do.
We revised our schedule: Shaina would bear one by me,
one by Etana, the third by me and the rest by him.

We made our wedding modest, inviting just family and
friends; I was not demarch yet, so it need not be public.
Strange, to put on the Shae-Arano-e wedding tunic, last
worn by my father, and kiss the crystals of two people who
were truly only my acquaintances. They shone, beautiful
in their finery, in the gazes of passion they exchanged, in
the joy of seeing their love celebrated. I had what I had; I
made my oaths with my child on my arm.

Sometimes, now they lived here, I felt I had been mad
to do this. Most of our half-moon of honey I worked,
cramming in the last of my matriculation, which had been
delayed by the war, and the transition. I stayed in the
offices till late at night, past when they made love; else I
crept out to the balcony, watching the moonlight over
Hetharin. Once, catching me weeping, they both made
love to me, and let me sleep cradled between them,
tossing a vote-stone for who would have the honor of my
head on his or her shoulder. In their happiness they were
generous. That's all I can ask, I thought. If I were a Lakan,
I would have an arranged marriage; this is one, in truth,
and friendship is better than many spouses have.

I had what I wanted: a marriage, a child and the pros-
pect of more, before my ascent; should I complain that it
felt too easy, undeserved, that I'd got it by my position,
that however we caulked them over with friendship, the
cracks of lovelessness remained? I had enough to love for
now, with the demarchy and Fifth, as he was coming to be
called. (If people shortened it to Chevenga, he got confused with me. As far as he was concerned, though, he was
Chevenga, I was Daddy, and that was that.) Should I of all
people complain that it all felt too sudden?

When the fire of leaf-turning on the heights spread
down into the valleys, the day came.

I slept alone, as the custom calls for. I woke early as I often do, but lay with my eyes closed, so that at dawn when the Keeper of the Arch-Sigil came, I felt the Crystal of the Speaker touch my brow before I saw it. "Fourth Chevenga Shae-Arano-e," she said. "Without the will of the people, what are you?" I had not known this was in the ritual, but I had the answer. "Nothing," I said.

"And with the will of the people?"

The obvious answer, everything, to complete the circle of nothing-everything, seemed too obvious. "Nothing," I said, "but what they will." She laid the crystal in my hands.

Naked in the courtyard, I found my friends and family my accusers, as I had known I would. To see every face so hard at once, though, brought back a child's fear of being abandoned; the thought came, "What I've done this time is beyond forgiveness," as if I were ten. Then I wondered who I was to hold the Crystal for all Yeola-e; the only one who could do that was my father, and he was dead.

I began breaking out in a cold sweat, which there would be no concealing. But the God-In-Myself was near, for the thought came, "You'd better be ready; your life's two-thirds over." I laughed inwardly, and remembered Tennunga, who had died young as well. Almost before I knew it, the brightness I had seen in him filled me, lifting me out of myself.

One cannot in truth even fight it. I had been afraid that I might have to struggle with my pride to kneel when the people called me out; as it was, the thunder of their joined voices drew me to my knees without my own will touching it, like a river current carrying a leaf, and I felt only joy. Then my body turned, and carried me into the Lake on steps of fire.

The Kiss is a gate, the demarch of old wrote, which once having opened and seen through one can never turn back from. Having passed through one is forever changed, for like all trials, it makes one know one's true nature.

I understood that now, as I chose my place. As deep as one's waist is best, I had been told. The fall sun had ceased to warm the water, so that it was icy on my skin. I would succeed or I would fail, and that would decide my life; though such moments had come a thousand times in the war, as they do for every warrior, this was in the presence of All-spirit, public; it would be the people I failed, not just myself.

I gripped the spear and the torch, from which a spark fell to hiss for an instant on the surface. I looked down; the ripples made gold circlets and ribbons on the brown bottom around the shadow of my head, and I heard Shininao's wings. Death lay there, or so it would feel to my body, that housed my soul. Sacred death: acquiescence. I suddenly knew that as a child, trying this, I had not truly believed in death, only known that my time was short.

The crook of the fire-dish was cold, half-clutching my sword-wrist, as I knelt; the icy water burned me up to my chin. The crowd was silent now, waiting; but they seemed very distant, and I was alone. The Ritual Monk's hands on my shoulders were warm, the hands of a mother; then they were gone.

I called to the God-In-Myself right away, barely after bowing my head. Like a fool, again, I'd taken a deep breath out of habit, and made it longer for myself. The first painful urges for air came; I put all my strength into my fingers around the spear, and thought with horror, I don't feel the God's hand on my back.

It's only a child, the bitter thought came to me, who wants a voice from the sky. You are alone. If you are forced, how is it true acquiescence? My body screamed "Save me!", used to fighting to the end, much more now.

A child is ruled by instinct, and accepts all; an adult can question. Why should I pay, I thought, for Notyere's treason? Did he, two hundred years ago, make me untrustworthy? Yet these are childish thoughts; the sacred trust was broken; the people cannot know my heart except by what I prove. But what do I have to prove to them, any more than I ever did, or he? This is like training until exhaustion, or being flogged to falling; I will always fail, in the end; I know nothing, despite all I have posed; I am nothing, so why struggle? So the debate, that I had thought long over, went in my head. One does indeed find one's true nature. In the end, it came down to my asking myself, "Can I fail, at *this*?"

I came to know how much worth I put on myself, by the agony it was to cast myself away. Then the hand did come, pressing between my shoulder blades; the hand of a murderer, I thought, my own murderer, my God, myself. Choice is not enough; one needs the deeper compulsion to bear this; yet I chose the compulsion. So the snake grasps its tail in its teeth. The time at which I am truly suffocating, I always feel a black snake in me, coiling in a dance with the singing wind: a thing of evil, for destruction is evil, and death is the destruction of all one knows. Here I am, the God-In-Myself says, laughing; and you always thought I was so bright. I am as dark as I am light, I am of death as I am of life; the Void is nothing, as everything. If you don't see this you are still a child, who cowers away from the full truth. I had been at eleven, I saw; it would have been unbearable.

That is what a demarch is, in the end; the one who faces the Void in full, light and dark, to learn what he must be for the people. No lesson had taught me that; in fact all I can set down here is words, and any Ascendant reading this fools himself to think he has stumbled on the key and can seize it, or has learned anything at all. I'd been told a thousand times, as you have. I had to do it, as you will.

I remember opening my eyes as I struggled, feeling the burning water swirl but seeing only dark, and knowing my senses were fading because all my strength was in my fingers. I remember the warmth of the Ritual Monk's hand again, clasping my mouth and nose. Then peace, and the music full of colors I knew from before, so engrossing it made me forget my name. The crash of light, noise and pain that tore it away I resented at first, and tried to fend off with my arms; someone's mouth was on mine, tasting of lentils, many hands touched me, I was cold all over, something flat and hard and heavy lay against my back. Then my ears cleared, and in the roar I heard the name I had forgotten. I was lying on the pier, the monks reviving me; the smoke-path in the sky I trailed down to a great tongue of flame on the fire-dish. I had succeeded. "Can you hear me, demarch?" someone was saying: slowly I realized he was speaking to me.

I was through the gate, that changes all. I would never be the same, I knew, nor anything I saw or touched, said or did; I had changed so much it seemed strange that my hands and body, as the monks wrapped me in towels, should look the same as they ever had. My sword-hand was strangely heavy; on my third finger was the demarchic signet, put on while I was unconscious, as per custom. I wanted someone, especially my mother, to hold me, my hand at least; she was not in sight, but the monks, sensing it, or knowing from before that a new demarch feels like a butterfly just out of the chrysalis, infant-tender, handled me gently.

All across the square, arms danced in the air, streams of wine and flowers and kerchiefs flew; I raised my hand to the people, and the roar doubled. No more distance; I was theirs now, one with their fears, their dreams, their whims; I felt the bond, shining and steely as chains, as hands clasped mine through Terera and all up the path by the falls.

Donning the white linen robe, I went to the sacred place on Haranin for my meditation. That heightened state, like the thick of battle, doesn't lend itself well to being remembered. It seemed all my questions were answered, and those that weren't would be in their time, or the answer I would choose. No vision came; it seemed to me I'd had the relevant one already, at seven, plenty foreknowledge for one life. I needed mostly to calm my ecstasy, which I did. Then I went down to the Hearthstone, to brand myself. I made the first mark, as is custom, over my heart.

1   Firso Shalev, of Brahvniki
2   Ixtak, of Laka
3   Dinosti, of Sria
4   Lobryr called Flame-hair, of Kurkania
5   Nikonial Curlionaiane, of Tor Ench
6   Stevahn called Argent Qualities, of Brahvniki
7   Ozbo called the Beast, of Nellas
8   Seliko, of Curlionaiz
9   Manthas called Hero's Finger, of Ungilia
10 Ganon Ian, of Tor Ench
11 Kuun Veersh, of Roskat
12 Helmuth called the Thane, of Oestmark
13 Iron Horse, of Kurkania
14 Kikro the Gallant, of Sria
15 Onkeng called Flashing, of Laka
16 Heinofenas, of Nellas
17 Biorio called Monkey's Shadow, of Sria
18 Gasroli called the Gourmand, of Sria
19 Riji Asadji called Klifas, of Tor Ench
20 Freni-danas called in-cendiary, of Kurkania
21 Walu-chou, of Rand
22 Lord Rhiored, of An Glyn
23 Boryas called King Long Legs, of Soldenkor
24 Ulszan Zeyk Steb, of Mogh-iur
25 Loiadas, of Nellas
26 Chachima called the Wanderer, of the southern desert
27 Darilas Isitlas, of Elmira, Tor Ench
28 Fanglet the Whippet, of no one knows where
29 Wiloo called the Cannibal, of Ungilia
30 Sir of Cliches, of Tor Ench
31 Spyranedas called The Pirate, of Nellas
32 Iliakaj, of Tor Ench
33 Kven Frel called Bug-eyed Chaos, of Doss
34 Kazhishna, of Laka
35 Anasano called Moonface, of Tor Ench
36 Kyera Shae-Lemana, of Selina, Yeola-e
37 Kadisias, of Nellas
38 Rao Erasako-e, of Akara, Yeola-e
39 Arno of Faiji, called Smeg-head, of Tor Ench
40 Minao Alcheringa, of Enkara, Yeola-e
41 Ana-e Verachake, of Selina, Yeola-e
42 Manadias called the Slaughterer, of An Glyn
43 Esora-e Shae-Barao, of Halthelae, Yeola-e
44 Fushu, of the Moryavska
45 Crad Killodny, of Tarano
46 Akara Sikora-e, of Asangal, Yeola-e
47 Marya Kosalena, of Shilishai, Yeola-e
48 Tyera Shae-Nekari, of Tinga-e, Yeola-e
49 Ini-tai Shae-Chire, of Miniya, Yeola-e

Book II

I

It seemed impossible that I could know anything I had before. So, as a new demarch does, I began tentatively. Then I began to feel I was still myself, remembered my training, and settled into it.

My friendships changed, as couldn't be helped. I felt it when I did my first inspection wearing the circles of the First General First, and saw my old clutch all standing stiff and as afraid of my words as if I were my father. The bureaucrats who'd scatted me away from their desks all my life now jumped when I called, and I stopped hearing the office gossip. Aside from family, the closest to me now were Chinisa, who had been my father's secretary as well as my aunt's, and could organize a demarch's life in her sleep, the five high ministers, who had all been experts before I was born, those Servants who made it a point to fraternize with me, and the three demarchic news-scribes of the Workfast Proclamatory, doing their work of tripping me up as best they could. I made all those I could persuade call me by name.

Only Mana thought me unchanged, and so did not himself change. Great ability lifts one apart from others, he had always said, so that one needs an earthbound friend, and he would be mine. He was right in the need, but wrong in the cause, because I never told him. Had I, he would not have believed me. He was an Athye's Athye, one who credited nothing that could not be shown him. Speak of the Hermaphrodite or the Twin Hawks as anything but symbols, or claim to have powers you could not immediately test, and he'd grow an uneasy grin like a foreigner's in the heart of Yeola-e, and make some deflating joke or argue that it could have been chance or power of will. The God-In-Him was a perfect sword-stroke or a flawless Enchian conjugation.

So with him I could live as I had before seven, remembering that life could be another way. He was my strongest tie to innocence; I could forget in his laughter, as in good wine. Call it avoidance; but we all get drunk now and then.

As a demarch should, I learned what spirit my ascent was taken in, partly by walking disguised in Terera Square. Because of my name as a warrior, they expected peace for a long time. It had a shade of a new love affair, too; they were besotted with me, for reasons that my mind had names for but my heart could only feel bewildered by. I'd had enough affairs to know the danger of that, though, so I held back from posing, and kept my head fairly low. My first half-year of demarchy was uneventful, as I hoped my whole term would be.

There were Lakan border matters to clear up, and an earthquake in Enthira. My first news of it came when I reached for a paper that had fallen under my desk, and was lurched almost out of my chair; in my cup the tea quivered, though nothing moving had been near it. That night I lay sleepless waiting to see if a runner would come, and from where. The town was all but razed it turned out, and some four hundred people died. I went there with the Demarchic Guard, and pulled the living and the dead from under their fallen houses for three unbroken days.

I made short state visits to Kranaj, Astalaz, Ivahn and Bitha Szten, head of the largest clan of the Schvait Confederation, which is as close as the Schvait have to a head of state. They all treated me entirely properly and well. It was not necessary, I was assured, and in fact some questioned the safety of it or accused me of running to them like a valet. Krero said, "I understand, Cheng: a state visit is almost the only thing you can do without the people's orders, so you being you of course you've got to, right away." When I got angry, he asked if I'd got so uppity I couldn't take a joke. But my only thought was, as a person does better with friends, so does a nation. History proved me right, I think.

The rest of it was sorting out what Tyeraha had handed to me, and learning those things no rehearsal but only the work itself can teach. I went to the same fate my father had before me: sitting in the demarchic chair in Assembly and knowing I was the youngest here by far. Once they knew me beyond formality all the Servants called me "lad." Of course people tested me, as children do a stepfather, but I kept my wits about me, showed the fist of the law when I had to, and got a name for strength and cutting to the heart of matters. Having been to war is good for that.

Shaina, Etana and I settled in to a good bond, earthembracing for them, light and laughing for me, and full, naturally, of political shoptalk. Fifth Chevenga haunted the Hearthstone, though people said he was more shy than I had been. Though some still frowned on how I'd got him, no one could deny he was full-blood Yeoli, and mine. It helped that he was quick. When people not related to him noticed it, I knew my first thought had been true. He spoke in full sentences, or more often in questions, with a perfect accent, and his little hands were into everything. My grandmother minded him in the day, as she had me.

About two months past the winter solstice, Shaina conceived, and I began the joyful desperate wait for my second child. Having a boy I hoped for a girl, and all the signs, the feathers laid over the womb and my mother's hunch and even something Jinai Oru tossed off in passing, predicted one. The drawback was, since I lay with Shaina only for conception, by our agreement I was out of her bed for two years at least. There are needs permitted to a youthful Ascendant or a warrior in the field that a demarch, especially married, is expected to have mastered, for all his body might tell him that was only yesterday. To borrow the Lakan idiom, I practiced my sword-grip a lot. As well I threw myself harder into my work, and raising Fifth; I moved his crib into my Hearthstone office, and began staying there late into the night.

Mana and Kunarda both got accepted into the Elite

Demarchic Guard. Krero continued climbing in the greater
Guard, making centurion; Sachara kept up his training but
studied classics, with the aim of teaching. Nyera bought
into a weaving workfast in Thara-e and moved there. All
but Krero courted, and took falls; none married.

When one has a name as a warrior, one also gets a name
for being warlike; those to whom war is alien, to whom I
looked frightening with all my muscles and scars, will
think such things, and make them part of the common
opinion. I let the back of my hair grow past my shoulders
and the forelock fall to a peak between my eyebrows, wore
loose long sleeves, and spoke of how well war teaches the
necessity of peace. Having Fifth in tow so much helped as
well, showing my tenderness. The talk lessened. But I was
all the more inclined, I think, to prove the truth of my
words with actions.

"You'll *charm* our enemies into leaving us alone?" my
shadow-father had asked me mockingly; yet knowing a
person does make it harder to hurt him, as I had learned.
Arko's attention was on the east, no doubt of that, as
anyone watching the sea knew; but they raided all nations'
ships, not just ours. No king in the region had done a state
visit to Kurkas for better than ten years; it struck me that
he might turn his hunger away from one who did.

The day I considered it publicly, a hand caught my
shoulder as I was walking down a corridor, and spun me
around so hard I went into stance. "You headstrong little
fool, are you mad?" Esora-e exerted political influence as
subtly as he had parental. "Can't you see? Those blond
child-rapers, every one of them, their oath isn't worth a
rhetorician's fart, they'd cut your throat or sell you in a
blink, and then we're stuck without you!"

I lifted my sword-hand, and looked at my third finger,
feeling my cheeks turning to flame. It is there, is it
not, I asked myself; yes, I see the bright hard white, I
feel the weight, it's familiar, I did the Kiss of the Lake;
I am indeed a demarch, not a ten-year-old. "You see
this?" I said, holding the signet on my fist under his
nose. "Do you know what it means? It means I need
listen to you no more than I need listen to the other two
thousand people in Yeola-e. So get in line." I walked
away. Every time he approached again, even if more
politely, I said, "Chinisa has the audience list," and threat-

ened to set the guard on him if he persisted. Even now, I was thinking, he doesn't respect me; at least now I have the means to teach him to.

My grandmother said that though Kurkas had always been high-handed he'd never broken an oath of safe-conduct that she knew of; still, she doubted it would do any good. "If you do go," she told me, "make very sure it doesn't seem you've come begging, or we'll end up being slapped with either tribute or war; if he doesn't spy weakness his ears in the walls will. But don't tempt him into treachery with anger, either; make him see the steel in your spine without ever letting the diplomat slip. You know the rule: high stakes, no mistakes."

My aunt said, "Ask Jinai. Why, you haven't even got him to do a general seeing for your term yet; what's keeping you?"

This demanded it, so I went, this time ready with paper and an Arkan pen. Jinai seemed smaller, because I'd grown, as I faced the blankness of his wall again, with his meaty hands adjusting my shoulders like a spyglass; he could no longer look over my head, but only beside it. I remembered as he began murmuring in his way that last time he had foreseen me going to Arko anyway.

"Plans, intentions, theories, vagaries. Where is augury? The die has six faces, but can land with only one up; there are a thousand paths, but Fourth Chevenga Shae-Arano-e and the world can walk only one . . . urk!" Without warning he gave me a quick shake, as one would to wake a sleeper quickly. "Shit." I heard a slap; his palm on his own head. "Wooden block, you! The die has six faces. . . . Child-rape. Maybe I'm having a bad day. No, that doesn't make sense, everything was like sharp leaves and sun and crystal last time through you, you're like that, besides I never have *that* bad a day. It can't just be a wall, shit, I'm sorry, demarch, I'm so sorry, forgive me, I can't see a cursed thing."

One could not tell him to try harder; he was not one who could conceive of trying any less than his hardest. Cursing and chattering, he strained, his cool hands turning sweaty. Finally I said, a little quietly as my aunt had taught me, "What does it mean, when you see nothing?"

"That you can't bear to see it," he said, in the unhesitating way he had when speaking true.

I stared at him over my shoulder, prickles sweeping all
along my spine and limbs. His flat blue eyes blinked back,
as if he'd forgotten already; there can be no more answer
in them than a voice from the sky, I thought, for it is only
the God-In-Him hearing the voice of the future that knows
anything, not him; I'm a fool to look for it.

"Whether I can bear it or not, Jinai, I have to see," I
said. "I am demarch; what I wish doesn't matter."

He clasped me again, and took a long deep breath.
"Demarch. Poor Chevenga. Arko. Arko. Should you go to
Arko? I don't know why you're asking, because you're
going." I started scrawling in shorthand. Every word; sometimes, my aunt had told me, there were meanings in them
one only caught after several readings. "I can tell it's Arko
because there are blondies everywhere and your thoughts
are thinking of it as Arko-ness. I mean, I'm sorry I'm not
being clearer, the die didn't give me a gift with words, but
you know what I mean, it's Arko."

"What's best in the end," I said, "to go or not to go?"

I was hoping for another quick truth, but he said, "I
don't know. I see a porridge of things, terrible things like
bad dreams, things that don't make sense. You don't want
to know."

"Yes, I do." I took a deep breath and told myself, no use
being short with him. It was fear making me angry. "Jinai,
don't think for me, don't clog up the stream, let it all flow
out to me, and I'll do the thinking."

"But you don't like more foreknowledge," he said casually. "I see a blob of jam of some kind of berry I don't
know but they're turning into worm's heads swimming in
blood and crawling out off the plate . . . and there's the
black lightning bolt with the fork that never goes away,
again. Pain. So much pain. You'll do the thinking, demarch,
you'll know what it means, I know. Fighting. Shakora,
All-spirit, Shakora! I see someone saying the whole city is
dead. You, fighting a man with blue eyes in red and gold
armor. Another battle."

Trembling settled into my limbs. One could not deny
his brilliant record. "Jinai, is this if I go, or if I *don't* go?"

"I don't know. You said you'll do the thinking!" I forced
my teeth closed, and signed go on with my pen. He froze,
then said in a whisper, "Demarch, there's something you
probably wouldn't want to know but should because it

might affect your plans . . . should I tell you?" One could not howl "What did I just say?" to him, either; he might not know. "Yes," I said.

"You are . . . with you I never see things past a certain time. That means . . . I should warn you . . . it has to do with . . ."

All my breath heaved out of me, of its own will. "I'm going to get my ear pecked young," I said. "I *know* that. Shit on *me*, Jinai—*should I go to Arko or not?*"

"Sorry, demarch, sorry . . . I see a . . . I don't know, a thing with metal and wood bits that's alive; it's moving all over and making noises and I'm thinking, I mean you're thinking, it's a blessing to all the world. And the wing thing, that too. Arko-ness is all twined with the rest of your life. Yes, go, you will go, you have to go, the people will you will go, you're going. That's all, demarch, I'm sorry, I'm sorry!" He sat down hard, spent, burying his face in his hands. I could only hug him and reassure him he'd done well, until his smile came back.

That night I stayed at my desk until dawn, reading my notes a hundred times by candlelight and straining to see the shape of the future in them, while Fifth smacked his lips and murmured in his sleep beside me. I was going to Arko; Jinai was certain. Yet if I did not write and send the letter, I would not be invited. Would I be called there later, of necessity? Arko-ness was twined with the rest of my life; but I'd never even seen a free Arkan except in Brahvniki. I read, each time expecting the words to transmute into something I could believe and understand. The black lightning bolt? Shakora, the whole city, dead? A wood and metal animal, the wing thing?

It all writhed and swam in my head until false dawn; then it came to me I was missing the point, trying to choose. If Jinai was right, I must go. The shape of it was this: whatever I went through would pay for greater good in the end.

And Arko was coming, soon, whatever we did; I'd shied from it, but with the thought everything fell into sense like a latch dropping. Whatever my people thought, the time was right, Yeola-e weakened by war and plague and with a new and very young leader. It struck me that I might be the first in the world to know, if Kurkas hadn't thought of it yet; or the only one to know, since Jinai didn't.

It was then, I think, I first truly learned the meaning of empire. My people had raised me as high as they could; I lived clothed in silk and ivory, my name spoken by two million; I need only say the word and all the warriors of Yeola-e would march; I was the embodiment of my people's soul. Yet in the face of Kurkas's power, I felt small.

Shock sank into my heart. Out of peace, just by my asking for augury on peace-making, had come news of war like a venom-snake out of a hearth. But only to me. Later this morning, I would sit in Assembly again, and everyone around me would speak and think as if all were the same as it was yesterday; indeed if I showed otherwise, questions would be asked. Why is it my fate to know what no one else does I wondered, and for a time indulged in pitying myself; it was late. Once or twice I slapped myself in the face, hoping to wake myself from the dream. Yet only a fool expects troubles to be over because he is tired of them. The die rolls as it will, and slaves and demarchs alike are nothing to it.

My thoughts trod a circle, but in time I understood. In the ancient tale, when the tyrant's machine-monster big as the world finds the warriors, obligation forbids them to flee, but holding their ground against it will be death. So they fly into its face, and because to its builders that was the path unconceived, they win. In the morning I had Chinisa scribe the letter, sealed it and watched the courier dash down beside the falls.

Some called me brave, others, reckless. "I knew we couldn't talk sense into you," my shadow-father said. "We never can." Others thought I'd be spat on in reply, or ignored. As it was, answer came within three-quarters of a month, good time from the City Itself, in a packet of silk with the sun-clasping Arkan eagle all over it. I had not thought such curlicues possible on stationery, nor gold ink. He would be delighted to meet me, he wrote, and welcomed me with all proper honors to the Marble Palace. As I had asked, there were five copies of his oath of safe-conduct, in Arkan and Enchian. I'd heard they had writing-machines, like before the Fire; these looked as if they'd been made by one. My request had been something of a test; if he'd shown displeasure at my suspicion, I would not have gone. I showed them to my doubters.

I kept one to carry, put one in the archives, and sent
the other three to Astalaz, Kranaj and Ivahn; let them be
witness, if something went amiss. It occurred to me I
wasn't necessarily doing any of them a kindness with this
trip; what Arkan trouble I turned from Yeola-e must go
elsewhere. But for me my people must come first.

I'd thought I'd go by ship, but Kurkas promised me over-
land would not be much slower. One hears much of Arkan
roads, built smooth and wide from one end of the empire to
the other. He wants to show them off, I thought, let me see
how fast his armies could get to our border. Well, no knowledge hurts. He would send an escort of twenty warriors,
and I was welcome to match that number; in the orderly
Empire, he assured me, that should be defense enough.

Krero's duties kept him here, as did Sachara's studies.
Mana insisted on coming, but this being a peace-mission I
forbade anyone else of the Elite. My little sister Senala-e
and little brother Naiga wanted to see Arko, so though
they were barely warriors I took them. The rest were all
volunteers of the Demarchic Guard, most of whom were only
acquaintances. I took nineteen, to remind Kurkas that I could
be counted as a warrior; no Arkan Imperator had fought
with his own hands for better than two hundred years.

So in the freshening of late spring, we set off, the peace-
sigil hanging from our necks. So little I knew my people;
but they turned out in hundreds in Terera to cheer my
way.

At the northern border, where the eagle on an open
gate faces the pass under the stone circle, so little Arko
fears invaders, we found the Arkan escort in their scarlet
armor waiting on the poured-stone road. They were truly
an honor guard, all wearing the same breastplates and
mantles of, All-spirit help us, purple, their horses all the
great pure white Arkan strain. The eagle standard they
carried was gold-leafed. I just put approval on my face,
taking it as homage. When the greeting was done I heard
one looking at me whisper to another, who snickered; but
I was above noticing. Learn from them, I told my escort,
and myself.

The leader, who looked about thirty-five, gave his name
as Ethras Innen, *Aitzas;* that and the length of his hair,
which hung in a braid down to his waist, told me he was of
the noble caste; the rest, whose blond braids fell no lower

than their hearts, were *solas*, warriors. All had chins shaven
as smooth as boys. No wonder they so love uniformity, I
thought, looking into that row of blue eyes; they are born
with it.

Though no one wore a helmet, they all had on their
gauntlets; when they didn't, as we learned camping with
them that night, they wore gloves, even around the cook-
fire, and even so would hide their hands behind shields or
under mantles. When I'd thought Lakans were shy about
their bodies, I'd known nothing. We never saw them
bathe, though they did every day; they'd creep off one at a
time, not even letting each other see, as if being clean
were a crime. Once, just to see what would happen, I
invited Ethras to swim in a lake with me. He informed me
that in Arko, decent people do not swim, having baths.
Interesting to know, if one ever fought with one near deep
water.

Every day at noon, a bell tolls in every village in the
empire. When they heard it they would pull up their
horses as one, dismount, bow their heads and touch their
gauntleted hands to their hands, palms up and cupped.
They would chant a prayer together, and stand for a time
in silence; then Ethras would bark, they'd mount up, and
we'd go on. "Noon observance," was all he said, though I
did not hide my fascination; I knew next to nothing of
Arkan religion. But since it made him uneasy, I left off.

He spoke Enchian in the stiff, pinched *Aitzas* accent,
and styled me *"Amaesti,"* apparently unable to say
semanakraseye if his life depended on it. He was too
solemn a person, too, his eyes expressionless whatever
they looked at, and making him laugh was impossible. I
noticed the rest stood off, from him and four or five others
of similar manner.

A year later, I would know the signs, as I knew my own
face in the mirror. But I'd hardly met Arkans yet.

On the fifth day, we rode through the town of Roskat.
This was only a recently civilized province, he told me,
and there were still bandits at large; yet we should be safe,
being too many and well-equipped for them to take on. I
knew history from my side; by civilized province, I knew,
he meant conquered nation, by bandits, rebels. There is
much Yeoli blood in Roskat, and they have always considered themselves our kin in spirit; seventy years ago when

they fell it was in spite of our aid, and I suspected it might be a bone of contention with Kurkas that we still harbored their "bandits." The town had the miserable look of a spirited people yoked; anyone with dark hair had a long face, slave-coffles were common, in the town square three naked Roskati corpses hung on poles, their severed heads laid at their feet, and no one near looking shocked, as if it were common. Whether they feared for me or envied my freedom when their eyes caught mine, I could not tell.

Half a day past the town, we rounded a corner to find the road blocked by twenty warriors on horseback.

They were rebels, for Arkan law forbade Roskati weapons; but their spears were up. Their leader, a stocky dark-blond man who looked a careworn forty, began speaking as soon as we pulled up, calling in Yeoli, "Fourth Chevenga Shae-Arano-e! Hear me!" while his eyes ran over us trying to discern me.

Ethras's voice, closer to me, drowned him out. It was Arkan, but sounded imperious and threatening; again I wished I'd learned the language. "Excuse me," I said in Enchian when he paused. "It's to me he speaks, Escort Captain. They've offered us no threat, but only want to speak; even if he is a bandit, where I come from the accused are permitted their say. I will hear, and judge. There's no danger; they're half our number."

"They're not to be heard, but chased down and beheaded!" he snapped.

"Very well," I said, "I'll listen, *then* you can send for someone to chase them down and behead them." At a loss for words he stared at me, his face more impassive, if that was possible, than ever. "I'm Fourth Chevenga," I said to the Roskati, in Yeoli again. "Who are you, and what have you to say?"

"My name is Mirko of Roskat." He gave no titles; the Arkans' stiffening at the name was all I needed to know. He pitched his voice for all of us to hear. "Your people have always been friends to mine, demarch. Let us be friends to you then, and warn you: Kurkas"—he spat— "will betray you the moment he sees advantage. He has us, a hundred times."

"Whatever the cutthroat says," Ethras said icily, "he lies. They undermine peace everywhere. He seeks to embarrass you, *Amaesti*." I drew the certificate from my pouch, and held it up for all to see. "You mean to say, Mirko, that this means nothing?"

He spat again. "Forgive my rudeness, but what means an oath, to a snake? He plans to betray you, demarch. It's bad form to stop you this way, I know, and would be bad form for you to turn around; but I fear for your life. If they object—they are half our number."

"*Amaesti*, listening will do nothing to recommend you to the Imperator, nor aid the cause of peace." Ethras, his voice cold as snow. I looked at him hard and said, "Do you threaten me, Escort Captain? If their words are wind, why do you fear my hearing them?" He drew his head back and high, raising the nose, in a way I had come to know as Arkan; then looked away, his blue eyes seeming settled. Mirko's were more honest.

"If he does not mean to betray you, demarch," he said, "why does he send born and bred assassins to escort you? You don't know the signs of the Mahid, the Imperator's black dogs, but we do. We've suffered their work long enough. There are several among you; the commander is one. Have you noticed, they never smile?"

"Cheng," said Mana, behind me. "I don't like—" Then his voice was lost, in my own. Whatever Ethras was, he had hands like lightning; his dagger was out and would have been in my back in the flash of a thought, had I not had weapon-sense. I think, as several other people afterwards suggested, that he did know Yeoli, and understood all we said.

In the memory, my shout of "*Chen!*" seemed to last an eternity, going on and on like the squeal of a cartwheel. His act had been a signal, too; all the other Arkans had picked a Yeoli, and done the same. I heard their massed cries through mine.

The world turned into a blood-haze, my last clear sight Ethras's face, blank even now, tipping and falling away; I'd struck off his head. So far, I'd always fought with open eyes and calculation; I'd never gone berserk in my life. Now I heard nothing but my own unbroken war howl, felt nothing but Chirel flying in my hand; my mind didn't even know when my horse threw me, though my body must have. I didn't think, "I will take as many as I can with me"; there was nothing so coherent. All around me was death-fighting, inside me was death-fighting, I was death-fighting, made only of blood and steel and movement; I knew no other existence, never had and never would; life was death and death life, so if they killed me I wouldn't notice, being still in my own element.

Yet somehow, clear above the din as a thrush's song against mountain wind, I recall my sister screaming "*Cheng!*", and a guard I'd only come to know on this journey, lying on the poured stone of the Arkan road, his hand clutched to his sword-side ear and blood pouring from his mouth. My rage was like a dream, from which I did not want to wake.

Then the next head I raised Chirel to cleave in two cried in Yeoli, "Stop! We will not hurt you!" and was a woman's, of some thirty perhaps, with brown hair and black eyes. It was over. The Arkans were gone, dead or fleeing; the rebels had charged in to save me. Only they moved, checking the fallen, seizing milling horses. The sweet scent of the Roskati forest was corrupted now, with wound smells. Both her hands clasped my sword-hand, while I stared, mind numbed; she wore a battered leather kilt with a cloth of sky-blue, and I remember thinking, *sacred Roskati patterns*. "It is ended," she said, "you need not fight more. Can you hear me, Chevenga? It is ended."

I let them take Chirel, wipe it clean, and give it back to me to sheathe. With my body still, my mind had slowly begun moving; but what it found, wherever it reached, was too terrible to touch. I heard Mirko's voice, shouting orders in Roskati. "Come," the woman said. My feet were rooted; I heard Yeoli moans. Then two big hands fell on my shoulders; after looking into my eyes, Mirko shook me, respectfully but hard. Hooves clattered away; he was splitting his people apart, to make the chase more difficult. "Come to your senses, demarch, lad. They're coming, they won't be long, we must get into the woods. Your people are all dead, or wounded worse than we can help; we can't go to the Haian, that'll be the first place they look. You have to leave them, else they'll have guarded you for nothing. Come." It's both a clip and a lilt, the Roskati accent, I thought idly, and went where his hand pulled.

I put all my thought into running, being dog-tired already from raging. We were five, including Mirko and Vaneesh, for so the woman was called. He followed no path, seeking ground no horse could go; we crossed a swamp on fallen logs, and for a time dashed through the shallows along the path of a stream to obscure our scent-trail. Here and there were ruins of old farms, a house fallen to a heap, a broken stone fence overrun with brambles. Then we came into forest and slowed to a walk. The boles of the oaks were wide as houses, the mat of green leaves above so thick they cut off the sun as completely as a roof, so I could not know even what direction we took. There was no underbrush at all, just a bare brown thatch that thumped under one's feet. One could see clear for a long way around; now and then I saw a herd of boar in the distance, or a family of deer, the young with spots, leaping gracefully away.

The light began to fail, and Mirko lit a torch; as full darkness blacker than black fell, it began to rain, the first sign a distant pattering on leaves high as a cliff above, then eventually fat drops leaking through to us. Still Mirko knew his way, saying now and then, "Keep heart, we're close." Finally he halted, and made a call like a nightingale's three times. From somewhere ahead came the hoot of an owl, that I realized had first sounded a moment before his. "We're here." A little further on was a camp-fire, and then several more, with tents pitched among the great trees. I heard a horse whicker, the rasp of stone on steel, the buzz of talk; in the firelight I saw rope ladders dangling, and looking up found houses built in the branches. "Until we win back our lands," he said, "this is home."

Vaneesh pulled my hood further down over my face, and said, "Keep the signet hidden. No one here would betray you willingly; but Arkans have a drug that makes one tell the truth. No one will ask." It was as she said; everyone hailed Mirko, and made signs of respect to her as we would to a sage, but seemed not to see me.

The rain had not reached this far. We joined a fire, and they ate; for the first time I saw the Roskati custom of offering the first bite to one's neighbor. That required that I eat one mouthful; but though I'd had nothing since morning and the pork was good, "the best meat, from close to the bone," as Vaneesh said, all food tasted foul to me, and I could only get down a little. We'd come in late; everyone else was turning in. When they were all gone, Mirko laid his hand on my shoulder. "All day, you haven't said a word. You can't bear this alone, and we are willing to shoulder some of it. Let out your heart, lad." His words drifted through the cloud-white blankness that was my mind, and out, without catching. Then one of the others handed him a skin, which he gave to me, saying, "Drink." It was some kind of Roskati liquor, hot as nakiti but darker-tasting.

I drank as he urged me; and they pressed me to speak. The stuff was as strong as nakiti too, and soon spread its glow through me, poking my emotion. "You needn't be the diplomat, you're among friends, lad," Mirko said; I fixed him with a fight-stare, and said, "Call me lad one more time and I'll kill you."

He stiffened; Vaneesh clasped my hands, and said, "He means nothing, demarch, it is only affection. Is it permitted to call you by name?" Then to Mirko she said something in Roskati. It is kin to Yeoli, with some loan-words; I heard the word "deranged." His eyes softened a little, but he said, "Demarch, you might remember who saved your life."

"Call me Chevenga," I said. I heard my own voice, like a dead man's, had he one, desolate, broken with his last struggle. "I am sorry. Forgive me." I kissed his hand, and pressed it to my brow. Then my heart took me.

They let me heap dust on my head, but held me from beating my brow on the ground or crawling into the fire. I railed and screamed, cursed the day I'd been born and my life for being so full of mistakes, and in between apologized for being such a sight, to which they'd answer, "Drink." When I paused, they got me going again by asking me to tell about the dead, or how I would break it to my family. With the wholeness that drunkenness can sometimes lend to thought, I thought it out: I'd killed my whole escort, two of my sibs, my best friend, by letting myself be done as easily as a baby; I'd be remembered as the worst fool in Yeoli history as long as it was read; from my journey of peace I'd bring home the news that war was certain; if they were wise they'd impeach me, and, my obligations done, I would leap off a cliff; nothing else was conceivable. From my pouch I drew again Kurkas's certificate of safe-conduct, sealed and ribbanded and device-written, and saw the gold glitter in firelight, and thought even as I poured out my soul; this must all be a bad dream, none of it can be real.

The secret darknesses of the heart I was showing got deep enough for Mirko to send away all but Vaneesh, and swear silence without my asking it. I remember trying to tear off the signet, crying, "Don't believe I am a man, it's all sham, all fake, I've been lying since I was twelve; I'm a child, nothing but a child, weak and stupid and throwing tantrums, I'll always be a child till I die!" So it went until I was exhausted; then they made me drink a full pitcher of water to stave off hangover, helped me up into a tree and put me to bed.

When I woke it was still dark; I almost reached over to where Mana should be lying near me, then remembered. Tears came too fast and hard to stop. Then a warm finger touched my shoulder, and Vaneesh's voice said my name, close by my ear. She slipped her arms around me, skilled in gentleness, and drew my head onto her shoulder and its hearth-heat. I buried my face in her neck. "The Goddess has three forms," she whispered, "all of which I can be, when they are needed. You need the Mother; perhaps the Lover, too." It came to me then she was naked.

I untangled myself from her, and turned away, though I hadn't touched a woman for months, and my body cried out. "You feel stained with death, so you shrink from life," she said, stroking my side under the woollen blanket with a touch as tender as breath. "But the only answer to death is life. You will die too, in your time; life spares no one. But now you live, whatever you deserve, and that is immaterial. There is more to do, your people still need you; who are you, to judge yourself?

"Your body knows that, and is wiser than you right now, so I speak to you through it; let it lead. They died to save you: tell me, do you think they'd have you suffer your life now, or celebrate it? Grieve and celebrate and live, Chevenga." For a time she caressed me as I lay face down weeping, and in time, though it felt to some part of me like surrendering up what shred of decency I had left in me, I gave myself to her hands. Though we'd been strangers yesterday, it felt as if she loved me with all her soul and always had. It cleaned me of my self-hate, and let me see clear. She was right: life was greater than this, I was still needed; in the face of it I saw my emotion dashed down for all it was, emotion, felt the ecstasy of life and the breath of the God-In-Me. That, I saw, was her mastery, the face of the God-In-Her; no wonder her people so cherished her, and the Arkans so feared her. I wept again, but with grief pure of recrimination, and then came to myself enough to hear sense. Jinai had told me the end good would cost some suffering, and I had chosen to accept that; my guard had volunteered knowing they risked dying, for Yeola-e or for me.

My troubles were nothing, anyway, to hers. The priestesshood was in her family, passed down through the female line; at eight she'd seen the secret temple where she'd lived burned down by Arkans, and her mother raped and killed before her eyes. Yet she'd felt the vocation all the more strongly, and now lived entirely underground. She'd conceived five times; two had been stillborn, one had died of a wasting sickness, one had been caught by Arkans and taken away in chains to no one knew where, and the last was a boy, who she was training as a priest in case she never bore a girl. Yet still, she had such strength.

We spoke until exhaustion took us. When I woke next it was late in the day; they'd let me sleep as long as I needed, though she was gone. I washed, ate and turned myself out as well as I could, and found Mirko waiting.

To his mind, I was better off traveling home with just two people who knew the way rather than a large guard, which would be slower, more easily noticed, and most likely outnumbered anyway if we ran into Arkans. He'd picked them already, ones who did not know my name. I agreed, and thanked him. Clasping his hand farewell, I asked forgiveness again for my behavior. He brushed it off, saying, "Nothing happened last night." We wished each other luck, and said, "I hope to see you again, in better circumstances." For him, I understood, that meant as king of Roskat. I could not credit that he had no rivals; but it was not my business to ask now. I embraced Vaneesh, and was on my way.

It is perhaps best that such prophecies are unclear; that it is concealed from the asker how much he must suffer to attain the good. Else he might never brave it; he is only human, after all. I was blessed, thinking I had only to grieve, and face my people.

On the second night, Nikroda, one of my guides, woke me, crying "Ishulta!"; the name of the other. "It was his watch; where is he?" We lit torches, but there was no sign save broken underbrush a little away from the fire. "He must have gone to piss too cursed far away," Nikroda said, "and an animal got him."

"So quietly?" I said. "I sleep light, and I heard nothing. He should have called to us."

"The leopards that live here know how to snap a man's neck silently," he said, "so his fellows don't kill them." In the morning we found blood, and followed the trail, but it went back the way we'd come, and we'd likely find only a corpse. Nikroda knelt to do some Roskati ritual; then we went on.

Suddenly he cursed, and broke into a run. "I heard a dog bark," he hissed through his teeth. "We must get to the stream." Not knowing what else to do, I dashed after him. We came to a long downslope, which appeared to fall off at the bottom, but since he didn't slacken his speed, neither did I. Suddenly, to my astonishment, he flung himself into the air; the hill fell away beneath my feet, steep and muddy. A rope hung in the clearing, like those which children set up beside lakes, to make swinging dives; he caught it, and swung away, while I hurtled down. I kept my feet, sliding, but could not stop; at the bottom where I thought I'd be safe the ground seized me, up to the waist; then to my horror I felt it drawing me down.

He swung back and alighted nimbly on the bank, looking at me with no surprise at all on his face, only reckoning. I'd been betrayed again. "A good place," he said. "We get Arkans to chase us here." I just said, "Nikroda, why?"

He sat down on the grassy slope, breathless; it had been a hard run. "I've figured out who you are," he said. "I know my history. My grandmother taught me. She saw all her family burned in their house, do you know that? When Fifth Inatanao could have saved Roskat, with a thousand more warriors. *She,* I understand, was your great-grandmother."

I felt my jaw drop, as with a will of its own. I knew my history, too. "She sent as many as she could—do you think we had no battles of our own? She was demarch; she had to think of her own people." Truths fell into place; he knew who I was, had heard the tales, and so was too cowardly to attack me; perhaps he even knew I had weapon-sense, else he'd have tried to slit my throat in my sleep. He had a studiousness about him.

"As are you," he said. "You'd sell Roskat to save Yeola-e. The people wills, isn't that the saying? At least now a Roskati will have got something from a Yeoli."

"You mean the reward the Arkans give you when you bring them my corpse." My only chance of life, it seemed, lay in changing his mind somehow, so I should beg, or promise him a greater reward, not insult him; but my heart, still laid open, ruled. "What always hides like a rat under the indignation of the traitor: greed. You'll have got something from another Roskati too; what's a fair price to your mind for killing Ishulta? A horse, a new barn, another strip of land?" No wonder I'd heard nothing. Probably he'd used a Roskati snap-rope, breaking Ishulta's neck; he had one.

"I hardly knew him," he said, shrugging, as if that excused anything. The mud was up to my chest now; having been taught that very slow swimming was the way to last longest in quicksand, I did so, aiming for the nearest knoll of grass. He sprang up frowning, loosening his sword in its scabbard. My arms were mired; he'd stick me like a trussed pig. I stayed where I was, where he couldn't reach me, and felt the cold mud creep up over my shoulders. It smelled like swamp, with meat-rot as well; I remembered what he'd said of leading Arkans here.

"Arkans killed your grandmother's family," I said. "They threw the torches. Now you'd take their money, for my life."

He shrugged again. "They were enemies. You'd expect it of them. They're to be used; their gold's still gold. *You* claim to be friends." Yawning just to hurt me, he said, "I suppose I shall have to fetch them. They aren't following us; did you really think I heard a dog? I don't think Yeola-e will miss you, anyway, you've swallowed every hook, just like you did with Kurkas."

That stab went home, and I had no more words. Nor were my tears the path unconceived; he only laughed at them. I began truly thinking of my life as finished then, and resigning myself to that. All my training, striving, expectations, I thought, to make me this: a corpse to be sold to Arkans to fatten a Roskati traitor. I thought of my family, my parents, my new wife and husband; Fifth, and the one to come; my people, at war with Arko. The mud touched my chin; then my foot found something hard.

I did not want to know what it was; I could know whether it would hold my weight if I put all on it. But if I tried, I saw, found it good and stopped sinking, Nikroda would devise some way to make sure I was dead before he went, stoning me or heaping dirt on my head. The only course came to me: to go under bending my leg beneath me, hold my breath and pray he left before I smothered; then put my weight on the foothold, and pray it bore me.

So I called him a coward, a traitor and a few other things, seeing no harm either way in satisfying myself, and just before the mud flowed in over my face, took three great breaths and then the deepest lungful of air I could. I thrashed and heaved, to make it look good; it was not hard to do with sincerity, once my eyes were covered; quicksand becomes darkness then, pressing cold and heavy on the skin, seeming to search with wet fingers every fingerwidth of one's head and body for deadly entrance. I pity those who have suffered this without hope; but I knew it would be worse for me if my foothold failed, having harbored hope.

My Kiss of the Lake training stood me in good stead. Still, he stayed a cursed long time after I stopped moving; I was close to truly thrashing, which would have ruined everything, when I felt his sword in its hip-scabbard turn and go. It took all my will not to spring upwards, but straighten my leg slowly. The die was merciful; the thing stood firm.

I wiped my lips and gasped for air, then wiped my eyes. A double arms length of quicksand still lay on every side of me; so I struck out for the grass again, with a slug-slow breaststroke, not knowing what else to do. I sank again, but my hand found a root, and I pulled myself out onto the bank that way.

For a time I lay with my heart racing, and tears washing the grime off my face again. Then I shook it off, and thought. If I went eastward, steering by the sun and the streams, which I knew ran north-northeast here, into the Ereala, I would come to Yeola-e. The Arkans, once they raked the pit and found no dead Chevenga (let them find their friends instead, and Nikroda get what he deserved), would track me with horses and dogs, like a runaway slave; so I should make it as difficult as I could for them. Where the forest was thick enough to travel through the branches like a tree-ape, I did, and used the stream trick at every opportunity. I ate lightly from my pack and from berry bushes, expecting to take longer than I would have with guides. It was utter wilderness, reminding me at every moment I had no real clue where I was. Best that no people saw me, though, in Arkan territory; for all the dirt and ashes on me from living like an animal, I was still dressed like a demarch on a state visit, in silk satin and ivory filigree, demarchic signet and the collar with the steel circles. Being alone I could not escape my own thoughts, but also had no one to impress; so when a memory of Mana or Naiga came and grief stabbed, I just wept as I walked. As well, I composed what I would say to my people.

The next day I came to a cluster of villages, and went around, staying well away. The people weren't Roskati: they seemed primitives, wearing skins, their houses of bark. Soon after that I came to a stream whose bottom was covered with strands of some kind of white water vine and whose water looked clear and good. I knelt for a drink.

The plants that grow in that stream, I have never seen anywhere else, in any country or climate, and no scholar knowing botany I have asked has ever heard of them. I think they were the spawn of some Fire-altered seed, or the work of some mad clan of plant breeders, long dead, one would hope. I drew up the first double handful of water, and drank; then when I dipped my hands again, I felt them seized as if by living wooden cords. The vines had tripped somehow, like the leaves of fly-catching plant, and bound my fingers and wrists fast in the water.

I tried to tear free with speed first, too late, then main strength; the roots were well-grown into the rocks, and clung with a grip like steel. I thought of biting myself loose; but then my head and neck would be seized, and I'd be strangled and drowned in a moment. This plant's usual way of nourishing itself came to me then; any animal that drank here would be killed so. Yet I wondered why I saw no bones. There was no way of reaching a knife, or Chirel; kicking at the vines would get my ankles caught. I ran back over my luck. Betrayed by Arkans, saved by Roskati, betrayed by Roskati, saved by some dead Arkan's skull, only to die of thirst with my hands in clear fresh water, killed and eaten by a cursed plant; I almost wept, and almost laughed.

Then it occurred to me I could call for help. These people might just as well immolate me for some god as set me free, but better that risk than certain death here. So I called.

They came. The moment they saw me, they started a high wordless ululation, that in a moment was echoing from other throats all around in the forest. A crowd ringed me. No one moved to aid me; but they might be waiting for someone more qualified. Trying to raise my voice over their tuneless song I cried, "Do you speak Enchian? Yeoli? Lakan? Arkan?" None answered; and though their faces all gazed at me full of seriousness, the note, I noticed, had more of a festive tone than one of alarm. It was hard to tell; they did not seem even to have expressions I could recognize.

I knew the die had rolled bad when two young men uncoiled ropes; yet my heart went numb. They came from behind, took me in a stranglehold, and persuaded the plants to release me by dropping thick fresh chunks of meat all around my hands; the tendrils seemed more drawn by bleeding flesh than unskinned. Well-rewarded the weed was, perhaps as well as Nikroda would have been, in its way—fed a whole pig's carcass—for capturing me.

I hadn't thought people so backward existed. They plundered me of my pouch, all the cloth on me and my boots, but left everything else including Chirel, seeming to have no use for metal. They couldn't make out what my father's ivory comb was, I could tell by their motions, and gave it back to me out of fear, I think, sliding it through a loop on my scabbard. I knew, of course, what it meant to have my body felt over by quick rough hands, my privates measured, my mouth forced open and my teeth peered at. A slave again, I thought, and felt all those bitter thoughts I'd had in Laka run through my mind again.

Four young men led me back west, through land sickeningly familiar. They kept me bound hand and foot and never for a moment let go my arms, knowing me for a fighter. They took me to an Arkan military outpost we'd passed through; so they did deal with the outside, after all, which must be keeping them in ignorance of the worth of metal. I wasn't about to enlighten them. I went on the auction block; that alone I took to mean no one recognized me, else I'd have been taken through some official channel. Buyers fingered the signet, and my brand-scar, which was still new enough to be pink; but none made anything of them, knowing nothing of Yeola-e. Still the bidding over me, and Chirel, was furious; it seemed we were a package. I thought they might want me as captive warrior in some campaign, in which I saw good prospects of escape. That will show you how innocent I was of Arko.

I was bought by a man who used only the name Daisas. The Arkan way of breaking new slaves is very different from the Lakan. He hacked off my hair, which I'd been expecting; then, right there, uncaring who saw, he flung me down, and while his apprentice pinned my neck with his foot so my face was in the dust, he did me as the Lakan raider had done Rigratora-e. That was how it looked, I recall thinking; so this is how it feels. He was like an animal in rut, panting and grunting, taking delight in my pain. Nor did anyone around seem taken aback; those who watched did absently, by which I understood it was customary. It was harder to bear silently than a flogging; the physical pain is less, but the shock stabs to the heart. "Get used to it," Daisas said, in rough-cut Enchian. "You are a slave of Arko now, and always will be, for you were born to be as are all barbarians. To serve Arko will be your life, for all else is death."

He had a mule and just the one apprentice, a sullen-faced boy of fourteen or fifteen, so on the journey I thought of escape; but he'd judged me a fighter too. He bound my arms using a pole behind my back, and put me in an Arkan slave-collar, one of those with the screws that can be tightened against the windpipe, the throat-arteries, and the nerves on the side of the neck, whichever the slaver chooses. He never whipped me when I fought him, just tightened the collar until I was choking or dazed or my skull screaming with pain, a punishment almost worse, for it brings home one's helplessness so hard. I tried feigning stunned as we marched to get him to loosen it, or exhausted, stumbling and going glassy-eyed and so forth; but he had seen all that a thousand times.

At night he "consummated the bond," as Arkans call it,

often. They have particular ways of breaking Yeolis; what they do with one's crystal doesn't bear writing down. He ground my face in the dirt, made me eat it and breathe it. Sometimes he forced me to climax, at the same time as some torment; I had not known this could be done, and the first time was a shock beyond description. There is a word, *fikken*, that only the Arkan language has, that I could not have conceived before I went there; it means both love-making and its rotten shadow, rape, as well as to harm in an unspecific sense; both pain and pleasure. Though I was yet to learn the word, Daisas taught me the meaning: pleasure for one, pain for the other. Arkans are right, to consider it obscene. Once the boy thanked me, for being here; "it keeps him off me," he said.

All through this, I still wore the demarchic signet. When Daisas asked me what it was, I said the sigil of my family, so that when he took a mind to make use of it in breaking me, he wounded me worse than he knew. He pulled it from my finger and slid it onto his own, then held it before my face as he used me, and said, "This is yours, so now it's mine, because you are mine. And one day all Yeola-e will be ours, to serve Arko, and I'll sell off all your family, yes, your little child and your granny too."

Afterwards, when he'd put it back on my finger, I knelt in the firelight, thinking. I was long past tears; my eyes were deserts these days. He was right; on my finger, it was still not mine. It was Yeola-e's; on my finger, it could only be defiled. The best thing to do came to me.

I remembered Saint Mother's words, about the sacred sword: "This is nothing but a piece of steel, without a living hand to wield it." The meaning of the demarchic signet didn't reside in it, but in Yeola-e, in Assembly, in the vote, in thought and choice; in me, while I had been demarch. Here, now, I was not; I had left that life behind, at least for a time. By that night, I had learned I was being taken to the City Itself; it seemed I would visit after all. There, where people might know it, the signet would be nothing but a liability.

Even so, it took a long time of meditating to force myself. Part of my heart at least felt I was throwing myself and all my hopes away too. It was hard to get enough leverage with my hands bound; all the force had to come out of my wrist. Somewhere in the forested hills of north-

ern Aijia, as Arkans call the province, there is a shallow
marshy pond, at the bottom of which lies the demarchic
signet of Yeola-e, carved five hundred years ago. Daisas
punished me, though not severely, when he noticed it was
gone. I had thrown away a piece of his property, but one
of little value.

II

So I came into Arko, still wearing the peace-sigil as I should, but chains and collar too, with slavers instead of an honor guard. Daisas put a shirt on me, out of courtesy to Arko, I think, and though I thought he would want to have me most in hand now, loosened the collar completely, so that I remember well my first sight of the city.

It was set in a great depression in the earth, bounded all around by granite cliffs eighty man-lengths high, the far ones distant enough to fade cream-grey in the heat-haze. It was as if I saw all the cities I had ever seen all added into one: the whole pit but the blue lake and a ring of green woods was filled with a carpet of white buildings, bulging high in the center like tall trees in the heart of a forest, reaching higher than I had thought buildings could.

Much Arkan commerce goes not by the gate but by the *lefaeti*, the lifts, of which there are twenty. All ado that surrounds them aside, each of the ten old ones is simply a fenced platform hung from a great cable, by which it is raised and lowered from the cliff-edge to the pit-floor. The modern ones each have two platforms balancing, one up and the other down; as this makes the work twice as fast and much easier, the inventor was raised from *fessas*, the third of the five Arkan castes, to *Aitzas*, the highest.

As we were lowered, it was all I could do not to gape at

the cliff-face. The living stone, the bone of the Earthsphere itself, was dressed to as shining a finish as a temple keystone, from not far shy of the top to the bottom; I saw my chained and collared reflection, and as we went lower, that of the sky and clouds, as in a mirror wide as a mountain. Daisas laughed as he saw me gazing, and said, "Your first look at civilization."

Through streets that seemed endless he led me. Though I did not know it at the time, it was the *fessas* quarter. As the *Aitzas* in my escort had worn their hair waist-long and the *solas* heart-long, every man here had his cropped just above his shoulder. They all wore gloves; hands are private parts in Arko, I learned then.

I would lie, to say there was no beauty. Arko's climate being hot and still, the houses were built airy, yet a good half of the windows had flawless glass. Arkans love art, and though in the poorer districts it was often in disrepair, at every corner was a mosaic or marble statue of some scene or person, full of luxuriant curves in the Arkan style. Street artists and musicians were everywhere, dashing out charcoal-on-paper portraits or crooning to the strains of a lute for copper chains—Arkan currency is all chains—nimbly thrown around their necks between strokes or chords. One artist tried to persuade Daisas to let him sketch me.

Arkans are also in love, so much as to dazzle away one's usual standard of excess, with gold. Everywhere I saw their elegant and simple script, even on house-signs, it was engraved and gilded; I began to think there must be a law. Temples were easy to tell; even the small ones, besides being built with all their angles pointing skyward, bore a great disc of gold over the door. I saw sun flash from a tower on the distant white parapet that stood like teeth beneath the far cliff; the roof was gold-leafed. The Marble Palace, I guessed. I had heard they'd carven the eagle in big on the cliff over it; that was no readiness for seeing it though, now we were close enough for it to be clear, each wing wider than three houses on top of each other, and long as an archery range.

As in Laka, women were few to be seen in the streets, Arkans considering the house their only business. But pairs of men walking close together were common. I remembered the Arkan custom. If a man and a boy of ten walk holding hands in Arko, they are as likely lovers as father and son; if the boy is better dressed, the man is his chaperone. I should add, though, that one should not take "lovers" as meaning "equals." To the Arkan mind, every bond has, and should have, one superior and one inferior.

I drew stares from the beginning. Being in the capital of an empire that had conquered so many races, I was surprised to see nothing but blond hair and blue eyes; perhaps there was a law about that too, to which I was for some reason an exception. Yet passersby, rich and poor, felt my arms, fingered Chirel with their gloved hands, and spoke with Daisas, eyes on me. Being in chains, I was anybody's meat—sometimes the touch was a grope, which Daisas would slap off possessively—but it was as if all Arko could buy me. Of course I could get no clues from their words.

A huge round building five stories high and wide as a palace loomed; soon I saw he was taking me there. It went far beyond what I now knew as the Arkan standard for garishness, even; I would have thought it could only exist in a story. The outer walls were ringed with niches, each of which held a statue of a warrior in stance or a grave, sitting king; all else was covered every finger-width with low-reliefs: animals, hunters, warriors, winged creatures frozen in furious motion, swirling plants and stars and running patterns, all painted with merciless flamboyance, their brilliant colors only slightly muted by the patina of age.

I suddenly knew where I had seen such extravagant whimsy before: the Sinere Circus. Its carts and props were painted so. But that had been just paint; here was gold-leaf, jewels, towering marble columns that proclaimed grandeur, as if to say, "Here in Arko, we need not spare expense even on our frivolity." It made me feel drunk.

Daisas took me in through the gate, which was inlaid with ruby-eyed dragons. The lintel was emblazoned with a sigil of a sword and chain entwined as well as Arkan words, in gold of course, which I would have given my hair to read, right then. The guards did not seem surprised by my looks. Inside was less ornate, as with the circus, but still quality. He led me a little way along a colonnade; beyond the red and gold-painted columns was a practice yard, where some twenty warriors of all races exercised. The walls made their number seem greater, being carven and painted all around with men just like them, as if to celebrate the tradition of the school. Yet they were watched, by men scribbling with Arkan pens on paper—they have paper to burn, in Arko—as no students are watched. One of these glanced at me, and though he looked seedy his once-over was so expert I felt stripped. But he was measuring me as a fighter.

Finally it all came to me: what this place was, why I'd been fingered in the street, why I had been bought together with Chirel.

As a boy in the School of the Sword I had heard mention—several times, before I'd believed it—of how warriors fought to the death for crowds to watch in Arko. Once we knew it was not a fanciful tale to tickle our morbidity, we'd spat on the thought, taking it as yet another evidence of the Empire's depravity. Yet inwardly, we'd been darkly intrigued, as the naive are with, say, human sacrifice, or children with ghost stories. In the end the Mezem went too far beyond all the bounds natural for us to truly believe in it at heart, leaving us helplessly fascinated, just as its decor went so far beyond excess as to overwhelm one's sense of proportion, so one could not judge it by one's own measure. If you wonder why it took so long to dawn on me: it had been too inconceivable to enter my head.

Daisas barked, and yanked my rope; I had not known I'd stopped short. The implications showing themselves slowly brought a creeping sickness. I who had been demarch, trained in the School of the Sword to save my people, would be made Arko's pit bull, my life given to the amusement of a crowd, my skill turned to taking other lives for it. If there is any time in my life I felt the full weight of slavery, this was it. In my conception of what misfortune treachery would bring me, I had been a child.

Then I thought, one can be made to work, with the stick or the lash; but who will put Chirel in my hand, and try whipping me? No one can force another to fight.

Daisas led me through a door into a tall bare room with a gallery, from which three ancient Arkan men peered at me. On all three noses perched two discs of glass attached by wire, this to magnify the world for their failing eyes. I had never seen spectacles before. Daisas addressed them with a marketplace smile, no doubt boasting my virtues,

while his apprentice attached one of my leg-cuffs to the
chain—iron, no less—fixed to a ring in the floor, and
unslung Chirel from my shoulder. Two men with the
manner of horse-grooms unbound my arms, leaping back
as from a stallion; then one took up two wooden swords,
threw me one and came to me in stance with the other.
This was the slave-block for gladiators; the goods must be
properly tried, to settle a price. That was why Daisas had
loosed the collar; the more awake I was, the better account I'd give of myself, and the more I'd be worth.

My arms were stiff as bones, which the man seemed to
expect. I shook them out and flexed them, then threw the
wooden sword into the dust, and said to the elders in
Enchian, "I will not fight, for a crowd." The tester didn't
seem too fazed by this; clearly I wasn't the first who had
refused. He mimed a thrust through my heart, which I let
him do; then fetched me a few blows on the ribs, hard
enough to hurt, in the hope of angering me. I stood still;
I'd had worse in training. The old men exchanged owlish
glances. They looked noble fools, awarded this sinecure
for favor, or incompetence in useful work.

He tossed me the wood again; as he came in poking, I
threw it down again. Daisas caught up his hawker's patter,
oversmooth; under his pasted-on smile was a scowl. At
every refusal, my price dropped. Then suddenly he went
silent, as if noticing some luminary had entered the room.
I heard a jingling and a giggle, the kind a child makes
pulling legs off spiders.

A plump boy of ten or so stood in the gallery. Not that
one should slight him, with such a plain word as "boy."
One could barely see his clothes for jewelry. Chains,
pearls, tiny figurines, gemstones of all hues and gold mail
shimmering at every fidget, coated him from head to foot.
Astalaz in audience would wear perhaps a quarter as much.

There was a strained silence, as he went from elder to
elder, patting their heads, tweaking their shoulders with,
to my surprise, bare hands, while they bowed with an
obsequiousness that seemed desperate. Everyone else had
gone to their knees, hissing something at me. It was a
certain pleasure, to find myself standing over all these
Arkans, so I pretended not to understand. I'd heard Kurkas
had a young son, the heir in fact; it seemed we were now
graced with his presence.

He plonked himself down with his little gold-clasped feet dangling over the edge of the gallery, his eyes fixed on me, intrigued, I think, that I didn't kneel; if one goes through life with everyone bowing and scraping, I imagine, someone who doesn't is novel. His features were plain enough, with a spoiled look, no surprise. As I stood trying to think how long my parents would have combed me for behavior a tenth as rude, he said in Enchian, "What is your name, barbarian?"

"My name I shall not tell one who calls me barbarian," I answered. I'd thought of this on the way, and decided to be a little difficult, then give an alias. In the corners of my eyes, the Arkans all seemed to cringe without moving. It struck me I might be acting recklessly; yet if I seemed to have nothing to lose, they'd think I did.

"Well!" he huffed, but without real anger; truly I was nothing more than a novelty for him. I saw he liked me for it. "It doesn't matter if you don't have one. I want to see you fight."

"As I have told these gentlemen," I said, "I will not, for you or anyone else to watch." The handlers were already moving when the boy said, "Make him!"

They tried harder this time, even hitting me between the legs once, just hard enough to bring agony without disabling. I did nothing but keep the blows off my head with my hands. Finally Daisas, fuming, came stamping and thrust the sword at me, shouting, "Fight, you *fikken* dirt-hair, you're a *shennen* warrior, anyone can see it, damn well fight!" I'd fought him plenty while he was making me eat dust on the journey. But he seemed to have forgotten I had something against him, unlike these others, and my hands were free. I grabbed him by the collar. He froze like a rabbit, his gaze trapped in mine. I held him just long enough to let it sink into his mind that he was dead, then hand-heeled him, the strike that drives the nasal bone up into the brain.

A pointless act, I suppose; but my heart wanted it, and I saw nothing to lose. The handlers yelled back and forth, wondering what to do, thinking to rescue him; I stood back from his corpse to let them take it. Meanwhile Kurkas's son was cheering, his wrapping of jewels flashing with his motion. "Bravo! Well done! Beautiful! Silence!" It came immediately.

"I hereby decree that this gladiator shall have a name," he announced, in both Arkan and Enchian; like me at that age he must have heard too much formal bureaucratic speech. "And therefore by these presents since he came alone and is so fast his name shall be *Karas Raikas*; and furthermore I declare my glorious self to be his first fan." With that he threw me something that flashed gold; catching it I saw it was a ring, that might barely fit on the tip of my fourth finger if I pushed hard. Then he skipped out.

So it was, the Mezem got me at a bargain. I found out later that Daisas had an heir, but he was underage and could do nothing, though by that one blow I had shown myself to be worth a small fortune. The testers, now knowing themselves lucky, stood out of my reach, and one said in bad Enchian, "Look, Yeoli, we're going to have to get the blow-darts with the stun stuff in them, and it can leave an awful headache when you wake up, so don't you think it would be less complicated if you just came peacefully?" They wouldn't come close until I lay facedown on the floor and clasped my hands behind my back.

Once they had me chained they took me further along the colonnade to an anteroom. They paused to talk to people nearby, so I got slightly ahead of them; then the air before me was a solid wall, shattering around my knee and head. I had never seen or conceived a door of clear plate glass before.

Someone laughed; someone else said "*fikket*." I felt a warm trickle on my head and back, then pain. Gloved hands held cloths to me. Then what I saw to my sides seemed to throw me into a dream, being impossible: I was one of a spear-straight rank, fading off into a dark green haze, of Fourth Chevengas, hair hacked, faces stunned and streaked with blood. The anteroom of the Gladiator's Quarters has on its walls what are known as the Legion Mirrors, reflecting each other and whatever is caught between them, infinitely. It is a constant amusement of the guards posted there, to see the mirrors' effect on hapless foreign primitives brought through. I didn't disappoint them. Suddenly the weight of the place fell on me as heavy as stone; the air went half-dark and the room with its smoky gold-leaf moulding and pillars and ranks of my staggering selves began to spin.

Hands steadied me, drew me into a room with a padded

table and shelves of healers' things. When I lay down my eyes cleared. The man who came was a middle-aged Arkan with *fessas*-length hair, the blond shot with grey and thin on top, the blue-grey eyes round and careworn. His hands were thick, but so tender, and his apology for taking off his gloves so caring, that I suddenly found myself near tears. I had all but forgotten touch that was not cruel.

He had me unchained, despite the protests of the handlers, and while he stitched the worst of my cuts, had two of his apprentices wash me from head to foot. It was odd to be worked over with such concern by a boy with his hair cropped and waxed to stand up like cat ears. But the style of the Mezem is all extremes. Nor did I care while I felt Daisas's touch cleaned off me.

The healer examined me all over, being as careful not to hurt me as if I were someone of import, and knowing without words where a new slave in Arko is injured. He was even civil enough to tell me his name, speaking in soft Enchian: Iskanzas Muras.

The room he led me to had bars on its windows. "You're counted a troublemaker, lad, because you killed your slaver," he told me. "But you'll be out of here once we've talked, and the bed's good. Lie down and rest, now. What's your name?"

"Karas Raikas," I answered. An alias forced on me, there was no reason not to use. He gave me a look as if he'd bit into a sour apple, and raised his brows in questioning. Denied their hands, Arkans are very expressive with their faces. "When I was tested," I said, "a child who I think must be Kurkas's son gave it to me."

"Ah, Minis," he said, when I described the boy. "Yes, you're right, he's the son of the Imperator, He Whose Arm is the Strength of the World. That's the proper style, you never call him by name, better learn that right away. With the boy, abase yourself, or don't let him notice you, and you'll generally come out all right." I told him what had passed, showing him the ring, and he looked worried; but clearly there was nothing he could do.

Next he explained the rules. They set one free after fifty victories; that he told me first. When I asked him how many made it, though, he went evasive. Fight days were once every eight days, five fights a day, always to the death, the matches made by lot. As for those who refused to fight, they were dealt with simply: tortured to death. At best, he told me gently, it takes three days.

Nor would it be immediately, but only when the next moral objector, as they called them, came, so my death could be shown him; it seemed some wretch already lay in chains waiting for me to witness his, unless one of us changed our minds. And though gladiators have the run of the city, he said, there was no way out; he explained how well the *lefaeti* and the Gate were guarded, and how smooth the walls were. Arkans don't call them cliffs, but walls, as if they built them. They have a habit of thinking they made the world; or at least they did then.

I took a risk. "Iska,"—I'd gathered he was called that— "have you heard any talk of war, between Arko and Yeola-e?"

After giving me a look of "why should you ask?" as if it weren't every Yeoli's business, he said, "Well, not until recently. I guess you'd know, your king, Fourth I forget his name, was coming on a state visit, worried about it, I guess. But they were attacked by rebels, and he got killed. Apparently he had a very good name as a warrior and a commander; now that he's out of the way, He Whose Arm is the Strength of the World is looking more closely. So goes the talk, anyway; and there's lots of tales in the Pages of Yeoli barbarities and so forth, always a good sign. Which might make you consider that your country needs one like you alive—Raikas, are you all right? What is it, dizziness, pain?"

I ceased seeing and hearing him, or the world. It was a sensation not unlike being struck almost to unconsciousness, the mind deadened, the senses faded to a sick twilight. *I misread the prophecy,* I was thinking. *It meant war would come if I went.*

My heart beating in my chest seemed an abomination, a cancer to be cut out; somewhere my hands could find, there must be a knife. Then I remembered, death had just been offered me, one whose pain might at least begin to touch what I deserved. I remember the sense of freedom in saying it, broken though my voice came. "I won't fight. I refuse."

He brought in someone else, a middle-aged Ungilian made all of whipcord with a wreath of gold chains around his neck, and eyes that looked as if they'd seen every war in the world and enjoyed half of them. Koree, he was, the fighters' Teacher. He had won fifty fights, which was why the chains, one per victory.

We argued. I can hardly remember: only that he held that it was no different than war, since I would be fighting for my own life, hence my kin, and my country; not the thing to say to me then. It all seemed far away and trivial. The motion I remember, as he had me bound and took me downstairs.

It is clever, the Mezem's compulsion, playing first on what is often in an objector's heart, his mercy for others. They bound me to a chair next to where the previous one, a Srian whose name was Sakilro, lay shackled—being a Srian he was almost too long for the table—and while the torturer readied his things, Koree said, "If either of you says he will fight, this will stop."

From his screamed words in bad Enchian, I learned only that Sakilro had recently sworn some high oath against bloodshed, and was certain of a worse fate after death if he broke it, something by my upbringing I should consider outlandish, which one might call fanaticism or atavism, as Koree did. But it was his will. On the first touch of the iron, seeing him flinch in his chains, I cried out, "No, wait!" It was my own death I wanted. Koree ordered a halt, and said, "Will you fight?" I sat trembling, thinking; if I said yes, Sakilro would be kept for the next objector; in the meantime he might change his mind, in which case I'd saved him, as Koree made sure to play on. But who knew how many others before me had watched him suffer this much, and broken, prolonging his end? I saw: only he could choose which way was right. "Sakilro," I cried, hoping at least I'd pronounced his name decently, "what would you have me do?" I thought they might try to stop him from answering, but they did not, thinking perhaps his pain might make him answer what they wished. His dark lips curled back from his teeth, and he cried, "Refuse!"

So I did, to the end. It took three days. In the times he seemed to lose resolve, I would cry "Never!", and lend him mine; I knew he'd only be heartbroken when he came to himself afterwards if he gave in. Let him die, I was thinking, with one person near who understands. I knew nothing of him or Srians, and could not even touch his hand; but he was my only friend in the world for four days, and I his; better to die than fail him. Some believe whatever a person holds the afterlife to be, it will be for him; never have I hoped more that this were true. I only saw his ebon-black face as it should look, smooth and unriven with pain, when he was dead.

The night of the day Sakilro died, I sent Iska's apprentice out of my cell, knelt on the bed and meditated. In calm, I saw I'd chosen too quickly; it was emotion making me think I'd misread Jinai's prophecy, not reason; there was no clear proof. My people might need me yet; I could not know. So I must stay alive. I would look for ways out, I decided, and fight if I found none.

So I told them I would. Iska asked no questions, but brought in a youth of fifteen years or so, with the kind of fine smooth face prized in Arko; I'd seen it on statues and mosaics on the way here. His lips were darkened with paint, his eye-lids shaded faint purple-blue; the edges of the two sweeping wings of his white-blond forelocks were black as my own, dyed. He was dressed better than the healer, all in black satin, the earrings and bracelets gold. On first glance he seemed to hate me, as if I had done him some injury; I wondered if he had known Sakilro, and thought me his murderer. Iska introduced him to me as my boy, meaning valet, companion, guide in the city, paramedic and only friend all at once; my servant even though I was a slave. His name was Skorsas Trinisas.

He took me from the cell into a room in the fighters' corridor proper. I saw them as we passed the lounge: men of all races, in all manner of circus dress, green hair, nose-rings, painted eyes, satin robes in every brilliant color. All wore their victory-chains showing; those with the most, I noticed, also had jewelry, mostly metal, of course. It seemed these slaves could own property. They were mostly taller than me, and larger-muscled; clearly the Mezem usually picked for that. I felt myself stripped naked again, as they all measured me; but this was for good reason, so I forgave it.

Suddenly Jinai Oru's voice came to me, from a blank-walled chamber in Tenningao, five years ago. "A death-duel against a man with black skin and blue hair, with a yelling crowd all around you, whose edge goes up to the sky." In the light of foreknowledge, I thought, all considerations, plans, worries, choices, are dust-specks in a sun-beam. This was already my destiny, *then*.

The room had a plain bed, a night-cabinet, an empty wardrobe and little else. The walls, which were of stone, were scrawled all over with scratch-marks. Looking closer I saw each was a name or a sigil, and a tally; the gladiators' records, of how long they had lasted. Up high was a very long line of marks, framed, some great one's. This must be all they leave, I thought.

All morning I spent learning Arkan from Skorsas. The greenhands, as new fighters are called, exercised in the afternoon, after the midday meal. Once I'd consented, I could eat with the others, and found that gladiators are fed well, and get as much as they want. Of course Lakans fatten cattle, too, before sacrificing them. It would be two weeks training at least before my first fight; that would be against one of the other greenhands, and in the training-ground instead of the Ring; only then does one enter the stable proper, as it is called.

So in the frescoed ground were about twenty of us, all eyeing each other wondering which one we'd have to kill. Koree ran us through exercises to tear out one's heart, then sword-work with wooden swords. Then he had us all get our true steel—since no weapons are allowed in the Gladiators' Quarters, they are held in a room known as the Weapons Trust—and came out brandishing his own. I should have known, he would call me out first.

As Sakilro had been killed, it was Koree I had thrown all my rage at, not caring what could be taken as insult. It had got under his skin, for he'd had me gagged, and railed at me in his bad Enchian that he did not choose this but was required by law, he only did this work in the hope of getting others through alive as he had been lucky enough to do, and did I think he enjoyed it? In my times of sense I had believed him, and understood; as Sakilro held to his truth, so did he.

I'd never told him that, though; he knew only my bile. Now as we faced each other, unsheathing swords, I wondered whether he meant to humiliate or hurt me, valuable a chattel as I might be. He didn't look easy to beat; though he couldn't be less than forty-five, he was spry as a youth, had skill like an old Teacher's, and being here would know tricks I couldn't conceive. There was no ritual to show we were on our honor; he just said, "Right, boy, come on."

As I had expected, I had over him only the blessings of

the young, strength and speed, and the advantage I can almost always count mine, weapon-sense: all of which finer skill can defeat. But it turned out he wasn't out for revenge, just to test me. Learning that, I didn't much want to win; it seemed callous to show ability to the other greenhands, into whose hearts it would strike fear.

Half-action, it was, that no master would fail to notice. He called a halt, stepping back. Now he looked angry. "You said you decided," he said. "You *fikken* lie, make me a liar if I beat you. Well, you're worth nothing if this is not real to you, so be it. From now on, boy, my sword goes in, it goes *in*, you're buzzard-shit, right here and now. I've had it with you."

No one had told me he was not permitted to kill me; I was indeed worthless, here, if I wouldn't fight. It was no bluff; the blows came too hard for him to pull if I missed a parry. If I tried nothing, it would only be a matter of time. As in the Ring; he was teaching me.

So I looked for openings. In time I found one. We froze with his sword far off-line, and mine at his throat; whatever he could do to me, I knew well I ought not to kill him. He smiled; on his skin-and-bone face it was like a skull's rictus. "Good! Very good!" I sheathed Chirel and turned to take my place in the line, which was silent as a funeral ground.

"Ay!" I found myself whirling like a foot-soldier at a decurion's bark; Koree certainly had the gift of command. "Did I dismiss you?" His sword was still out, his eyes still alight with sparring-fire. "*Again*. Get back here. Or do I have to come and get you?" The line around me stepped away out of his reach as he approached. I drew Chirel; it was that or run.

He'd seen Yeoli Unsword before, no doubt; but he could not know it as well as I. A hilt wouldn't tear easily out of those rawhide fingers; I used everything I knew, waiting for the perfect angle, listening for the dead moment between his breaths. It worked; his sword landed in the dust with a pleasing thump.

He swore, and cackled wickedly; I turned away to the line again. By weapon-sense, I knew when he snatched his blade up; but thinking I needed warning anyway, he made a war cry to stop the blood in the veins as he charged. I turned and did the wrist-parry, turning his crosscut high with my shield-arm wristlet, and pricked him over the heart.

He stepped back, with a look that made me feel like a boy again, thrilling to see it on my Teacher's face. Then he gave a whoop, and tossed his sword straight up into the air, laughing like a child. Before I knew he had grabbed two handfuls of my hair on either side of my face and was knocking his head against mine, half roaring, half laughing; I didn't think to resist. "You idiot! You killer mountain boy idiot! How could you *think* of refusing? How could you even *think* of it? Most of the men here would sell their mothers for your talent, and you, you little curly-haired son of a bitch, you could *fikken* make it out of here! You could *fikken* make it, you jackass, you could *fikken* make it, you piece of shit, you could *fikken* make it, you mouse-brained, snot-nosed, dog-raping . . ."

Over his shoulder I saw the faces of the greenhands. All down the line were eyes from which the veil of hope had been torn away, to show their true fate: Shininao, waiting only a few steps more down the path. But it was me they looked at.

I tore out of Koree's grip, and away. In the colonnade a clutch of men accosted me, yelling questions in a jabber of Enchian and Arkan. I broke through, uncaring who I bruised, with Skorsas trailing, chattering. In the baths—Arkans like to wash in a rain of water flowing from a high cistern—there was cool water, to wash the burning out of my eyes and my guts.

The moment I had on the black satin robe Skorsas gave me, he tried to pull me out to the doors, exhorting in Arkan. "He's trying to say the writers want to speak to you," Iska said, as we came to his desk. "Do you understand, we have a machine here in Arko, that writes? Every week, all the news is written on paper, many times over, for the citizens of Arko to read. They want to write about you. For all the people to read, lad, do you follow me? If you want them to write anything slightly resembling the truth, it's best to speak to them."

I spun on my heel, Skorsas shrilling all the way. I was none of their business, and had no care what was said of me; Arkans were not my people, for all they thought I should take their leers as honor. Now the fighters with many chains, who'd ignored me before, looked measuring.

This room, I'd been told, was mine; so I slammed the door
and shot the bolt.

That night I could not sleep. Pacing, I heard through
the door to the adjoining room, which was Skorsas's, a
muffled moan.

He'd been teaching me the colors in Arkan today, and
when we'd come to black, I'd asked him, as best I could
with my few words of Arkan and gestures, which he was
worldly enough to tolerate, why the black in his hair. He
seemed somewhat offended at the question, but as he
seemed offended sometimes even by the sight of me, I
took no notice. It turned out he had been in love with his
fighter before me, who had won eleven fights; dyeing the
hair black is an Arkan mourning custom. The man, whose
name was Tondias, had only been dead a few days, it
turned out; no wonder the boy was not at his best.

Now I heard half-smothered sobbing. I thought of how
young he was; my lost loves of that age had broken my
heart just leaving me, not being run through in front of my
eyes as well as a slavering crowd's, and I'd had comfort.
No one consoled him.

I tapped on his door, and when he did not answer,
tiptoed in. Hot though it was, he had his pillow wrapped
around his head as if he wanted no one to hear, though I
could conceive of no reason he could be ashamed of grieving. The tiny cot shook with it. Not knowing words, I laid
my hand on his shoulder. After a time, his weeping cut off
and he went stock-still. Slowly his face peeked out, his
eyes white all around the blue. To my shock, the black
locks were shorn off.

When the sight of me sank in, he shrieked, clenched his
eyes shut and flipped off onto the floor on the other side of
the cot, clutching the covers around himself. What Arkan
curses he flung at me, keeping his eyes clenched, I cannot
know; I kept hearing the words *fikken* and *shennen*, though.
Finally he made a gesture, a violent thrust away. At last it
got into my thick head: I was stark naked, in front of one
whose people cover even their hands.

He'd promised we'd shop for clothes tomorrow, and in
the meantime hung several other robes in my wardrobe,
which smelled as if it had been filled with rich scented
clothes before; this had been Tondias's room as well, I

saw. As I threw one of them on, I wondered if he'd worn it; it was too long for me, trailing on the floor. No wonder Skorsas doesn't like me, I thought; as my stepfather was at first for me, I am an intruder a thousand ways, and not knowing it, have likely been callous a thousand ways. How do I comfort him?

You might wonder why I wanted so to make peace with an Arkan I'd barely met whose manner had been coldly civil at best. I felt for his loss, and his aloneness in it. But as well, one must cultivate what one has. I was far more alone than he.

I belted the robe and folded my hands inside the sleeves. He was sitting up against the wall, wrapped thickly in bedclothes. It didn't help much; he looked at me as if at a murderer, and cringed away when I knelt beside him. Fine peace I'll make, I thought, without a common language or the use of my hands.

His eyes were more afraid than angry now, obsequious again, and I caught the Arkan words for "I'm sorry." It came to me that if caring for me was his trade, he might be in trouble if I complained, hence his fear. Too Yeoli not to sign, in the end, I brushed it off. He flinched, as if I might hit him.

I made him understand in the end with a smile; all people on the Earthsphere share that. He looked like a child spared the comb; but with that gone, the grief came again. Skorsas was what Arkan men call a beauty; I think I sensed even then that before coming here he had been a pleasure-boy. On those fine lips and white-blond brows, more truc now with the paint washed off for the night, emotion showed clear and keen as through Arkan glass.

I'd learned how to say "Why black?"; now I could say "Why not black?". It was for my sake, he made me understand. By Mezem custom, for a boy to wear mourning dye is very bad luck for his fighter. His time of grieving was finished, and from now on, he promised, he would devote himself solely to me.

He'd taught me the Arkan for no. Perhaps he'd never lost anyone close before, and did not know what a brutal thing the Mezem law asked of him; perhaps he was denying it to himself. As best I could, I told him if he'd truly loved Tondias his time of grieving wouldn't end for a good year, whatever the rules were, I knew it so he need not hide it, but I would keep it secret, and he need never forget Tondias for my sake. He stared at me for a long time; I swore on my crystal, hoping he knew or could tell that was sacred. He stared for a long time more; then his eyes brimmed, and he pulled the blanket-edges in over his face.

I spoke his name, and held out my arms when he looked. Better to let him come if he willed, like a shy colt. After a time he did, and wept out his heart like a child, sometimes clenching the satin of my robe, sometimes beating my chest with his fists, as I hugged him. In time he fell asleep on my neck, so I lifted him into bed and tucked the covers in around him. It made me think of Fifth; as quick as the thought, my own tears came, piercing.

But I was thinking of Tondias too, as I could not help. Arko does well for a gladiator's body, I thought, feeds it, clothes it, trains it, all well. But at death, he is cast off like a worn kilt, his name forgotten as if no one ever knew it, his presence vanished as if swallowed in bottomless quicksand; even those who loved him are required to forget him after a scant few days. No wonder fighters scratch marks on the walls, even the illiterate; for where else is Tondias? He lived here, for some four and a half moons, and this room must have been full of his possessions; but now his touch is cleaned away; all of it is mine, even the leftover clothes until I die. He gave his life for Arko's pleasure, and Arko effaced him; and so they mean to do with me.

III

The cliffs of Arko are polished smooth as a dead-still pool, and their bases, all around, are patrolled by guards, lest vandals mar the polish. To climb them was conceivable with pitons, as I had thought out at night, even if one had to drive every one of them into mirror-clean rockface with a hammer. Still, I had no way of getting any—a Yeoli captive entering a shop selling such things could hardly avoid suspicion—and, more fatal to the plan, it would be impossible to do silently.

The *lefaeti* were well-guarded, as Iska had said. They are worked from the top, and the guards there have a clear view of the bottom, so that if one were to commandeer one, it would not be raised. At night, they are kept raised, even the double ones, and no ropes left hanging. The other egress is the great corridor bored through the cliff, commanded by the Gate, which is some seven man-lengths high and four wide. At night it is bolted well, from the cliff-side; there are actually two gates, between which is a tunnel and a barracks carved out of rock, where the guards sleep. Every load that goes out by either way is inspected through and through, sometimes with spear-points; every person must show his bare face and papers. Little trouble, to forge or steal papers; but unless I found a way to turn my eyes blue, they would betray me.

All these things I learned, the days before my first fight.

I notice that writing of the Mezem I keep falling into the present tense, as if it were graven stone, unchanging, and I were sealed into it forever, as into a crypt. Anyone else who has been through it will understand. Whatever else one's life is, even the demarchy, the Mezem etches itself into the soul, and stays forever. To write of it carries one back, making the present tense seem proper, so I hope my lapses may be forgiven.

It is a life more vivid than life, yet seeming less real; being always near death one's eyes see everything hard and clear, yet one's mind is in constant disbelief. Since one never thinks ahead more than eight days, time slows, sometimes passing like syrup, and indeed loses its meaning, replaced by the number of one's victory chains. Other than those of the boys, who are as present and unobtrusive as air, the faces in the quarters are ghostlike for all they appear solid and alive. Most are soon gone, while those that stay are to be feared; the more chains hang around their necks, the deeper death seems worn into their features.

As for myself, I didn't even know the meaning of the name everyone called me; since every time an Arkan first heard it he gave a sour look or bit his lip as if swallowing laughter, I guessed I shouldn't want to. Skorsas took me shopping for clothes. He had money, it seemed, for we went to fine shops, with full-height mirrors. He had colors picked out for me already, and wanted of course to dress me in the style of the Mezem, garish beyond any decency or reason. "Why do I resist this?" I asked myself, gazing at my image, if that could be me, in a deep red puff-blouse with sheer lace in front down to the navel, showing my skin just enough to be enticing. "I am this." Right there I shouted, "Dress me as you wish, just don't drag me in front of any more mirrors!" Through enough gestures to make me sweat, I made him understand. He never did again, and had the one in my room taken down. So I became invisible, to myself.

I will write very little of my fights. They have been made too much into public shows already, by their very happening; I won't reveal those deaths to more eyes. One collection of scribblings regularly printed by the hundred on the great Arkan machine was the Watcher of the Ring, a collection of tales concerned entirely with each eight-day's fights and other current doings of the Mezem; in old ones, lingering on the shelves of libraries, may be found detailed accounts of all my fights, for those interested.

Of my first, I will say only that he wounded me. Because it did not seem real to me that in front of all these hawklike blue and grey eyes and Arkan pens scratching writing-boards, not on a battlefield, I could be death-fighting, I didn't truly feel I was, until I saw in the bottom of my sight my own blood streaming from my leg, and his blade, moist with it, coming in harder, encouraged. Then I killed him. In the clinic, while Iska stitched me—the cut was two fingerwidths deep—and Skorsas fed me some sweet drink full of painkiller, I fingered the one fine gold chain around my neck, and swore to remember the man's name, Firso Shalev of Brahvniki, all my life. No one else would.

My second fight took place in the Ring proper. I had seen it already, watching a day's fights from the fighter's box. The great bowl of stands is deep as a valley and holds fifty thousand Arkans, the nobles in the closest seats, of course, the poor massed against the blue of the sky. The ring is circular, some twenty paces across, and covered with sand the color of gold. It is bounded by a trench two and a half man-heights deep, in which, during fights, a pride of hungry lions wanders. The seats are fenced off from it but the ring-edge is not; step too far and the other man wins. Three bridges cross it: two at east and west for the two fighters' gates, one at north for the winner to receive his chain. My feet still know every rise and hollow; I could walk across with my eyes closed, and stop with my toe-tips touching the edge. I could do it in my sleep; I know, for I still have dreams.

At the south is the Imperator's box, with its sliding plate-glass doors bordered with the sigil of the Aan family, the golden sunburst. I hoped to see him in person, my oath-breaking betrayer, but he did not come that day.

I hardly remember the fight, except for the bright-haired crowd; somehow it is that I remember most vividly, of all things I saw in my stay.

The most eager come in the moment the gates are opened, a good bead before the first fight starts, dashing down the aisle steps to their places. The stands hawkers begin crying their wares, sweetmeats, sausage, nuts, wine,

Arkanherb, banners and kerchiefs with the names, colors and likenesses of favorite fighters, mourning dye for afterwards; the bet-carriers thread through the seats, obsequious among the *Aitzas* in their jewels and gleaming sheets of blond hair, rude among the ragged and shorn *okas*. As the stands fill, tiny flames flash everywhere as pipes are lit, and the air soon fills with the spice-sweet smell of herb smoke.

They sit silently through the various ceremonies, the boy choir's singing and the priests' litany, and cup their palms as one for the silent noon observance. Once that is done, it becomes a great party, with the whooping and whistling and blowing of horns. If a great favorite is listed, they will chant his name; if two rivals, their factions will try to out-shout each other.

The poor are loud and rough and comradely, though they sometimes break into their own fights, two bristle-haired men posturing, then flailing dark-gloved fists while everyone near eggs them on; that kind likes to come here. The rich, with their cushions and hand-cloths and lap-dogs, behave with more decorum, but yell the more cutting words down to the fighters, knowing they will be heard. Men and women alike come, even whole families, with children, and no one considers that out of the ordinary.

Once the herald has spoken the traditional words, "Step forth ye two, one to receive the chain of victory, one to receive the sword of death," fifty thousand pairs of eyes follow every twitch of blade or shift of foot; fifty thousand voices gasp with every feint, roar with every flurry, exhort, sneer, warn, laugh, shriek. There are the purists, who applaud the fine moves and yell advice as if they were Teachers, and the blood-bats, who in the way of that creature make themselves apparent on the first wounding, and love best the goriest death. One may see an *Aitzas* with a lace-decked pleasure-boy, soon to disappear under his master's robe when the main fight starts; quite openly the man will cry out in ecstasy at the killing or crippling blow. Yet when a favorite dies, they keen and pull and blacken their hair just as if they'd loved him (I had not yet heard of mourning dye that can be washed out). It's a disservice Arko did itself, I suppose, giving me that for a first impression of its people.

So I stood at my gate, with Skorsas at my shoulder chattering encouragement, and once more it seemed I should be able to slap myself, and wake up in my bed in the Hearthstone Dependent. Or at least walk away; that I could be forced after all, that my body would presently do what was so against all I knew, seemed impossible. Able neither to do nor flee, my limbs locked, as if joined with stone; I hardly heard the gong sound or saw Skorsas throw open my gate, and stood flat-footed, while he shrilled at me. The other, a Lakan by the name of Ixtak who also had one chain, came out in stance, stood for a moment, then seeing I wasn't moving, charged me; if he could trap me still in my gate, he'd get me easily. The crowd flapped its lips at me, the Arkan way of disapproving, for cowardice. I came out in the last moment, yet still it didn't seem real, this time more like an all-Yeola-e unsword tournament, with so great an audience; some other part of me thought absurdly, "I'm All-seeing Rao again!" I had to get wounded again, my sword-arm this time, the first blood of the day since ours was the opening fight. That drew a cheer, but so did my switching hands and being able to go on with the other; I didn't understand yet that it was two different factions, or perhaps two opposed sides of the same souls. In the rest break Skorsas smeared the cut with some stuff that stopped the pain as if it had never been, and bandaged my arm tightly with quick hands. He refused to let me see, in case that unspirited me, a Mezem tradition; then the gong sounded and Ixtak charged again. I killed him.

One goes through the north gate and climbs the stairs to the box of the Director to receive one's victory-chain. I never knew the Director by any name; all I knew of him was that everyone rolled their eyes in the Arkan way on mention of him, and that the Mezem is truly run by Iska, Koree and the chief chip-seller (the seats are bought and sold by means of graven wood-chips, each representing a particular seat). He seemed a witless *Aitzas* effete given this sinecure for some favor, like the men in the Hall of Trial, but thought grandly of himself. I bowed my head to take the chain from his fat hands, then turned. "Young barbarian," he said in Enchian, yet slowly as to an idiot, "what do you say to someone who has just given you something?" That as I stood dead-tired, wounded, having just finished fending off death by a hair, almost in tears for having given it to someone in the same place as I, and feeling the stink of blood-lust from all around sink into me. I answered the two words that Skorsas had taught me to say to those I wished to offend, and turned away, to gasps all around.

In the clinic as he stitched me, Iska said, "You can't keep doing this, having to get wounded to know where you are. It's not good for your health." My third fight, against a Srian three-chainer named Dinosti, I hesitated in my gate again, and like Ixtak he rushed me. At the last moment I went out, sidling along the edge of the trench, where the smell must be smelled to be believed. He slightly turned his charge, thinking to bowl me backwards into it; as he was almost on top of me I whirled aside, stretching out my leg. He went in headlong with an astonished cry, that soon turned to screams of pain, clear over the crowd-roar. So, I could tell myself the lions killed him, not I.

All the way into the baths, men with note-boards chased me, shooting questions like arrows. Some even knew Enchian. "Raikas, how'd you do that? Where'd you learn that move? Where were you trained? Aren't you glad now you changed your mind? Do you think you'll make fifty? Are you happy you won? What's your real name? What's *fikken* wrong with you that you won't give us a single *fikken* answer? We're your name in town, boy, however little you understand, so smarten up." Skorsas was thrilled, and treated me like a war-hero returned home. This was a month into my stay, so I understood enough Arkan for him to tell me I was the latest sensation. After I'd sparred Koree, it had been predicted I would be the next great champion; that had faded after my first two fights, but had started up again.

Iska asked me, "Do you read? Yes? Then you *should*." Both the Pages, which is Arko's main source of news and comes out every four days, and the Watcher, make an Enchian version. The Mezem traditionally gets one of each. Out of curiosity, I suppose, I pulled the last month's out of Iska's library.

I wavered between laughing and throwing up. In the first Watcher I found, "Luminary to be: Lightning Loner"; wanting to find out who they were touting, I read, until I came to "this mountain warrior, of ebon curls and smouldering eyes," who had beaten Koree three times in a row sparring. So that's what Karas Raikas meant. It was a name a child spoiled into believing he was clever would give; no wonder people bit their lips. Forever after, I always thought of it, when I did, in the Arkan; it retains a certain grace that way, left over from the time I'd not known its meaning.

I was a fascinating creature, I read: mysterious about my true name, holding out stubbornly in my refusal until the victim I watched was dead, then changing my mind like the wind, and shaming Koree in the next breath. They spun off all sorts of tales about Yeoli mysticism and how ancient mountain masters could blow down walls with a sharp breath, kill with the touch of a finger and parry swords with bare hands. After my second came a debate on whether I was a coward or not; some scribbler seriously argued that I'd faked it all, even the wounds, to conceal my true ability. All agreed that my skill had depths unplumbed. It was then I resolved to do the quickest and least necessary in every fight.

I carved my tally on the wall, after all: the initial "Che," and in irony, I suppose, the sign of peace. As I was doing the second tick, Koree came to my door. "You're due twenty lashes, by order of the Director," he said.

Knowing I'd done nothing wrong but what they'd forced me, I resisted, breaking off the straw from a broom to make it into a staff, while Skorsas begged me not to. Presently Koree and four guards came down the corridor with sticks of several lengths. I held them off easily enough at the door, though it was tricky, with them wearing full armor. Then Koree sent two men around through Skorsas's room, and I had to retreat atop my bed, while Skorsas cursed me from his hiding-place in the wardrobe for griming the sheets. Koree was one who fought with a grin on his face like an old wolf's. Finally when my stick was tangled, his came free enough to find my temple.

The Arkan whip is nothing like the Yeoli that leaves no scar, or the Lakan that cuts with a fine leather strand. Its tail has ten stars of steel in it, to drag through the flesh at every stroke. As I'd suspected, twenty lashes was serious. Still, I managed to hold my silence. I didn't know that Arkan custom always adds the one extra for assurance of good behavior, though, so the twenty-first caught me relaxed, and flayed a cry out of me. Nor did they unbind me then; Koree had yet to punish me for resisting. Being too old and tired to flog, as he said, he rubbed a palm-full of salt into my back, making sure to get every cut. "It'll clean out the festers," he said, "so think of me as your healer."

It wasn't over even then. The same four guards, recovered, let me down, but bound my wrists and ankles right away, grinning grins that reminded me of Minis. I remember Skorsas following them as they dragged me, calling them all manner of names for doing this, until one said something that shut him up fast as a gag; that they'd make me feel every word. They took me to a bare room behind the barracks, and with gauntlets on like true Arkans, beat all but life out of me. I remember only the walls and floor and ceiling advancing and receding, and a front tooth, that I muddily realized must be mine, being crushed on the stone floor before my eyes.

Every time I walked by their posts afterwards, those four would grin smugly, in pride at having bested one man in chains and already weakened, I suppose. When I was training again, I challenged them, Arkan-style: a slap across the face with an ungloved hand, no trouble for me since I never wore gloves. All four of them at once, with swords, I proposed, suicide against people with a shred of courage, but I read them right. One quit his job and left for Korsardiana on urgent family business. The other three protested deadly weapons, arguing that they were constrained by their positions not to kill me, while no such restrictions hindered me. True enough, so we agreed on the weapons we'd been born with. I left each with a gap in his teeth; from then on their manner was changed. No great accomplishment; they were not warriors. If you wonder how I know the pretext of the one who fled, it was by reading the whole story under Miscellanea in the *Watcher of the Ring.*

As I lay in the bath afterwards, my scraped knuckles scalding, I thought, I've been here a month and a half, and have twice as many scars as I did before already; yet I've given far worse than I've got. Thrust a person into a barbarian's place, and he becomes one. Suddenly the sight of Assembly Hall and the great crystal in my hand came into my mind, and my own voice saying, "By the will of the people let this become law." The baths are a good place to weep; one can splash water over one's face if someone looks.

The night before my fourth fight, I could not sleep. Skorsas offered me water, wine, herb, sleeping drug, a massage, to no avail. It was a child's act I did. I was matched against Lobryr Flame-hair, of Kurkania, who had four chains; with a trembling hand I knocked on his door. When he asked what did I *fikken* want, I said, "If you kill me, I will forgive you, since you were forced; if I kill you will you forgive me?" I suppose I expected a tearful yes. It's hard to imagine I was ever that young. Instead, from within came quick footsteps; then the door flew open, and he seized my collar and threw me back against the wall.

"*Forgive* you? Don't ask forgive you! I going to kill you, hack off your head, the lions eat your bones!" I tried to twist free, then nerve-grabbed his hands, and we were fighting. The guards pulled us apart; this must be saved, after all, for an audience. As they went away, I heard one say laughing, "Some of them just can't wait, can they?" Several other gladiators glared from their doors; it was unwritten law not to break each other's sleep. I had broken Lobryr's. "Start again, you puppies," said a cold low voice, "and I'll disembowel you both." That was Suryar Yademkin, whose chains were a golden wreath, twenty-seven; one was for Tondias, Skorsas's dead love. He could say such things.

In the fight I ran Lobryr through lower than I aimed, and he did not die, but lay writhing, his teeth set against any sound, since the crowd sneers "Coward!" and spits on one who cries out. All that I'd felt last night came back in a flood; my hand lost all strength to give him mercy. I knelt beside him, gripped his shoulders; from the crowd came mocking boo-hoo's. "Forgive me," I said, quietly so only he could hear. "I was forced."

As last night he had answered in fear, now he answered in bitterness, pain turning his words to shrieks, his twisted face soaked in tears, and blood from his nose and mouth. It would be wrong, I think, to repeat the things he flung at me, and I have done him enough wrong. Now, finally, I saw my last night's folly for what it had been to him: cruelty. In the end he tried to crawl to the lion-trench, saying they wouldn't be too cowardly to finish him. I put my hand over his eyes and did it.

I always wept after a fight, more with horror than with grief, since I had not known the dead. This time it was beyond that: at midnight my hands had not ceased trembling for all I'd had a long bath, my insides felt empty as if each organ held only air, and all I perceived seemed unreal, as if I were drugged. I won, I thought, again; why fear?

As I write, the line of memory is broken; yet I remember my awareness being that way at the time as well, as if parts of me had fallen away randomly, like flesh from a dead man's bones, or gone invisible, like patches on the skin of numbness that one can recall no cause for, nor even when their feeling went.

That's it, I thought; I no longer know myself. I sprang out of bed, and went to the Legion Mirrors. Too close to see the line of images, it being hidden behind the one, I examined my own face. It was all there, familiar, Yeoli, the same one the Assembly Palace carver had graven for my official portrait; the eyes looked tired and anguished, but I'd seen that before. Smouldering? Perhaps when I'd fought the guards. I haven't changed, I thought, gripping my crystal; whatever fix I might get myself in, I am still myself.

That was four fights in: I had forty-six to go. Thinking that, I understood my fear. If I felt so shaken so soon, how would I bear more than ten times as much again?

From then on I knew I would have to do more than trust myself unthinking; I would have to cling, hard, in full awareness, to what I knew. I crept out onto the training-ground, where moonlight had softened the harsh hot red-brown of the sand to a misted blue, and cooled it under my feet. Arko's heat-haze is chilled away on some nights, such as this; the air stands so still it seems to hang like clear glass, and every sound, even quiet footsteps in sand, comes crisp and ringing.

The same bright pitted moon shines over Arko and Yeola-e, the same constellations wink down; being familiar, they were a comfort to see. To eyes up there, I thought, Arkans and Yeolis, and indeed all humanity, must seem one; anywhere on the Earthsphere, even around the other side where All-spirit knows what kind of people live, any slave torn from any nation may see something of home just by looking up. The thought was comfort in itself. I knelt, and clasped my crystal, and called the God-In-Myself, knowing it was no indulgence this time, I was truly in need. Just enough of the wind and the harmonic singer came to my ears to tell me, "I am here."

Four days after my fifth fight, I saw from the training ground, as one often did, two slavers coming along the colonnade with a new man in chains. My sparring-opponent could have whacked off my head without my noticing, and almost did; I'd never thought to see that jaunty style of walking again. It was Mana.

I ran away from my man, so the thicket of fighters was between the colonnade and me, then when he chased me, let him throw and pin me under him. He must have wondered how he got his way so easily. If Mana saw me, I knew the first thing he'd cry out: my true name.

When I got up he was gone, into the Hall of Trial; he'd be back out again, I could not know precisely when. The punishment heavier than push-ups but lighter than a flogging was being expelled from training; one who did not keep his edge in practice was likelier to lose. I stayed lying in the dirt. Koree could smell laziness as a buzzard can meat, and because there'd been whispers that I was his favorite, he was hard on me to prove otherwise. In an instant he swooped. "What's this, think because great promise you can sleep in training? Fifty push-ups, cockerel." I told him the two words Skorsas had taught me, for when I wanted to offend. That did it handily enough; I went.

"What in *Hayel*"—the place where Arkans who have sinned go after death—"did you do that for?" said Skorsas, when we were in my room. I could think of nothing else, but to be honest. His work, and the public loyalty his position required, had always been faultless; but as well, I'd comforted him in his grieving several times again, and as far as I could tell, he'd ceased hating me. He'd been particularly kind after I'd been beaten; when I cried out in the night he came and took my head on his shoulder. Now I decided to truly trust him.

One does not make friends with other gladiators, I should explain. The matches are made by lot, but not always; I'd seen and heard already, how two high-chainers won't get matched against each other for months, until, strangely, one's fiftieth fight. If two have a feud, they'll invariably be matched, for the crowd loves a grudge; if two are known friends, it's just as inevitable, for the crowd loves tragedy.

"That Yeoli . . ." I said to Skorsas.

"I perked my ears," he said, or some such thing. By this time I could understood about half of his Arkan. The language has five different forms, all depending on the castes of speaker and listener; I refused to learn any but that which one spoke to equals. If I offended the rich and honored the poor, so be it; they got too little, respectively, as far as I could see.

"His name's Mannas Something-I-Forget," said Skorsas, "he looks really good, everyone's saying he reminds them of you." No surprise; we'd had all the same Teachers. "But he's something political, so they put him in the cells, and I bet he's off to the Marble Palace for a prick of truth-drug sometime soon." My heart came to my throat; what if he had caught a glimpse of my hair or my hand, which he'd know? But that was before he'd gone into the Hall of Trial. He must have answered honestly about why he was in the Empire, I thought, as he did his name; he wouldn't have, knowing I was here.

"He knows me," I said. "If he sees me he might say my name out. My real name."

"Shit of the saints," Skorsas breathed. "*You're* not something political, are you, jewel of the Mezem?" He'd started calling me that. "*Fikket*, you could be the missing king of Yeola-e, and *then* I'd land in the shit—I don't want to know!" I just said, "Will you watch him for me? See when they take him to drug him?"

It was that evening, at dinner hour. He was gone for three beads, by Iska's bead-clock, on which the Mezem runs. I ate in my room, the story being that I was in a mood. Even afterwards, I saw, it might not be safe to see him; he might be questioned again.

Skorsas spied for me. Mahid had taken him, and they did not announce their intentions; but he said, "He got truth-drug-scraped, I'm sure." I used the first Arkan words I'd learned, and the ones I still used most often: "What does that mean?"

"They fill you with the drug. Then they ask you, 'What's the fact you know that you'd least like us to?' When you've answered that they ask, 'What's the fact you'd *second*-least like us to know?' And so on, down to your birthmarks.

People who've had it done always look like someone did a grape-pressing dance through their insides." Scraped is a good word, I thought. The sight came to my inward eyes of the inside of a skull, cleaned raw; I turned it away. Yet if they did that, they'd likely not take him again.

I waited till late, slipped by Iska's desk when he was looking through his phial-drawers, and gave the cell-guard a bit of silver chain Skorsas had given me. Beyond the window-bars of the one locked cell it was pitch-dark; but I knew his breathing, from a hundred war-camps. "Mana." He moaned; sheets rustled. "Mana. Don't say my name." I had to raise my voice a little higher. "Mana, *chen*. Give me your candle and don't say my name, that's an order."

"All right, all right, Che—millennion," he murmured, heaved himself to sitting and fumbled on the cell's night-table. "You and your cursed mysteriousness . . . here." I lit it from a wall-torch, gave it back through the bars.

He had two months of beard, and his forelock was hacked off; otherwise he was just the same. Tears stung in my eyes. Now it came to him where he was, for his face went pale enough to see even in candlelight as his eyes fixed on me. I grabbed his hand where it clutched a bar. *"Don't say my name."*

"Saint Mother," he whispered. "Sweet Saint Mother help us."

"They don't know who I am," I said. "That's why I keep telling you not to say my name." We clasped wrists and pressed our brows together, the best we could do through bars; the guard was looking the other way. "Mana, heart's brother, you're alive, I thought you were dead! What happened?"

"I faked it," he said. "A kindly Arkan couple took me in, saved me, nursed me, and sold me to a slaver." I told him my tale. When I drew back his eyes were the fierce imp's I knew. "Another fine scrape," he said, laughing. "If we could get out of your grandmother's reach when we hit the back of her neck with that snowball, we can get out of this." Nothing in the world could have been more heartening then; it was as if we were on the Lakan border again, in a camp full of friends.

Under truth-drug, he'd told them he didn't know what became of me. "Good," I said. "Mana, you don't know me. You've never seen me before, though we got taught the same style, classic Yeoli. For Mezem reasons as well as Yeoli; they don't always match by lot."

I always wore my chains under my shirt. His hand was on my shoulder; now it shifted in, and fished them up into the light.

What could I say? He was here; he knew the rules. To Arkans I could claim I was forced; he was a Yeoli, who knew I'd chosen.

But when his grey eyes flicked up to mine, I found not horror or dismay, but gentleness. I'd forgotten how well he knew me. What I'd taken days to come to, he saw in a moment. "Don't reproach yourself. You're doing right. Yeola-e needs you. Listen to me, Cheng; the people wills." I just signed chalk.

"I don't know you," he said, grinning again. "Who are you?"

"The ebon-curled and smouldering-eyed Karas Raikas."

"*You're* Karas Raikas! All-spirit! No wonder these people keep saying I remind them of him." We laughed; then the guard cleared his throat loudly, and we agreed to meet again.

I watched his first fight, nothing suspicious since we all watched each other's fights, and indeed were expected to, while the writers hung around saying, "You know him, don't you, Raikas? You're both Yeolis." I would answer, "That's like my saying to you, 'You're from Arko? Do you know so-and-so?' There are two thousand thousand people in Yeola-e; do you expect me to know all the other nineteen-hundred and ninety-nine thousand nine-hundred and ninety-nine?" Skorsas and I had been working on numbers. No surprise, Mana didn't hesitate as I had, and won unscathed.

He got the room across and three down from mine, so I could easily slip him notes. In the forest around the city are private places; in a green clearing one could imagine, if one tried, was in southern Yeola-e, we made our proper greeting embrace, which turned into a wrestling match in the moss. He showed me the scar Ethras's man had given him, as good as one will ever see on a body still living; he'd twisted fast enough to keep the back-thrust out of his entrails, but it had cut a little into his kidney. His benefactors had even paid a Haian to heal him, an investment, I suppose.

We spoke long of the Mezem, comforted each other for

our slavers' torments. Trust him to know the best taverns in Arko already. Barely a word into it, he said, "Don't let this claw you down, Chevenga. You start sinking into a pit, and I'll pull you by the hair with one hand and the balls with the other."

"Why do you say that?" I said. "Why should you worry more for me than for yourself?" I suppose I should have known; but I was afraid he'd seen it in or on me somehow, and wanted to know.

He pulled me to him, pinned my head against his shoulder. I supposed we touched so much because we were both starved for it. "I know you," he said. "Having to do anything you feel stained by, you feel like a knife in your heart. And this will go on long."

"It doesn't show then?" I said. "I haven't changed?" He just said laughing, "Of course not, you idiot," and tickled me silly.

"You haven't changed, that is," he added, "except for the teeth. Esora-e will turn somersaults over that. . . . Where'd you lose them?" I told the tale of the four guards, then asked him what he meant. "You know. The old boar couldn't stand a necklace with metal links on you; what do you think he'll say to teeth of gold?"

"*Gold*?" It came to me that Skorsas had arranged everything with the healer who did dentistry, and I'd understood less Arkan then; I'd just sat in his chair, I recalled, keeping my eyes and mind on anything but what he was doing. It had never occurred to me he might not remake my teeth with ceramic as a Haian would. I hadn't looked in a mirror since then, except once in the Legion Mirrors, with grit teeth and closed lips. I turned to the sun, grinned and held my hand where it should reflect; sure enough, there was a golden shine.

In the image of their desires, I thought, they will remake me. But this time Mana of the earthly and simple was there, to see my face and cut the thought short. "See?" he said. "You're taking too much on your shoulders, right now. So you look rich in Arko, where money's everything, and Esora-e will hop when you get home—so what? You can always get them done over. Cheng, be easy." He was right; I thought no more of it.

Yet one thing never came up, under that sweet warm sky: that we might be matched against each other. Neither of us could bear to mention it, I suppose, because, other than pretending we were strangers, there was no plan to be made against it.

At the start of a fight, each fighter declares his preference of weapons; a toss of a die decides in which mode they will fight for the first round, after which it alternates. Yet the judge, who sits by the Director (and is, I should note in all fairness, a true student of the Ring) might instead command them to fight each in his preferred mode, if he thinks that will even the odds, and be more interesting. This is called Judge's Clemency.

I always bid clean blade, which means sword and no armor. For my eighth fight my opponent, Seliko, a half-breed of Curlionaiz with three chains, bid full armor, shield, spear, sword and two daggers. "Finally we'll see Karas Raikas in the ring for a decent amount of time!" the judge said, and called Clemency.

One may beg mercy, that is, ask for one more item, weapon or armor; one gets flapped at, but neither I nor Skorsas, who'd turned ghastly pale under his face-powder, considering it his mistake not to have foreseen this, cared for my honor right then. I asked for my wristlets, though he thought I was mad not to take a shield. The crowd cheered me, taking it as gallantry.

I made Seliko chase me all around the ring; he'd tire before I would. When he was spent enough to get frustrated, I wrist-parried one of his spear-thrusts, and grabbed the shaft below the blade. He had the habit of throwing his shield too far if he were rattled, so I did a low side-cut to draw it down, and kicked him in the face, which was the true finish.

From then on I couldn't walk through the streets of Arko without hiding my head in a hood. People seemed to think I was obliged to greet them, answer the silliest questions, sign papers and kerchiefs and waxboards, as if I'd chosen this. Many chains had been won on bets, so a rash of gifts came. That is how a gladiator acquires riches—that, and taking the riches of those he has beaten, his right. Skorsas wondered what disease I had, refusing to wear metal jewelry. The chains were bad enough.

One doesn't want to be in a street of houses in Arko anyway, at the hour of noon. Praying isn't the only observance they make then; in the time when everyone else is silent one will often hear a child's scream, that goes on longer than one would think a child had the strength for. The chimes of noon, Arkans call it: a girl at first threshold, seven years old, being cut. What Yeolis would call maiming, Arkans call purification, as if a woman's sexual pleasure were dirt or corruption. All my time as a gladiator, I never touched an Arkan woman. I told myself it was because I didn't like Arkans; in truth, it was at least partly in fear of the devastation I would find between her legs. What would I say? How could I give her pleasure, or take any, when I wanted to run out and be sick?

I began getting love letters soaked in scent, kerchiefs with lip prints on them, life-epistles of unbelievable tedium, invitations. Many came from followers of those I had killed. It is an ancient Arkan principle, too barbaric now even for some of them to stomach, but still partly encoded in their law, at the time: who kills, becomes. That is to say, who kills your father becomes your father, taking ownership and responsibility of his progeny; who kills the Imperator in a coup becomes Imperator; who kills your favorite fighter becomes your favorite fighter. Nor were they feigning it; why go to such trouble? Those who had loved Seliko now truly loved me.

Skorsas almost fainted when a velvet-bordered invitation came, from one Mil Torii Itzan. He, it seemed, was one of the most famous party-givers among the *Aitzas*. The inspired host always brings in a prized gladiator, to brighten up the decor, and provide sure amusement. "*What?*" my boy said. "You're *not going to go?*" By his face you'd think I'd pissed in the offering-bowl.

"You mistake me for one who cares fly-dung whether this fellow's offended," I said, which made him flinch as if he'd been wounded. This is a youth, you understand, who when I decided to crochet myself a half-poncho—could there be anything more innocent?—promised me he'd die of shame if I did it in public, because in Arko that sort of thing is women's work. So I learned, crocheting in the Fighter's Box while watching other men's fights was a sure way to get rid of Skorsas; he lived, though.

"Still, someone has to convey my regrets," I said. "I don't care what you tell him. Have a good time." As he was primping himself on the dread night, I heard a choking groan; worried he was sick I ran into his room, and found him in horrified tears, moaning about fatal flaws and weeping pustules and how it would draw every eye like a beacon-fire. A pimple had come up on the side of his nose. I nearly fell over laughing, while he snifflingly called me a callous barbarian. One could forget he was fifteen.

The next morning, he described pleasure-boys in gold lace gloves who would pass you oysters from their mouths, a shower of rose petals, a waterfall of wine. I took it all as herb-dreams. I'd never been to a Mil Torii Itzan party.

As I came off the training-ground, a writer chased me. Though by custom they had to write praisingly, they all hated me; I gave them slighting answers or none at all, and had struck one once. Though I'd given him fair warning—"I'll hit you if you follow me", and he'd followed me—it is a thing which, as Arkans say, is just not done. Yet the more they hated me, the more simperingly they lauded me in writing, taking joy, it seemed, in hypocrisy.

"So!" this one said, pen poised on paper. "I hear you weep after every fight, Raikas! Why, when you win?"

How he'd found that out, since I did it only in the baths or my room, I could not know; at least not until I read that day's Pages. The Serpent's Tale, as they call the page entirely devoted to gossip, had a detailed account of Mil Torii Itzan's party, and how Skorsas had boasted of me. "Not only is he the bravest, the strongest, the best-looking," and so on and on, "but he has the kindest heart. . . . He weeps after every fight."

I called him to me. "Is this all you said?" He hadn't read it, he answered. With a look like a whipped dog's, he said, "I can't read," though I'd thought *fessas* got educated. I translated for him as best I could; the more I did the redder he turned. When I was done, he said, "Beat me, jewel of the Mezem. I'll bear it."

At the start Skorsas had had the habit of flinching if I raised my arm to scratch. Now he was getting over it; my promise I'd never strike him had helped. Iska would never do that either—threat of dismissal was enough to keep the boys in line—and one who has been beaten by those who raised him doesn't lose the habit so easily. I had to surmise it had been Tondias, whom he had loved.

"No," I answered. "Just tell me if this is all you said." He had no idea, he admitted, nearly in tears; he didn't even remember saying half of what was quoted. I bared my heart to him. "I don't want to get truth-drugged because you blurted some idle fancy."

"What?" he said. "That you're the missing king of Yeola-e? Raikas, they're not *that* stupid. Besides, you get truth-drugged, what's it matter if it's not true?"

I looked him in the eyes, feeling my cheeks begin to burn. He was too cursed quick. I trust him, I thought; they'd drug me before they drugged him anyway. "What if it is?" His mouth froze, in a stunned circle, scarlet with lip paint. "I've just put my fate, perhaps my life, in your hands," I whispered. "Perhaps you'll consider it your duty to turn me in; if so, so be it. I'd rather have it purposely, than inadvertently."

He made no move to go; instead he threw himself to his knees at my feet, seeming near to prostrating himself, but wavering. By Arkan custom, that is an obeisance for the Imperator alone. His Arkan changed, to a form even more obsequious than usual. "Celestialis, Blessed of Celestialis, king . . . great one . . . I don't know the proper style to address you, forgive my flea-brained ignorance, Celestialis, I've been doing everything wrong, I've been treating you like sh—excrement."

That was a new word to me. "You mean shit?" His jaw dropped again; in a blink, it seemed, I'd shape-changed into a person who would never swear. In this place, I thought, I'm a fool not to have expected this. "No, you haven't, Skorsas. You want to know how to treat me? Exactly as you have, not a speck different. Except . . . you have to keep calling me Karas Raikas in public. In private, will you call me Chevenga?" He hesitated, wanting a title; I refused to tell him one, leaving him no choice. The best he could do was "Shefen-kas." Hearing him call me by it was like warm sun on my skin after a year of winter.

IV

A few days after my ninth fight, I heard in the lounge a choked cry in Mana's voice, as he would make if an arrow in him were being pulled out. I could not come running, as I yearned to; absent curiosity was the most I could show. I strolled out as if I'd intended to already. He sat trembling with his face buried in his hands, the Enchian Pages lying before him.

Somewhere in me I knew, for shivers crawled out all through me from my heart. Still, one must learn the details. I peered over his shoulder; such closeness for news reading is not suspicious. Then I snatched it up. He sprang to his feet, and strode out through the Legion Mirrors in a rage. I sat in his place.

Hidden within the fear of news is the assumption that it will be no worse than one feared. Sieges on the strongholds at the border, I expected, a pitched battle in the foothills; it was an odd time to attack, with winter, which would fight for us, coming on. But they'd struck from sea, not land. In one great ship-battle at Selina, our full fleet had been destroyed, and the town taken; now they were pouring upriver to Akara, where Tinga-e lay wide open. We were already twenty-thousand dead.

As one's flesh is struck numb at first in a severe wound, my heart felt nothing, and my mind could think. I saw it like one of my teaching-games; Azaila seemed near me, a presence like a fire below me while I perched on the beam, and Hurai, saying, "*Think*, boy. Now—you haven't got all day."

We bear the burden of our customs; all through our war-history are times we'd have defended better by attacking, or foreigners have made use of it, raising armies near our borders without fear, and so forth. And while all the other nations around us have their island sea-bases, we are bound not to, for we'd have to take them. The Arkans had struck from Tuzgolu, and so taken us by surprise.

Yet Yeoli half-action was written all over it as well. The Pages wrote little news from abroad that had no bearing on Arko, but it had announced my aunt's reinstatement to the demarchy, awaiting my sister's coming of age, on the presumption I was dead. Two demarchic transitions and a third expected, within a year, and the mourning; Assembly Palace could hardly run with perfect smoothness. No doubt the Arkans had told Tyeraha the same, that I'd gone missing in a skirmish with Roskati rebels, and they were making every effort to find me or my corpse. She'd believed it; why not? I'd never told her my premonition of war with Arko.

So she hadn't expected it, or, worse, if she had, she'd sent warriors to the border. I could see them trapped by winter in the high valleys, cursing their own uselessness, while Arko stormed through the plains. Then the scenes began running before my inward eyes: a forest of red sails on a horizon, the cries, "To sea!", a ram splintering planking, the roar of fire in rigging, water boiling at bows, stained red; all the people of the city out on the shore to see their fate decided, their one great cry, as they saw. My heart ceased being numb. Next I knew, my eyes were half-full of sparkles and black streaks, and what I did see was the lounge ceiling with its crisscross gilding, beyond the Pages, which were still in my hands. I'd thrown myself straight backwards from my chair; I heard my rage-cry still echoing.

Faces stared, curious; a voice said, "Has Yeola-e burnt down or something, to set them off?" When Iska and Skorsas came, I got up and moved; I was afraid I'd kill any Arkan my arms could reach. Flames seemed to roar through every muscle, crying "*Move!*"; at the same time, a blade seemed to be working back and forth in my guts; it was not only they who should die. The training-ground was worse than where I was, the city too. I went at a full run to the woods. In the streets people sidled away from me.

Mana was in our first meeting place, sword in hand (we were allowed weapons outside the Mezem), gazing at it. I flung myself at his feet, my face into the dirt; I'd forgotten that gritty dark taste, since Daisas had brought me here. I said nothing. What could I: "I'm sorry?" "Forgive me?"

He knelt at my head; when he laid his hand on my shoulder, I shrank away. His comfort was mercy: injustice. His hands caught my arms, pinned me to him. "Cheng, don't blame yourself." You say that in kindness, I thought, as a friend would. "Fourth Chevenga, listen to me. The people wills." Or to keep me from giving myself justice, because you imagine I might yet be some use. As demarch, as if I were ever worthy while I played at wearing the signet. Better I'd never been born; but that was the stroke of the past, only the next best thing remained. He was saying, "It's not as if we've lost the whole thing; who says we can't beat them back?" His sword lay on the ground beside him; with one free hand I seized it, turning the edge inward. He grabbed my wrist, cursing, and we wrestled like two poor-quarter dogs over a bone.

Then just as fast he let go. "All right!" Anger edged his voice under its breathlessness. "Go on. You're our only demarch, while you live. If this is how little faith you have that Yeola-e can win back, if that's all you think of us, then do it. We're better off without you." I'd had my hands poised to draw the edge through my throat; now they locked, and reason came back.

We sat together, and talked sense. "It occurs to me," he said, "perhaps the Pages are as truthful about war news as they are about the Mezem." I slapped my brow; you see what state I was in, not to think of that. Now, the lies leapt out at me: our whole fleet could not have been destroyed, without their taking Asinanai as well, which they'd hardly forget to mention; Tinga-e would hardly be undefended; even if fifty ships with two hundred warriors each were sunk and not a single person swam away, that was only ten thousand dead.

Still, I doubted untruth would reach so far as taking a

city. We should not pretend Selina had not fallen, and
they were not sailing upriver. We would fight our utmost,
and still Arko would outnumber us; I remembered why I'd
made friends with the kings all around. I had; Tyeraha had
not. Kranaj knew her as sister of my father, who'd warred
against his father; Astalaz knew her as the demarch who'd
warred against his, herself. "Is there no way," Mana said,
"you can write to let them know you're alive?"

From the beginning I had chosen against this, afraid
that should the letter fall under Marble Palace eyes, it
would reveal me. Yet I might still have risked it; names
can be hidden in codes, letters within other letters. If you
will have the truth, it had seemed to me that to know what
I was in Arko would be worse for them than to think me
dead. Now it came to me: that was the thought of one
who'd let shame make him stupid. It would be even worse
news, now; but they should have all news.

So I had my plan, and he bound me to it, saying, "I am
your people, in Arko, and the people wills." We both
knelt to meditate, and went back to the Mezem, apart. I
remember no more of that day.

The line of memory picks up with cold and wet and
hardness pressing against my head and body, and the stink
of rot. I was lying, shivering, in darkness and a foul stream
of water; my eyes felt wrapped all around with thick wet
felt, as if my brain were made of it. I heard the rattle of
leaves blowing along stone, footsteps and the thump of a
walking-stick, distant laughter as if through glass windows.

"Young man." I woke once more, having gone senseless
again for a time, preferring it, I suppose; the voice, an old
woman's, sharp and definite, snagged my mind. Her stick
poked at my ribs. I lifted my head; it felt as if it should
keep going, dropping off my shoulders. "This is no place
for you. You're a foreigner, a Mezem boy, you should be
there. Come on, up. What a disgraceful state to get yourself into. No gloves even; tsk."

My body was heavy and stiff as wood, but weak as a
child's. We were outside a tavern. When I was on my
elbows, sickness took me; I barely crawled out of the
stream, so my vomit wouldn't flow onto me, in time. I
thought of Selina. Like feeling a wound, I had to remind
myself: we were at war. "Home with you." The hot bath
waited, a warm cup of nectar with something to bring peace,

Iska to examine me, Skorsas turning back my bed. The Mezem: home.

I didn't know the way; I didn't even know where in the city we were; she had to lead me. I needed her arm to lean on, too, while she leaned on her stick; she gave me a kerchief to hide my hands, and used another to cover wherever I touched her. I learned how she could walk alone after dark without fear when four toughs, instead of threatening, greeted her respectfully: she was the neighborhood midwife, probably the first pair of arms that ever held them. When we got to the gate, I said, "I should give you something in thanks; but all I can think of is to sign your kerchief." She accepted out of civility alone, I think.

I got along the colonnade by leaning against the wall; between the Legion Mirrors I tried standing alone. Misty in the dark I saw my rank, a hundred Karas Raikases to either side: a formidable force the writers would make that out to be, I thought, except we're all reeling: *Chen!* Straighten up! We should be in Akara. The first step of the march lurched me too far sideways; my shoulder bumped too hard into the shoulder of the next Raikas over, who somehow had fallen into me precisely the same way. I tried to check myself, lost my feet, and heard a muffled clank. From the floor I saw my sprawled reflection slowly rise, and the line of selves behind it shoot up like a whip and vanish; then I understood. The mirror, long and tall as the wall, had been knocked off its moorings, and was falling. I closed my eyes, and shielded my face with my hands. The crash, no words can describe.

Iska came running, Skorsas on his heels. "Yes, it's him." "Always, I'll be picking slivers of glass off you. Lie still." Servants came, gasping; a mirror so big is worth far more, say, than twice as much as one half its size. When I was clean of glass, they took me into the clinic. "I know you're not drunk, lad," Iska said. "I believe you", so I must have been protesting. He smelled my breath, tasted my spittle, looked long into my eyes. When they stripped me for the bath I saw him glance at the crook of my arm, but thought nothing of it. The water burned, driving away my chills in a moment. "Calm, Raikas," he said. "You've got more drug in you than what the Mahid fed you, but you'll be all right."

I went dizzy again, heard my head thump back against the wooden tub-edge. Something kept coming into my mind, each time with a flash and a chiming: the sight of an orange jewel, emerald-cut, that was somehow deathly urgent. Hands held me sitting, voices said, "Calm, lad, steady, what is it?" Somehow I made it clear to them, I remembered nothing later than the afternoon. "They didn't want you to, then," Iska said. "That's one of the drugs. . . . Two Mahid took you; they drugged your dinner."

Skorsas's face swam closer, all but weeping. "I'm sorry. I'm sorry I gave it to you; they took it right out of my hands and sprinkled it full of powder and said, 'Make sure he eats it. . . .' I just had to pray it wouldn't kill you, I'm sorry. . . ." I heard my voice, forgiving him. Iska, the one Arkan who used Yeoli customs on Yeolis, put his hand on my shoulder and said, "You were almost certainly truth-drugged, lad. The mark's on your arm. I hope you have nothing to hide." On the inner crease of my sword-elbow was a tiny red spot like an insect bite, from a syringe, the piercing instrument used to put fluid straight into the blood. The candle-flames all went dark; when next I knew they were lifting me out, and Iska was saying, "I can't give him sedative, he's got too much needle-piss in him already."

I slept in ragged patches, full of nightmares, through which the orange jewel flashed in and out like a fish in stained water. In the morning there was something in my juice, that dulled all my thoughts and feelings; but I welcomed it. I trained, but was forbidden to spar.

Likewise next day. Mana must have been there; but I didn't see him, as if he were a ghost. As sparring-time came, and Koree set me to practicing forms alone, two Arkan men in black with long hair bound in fighting braids came along the corridor, in step and smooth like cats; they were armed with daggers, and tubes for blowing darts. The usual colonnade hangers-on casually scattered. "Celestialis dump its commodes," said Koree. "*Them* again. Who the *fikken* they want this time?" We learned soon enough; they came straight across the ground, to me.

Koree must have felt my intention, for he said, "Naw, lad, don't fight them. Always make it worse if you do. You're too fuddled to make good account of yourself anyway. Don't be scared, don't forget: you're too valuable a piece to die anywhere but the Ring. They just want knowledge out of you, for the war." Never until now, I thought, have I truly known what fear is.

Mahid always say the same thing: "Karas Raikas, you are required." With quick hard hands they clipped my wrists into manacles. In the streets everyone stayed back from us, turning their eyes away, as they do from Mahid and those they arrest.

Thus I got my first sight, that I can remember, of inside the Marble Palace. It was not as tall as the Palace of Kraj, but sprawled wider, a city under one golden roof. Its ornateness was restrained and refined, after the exuberant gaudiness of the Mezem, but of higher quality. They stripped me of everything but my chains, and bathed me in a shower-stall all of marble, with water-spout of brass. Somehow as I was looking at that, my heart ceased to feel again, and the fear went like a stream of water shut off. I became the spectator of my own life, from afar; yet the actor playing me knew all my moves and lines, and made them perfectly.

In a small room, they made me lie on a table like a healer's but with shackles, and locked in my wrists and ankles. An old man in a white satin robe with the deft hands and careful manner of a healer opened a box, drew out several vials and other shining things. Thus—how else?—I first met Amitzas Mahid, the Imperial Pharmacist, as he was titled. A middle-aged Mahid slid a thing like a harness with two vices in around my head, and clamped it tight on my temples and cheekbones so I could not move my head a hair's-width. Watching him was a boy of about fifteen, his bare arms bright against his Mahid black: an apprentice.

That was the first touch of the hollow needle I can remember, as well: he pricked four times around my eyes, and in a short time I could not move them either, but only stare at the spot of ceiling I'd been looking at when they'd gone dead. It was when he lifted the syringe with a curving needle a good hand-span long that I asked him what he was doing. He closed my sword-side eye, washed it with some sharp-smelling liquid, and answered civilly that he would explain when it was done.

I felt nothing, but saw it all from the other eye: his hands, delicate and steady, placing the point under the brow-ridge, and threading it in around my eyeball. I heard the faintest click, on bone deep inside my head; his hand stopped, adjusted, began again. It was more than a finger deep when he pressed whatever was in the syringe into me. Once done he bandaged both my eyes closed, and explained as he had promised.

Grium sefalian is the Arkan: it means "seed of the head." They say it is older than the Fire, brought down from their first home in the sky, along with all other substances they alone possess. A living thing, like a yeast, that grows by feeding on the flesh of the brain: unchecked it kills, bringing madness first. A year ago I might not have believed this, thinking they meant to torture me with a tale, but I'd seen many things since then.

I had forty-one fights to go, a year and a month, perhaps. This seed was timed to kill in two years. "It is the will of the Imperator," he said, "that you be informed: on winning fifty fights you will be administered the antidote." I understood. All ways of escape for a person alone, I'd tried; but others can open, to one who makes friends. This closed those off, too.

I was to lie in their care for two or three days, the Pharmacist told me, then back to the Mezem. They unbound me, lifted me onto a litter and bore me off somewhere; just raising my head showed me why they didn't fear my resisting, for I had to lie back sick in a moment. Still, the bed they laid me in had a neck-restraint. The middle-aged one and the apprentice stayed.

I still felt nothing; too weak, I suppose. Once I'd got him to give me water and a *katzerik*, the Arkan smoking-stick made of shreds of tobacco leaf rolled in paper—yes, I was smoking them in an unbroken line by then; no gladiator who ever lived didn't, as one can see even in the frescoes—I got speaking to him. He was permitted only to answer my questions, the other, his uncle and teacher as it turned out, watching him with hawk's eyes.

His given name was Ilesias, same as the composer. From him I learned that the Mahid were a clan, of *Aitzas* caste, whose stock in trade was simply ultimate loyalty to the Imperator, and the willingness to do anything he commanded. They served as spy chiefs, torturers, concubines, messengers, anything that demanded someone utterly trustworthy, most in the City, some out in the Empire or beyond. A perfect Mahid, he taught me, thinks only the

fifty maxims he has been taught from childhood, feels and
does and is only what the Imperator's will requires. I
gathered the training was rigorous and brutal.

Eventually his uncle left him alone with me, and he
unbandaged my eyes, to which feeling had returned; the
one was sore from front to back. I had spoken with him
first mostly to make trouble; his soul cried out to be
subverted. When I repeated a rumor I'd heard, that
Kurkas had never been weaned—he'd known at two he'd
have absolute power, threatened his mother into keeping
going, and now had a stable of slave wet-nurses as well as
the finest in Arkan cuisine—I could almost hear his brain
creaking in his skull as it flinched away. But I found myself
concerned for him. Over the day we made friends; he
even consented to take a message to the Mezem.

On the second day, I saw I'd got him into trouble; he
was deathly tired, and dreaded speaking even a word. It
turned out his superiors had told him he was to torture
and cripple me; in that sort of way young Mahid are taught
not to make friends. I told him they wouldn't waste the
grium sefalian if they didn't mean me to keep fighting, but
just toss me in the dungeon. When the orders came to
take me back to the Mezem, he nearly fell over.

Skorsas and Iska took me off his arm at the gate, put me
straight into the bath. Now, in a familiar place, I came
down from the dream, and could no longer avoid seeing all
the world had changed, like a house twisted a fingerwidth
off its foundations by an earthquake; now I wept and
cursed and threw up, and would have smashed my head
against the tiles except I'd been warned against moving it
quickly.

Skorsas passed me something that flashed with gold,
saying, "You should see this." His face under its powder
was pale. It was a parchment, sealed with the Arkan eagle;
the writing within was in golden ink. I remember thinking
blearily, "As if it isn't clear enough that they know who I
am." It was a dinner invitation from Kurkas Imperator,
addressed Fourth Chevenga.

V

I was too muddleheaded to know Mana was trying to
see me; finally, two days after I'd come back to training,
he climbed in through my window at night. It looked out
over a neglected courtyard full of whatever gladiators throw
out their windows; he'd got onto the ledge by sneaking
through someone else's room.

Even after I told him everything, he hit my shoulder
with a fist, and said, "We'll get out of this, Cheng." To his
grin I could only grin back, which makes one feel stronger
in itself. We wrote our letter, ostensibly from him to his
mother, to send through a Haian he knew in town. I did
the fancy border, all in shorthand made to look like patterns, telling my aunt everything. I suggested she at least
try to make allies, which my being alive might help; and
that of all Yeoli things it would be harmful for Arkans to
know, she should change as much as she could, as quick. I
had prided myself on having it all in my head.

"An invitation from the Imperator," Skorsas had said to
me, "is a summons. What do you want to wear?" In truth,
I'd come somewhat to look forward to it, for what I'd learn
if nothing else. I had been scheduled to meet him after all.
After some thought, I had Skorsas get a shirt tailored in
the proper demarchic style, with the keyhole collar. I said
black, with the white border, but forgot to tell him not to

have it embroidered, with fine patterns black on black, all over. When he answered my question, how much it had cost, my jaw dropped; I'd never worn anything so expensive in my life, not even armor. "Now," he said, "about jewelry . . ." I decided to wear only my peace-sigil, as a reproach.

I did see Kurkas, as it turned out, the day before. I'd given up on seeing the Imperial box tenanted some time ago; apparently he did not come to fights. But for my tenth, he was there.

Warming up, I felt my stomach go tight, when by the bustle in the box I knew. It would have been different, when he'd known me only as Karas Raikas. Now I was the captive king brought in chains at the head of the triumph, and made to dance for my master; even if the crowd didn't know it, it was enough that he and I did. Even letting him see my skill chafed; it was no threat to him, here.

There was little to learn by seeing, except that he dressed with more restraint than his son, and tended to fat. I was surprised to see his hands quite naked and pink but for flashes of gold, the Imperial seals. It turned out that since the Imperator is divine, the Son of the Sun, all parts of him are sacred and need not be concealed; the same for his son. Minis was with him, jumping up and down for me. I put it all out of mind—as gladiators say, slip of thought, feed the lions—and did what I must to get out of his sight.

Next day, Skorsas spent all day making me ready, terrified that I make a less than perfect impression, as if that could attain even the end of my list of concerns. In hooded robe, I went to the Palace.

Last time, I'd been in a plain wing. What was in the Imperial complex beggared the mind. Ceilings were crusted with gold; marble stairways flowed up in curves like waterfalls and flames; windows and skylights were lace-works of glass; the walls were filled with great artworks, portraits staring and battle scenes writhing, all but alive; the marble statues seemed frozen in acts of life, which they would continue the moment one looked away. I would not have thought there could be so many riches in all the world; of course, all the riches of the world Arko has taken, I thought, come here.

The precautions that surround the Imperator beggar the mind too. I went through three anterooms, each richer

than the one before. In the first I was stripped, and
searched to the skin and deeper, though civilly and with
apologies; in the second some ritual was done over me by
priests, to purify me sufficiently to enter the Imperial
Presence; in the third, I was instructed in how to make
the prostration with grace pleasing to the Imperial eye,
and warned by a friendly Mahid that the room was stud-
ded with spring-darts, their triggers under the fingers of
invisible watchers, so that the slightest threatening move
would be instant death. Beside the final door stood a
grotesque statue in bronze, of a twisted grinning bald man
holding a bowl; the butler who'd led me in whispered,
"That's Lukitzas, honored barbarian. Give him a chain
and he will bring you luck in the Presence." I had brought
no money, not having expected to need it. "Touch his
head then, and take your chances." I did, and the door
was opened for me.

They were no idle threat, the spring-darts; I weapon-
sensed them, built into walls, molding, tables, sculptures,
their mechanisms coiled like snakes, aimed everywhere
but at the chair where he sat.

I did not do the prostration, nor any obeisance, wanting
to see what he would do. "Well, here you are!" he said, in
jovial Enchian. He didn't have a carrying voice; no doubt
he used heralds for his speeches. Close up, if one looked
through the finery, he was plain enough, his wide shaven
face smooth for fifty, his hair greying a little and thin on
top, his eyes a bright blue, not brilliant but not foolish
either, calm and contented but with a touch of petulance.
Dressed up as a god, but still a man, with moles, a
birthmark on his cheek, hair on the backs of his hands
under the seals like anyone else's; one could imagine him
a relative of Iska, a mere *fessas*.

That I had expected, though. Knowing all he held in his
hands, I looked for its mark on his face, the furrows, the
gravity, the weight on his shoulders of his enormous power;
but there was only that flat smoothness. I was suddenly
reminded of his son. Is this all, I found myself thinking,
after all I've come through?

"Looking more alive than last time we spoke, I see,
even if less honest," he went on, smiling. So, he had a free
tongue, never something to complain of in an enemy; the
night I could not remember, he'd seen me truth-drugged,

I knew now. "Fourth Shefen-kas. A fine fight that was yesterday; very impressive—I see why my son called you Lightning. I suppose you don't need to prostrate yourself, by diplomatic protocol we're equals, aren't we, for now; sit down, my boy, sit down, and drink."

I sat, and took up the wine, which was in a vessel of pure glass, on a table of pure glass. It had almost escaped me, what he'd said, so fast had it gone by. *For now*. By those two words, he'd meant the death of Yeola-e, the enslaving of my people, the smashing of every circle-stone, crystal and sword, all the death and fire, sweat and pain that would take; to me, my ultimate failure, far worse than death. Yet he hadn't said it to hurt me or put me in fear, else he'd have drawn it out, examining my face. He'd said it absently; he wasn't even looking.

I had sworn not to be afraid, and had not been. But now my heart went to water, sending chills flowering all over my skin. I took a draught of wine in the hope it would keep me from paling, then put it down so it wouldn't show the trembling of my hands; but his eyes were on his glass, which he sniffed. "Yeoli," he said. It was only by what was left of the taste on my tongue, at first, that I knew he was speaking of the wine. It was Tinga-eni. "Fifty years old, they tell me. Many things to offer, your home has. You not the least; you fascinate me. Speak. Shefen-kas . . . am I pronouncing it right?"

To do what I had planned, call him down for betraying me, almost seemed trivial in the face of all this, ill-mannered like bad humor at a party or a child's sulk; the peace-sigil, a reproach he would not understand, seemed a toy. It was like a dream, my head going light with my own helplessness while the wine sunk hot into my heart. All the time, in the Mezem, I fought off the sense that my whole past life had been entirely fantasy, and only this was real; never had I felt it so strongly as now.

It was words of Mana's, returning, that shook me out of it. "You are our only demarch." If someone doubts the reality of Hetharin, I thought, let him try running up it. "Kurkas," I said, forgetting the abasing addresses I'd been taught. "You gave me an oath of safe conduct."

He looked for a moment as if he did not understand me, or had forgotten; then said, "Yes, I did. Of course I did." For a moment a silence of misunderstanding hung between us. Since it needed saying, it seemed, I said, "You broke it."

In the same even tone, with pale round brows unmoving, he said, "Of course. My Shefen-kas, you gave me such an opportunity, coming here; should I have let it pass?"

I sat speechless. Once on a month away I'd been eating dinner with the family when one of the boys, having finished his cup of watered wine, reached for mine and drank a good half. "Why did you do that?" I asked, astonished. With utter innocence he replied, "Because mine was empty." This was just the same. Whatever I say will touch him as much as it would the polished cliff, I thought. I felt, not chained, for chains can be held to; but dangling in air, my hands grasping at nothing.

He wanted, of all things, to talk Mezem. "You have ten chains now?" he asked. "Before you go into the Ring, Shefen-kas, do you feel fear?" I stared at him, and thought, I stand on one end of the world, and he stands on the other, if it's even the same world.

It went on this way. I'd been forestalled from getting angry at him, from the start; or perhaps it was that I didn't know how, in the way one wouldn't with a creature from another Earthsphere. I found myself humoring him, though it gave me a dull sense of being raped; and we ended up speaking as any gladiator and Ring patron would, about odds and techniques and who looked good. The food came, course after course of Arkan delicacies, which the servers would announce as they uncovered: hummingbird tongues in saffron sauce, black caviar in red aspic jelly molded in the shape of an octopus swimming in white sauce, ginger sorbet to clear our palates, chocolate truffles with gold-leaf (real gold-leaf, thin enough to swallow). The final course was, for me, a small covered dish of cheese, for him, a naked woman, who, once she'd done the prostration, took his head on her arm and put her breast to his lips. It's true, was all I could think. He stopped sucking for a moment, to say, "Shefen-kas, what you have is also this, in refined form." I had to fight down my gorge. Cheese of human milk—somewhere a child was starving, for this. Will it starve any less, I thought, if I refuse? But Kurkas's eyes were closed, in happiness, so I fed it all to the three

long-haired white cats—blue-eyed, of course—that had
been writhing around my legs.

When he was done, kneeling servants had washed our
hands and we were alone; we went on to worldly matters.
For him, that was Arkan matters; he spoke at length on
the spirit of Imperium, of Arko, of which he was the
embodiment. I soon got the same measure of him I had
when we'd talked Mezem. He had no great intellect, and
knew barely anything beyond his borders—what was beyond
his borders was unimportant, except that it should soon be
within them—but his belief in his own genius was so
complete and sound one could not begin to shake it, and
in fact found oneself unwilling, and half-convinced.

Eventually I said, "What do you plan to do with me?"
Feeling no qualms about it, he might give me a straightforward answer. He did: "Ransom you."

"But I could get killed in a fight; then no ransom money."

He did the Arkan head-shrug, as if it were entirely
natural that I address only his concerns. "Watching you
fight grows on me. If you die, it's good for us too. Shefen-kas,
I've grown to like you, I won't have you worrying. I'll
make everything end for the best; trust me." So, had I
revealed myself at the beginning, before he'd seen me
fight, I might have been taken out of the Mezem. No
use to look back on the stroke of the past.

Soon after that, we made our farewells. Never would I
have believed, I thought as I stepped back through the
gate, that I would be in any place that made the Mezem
seem plain and real.

Skorsas ran to me asking how I was, and should he call
Iska; it seemed people did sometimes come to harm at
Kurkas's dinners. I just said all was well, asked him not to
disturb me, closed my door and doused the candle, so I
could kneel in darkness.

I have met someone, I was thinking, whom I understand
less than anyone else I have met in my life; whom, by any
measure of understanding from the shallow to the deepest,
I do not understand at all. If ever there was a call to be the
other, it was this.

I meditated for calm. Then I thought of the Marble
Palace, still glittering in my memory; of Minis, swaddled
in jewels. The son would lead me to the father, again:
Kurkas had been raised the same way. I thought of the

Mahid, bred to be blind obedience incarnate, the scarlet-armoured armies, claimed to be a *rejin* of *rejin*, a thousand thousand, from Tuzgolu to the gates of the great western sea, their wills relinquished to him from birth. I thought of absolute power: no impeachment, no vote, no law to bind him, in fact the laws his to change at a whim; every person who came into his sight falling face-first to the floor; all near him considering him, all of him and all his will, divine.

It took time; my heart shrank back from every step. *I am the Imperator of Arko. The Palace, the food, the clothes he would wear, eat, see, live anything that he could dream and hands could make. I may have all I desire; I always have had all I desired. What I desire and what I have are one.* No one ever gainsaid him, no one spoke but what he wished to hear. *I am always right; I am the only wisdom in the world. All other thought flows from mine. I am Imperium; I am Arko. Arko's borders are mine; to expand them is to enlarge myself.* For one with absolute power, underlings are as subject as his own body: they are his eyes on the border, his feet on the necks of the peoples he crushes. *There are no bounds of property; all that is yours is mine, including you, Fourth Shefen-kas, because all the world is mine.* As I sat in darkness my mind rose, soared across the Midworld Sea to a thousand outposts; I saw my hands in Tuzgolu, in Kurkania, in Tebrias, attacking here, trading there, working the whole great device with divine brilliance, as I had been born to do. Nor could he fail; for if he did no one would tell him, blaming anything but him. *I am the world; I am perfect; I am God.*

But we are all small, I argued with the role. We are blind, we slip, we bleed, in time we die. No human soul is great enough for this. I looked down at my own naked body in the starlight, to see how slight and scarred and dark it was.

To be the other I had imagined the golden seals on my hands, sun-bright and heavy. They were still there; but shining with a light that lived, and so in its subtle faintness was a thousand times brighter and warmer, was my own skin. I felt it as I saw it, bathing me inside as well as out with gold; to know it as myself was ecstasy.

I am God. I am Imperium. All else is training.

What seemed a fist of wind struck me; I lay on the stone

of the floor, face down, gasping, sick and trembling like a
vessel of water shaken. For an instant, it seemed, my
shape in gold wearing the seals stayed kneeling on the
bed, real enough to reach for; then it flashed away and
there was only the Mezem darkness with its sense of
defeated ghosts. God-In-Me, I prayed, clasping my crystal, I understand him: he believes it, entirely, how can he
not? For a moment I believed it. But let me die before I
do again: for I wanted it.

Two days later, I met Riji Klifas, whose use-name means
Mangler.

I'd heard of him, as all gladiators had. He was still
considered the Living Greatest, the best fighter alive,
though his time was ten years gone. Coming to the Mezem
by choice, as some do, he had soon won a name for being
extraordinarily cruel to those he defeated, making their
deaths as slow and wide-festooned, as the Mezem expression goes, as he could. Needless to say the crowd slavered
over him. After winning his fiftieth chain, he'd married
one of his woman fans and settled down in Arko as an
Aitzas—no slight feat for an Enchian—and, if you will,
began teaching philosophy in the University. As limitless
as his savagery, it was said, was the brilliance of his mind.

I should add here: some time before, I'd found out
Skorsas's illiteracy was a constant haunt to him; being
fessas, it seemed, he ought to have been educated and
apprenticed to his father's trade, which was goldsmithing,
but his father had got addicted to Arkanherb. Among the
things forgone when they'd gone down in the world had
been Skorsas's education. So, though he didn't think it
possible, I undertook to teach him how to read. Outside of
training, since I didn't go out at night, I had little to do,
and had contented myself with such things as a tactical
game one plays alone, with Arkan paper cards.

Tutoring Skorsas meant not only learning Arkan script
myself, but prowling through libraries. Once I'd given
proof I could read, they let me borrow what I liked, so I'd
come out with a stack of children's books on one arm and a
stack of Enchian translations of Arkan strategy and tactics
on the other. (At the entrance to one wing of the library,
which was bordered in black, an officious man demanded
to know my age before he'd allow me in. This was the

Second Portal of Propriety, he told me importantly. In truth I wasn't sure of my age, sensing my birthday was close to now but not knowing the Yeoli date; Arkans keep better track of solstices than equinoxes. As was my habit I gave the older count, twenty-one, which happens to be the Arkan Third Threshold, or coming-of-age, so he let me in. It was a disappointment, in truth, to find out what Arkans considered too hoary for twenty-year-olds to read.)

At any rate, I ended up with a name for bookishness, which Mezem people kept saying reminded them of Riji Klifas. In fact, having heard of his success and seeing mine, a few other gladiators took up reading, imagining it might contain some secret of victory.

I met him on the training ground. When I asked Skorsas who the man was who stood alone while everyone else crowded down at the other end, he went beyond pale, almost green. So, I thought when he told me, that's fifty chains: I want a closer look. I went to Riji and greeted him.

He was the same height as me, and of similar build as well; but his face instead of sharp was broad in the cheekbones, like a lion's, his mane of light brown hair tied back in a club. His eyes were bright green with a touch of gold, and deep-piercing as a great fighter's or philosopher's are. He smiled, but refused my hand, saying that would be inappropriate, since he was returning to the Ring, and asked where my boy was. I turned, surprised; usually he was right behind me. Now he was nowhere to be seen. "Skorsas!" the Enchian called, as if to his own boy; but it was only when I spoke that he came, from behind a pillar. He was trembling, and would come no closer than half behind my arm.

"So is it true, lad?" Riji said. "Do you hold to it? All Arko read it." It came to me what he was talking about; along with the rest, Skorsas had said at Mil Torii Itzan's party that I could beat Riji Klifas. My skin tightened all over.

The boy didn't answer. I said what was true: "If you don't mind, Living Greatest, I see no cause for quarrel. What this lad claimed, I never did." It's death to go into the ring fearing the other, so if it came to that, I wouldn't fear him; yet any difficult fight I could avoid was for the better.

He looked into my eyes, past my words. For fear, I
suppose; perhaps I should have shown some. Every Yeoli
warrior should have a foot that quick, and intent that
well-hidden. It seemed one moment I was seeing that
green gaze consider what to say, and the next I was
curling on the ground, in too much pain from between my
legs to move.

I felt something land across my hair: a money-chain. Riji
had thrown it there, making the Arkan challenge to a bet;
now he stood gazing at Skorsas, who had frozen like the
rabbit before the snake. Well, you're on your own for
now, lad, I thought. Just then he drew himself up, lifted
his nose as only an Arkan can, brought out his own chain
and knelt to smooth the two tenderly onto my neck. Riji
nodded, and strode away. There was nothing to do but
comfort Skorsas that he'd done the right thing, while he
aided me, rapping my heels with his fist and so forth. He'd
had no choice, in truth, and he'd done it with style, to
show his faith in me.

Yet even my agony was relief, in some part. No golden
idol gets this done to him; the world still was as I'd
thought.

As the Pages wrote, the Living Greatest had returned to
the Ring for no other reason than to fight me. I was
expected to take this as an honor; and in truth, I saw, it
was. Much was made, of course, of his not being in his
prime: he was thirty-five. Yet if prime is between twenty-
five and thirty, as Mezem experts say, I wasn't in mine
either.

It wouldn't be immediately; he had to do a few fights to
get back into form. I will say nothing of how they went,
except that he was true to his old name. My heart went
out to those men who died unspeakably as part of his
training. The crowd fell in love with him anew. The advantage was that I didn't get matched against anyone hard
in that time, since I was being saved for him.

Outside the Ring, he dressed and acted impeccably,
never a hair or a word out of place; he loved to discourse
on the finer points of civility and morality over dinner,
even with me. In the Ring, he wore his long hair in an
unkempt braid, and his fighting-clothes were shredded
rags, true to the part he played of the madman. Once,
seeing no other way to find out, I asked him why.

He was quite straightforward. "You are familiar with Haradas's concepts of the intellectual and the beast within each of us," he said. I was, having read some Arkan philosophy as well as strategy. "Most men let the two fight it out, and so are always locked in a struggle. I let them take turns, so that when I am the intellectual I can be purely the intellectual, and when I am the beast, likewise. You see why I came here; there is no better place in the world for that." True: and it explained the device of his sword, which had a head with a serene face on one end of the guard, a contorted one on the other. Perhaps he isn't mad, I thought, but in some way further ahead than the rest of us; but I am mad, if I think that justifies what he does in the Ring.

He was certainly brilliant. He spoke some ten languages, read and wrote six or seven, was expert on the Enchian lyre; sometimes he would play in the stands at dawn, strange dark melodies of his own, leaving me to wonder, since I was, as far as I knew, the only one who'd be awake, whether they were just for me.

Once when I sat reading in the lounge, I looked up, feeling a gaze on me so intent it was warm, and caught him drawing me. "You don't mind, do you?" he said humbly. Not seeing why I should, I said, "Not at all." When he was done, a bead later, he showed it to me, with a grin like a child's. It was astonishing, as good as any artist's; he'd caught me perfectly, my emotion, my coloration —how with black charcoal on white paper, I don't know— even my resemblances to my father and mother. I secretly hoped he'd give it to me; but he folded it away in a portfolio.

About that time a greenhand came in of whom enough fuss for five Karas Raikases was made, for no other reason than that she was a woman. Never before in Mezem history had there been a female gladiator, it was said, though I found that hard to believe; but then we were picked by Arkans, who, like Lakans, believe women cannot fight. No slight feat to convince them; I wondered how she'd done it. Her Ring-name was Niku Wahunai.

The story went round that she'd broken an oddsman's ribs by a standing double-kick with her ankles in leg-irons, and killed one of the testers by breaking his windpipe with the wooden sword. On the training-ground, I saw: one would have to be blind not to see warrior written all over her; she moved like water, and even as a man would have been muscular. Not hulking, but corded, the bunches and veins showing up clear under honey-brown skin; she was from some southern island. All through training one could see the men from lands ruled by men sneaking glances to see if she kept up.

She kept up, then won her first fight, easily. The writers wrote that she had ensorceled her opponent into weakening, "charming his barbaric loins"; that she was a man in disguise, or of an inhuman race, or altered by magic—anything but a woman of strong body and spirit who'd got good training, the thought of which somehow terrified them. Skorsas was almost more afraid of her than of Riji Klifas, especially when she was given the room next to mine. "You are a woman-lover," he said direly, "are you sure she couldn't charm your loins in the Ring?" I asked him whether he really thought I'd listen to my loins while my heart was in danger of getting cut out.

Yet once she ran into me in the corridor, coming out of her door too fast, and for a moment we had looked into each other's eyes close. Hers were black, two perfectly polished onyxes, but flashing bright with life, the kind one gets the urge to make laugh. So I felt, as a man; I forgot to feel as a gladiator. They gazed unwavering; I turned away, having seen what I had feared to; that she was beautiful.

It was bad enough, every eight-day when the matches were made, to have a friend here. To stand hiding my trembling before Fate's Helmet, as they call the bowl from which the lots are drawn, knowing that one lot held the name of a lover, would be unbearable. It should be said, gladiators play all manner of tricks on each other, subtle or unsubtle, outside the Ring as well as in, to win. They're good weapons she has, I recall thinking, those eyes; how many others has she put in fear?

Sometime after my twelfth fight, I was reading in the bath, late. The tub in the Mezem is a remnant from an earlier time, when Arkans found nothing immoral in communal bathing; fifteen people could sit in it, though rarely more than five did. It was late enough that most of the others were sleeping: I was alone, with my *katzerik* and my book, something I always found calming.

"Karas Raikas." I did not need to look up; only one person in the Mezem had a woman's voice. "Does anyone listen, in here?" Her Arkan was better than mine, learned elsewhere, though with a thick accent from a hot clime. She climbed naked into the water. Peering coldly over the edge of my book, I told her no if one spoke quietly, the truth, but turned my eyes back to it to make clear she was imposing. I still remember the line I was reading, from Etzakas's *War Histories*, "so the enlightened general will endeavor to set ranks in this fashion," for I read it seven times without it entering my mind.

She said, "I want you, Raikas. Will you make love with me?"

The book almost went swimming, then. I looked away from her eyes, took a long pull on my *katzerik*. Ripples on the water obscured her body from me, and mine, fortunately, from her. "No," I said finally.

"Why not?" She leaned closer. Even in steaming water, I felt a quick heat like a new-lit fire coming off her. "*You* want *me*. Why are you afraid?"

I stared, got caught in her gaze again. My heart raced and my innards went cold at once. Let her take the flush on my cheeks for anger, I thought, and slammed the book shut. My voice coming out icier even than I'd meant, I said, "Do you understand this place?"

"Yes, of course," she said lightly. "We might get matched. Do you think I'm an idiot?"

I unlocked my tongue and said, "And you ask why not?"

Her long black eyebrows hardened, the arches straightening out into two daggers. She had a name for a wild temper; having heard crashing thuds on the stone wall between our rooms from time to time, I believed it. "Arko," she said in a hissing whisper, leaning close, "has its chains on my body; that's enough. I won't let it put its chains on my soul. It's a shame you have, one like you. Farewell." While I sat back with eyebrows up, she sprang out, her lithe brown body cutting up through the water with barely a splash, and was gone.

Now that it was too late to voice it, my flush did turn to anger. Give it time, one-chainer, I wanted to say, who are you to call me to account, let's see how long you last. You don't understand; what I have suffered you won't, even should you make twelve chains. I fingered the spot under my eyebrow; greenhand, there are a thousand things you don't know.

But it soon crashed in and turned to ashes, being false, as I saw. These were justifications: the pale and bitter arguments of one whose strength was failing. It came clear to me then. The ripples smoothed, leaving the only sound a dripping water tap somewhere in the shower-stalls; I looked down at my wavering reflection, gold teeth winking, and saw my own impression of my strength and courage stripped away. I was full of fear, if not enough to freeze me, enough to stiffen my mind; for, good reason or not, it had ruled me just now. She was right.

The next day I avoided Niku's eyes, and she avoided mine; but I was aware every moment of where she was, even when I couldn't see her, as if she were a sword. I met Mana in the woods, always heartening, but did not share my trouble with him; in Arko one tells as few people as little as one can. So it grew; every sight of those rippling brown arms scolded me, every passing of that proud bearing, always facing elsewhere, while I sat in the lounge with my head buried in smoke and a book—for keeping to my room would be a retreat—etched reproach on my heart. In the training-ground we happened never to face each other. I began to wonder whether she had the better of me, should we be matched; could I kill her? Perhaps she had charmed my loins, fatally. No; it changed nothing; I had my duty.

Yet somehow I happened never to imagine Chirel in my hand running through her wiry small chest, or striking off that proud-held head, though I did that with other fighters, particularly Riji Klifas. I told myself I did not need to.

That night as I lay half-asleep, a scratching like a tree-twig brushing the stone outside my window sounded. I woke and tensed; the courtyard had no trees. "Raikas?" came the whisper, in her accent. "May we speak? There is much I didn't explain." She'd come along the ledge, easy from the next room.

I was awake enough to fight, not enough to think; I said yes. Taking that as permission to come in she swung her legs over the sill, their shine flashing under her open robe, and knelt beside my bed. Her eyes shone like black glass beads in the darkness. "I should say, I am sorry," she said. "I judged you, though I do not understand what it is to be you. Do you forgive me?"

Nothing could come to my tongue, but "Yes"; how could it? "You fear being matched against me. You need not; if you are, you will never face me." I asked how that could be. "I *would* not. I would do otherwise."

I have always been a good judge of honesty; by her eyes, that had never left mine, I would have believed her. But when I understood her meaning, it was beyond belief.

"You are saying," I whispered, "you'd kill yourself. You'd give your life to save mine." No reservations, she just dipped her head, yes. "You've hardly met me, you don't know me. For all you know I could be a child-raper, or traitor, or murdered my family in their sleep, back home; and you'd rather die than kill me?"

"You are none of those things," she said, with certainty like a child's of his parents' goodness. "Besides, my life . . . You know my people are never captured alive."

"Except for you?"

"There is a reason we kill ourselves. But I . . . perhaps you do not believe, in visions." I did, I assured her. "Lord Friend came to me, while I was senseless, and said I must come here, alive. That if I tried . . . he would not take me." Lord Friend, I thought: Shininao, in her tongue. "What would become of me, if I tried to throw myself under the wheels of the wagon, for instance . . . he showed me." My inward eyes clenched shut, against the sight of her crushed, that perfect brown symmetry broken, to heal twisted.

"Why were you to stay alive?" I asked.

Some tale of how she was destined to meet a handsome stranger, I expected; the same she'd told to Suryar Yademkin last night and would tell Dridas Danas tomorrow night. But she said the one thing of all that rang most true, to me who knew foreknowledge. "I don't know. He didn't show me that.

"That was the day I should have died. Each day, since then, is a gift, and a dream: free, nothing. If good cause came I should give my life again. You are that. I love you, Raikas."

My heart flared like a fire poked; but I said what I must. "You must think I'm an idiot. Last time you just wanted *fikken*."

"I thought I wanted only that. Do we always understand ourselves? If I said all I knew of you, it would seem like flattery, what a liar might say. . . . If you were not the man I think, you wouldn't argue with me, wanting me as much as you do; you'd just use me, without a thought. I understand, you suspect me. I swear, Lord Friend . . ." She strained, as if to say a forbidden word. ". . . *Death* witness. That is the highest oath of my people." In my silence she went on. "Which means nothing to you, of course. Second Fire come then."

All down my spine, the little hairs rose. "Lord Friend *Death*," I said, "is indeed witness to one who falsely swears that." She flinched; under her robe, her chest rose and fell fast; her little strong hands clenched the edge of my bed. "Don't say it if you don't have to; it calls his attention. Raikas, please, don't call it down, not on you."

The madness of this place has infected me, I thought; half of me believes her. The very preposterousness of her story recommended it; usually one trying to put one over on you does it more subtly. But I had one test left. As the saying goes, a dog smells his own behind first; none is more suspicious of others lying than a liar. "You ask me to believe you," I said. "What if I said I was the missing king of Yeola-e, and asked you to believe me?"

Her eyes seemed to set and fill with light at once, as at a revelation. "Are you?" It didn't matter; those I'd wanted to hide it from most knew. It was only in shame that I kept my secret now; bad though it was to be called Karas Raikas, Fourth Chevenga the pit bull would have been worse. (In case you wonder, as I did, why it had not been proclaimed in the City or the Empire, to lift morale for the sake of the war, or just to let people know the truth, I will say what I found out later: just letting people know the truth was not tradition here, and Kurkas didn't put himself out to do it, nor was he concerned about morale, being certain of victory.) I said yes. After a time she said, as if I'd told her not this secret but another far deeper, "That explains many things."

"Such as?" I said; now it was flattery I suspected. "You don't know me, to say what it explains." It would be so much easier, I thought, feeling a drop of sweat break loose and roll down my back in the hot night, if I caught you in a lie.

She said, "I have . . . You believe in visions. Do you believe in gifts too?" I signed chalk, forgetting, then at her puzzled look, nodded my head. "I have one. I feel other peoples' feelings. It isn't always, only now and then—but it comes more with you than anyone else, ever in my life."

I'd heard of Haian healers with such a gift using it to heal the mad. Now I remembered her asking me in the bath why I was so afraid, though I'd thought I'd shown nothing, how she'd seen Arko's chains on my soul more clearly than I had myself, how she'd been so certain of my good character.

It seemed the worst sort of gift for a gladiator. "Do you just know the other's feeling," I asked, "or feel it as if it were your own? That could throw you, in a fight."

"I can make a wall in my heart, against it. But you see? You see?" Her voice went like a girl's. "Don't pretend to be less than you are! Usually when I tell someone, their first thought is to worry that I'll learn their dark secrets. Yours was for me. Such a soul you have!" Reaching, she took my crystal in her small callused fingers, lifted it to the slight window-light. "Like this, so pure, so strong. Raikas, how could I not love you?"

It is, I thought, the part of me that loves you. "My name is Chevenga," I said. She pronounced it well, better than most, for she was thorough and careful with it, her voice like fingers handling something precious. To hear it was like a warm hand on one's brow when one is in bed with death-chills. I lifted the bedclothes for her, and said, "Then I give myself to you." To one who would die to save me, I could do no less.

VI

So my double life was doubled again, like Legion Mirrors, wheels within wheels. By day we disdained each other, played rivals. By night we bathed in passion, free but for the hands over mouths to keep silent. Sometimes we were wild as beasts, being young, and full of the fire of training and desperate to throw off our chains at least for a soaring moment; sometimes we were each other's healers, for as my slaver had hurt me, hers had hurt her. "*Mehishmanwia*," she would say, "I love you" in Niah; I would answer the same in Yeoli.

With love I took on fear, as I had known I would. It did not matter, that she had promised not to threaten my life, for now I feared for hers no less than mine. That brought another pain: like cliff-climbing, it felt safer to fight than watch her fight. But we could not be absent, as that would bring suspicion.

On the second night she spoke what seemed again as good as proof of her honesty; were she false, she'd have said it on the first. "I have a way out of here."

"You do? You have friends no one knows? Or can you fly?"

She laughed, and dug my ribs. "I can't tell you what way; it's a secret of my people. But it would work, I know that."

"Then why have you stayed so long?" I still half-disbelieved; the thought of her leaving left my heart a hollow ash for a moment, until I remembered how much for the better it would be.

"It would take time. I don't know how long, the way I'd have to do it; four, six moons, I think, or more."

"Then I will bid you farewell with my blessing," I said. If I live, I thought, perhaps we may see each other in the true world, outside these cliffs. Yet perhaps it is love that could only live here; it was too soon to say, so I kept my silence.

"What do you mean, farewell?" she said. "I'm taking you."

So it was I had to tell her, as I had wished not to, of the *grium*. I could forget the roughness of this place, in her arms that pulled me in so hard and so gently at once, in her lips as they kissed the spot under my eyebrow, in her hands brushing back my hair, the skin leather-hard, the touch tender as a mother's.

It was her nature to face what must be faced. "Perhaps they lied to you, and there is no antidote," she said, right out. "Have you asked a Haian?" She caught me out again, for having given in to fear. I had neglected to see to it, holding no hope of escape anyway. Now there was reason. "You will," she commanded me. "You must. Think of your people, Fourth Chevenga."

At least twenty Haians—all men, of course, since Arkans wouldn't trust a woman—practiced in the City Itself at that time. I had myself examined by five. Three said if there was an antidote, they didn't know it; two said there definitely was not. The most conscientious one, named Nemonden, agreed to write for me to Haiu Menshir, the place of the greatest medical knowledge. After my seventeenth fight, he sent for me to come to his house; the reply had arrived. The foremost scholar-healer in matters of Arkan drugs and poisons, Osuber of Haiu, had written.

She would not rule out an antidote known only to Arkans, and kept secret; other such things had been found out afterwards. But if there were none, two other cures were possible. Drastic, I thought as I read the precise Enchian hand, goes without saying. The first was a long regimen of rest and extremely strict dieting, including long fasts, "which," as she phrased it, "makes strenuous physical exertion impossible." So much for that. The other was quick, but dangerous, and required a trip to Haiu Menshir: surgery.

"Surgery?" I remember asking Nemonden. "In my head? I didn't think that was possible." He assured me it had been done by several healers on the island a number of times, usually to remove growths in the brain, though being the most invasive of treatments it was used only when death would otherwise be certain. People were sometimes saved, though some came out of it addled, which in my case would be as bad as death, or worse. I remembered how little time the Imperial Pharmacist had needed to afflict me with it. The shudders came, as they sometimes did when I thought about it, enough that Nemonden put his arm round my shoulders. So easy to destroy, I thought, so hard to create, or repair.

So that way was closed too; I could hardly beg permission of the Marble Palace to go to Haiu Menshir to get its own expedient eliminated, promising I'd be right back to finish my fifty fights. I could only wait until Niku's promised time, trying to forget that one's chances lessen as the condition advances, then go straight there on the way home. In the meantime, Osuber wrote, I could slow the *grium's* growth by keeping as best I could to the diet she laid out, and ingesting a certain drug. When I asked how I could do that, Nemonden said, "You do already. Not here, since I disallow it, but elsewhere, constantly, by what you told me. What is normally a noxious habit, that I urged you to stop, will stand you in good stead, it turns out." The stuff was in *katzeriks*; I got it every time I smoked. Some part of me felt vindicated.

He also recommended another Haian in town, Persahis, who was a psyche-healer. "I know you are not mad," he said quickly, as people always do when recommending psyche-healers, "but if you find yourself needing comfort or steadiness, as would be understandable in your circumstances, he is a strong soul who will cast with you." As well as Skorsas and Iska, I thought, I have Niku and Mana, two more than most gladiators have. But they were in the maelstrom with me, while Persahis stood on a rock outside, and so could see what we could not. I thanked Nemonden.

So Niku did her work, whatever it was, and I had my plan, whatever it was worth. She spent much of the day out, supposedly meditating, wandering the city or carving, for which she needed the peace and solitude of the woods. For every man she killed, she made a grief-bead; at home, apparently, they were hung on a sacred tree as memorials. Now and then she'd ask me for money, which I'd give her as I got it, in jewelry that had come with locks of hair and notes saying "A favor for my fancy," or "Wear this, Raikas, and think of me."

The chefs were willing to cook specially for me; I was kind to the staff, who were honest. No more red meat, and only a little white, a standard Haian limit which in fact I've been prescribed for most of my adult life; as well certain vegetables and spices were forbidden, and others required. I didn't like it; but then no one sensible truly likes smoking either.

Every now and then the Mahid would take me to the Marble Palace to be truth-drugged. What I told them, I have no idea; I wouldn't even know it had happened until I noticed a long string of the day was cut out of my memory, and Skorsas said gently, "They came again." Why they gave me the forgetting-drug, I don't know, perhaps as a torment; if anything, it was a mercy.

Suryar Yademkin made forty-nine, and was all white-toothed grins. He was a big dark bear of a man, whose rallying cry to himself was *senraha*, his word for home. Now it was *senraha* all the time, his joy spreading through the quarters like a warm flood.

At dinner the night before the matches were to be made, he suddenly stood up and said "Everyone!" We all stared; gladiators never speak more to each other at dinner than, "Pass the fish sauce, please." He lifted his wine-cup. "I hope you don't mind," he said in his rough Arkan, "but I want to do this before one of you is chosen, that this toast would be a curse to. Here's to, whether it be near or far, rich or poor, flat or mountainous: *senraha*."

A silence thick as night fell. All around I could see them thinking, *easy for you to say. It looks good, for you.* No one moved, not even to chew; eyes narrowed on him.

He stood alone, frozen; I saw his face begin to redden under the brown. Then a chair banged over backwards, and another man was standing with cup raised: Mana. His face was angry. "To *senraha*!" he barked, like a decurion. "It's what we all want, what we all share. So we will see one of us get it, most likely, and it'll bring no hardship to any of us but one, so what's the trouble? For once we can be big-hearted. Come on, you assholes!" He was looking straight at me, his eyes seeming to say "*You* should have thought of this." I sprang up, cup in hand, shouting, "To *senraha!*" Then Riji did, laughing that this was his home, but he'd drink to it; then all did.

Such a soul had Mana-lai Chereda. Need I say why I loved him?

Miracles happen in this world, even in such a part of it. It seemed to come to all of us at once that while two gladiators making friends put themselves in danger, all being friends with all others changed nothing. Dinner turned into a night-long party. I was very much behind it, spending more jewelry I never wore for the wine and the twenty women of the evening. While the boys and servants ran back and forth serving us, gaping and exclaiming they'd never seen such a thing in a hundred years, we danced and hugged and poured wine into each others' mouths like a victorious army. Riji brought out his lyre, and serenaded us with songs more filthy than we'd thought a scholar of his dignity should know. I remember the toasts: "To death, which we all will be to each other!" "To the lions, who will chew our bones!" "To the buzzard crowd, who'll dip their kerchiefs in our lifeblood!" "To life, may it last forever!" All night we laughed so hard we cried. When it ended a good nine of our thirty needed carrying to bed, like corpses already.

Next day truth came with sunlight, sharp into our hung-over minds; the silence between us returned. At noon came the wait before fate's Helmet, and the matching.

Yes, Mana, I spoke inwardly, I should have thought of it first. It was safe to assume, because they are saving me for Riji, that I wouldn't be put against Suryar for the only fight that stands between him and *senraha*. You should never have had to pay so, for your good nature. The Mezem evil always proves mightier in the end, the slaves who have bucked against their chains, slapped down with the whip, until the proof they are broken comes: they regret their act. All that eight-day I could not bring myself to speak of it to Niku; out of civility she did not mention it to me. As we watched Mana and Suryar take the Ring against each other, we all regretted it; for by it we had set this fight to be a tragedy, either way. The Director was only the director; we were the playwright as well as the actors. So it must be, to amuse the audience of Arko.

I shall say no more of the fight, which I watched stone-faced as I always must and always did, but that Mana won. It came to a contest of stamina in the end, and he, like me, had broken his limits with his heart running up mountains.

We met in the woods afterwards. There he, who had never before let the Mezem touch him even a trace, flung himself to the ground and piled dirt on his hair and wept in my arms when I seized him, crying, "I should have let him kill me!" Usually one can say, someone else would have got him if I didn't. Not when it is the other's fiftieth; his blood is on your hands alone.

"He never called me a double-dealer," Mana said to me, between his sobs, he who always laughed. "He could have. But he was too good. Near the end, Cheng, when he felt himself flagging, you know what he did to try to keep himself going? All-spirit, sweet Saint Mother, he said *senraha*, over and over again, *senraha, senraha, senraha*, then when I got him and he knew he was done, *senraha*. . . ."

My fight with Riji was soon after that. Eight kills, it seemed, were enough for him to get back in training, so he'd gone to the Director to prompt him, and now we were matched.

I hardly need say, it was very thoroughly built up. Chips were five times the usual price, and the market for them on the street was Hayel-fire hot, as Arkans say. The Pages predicted and speculated and wasted the precious power of the Press on all sorts of nonsense. The city made a holiday of it.

It was Skorsas's duty never to let his certainty that I would win slip, and he didn't; but I could see through that brass facade. It wasn't doubt in me, I saw, but his feeling that, if I did feed the lions, it would be entirely his fault. Once I told him I would not blame him, whatever happened, for Riji would have come back sooner or later anyway. It only made him spring up and away, saying he had to fetch something, so I gave over.

Gladiators usually never take sides in other fights; if the wrong man wins, he will come out fired up against them.

But I felt in the air a secret current of favor for me. On first sight it was practical: I killed quickly and without shaming, unlike him, so they'd rather bear my danger than his. Looking again, I saw they were thinking wrongly: if he won he'd go back into retirement, so they'd be rid of both of us. It was their hearts that ruled.

Then, the day before, it suddenly became open; out of Riji's sight, for he might stay on if he won and someone had offended him, they'd hit my shoulder as I passed, or give me a blessing in some strange language. Wishes have strength, whether they influence the falls of chance or the spirit of the receiver; I know it helped me.

The colonnade was packed with people all through training that day, writers, oddsmen, motley hangers-on. Riji lingered afterwards. Before they could envelop him, he called my Ring-name. "Shall we spar?"

We never had. He'd always happened to be at the other end of the line, or with someone else; when it came to me he wished to avoid it, out of civility I didn't press it. Now I regretted it. I should have refused him, this time. It certainly would have been most just, and if he taunted me for a coward in front of the writers, what of it? But sparring is for learning; if this was my only chance, I was thinking, I should take it.

So I said yes, and we went into stance. The clots of watchers that were just beginning to disperse froze, then rushed back, elbowing each other and whooping.

It was a lapse of thought, such as a young warrior will make. He'd planned this from the start, and so was ready for it, as for the fight; I'd had it sprung on me, and so was not. Suffice to say, his skill was faultless, as I'd expected, and his spirit, steel wrapped in silk. It finished with Chirel off-line, and his sword, with its sane and mad faces, touching my throat; he'd won. As if taking a trophy, he jabbed me, in the point over the artery, just enough to draw a trickle of blood.

"You think it will be different in the real fight," he said softly, wording my thought even as it went through my mind, his green eyes in a smile that anywhere else would have been compassionate. I suddenly felt like a student again, in the presence of the old master. He ran his fingers through his fifty-eight chains, making them swing and flash. "So did many others." He gazed for a moment at the drop of blood on the tip of his sword; then he walked away.

Skorsas ran to my elbow like a hound. "He must be running scared," he said. "I've never heard of him going to all that trouble." I didn't know whether this was true, though, after what Riji had said about others; they both had reason for falsehood. Men crowded around me like rats; for some reason their Arkan smell, from eating too much beef, seemed pungent as dung; I wanted to cut a path through them. "So, he got you! Do you think he will tomorrow?" "Raikas, how does this change things?" "Raikas, might this be your last chance to speak to the people of Arko, what do you wish to say?" The standard odds had been even money; now I could hear five-to-four, even four-to-three, for him.

In the shower, and for the rest of the day, I thought a thousand things. I couldn't meet Mana in the woods; the streets would be a gauntlet I didn't care to run. He made no great effort to speak to me, not wanting to seem as if he never hoped to again. Niku sneaked in through my window that night as usual, and we made love. "He is a *fahkad shkavi*," she said, meaning one who mates with sharks. "Kill him, *omores*." It made me feel strong, to assure her with an unforced smile that I would. She didn't stay that night, knowing Skorsas might well check on me.

Past the time I should fall asleep, I could not; and then the trouble he had intended came.

Fear is a squid, with a thousand tentacles. In the ink-darkness of late night, when even the trees are silent, when strength and faith are at their lowest ebb and the old or weak die, its tendrils reach. I lay measuring, weighing signs, telling myself I was truly better than he, he'd just been ready when I was not; then I'd feel the last stroke again, putting the lie to it all. Then I'd see I was afraid, and the fear of fear came: I can't sleep, I thought, he has me; by morning I'll be exhausted.

Fear is a sparring-partner that knows every opening in the black dance, is fire, licking at the pillars of the soul, and shadow, crouching behind every unevenness. Stamped out in one place it flares up in other; driven out of one corner by light it creeps around to gather behind, as often as not in disguise, as caution, as reason, as courage, as fear reflected in courage, as courage reflected in

fear: so on forever to impossibility like the Legion Mirrors.
Why, I thought, didn't I call him back to spar again? He's
left me with just that one memory, his sword in my throat;
I felt it again, on my skin and with weapon-sense, caught
myself fingering the scab, whipped my hand away. Perhaps I'd have beaten him, given myself another. Yet perhaps not; perhaps he'd have got me twice, making it twice
as certain. No, that's fear talking; I'd have got him, I know
it. But how can I? That's fear, too; no, it's sense; no, it's
fear disguised as sense, no . . . Fear is a dead end at every
path, a dam clogging and choking the flow of good thought,
twisting it against itself. I'm not stopping the bad thoughts,
I thought, the replayings of the sparring-match that will
etch that result into my mind and my muscles, making me
follow it tomorrow as sure as if I were planning it myself.
No one kills us, but ourselves. I meditated, which brought
calm while I did it; but afterwards they scuttled back. I
did not go to the window, and call, telling myself, "There
is no voice from the sky." Yet if I believed there were, I
thought, I'd be comforted; it's fear stopping me again. But
if I try I will fail, and feel like a fool. What am I afraid of?
Shininao is my little brother, I like to say. A thousand
times, I have accepted my death.

Fear is a disease, for as in a disease, the body rules the
soul; one cannot keep the sickness, the trembling, the
sweating, from poisoning the thoughts; one cannot forget
one is feeling them, nor that they aren't going away. I will
fail, I will prove too weak, I will slip, I will have lost . . .
some mistake in technique that my teachers taught me but
I was too stupid to remember, and in an instant I will die.
How many others, I thought then, have lain awake in the
claws of dread in this room? Is it the power of their ghosts
I feel, resenting my life, my victories? The Mezem is the
jaws of a monster big as the Earthsphere, eating all that
comes into them, first with madness, then death. Everyone knew the story of the gladiator who was so afraid of his
opponent he jumped into the lion-trench; but there are
subtler forms, the drink, the herb, the *katzeriks*, the
quirks, the superstitions, the fanatic religions full of illu-
sions; one saw them all around. We all knew the look of
man whom the day-in day-out fear had finally broken. He
went into the Ring looking for nothing but death, the

life gone out of his eyes already; he didn't really fight, but only made the motions, and got spat on by the crowd; soon he got cut down, putting an end to the pretense, his body following his eyes. We all hoped to be matched against him. Am I that now, I wondered; no, but I will be by morning if I don't sleep. I closed my eyes; but as good to try to force it as to catch the sea-tide in a net. It was far past the time of reason; every passing moment I lay awake was sapping my strength, killing me. Yet I could do nothing. Fear is a wall, at every side.

Finally, in frustration, in exhaustion, in horror, I wept in the darkness and tossed, my sheets thrown aside, like a child, even as I knew the motion itself would keep me awake. Fear destroys, I thought, one comes to a point where there is no turning back, and death is inevitable; I must be past it by now. *No, All-spirit . . .* the voice from within turned stronger. *No. You are thinking wrongly.* Calm—I need something I thought; there must be some way. I have borne this alone so far, in pride, telling myself I was capable. Forget the pretense; I can't afford it. I got up and put on a robe, and went to Iska's desk.

His eyebrows rose, to see me. "Don't tell me, lad," he said quietly. "You can't sleep."

"I can't sleep," I said, my own voice sounding hollow to me.

He looked into my eyes, and said, "You're scared shitless."

"I'm scared shitless," I said, feeling a smile tug my lips in spite of everything.

"One thing you are blessed with that will always stand you in good stead," he said. "You never deceive yourself."

I waited for him to mix me the sleeping drink. A failure, to have to take it, and it does throw one off slightly; but better than no sleep. Instead, he said, "Raikas, listen, and do exactly what I say. Do you trust me?" I said yes. "Will you do it?" His firmness was welcome: I said yes again.

"Go out to the Ring. Right now, *into* the Ring. Give voice and deed to your fear. Don't worry about waking anyone or anyone seeing you, but scream what you want to, yell, 'He's going to get me! I'm lion-food! I'm going to lose! I'm doomed!' Run around and throw yourself in the dirt and kick and scream and be totally undone until you can't any more. Then come back in here."

I stood staring at him, wondering whether he'd taken Riji's side. "You said you'd do what I say," he reminded me, his brows hardening. "You said you trusted me."

In the Ring, though the air was still warm, the sand had gone cool, under my bare feet. I stripped to free my limbs, and stood for a while naked, thinking, "What I am about to do is madness." But once I'd begun, precisely what he'd prescribed down to the words, it followed naturally enough. I can't remember all I yelled, switching from one language to another; a child throwing a tantrum with all his childish single-mindedness couldn't have done better; I did it until I fell. Then as I lay panting, for an audience of ghosts in the empty stands all around, I thought, this isn't going to help one bit. I'm being a complete idiot. Maybe he'll get me, maybe he won't; I will do all I can do, my utmost, and if it isn't enough, at least my people won't have to pay the ransom. Clarity came harder. I've been afraid of *losing*, I thought, not death; that's pride, vanity, hate; Saint Mother, who cares if he outdoes me or not, when my *life* hangs in the balance? That's the only thing to fear, and I don't hear Shininao's wings anyway. Fear is an illusionist, masking one feeling with another.

I went back in to Iska. "*Agh minigh*, look at your face," he said. "Are you that dirty all over under the robe? Well, you have time for a quick bath, while the drug's taking effect." He'd mixed it after all; I drank it down. "Now get to bed," he said when I was out of the bath. "Too bad if you don't like my shortness. You understand, I don't have so much sympathy for you, Karas Raikas, as for most. For once in your life you've had an inkling of how it would be to be matched against yourself. Now get."

I slept. In the morning I felt myself, as before any fight.

As I have said, there are five fights per fight day. The main event, between the two highest chainers, comes last. My heart goes out to those who die barely noticed, the crowd having its mind and voice too much on the fight to come. His and my followers were out in force, with their lettered banners and ribbons and blow-horns; I even saw black curly wigs. I wondered what Yeoli warriors fighting Arkans would think, to see that. Kurkas was in the Imperial box, with Minis; he came often, now, to my fights.

I bid clean blade; Riji bid his specialty, sword and chain. Every gladiator was trained in the Mezem chain, a weapon invented here, I think, to match the symbol. It is some three-quarters of an arm long, with a grip that clasps around the hand, and at the end five small spiked balls. Not a weapon to kill with, easily, but in a skilled hand it moves too fast to see, can hurt, and distract, tangle up weapons or limbs and curl over the edge of a shield. One used it in one's shield-hand.

Fear is the stuff of childhood, I thought, as Skorsas, bouncing and chattering, clanged open my gate, and the crowd leapt roaring to its feet. I just fight, that's all.

I had won the die roll, clean blade first. In his famous tatters and tangles he came out fast and furious right from the start—we'd tested each other's defenses last night—so I paced myself, parrying. He knew, as I did, that I could outstay him, and didn't want to let it get to that. His skill was the kind that teaches one even as one fights it, that lifts one above oneself by necessity. I remember feeling a kind of yearning as we circled and struck, that I could not put a name to. His spirit was the beast, killing for killing's sake, killing me for pride. But I had finished letting that touch me, on this same sand, last night.

Where two spirits cannot crush each other, skill will out. He had trained for far longer than I, in the chain; I'd seen him put a man's eye out with it once, and in the next round, the other. In the fourth round, when our fight had already gone far longer than most had expected, giving one and all his money's worth, he switched hands, sword now in left, chain in right, so we were mirrored. Something to change the pattern, since it had not served him well, confuse me, show his skill, perhaps; he was equally brilliant either way.

One keeps the chain spinning always, so that they both whir in the air like angry bees, invisible. I stepped in to cut; he parried going low and then something knocked my lead foot out from under me, stinging like an arrow: his chain. I had never seen a footsweep done with a chain before. Going down I held his sword off, and lashed with my chain; but I was off-line to aim between his legs, and so only got his middle, gaining nothing. My head was open, and we were helmetless; I could only clench my eyes shut in the hope that would save them, and expect death. Instead he threw his fist into my temple, and all went black for me.

I thought the screaming roar was in my head, at first. Chirel was far off, my chain still clipped to my hand. I heard words: "See what you've done, boy! He'd have made fifty, if not for your loose mouth." Riji Klifas, standing over me, speaking to Skorsas; by that I knew where I was, the cruelty of his words bringing anger sizzling through my pain.

I opened my eyes. A mistake: they instantly filled with fire. In the midday sun, the Ring's golden dust gets scalding hot; he'd flung a handful into my eyes. Before my strength came back enough to fend him off, he ground more in with the heel of his hand, holding my head by my forelock. Then he stood up, and backed away. Once he'd incapacitated you, he'd play with you, like a cat with a mouse; the better you'd been the longer he'd make it last.

I turned over and got up on my elbows, and for a moment could not tell up from down, the two seeming to spin end over end. I tried to shake it off, and threw up, making some people cry "Ugh!" as if I'd showed bad table manners. "*Raikas!*" my followers were screaming. "*Up, my treasure, up, my darling, up, for the love of all Ten Gods!*" Wishes have strength, even from them; again I won't deny, they aided me. He kicked me onto my back again, slid his sword under my belt and cut it through, flicked my kilt off. An earth-shaking sight, to an Arkan; some laughed, some whooped, some cried out in anguish, for opportunities lost, for the tragedy. I got to my elbows again, and this time he let me rise all the way to my feet.

Never have I been so glad I kept my mouth shut, about weapon-sense. Still, could I fool one so masterful? Only one way to find out. I set my chain to spinning, and blundered here and there as if I were trying to find him by sound alone.

Now and then he'd come close and laugh or whistle, teasing me, at which I'd strike or charge vaguely; then of course everyone took it on themselves to direct me, as if they could be quick enough, my followers to my favor, his followers every which way to befuddle me, and Skorsas, trying to make his thin youth's voice heard over all the others, crying "Jewel of Arko, listen to *me!*"

When Riji came close enough behind me, aiming to cut the tendons behind my knee, I turned, wrist-parried the sword, caught the chain, and kicked with all the strength in me where his stomach must be. I felt my heel go in deep, with a heavy thump full of burstings and partings within. He made no sound but the breath forced out, and fell, his sword tumbling, his chain dragging down on my hand. I wasn't about to make a mistake I'd just seen made, though I knew he was already dying of the kick; he made no sound still, his innards too crushed even to give out a gasp. He was too good to play with, as he should have known I was. I took up his own mad and sane-faced sword, searched through the rags with my fingers for his heart-beat, and finished him.

Skorsas's hands were on my arm in a moment; then I was in a press of shrieking people. The crowd had burst through the gates and rushed the Ring. He led me out; it helped when I set my chain spinning over my head. At least I could defend my hair, my fingers, my blood. Riji's corpse fell to the souvenir-takers. When a great gladiator dies, enough genuine finger-bones of his appear for sale on the streets of Arko to have come from an army; but ten fingers' worth are real.

In the clinic Iska tended my eyes; once he'd bathed and salved them he covered them with bandages. He was not certain, but thought my sight would come back in a few days. I asked Skorsas what happened to blinded or crip-pled gladiators. "A rich patron buys them from the Mezem and supports them in luxury," he said, too quickly. That was the lucky, I guessed; the unlucky no doubt ended up rowing or carrying stone or running on treadmills. Of course, I'd still be able to fight; but I still meant to keep my silence.

All afternoon I slept, Skorsas succoring me like a mother. Now he called me Jewel of the World; to his mind at least I had become Living Greatest. It seemed almost a waste, that a title so coveted should come to one to whom it meant less than nothing.

That night, Niku crept in, and without a word we seized each other and made love like two starved lions, so wildly some of my cuts bled again. "Live, *omores*, *live*," she hissed, silvery in the dark as we thrashed, "I hold you, I hold you, to life." When we were done, we both wept, though it hurt my eyes, with the feeling that has no name but feeling. It had felt like a sword through her heart, to see me fall, she said. "If he'd killed you I would have insulted him, so that he'd stay, and fight me. I couldn't have lived without killing him." No idle words; I knew her that well.

I did not know I had fallen asleep until I woke. My head was still on Niku's shoulder, the scent of her skin faintly sweet in my nose. But she was twitching, and moaning in her own tongue, "*Gh'yir! Gh'yir!*", caught in a nightmare. I held her and whispered soothing words to her, as we did for each other's bad dreams; gladiators have them often.

She calmed, pressing her cheek to my brow, and by a movement of air, perhaps, or a rustle, I felt another presence in the room, near my side. My breath froze in my lungs: of course I could see nothing. Not knowing what to say, if anything, I lay tense, my head raised, the air seeming to pulse and ripple about me; then Niku sat bolt upright, and gasped.

"You brown bitch," I heard the voice say: Skorsas's. I understood. In fatigue we'd both fallen asleep, forgetting he would come to give me more painkiller. "You figure you won't beat him any other way, so you'd try this. May you smother in Hayel."

She lay still and silent as stone. I swung myself up, groped in the air for his shoulder to get a fix, and backhanded him across the face so hard he fell; I heard him hit the stone floor through the rug, his hands smacking; then the sobs.

So I betrayed my promise to him, because no words sharp enough had come to me. Yet that is no good cause either; and though I might excuse myself saying this barbarian place brought out the barbarian in me, no threat had forced my arm.

"I care for nothing in the world but you," he breathed through his tears, from the floor. "I care nothing for my father, nothing for my Empire, nothing for anything, but you."

So it was. You might ask how could I have been so stupid for so long, how I could have missed the thousand signs. I stood feeling like a post, or a tree, no less blind, while the evidence flooded through my mind. He was Arkan, and a youth. He'd loved his last fighter, who'd been crueller than I. The devotion, the tenderness, the excessive dread that he'd doomed me with his words at the party, the words themselves; the looks he let linger on me, that I'd caught in the Legion Mirrors; even the first groundless loathing, that he'd never explained, the spitting on my sympathy; he'd hated me for making his heart betray Tondias, when the corpse was barely cold.

I had struck him for words he'd spoken out of love.

I knelt beside him, apologizing, asking forgiveness. At first he scrabbled back, then, when I cornered him against the wardrobe, let me touch him. "Those are tears, not blood, aren't they?" I said. "Do you need Iska?" Niku was at the window, ready to go in a moment, saying nothing because anything she said would hurt him; she had sense that way. He just answered, "You shouldn't be taking care of me, you're hurt, you should be in bed."

"Skorsas," I said, "you're wrong, that's all. There are a hundred things you don't understand, because no one's told you. Only one matters: I'd rather cut my own heart out than fight her. Remember that, if jealousy tempts you." He said, "If I had to cut *my* heart out not to hurt *you*, I would." Then, the city came for me.

I had wondered, why the street susurrus echoing dully in the courtyard beyond the window had been noisier than usual; Arko was celebrating my victory. Now there were drunken tromping feet in the corridor, and joyful shouts, mostly my Ring-name.

"Oh my little professional God," cursed Skorsas, springing up. "The buzzards are breaking in." "I love you, *omores*, I'll come back if it's safe," Niku said in Enchian, and I heard her legs slip over the sill. "*Raikas! Raikas!*" they chanted outside, without regard that anyone might be sleeping; angry shouts came too, and Iska's voice, wearily, "He's resting, leave him alone if you care for him," in between. "*We want him! We won't leave without him! Raikas, come out and party! They can't refuse, he won't refuse; there's too many of us!*"

The people wills, I thought ruefully. Voices got threatening, there'd be blood; I heard a fighter shout, "Raikas, call off your dogs!" Skorsas gasped when I groped to the

wardrobe, threw it open. "You're not going to—! Celestialis,
you're too good to the world, you're a born king, here, let
me help you. . . ." When I went out the cheering doubled.
Wine-stinking breath and body smells choked the air.
Hands grabbed my legs and I was off the ground; then I
was on someone's shoulders. Like a general on a horse,
I thrust my arm to the egress of the corridor with a grand
flourish, and bellowed, *"Out!"*, the blind leading the be-
fuddled. Roaring and whooping they took me, and all
night paraded me through every street and tavern, I swear,
in the city.

I should add the one bit of this tale that remains, though
I didn't find it out for myself until years later. I asked Iska
idly what sleeping-drug he'd given me the night before,
that had an effect so natural. He grinned. "Extract of
nothingness, we called it," he said. "The Haian term, I
think, is placebo."

VII

"I understood from the start," Skorsas said the next afternoon, when I had slept out my hangover. "You are a foreigner, you love women. I always knew that." His voice was hard and closed, with resignation.

A little later he said, "The writers are on the verge of disemboweling each other with their pens to see you. What shall I tell them?"

Some say I saw a chance; it's more true that I wanted to throw the rat-pack a fish instead of a fish-head, just to see it stick in their throats. "I'll speak only to the first one who swears on his hope of Celestialis he'll write all I say, and the truth of it."

To my astonishment, they found one; he recited the oath right in front of me. His voice was middle-aged, gentle and, most strange, *Aitzas*-accented; all other writers were *fessas*. He can afford to write truth, I thought. I wished I could see his face.

I took my answers off down my own path almost as soon as I opened my mouth, and could barely believe it when his pen didn't stop scratching, even as I said the Mezem ravaged and despoiled all who entered it and was a boil betraying the corruption running through every vein and nerve of Arkan society. He confessed to me he'd barely seen a Mezem fight in his life and didn't know what to ask, so I gave him all the pat answers; when that was done, just as I was thinking, "I've been had; he'll leave now," he turned the subject back to corruption. He didn't protest or even calmly deny, only listened and wrote and now and then asked me to clarify. I began to think he either was a spy, or agreed with me.

We spoke for a good two beads. What I most remember is his saying, "You don't belong here," to which I answered, "None of us do. Except those who choose." (It wasn't only Riji; actually there are a few, who come out of love of fighting or to seek fame. I'd heard a story lately of an Arkan, one Kallijas Itrean, who would have entered the Ring had his father not forbidden him.)

He told me he would write the account of the fight for the Pages and the Watcher, as he'd promised; then he wanted to write a book about me, of all things. I agreed to speak to him again. His name was Norii Mazeil.

As Skorsas salved my hurts again afterward, he said, "We've got to deal with the spoils, Shefen-ka." I'd forgotten: a fighter is entitled to all the possessions of the man he has killed. When Mana had killed Suryar, he'd acquired a roomful of clothes good enough for princes, none of which fit him, a house in the *solas* quarter, five slaves including three concubines, and a horse (all of which he freed or sold). Riji, it seemed, had been even richer than Suryar; without intending it, I was a slave-owner. I could imagine what could be made of that, if it ever got back to Yeola-e.

But he was married; that makes it simple, I thought. "Manumit the slaves and sign everything else to his wife," I told Skorsas, whose duty it also was to manage my money. For all I told him I did not consider myself owning it, he kept informing me with lusty pride how much it was increasing—he'd cached it all in clever investments—though with eyes downcast he admitted it would never match the hoard I must have at home.

I should say, once when I'd come in unexpectedly, he'd started so badly the ledger jumped off his lap; almost before I even asked any questions, he was on his knees begging forgiveness and admitting he deserved dismissal. It turned out he'd been filching, to save up to buy his family's way back out of the poor quarter into the *fessas*. I told him just to ask if he needed money, and gave him the whole jewelry box; I got no use from it. I thought he'd die of thirst, so much he cried.

"To his *wife?*" he said now. "You bizarre Yeoli. She's a woman, she's spoiled herself, so are his children. You're her husband, and their father. You could sell them all to brothels, if you wanted." I had forgotten: who kills, becomes. Already weak, I felt sicker. I could imagine her, a delicate *Aitzan* woman, in her house with the two little boys gathered near her, waiting to find out their fate from her husband's killer. I knew from the Pages, they'd had front row seats at the fight.

I sent Skorsas for their books. It turned out Riji had hired out his accounting, so I called in the accountant. I saw in a moment even without my eyes that he was looking to bilk an ignorant woman—they aren't permitted to read in Arko—and a slow-witted barbarian out of whatever he could; it started with his trying to charge me for this visit. I dismissed him right there. When my sight came back, which it did, thank the die, in two days, Skorsas and I started checking the figures; luckily it was all in Enchian, and the bankers he had dealt with used that tongue.

His funeral was the day after that. The notice in the Pages said only those he had known were welcome; he had known me, so I went. I would have gone to the funeral of every gladiator I killed, had they been held. His was the only one.

I wore my hood, and let no one else see me when I greeted the man who held the temple door. He looked at me as at a child-raper, and drew breath to cry out; I whispered, "Think, if you reveal me, what a scene this will be"; there were three writers trying to wangle their way in. "You're his friend, I understand; I will hide in the gallery, so no one sees me. My oath on it." With lips pressed tight, he said, "Very well, sword-buck. But take good care. If a hair of you is seen, I'll have you murdered. Don't think I don't have ways." I just nodded, and he let me pass.

As the saying goes, nothing reveals a person so well as his funeral. Elegies were spoken by his philosopher colleagues, by Koree, by the Mezem writer Roras Jaenenem; but no living fighters, or boys. Several of his paintings

were on the wall, the music and verses were all his; one
had to marvel. His corpse was covered to the neck, and
wore a wig that matched his hair, to hide its desecration.
A wreath of chains, fifty-eight no doubt, shone on the
shroud, though the original ones had surely been snatched;
someone was spending, out of love. I slipped out before it
was finished.

I was sure Sora, as she was named, would be better never
to see my face; but Skorsas assured me that she expected
me, and in fact until I spoke to her in person, would
live in fear. So I steeled myself, and went to the house.

It was a medium *Aitzan* place, but Enchian inside, the
woodwork all plain and dark, a sweet spice incense in the
air, the walls full of paintings, his and others', as if they
deserved to hang together, which they did. Everything
was quality. I was shown into the great-room with all
courtesy by the butler. Their forelocks still streaked black
with mourning dye, Sora and her sons came in. With her
eyes down, never on me, she knelt at my feet; the two
boys stayed back, silent, the younger clutching the arm of
the elder, who was about ten, and had Riji's face in small.
I remember the look, when his eyes, of the same pale
green, met mine: "When I come of age, you are dead."
True enough, I thought.

They were out of school for this appointment; "Let them
miss no more of their learning," I said, wanting to speak
with her alone. A slave appeared instantly to attend them,
with a bow to me as to the master of the house. When she
and I were alone, she offered refreshment, sensing, perhaps, my unease: a flask of nakiti, Kiaji's, the finest. I
poured two cups, threw back half of mine in one draught,
and asked her to take a chair, and drink, and look at me,
or not, whatever she wished.

I spoke my intention from the start: that they should
lose nothing, and live in no less comfort, except what I
could not replace, his presence. She did not seem to
believe me, at first, having expected horrors. At the first
sip of nakiti she sputtered. It had never occurred to me
this might be the first nakiti in her life; that she had taken
my permission to drink as command. Arko breeds its
women like that.

I went on, though to my own ears it sounded hopelessly
lame, about investments, interest, manumitting the slaves

but keeping them on for a wage, and how I would give her my own money if there were no other way. His Mezem gold had all gone to the house, books and art, of which I'd just promised to sell none; it was on his professor's pay he'd sustained the family, including the education and war-training of his sons. She did not answer, this all being men's business.

What I could not bring myself to raise, she did. "I pray, husband," she said with her eyes hidden behind the black locks of hair, "you find me pleasing." One could not imagine a murmur more cold and weak. Sickness cut through the nakiti glow, I itched to dash out the door, and never think of this again.

In Arko, it is respectable, though difficult, to be a widow; one's wealth is held in trust by the husband's nearest male kin, for one's second husband if one remarries, or one's eldest son when he comes of age. But Sora was no widow; she was my wife. Divorce is utter dishonour for the woman; since the house is the man's she is expelled to beg the mercy of her kin, who consider her a burden. What becomes of the children is entirely up to the man.

Yet if I left things as they were, she would either be abandoned when I went home, or claimed by the gladiator who killed me, until *his* killer claimed her, and so on, passed on from man to man of who knew what character until one made fifty, or more likely for the rest of her life. By Arkan law, the best I could do for her was kill myself.

"It's death, not love, which binds us," I said, then cursed myself for saying something so obvious. You'd rather die than touch me, I wanted to say, and I can understand that; but by Arkan law she must not feel that, so on my lips it would be an accusation. "I won't dishonor you," I said, finally. "Or make you suffer. There must be some way; I'll look into it." She just nodded, then said, "Perhaps you wish to see what is yours." Not knowing what else to do, I followed her. In my discomfort I'd drunk enough nakiti to be slightly unsteady.

I lingered in the library: there is nothing else I want here, I thought, but let me at least read these books. I had no wish to look into the children's rooms, or hers. She didn't show me the kitchen as a matter of course, that being a woman's place; is it because it is the man's places she's showing me, I thought, that his presence seems everywhere? In his studio, with its great window to let in light, stood an easel with a painting, unfinished, of a battle scene. Beyond that was a gallery full of portraits, some sketched, some in full oils, of gladiators. "When he killed them," she said, "he'd hang them here."

I didn't know what all this meant, until we went to his room. There, next to the bed where one would put the image of a loved one, hung a painting, based on the sketch he'd done, of me.

I forgot courtesy; or perhaps felt I deserved an answer. "Why did he do this?"

Her gloved hands pulled at the hem of her peplum. "I am only a woman, husband. Of art and swordcraft, I know nothing."

"What did he say?"

"To concentrate his attention, he said. If he could paint a man, he could capture his spirit, and so beat him. So he said."

I lifted it in my hands, and held it for a long time. Finally I said, "I would take nothing else from you. But this, you cannot want. May I?" Casting her eyes down, she said, "Why do you ask, when you know you need not? I will wrap it for you." Without the nakiti, I suspect, which had turned her cheeks bright red, she would not have asked what she did then. "I didn't think you would want it. Why do you?" After a while, I answered, "It captures my spirit."

"Not well enough," she breathed. Then looking up, knowing I'd heard, she covered her mouth with her hands in dread. "It's great art," I said. "I'm sorry, did you say something?" She shook her head, and her slip of tongue was a stone vanished in a pool.

As I was leaving, with the painting under my arm, I considered apologizing and asking forgiveness, for everything. But it was too insufficient to try, the effort worth spitting on, and all for something not my fault in the first place. In the end, as she had finished her formal goodbye, I just said, "I chose this no more than you did," forgetting that one bereaved wants to blame someone other than the lost. "I will do my duty," she said thickly, her eyes down, "whatever you decree that to be. But forgive me for what is beyond my strength. I will always hate you."

Skorsas found me an advocate who was understanding; searching through his books he found some obscure ruling whereby a husband could declare himself unfit, giving the wife a widow's standing. Being from Tor Ench, Riji had no male kin here, and, it turned out, was estranged from those at home; so two old friends from the University offered to be trustee. The elder, an old cobweb-head of a scholar who felt he should get it by rights, spoke of "that empty-headed woman" and wondered with a scheming look what use she might have, while the younger seemed to have been her friend as well as his. I signed everything over to the latter, and gave up on borrowing books; it would have forced her to see me.

"It is a tragedy to us all, though not to you," the trustee said, superior-to-inferior, in the way of *Aitzas*, when we were done. "We all tried to persuade him not to return to the Ring. Especially Sora." So much worse it was than I'd known, then, for her. "Yet I must add, you have been very gracious, young man, much more so than we expected from a Yeoli." I thanked him. That was all I'd wished for.

So I was finished with his affairs. Or so I thought. "You seem to have forgotten," Skorsas said. "You also have a position at the University as a professor of philosophy." Who kills becomes: having defeated Riji apparently qualified me for the work. Diverse Foreign Philosophy, the contract read, and a bonded post, which meant, in Skorsas's straightforward words, "If you can do it, they can't dismiss you."

"What am I to do?" I said. "Go there and teach?" I meant it as a joke; but then the idea seized me. A teacher, in Azaila's terms, which I followed, is one who knows something the student does not, and it struck me I likely knew quite a few things of foreign philosophy which Arkans wouldn't.

So I went to the University, found my way to the Halls of Thought, and declared that the Diverse Foreign Philosophy classes, which had been canceled, could go on. My superior I knew immediately: the elder of Riji's friends whom I had spurned as a trustee. He was surprised at first but turned all to courtesy in a moment, showing me to Riji's office, handing me the schedule (in Arkan, of course) and introducing me to my two assistants, who were both over thirty and held doctorates. I saw by the smile in his

limpid grey eyes, his plan: simply to throw me to the
wolves, and see how long it took them to spit me out.

First standing in the lecture chamber in Riji's robes,
which fit me, I saw why. This was a doctoral class. My
thin-shouldered beady-eyed students, all men of course,
with spectacles and gold bracelets and waist-long Aitzas
hair, leaned back in their chairs, dangled their feet over
empty ones, looked down their noses at me with the
assured smugness of those who know they will one day be
an Empire's ruling elite. They were all five years my
elder, probably ten years more educated, and a hundred to my one.

Still, they'd never come through the demarchic school
of debate, or the forge of Azaila's teaching; and if they
thought to intimidate me, they forgot what I faced each
fight-day. I remembered Azaila's way on the mountain, of
tossing us this way and that with his wisdom until our
heads were spinning, and enlightenment came. I did that
to them, beginning with, "You must excuse my poor Arkan;
I was taught only recently. Arko has only been on our
border since the 1348th year of our reckoning; my tutors
felt Arkan was an upstart language." That threw them well
enough for a good start. I recall the man who stamped out,
since it seemed he wanted only to receive an unbroken
string of knowledge into his head, and not use it; and the
one who, near the end of a bead of cut and thrust debate,
asked in a beleaguered tone, "Professor Lightning, sir, is
this going to be on the exam?"

They went away dazed and laughing, both; at the next
class there were half again as many, the one after that,
double. I understood: all these staid, stiff dogmas, unchanging for two hundred years and always given in the
same drab voice by the same drab codgers, bored them
silly, as such things will the young; my teachings, whatever they were, came to them like a splash of cold water in
the face. All through the University taverns, soon, it was
Lightningism and nothing but.

I would let them write their essays on whatever they
wished, no matter how revolutionary; I gave authorization
to enter the Third Portal of Propriety—that limited to
professors and students they allow—to anyone who asked,
for any book. Several times they were convened by my
superior on the matter of my incompetence; always they

spoke in my favor, some nine to one. (*Aitzas* in Arko are permitted a slight taste of the vote.) I'd tell them to come to the Mezem and cheer for me, if they liked me; when essays were due they'd vow to cheer for the other.

It all went well and was great fun, until someone tattled on me to the Marble Palace for sowing subversion. We'd wandered from philosophy to society to politics to Yeoli politics, I can't imagine how. That was enough; despite howling protests, I was run out of the Halls of Thought within a day. When my students gathered around me in a certain tavern to console and be consoled, I put out the secret word that I would go on with classes in a certain clearing in the woods; the Marble Palace couldn't forbid that. So the torch of Lightningism was kept burning. Some fifty stayed with me to the end.

The Pages and the Watcher both accorded me title as Living Greatest, and my fame seemed to triple. Gifts from those who'd benefitted from the odds against me poured in; at my fights one could see the crowd dotted everywhere with black heads; on the streets one could buy luck-charms with my figure, stamped out of a mold, porcelain in the poor quarter, gold in the rich. One tavern became the haunt of my followers, for no other reason than its name, the House of the Mountains. Going along, the master had my face painted on the sign, in the style that had become standard, following an engraving in the Watcher: straight frontal, the lines too square and perfect— they forgot I'd had my nose broken—the eyes wrought of pure sentimentality, huge, dark and sad to lugubriousness, and hauntingly following the viewer wherever he went in the room. I only know of the place because Mana insisted that I see it, and we crept in through the kitchen— threatening to show my face to the clientele, which might start a riot, if the master didn't let us—to peek through the service-slot.

I knew I was truly great when Koree threw me, smoothed the dust of the training-ground with my face and said, "Don't let it get to your head, cockspur. You can still die."

A polite letter came from Haiksilias Lizan, *fessas*, who wanted to paint my portrait; Skorsas, who insisted on going through my mail with me in case I missed anything (I was looking only for a reply from home) did his typical shocked gasp. It seemed Haiksilias was considered the greatest painter in Arko, and the portrait would be raised in the Hall of the Greats.

I sat, mostly to humor Skorsas; I did many things these days to console him for my not being his lover. To come closer to me without hope of love-making caused him no pain, he assured me, but the sweetest joy, every fingerwidth. "I know now I have no claim on you, or ever could," he said, twining his fingers in the back of my hair, one of the things I let him do now. "You're a king." To the Arkan mind no one has claim on a king, even a people.

So I let him hold my hand and gaze at me and speak endearments in public, so that soon we were a pair, in every way but one. Of course the writers made much of it, and our love became common knowledge: good, for it diverted suspicion from Niku. At first it bothered me, that he seemed to love me more the more I killed; then it came to me, it was the more I stayed alive.

One day an ornate little wooden box came, wrapped in silk; since they often had sweets in them, I opened it. It was lined in cushioned satin, very elaborately embroidered, all framing what seemed to be a tiny bit of meat, entirely desiccated. For some reason I found myself afraid to touch it. I read the note, seeking clues. The writing looked like an eight-year-old's; he—one could assume he— was scribing under great duress for his twelve-year-old sister, who loved me and wanted to dedicate herself so entirely to me that only this gift could express it.

About then, Skorsas came in. "*Kaina marugh miniren!*" he cried, meaning "dog mother of the Ten Gods," the most blasphemous curse Arkans have. His face was ashen. "Close that up! My blessed God, close it—you didn't touch it, did you? Oh, my *God*! Where in *Hayel* did it come from?"

I closed the lid, and read off the street and number of the house, which was in the *Aitzas* quarter. "Why, what is it?"

His tongue seemed to stick to his teeth, and his cheeks turned from grey to flaming red. "Celestialis . . . I don't think I can tell you, love of my life . . . But—no, no, don't ask Iska! We've got to keep this secret; that poor idiot girl will be in more trouble than anyone deserves, and . . . my professional God, what do we do?"

"I don't know how you expect me to know, when I don't even know what the thing is," I answered, hoping my calm would rub off on him. "Is it something sacred, that shouldn't leave the house?"

"No!—well, yes! It's sacred—cursed—well, cursed for a man to touch, or—Shefen-ka, it's a *women's* thing, it's the abomination, it's the vow, it should go to the man she's betrothed to, it's . . . Shefenka . . . Celestialis help me . . . Shefenka, forgive me, I beg you, but do you know anything about purification?"

I put the box down hard on the night-table, and vomited my guts out into the chamberpot. He knelt with me, steadying me in his arms, saying, "This shows how pure and clean-hearted you are."

The other aspect of the custom is this: what was removed is placed in a ceremonial container, to be presented to the girl's husband-to-be on her betrothal, symbolic of her fertility, given into his ownership. My vomiting-tears turned into heart-tears.

"We should send it back," I said, when I'd mastered myself. He ruled that out: her father would find out then, and she'd be disgraced for the rest of her life, for nothing more than childish stupidity. In the end, he agreed to sneak it back to her. He had to argue with her for a good half-bead, balanced on a third-floor windowsill.

It happened three more times. Once the girl's father stamped in and caught Skorsas at the window; "but," as he told me smiling, "he was one of my old clients, so didn't have much to say."

One night I lay noticing, how my mind felt off-kilter more and more these days, as if it had been stirred with a ladle and left to fall almost back into its old pattern, but not quite. One can hardly avoid it here, I thought; so reminded I did my own observance again, kneeling with crystal in my hand. Then as I lay down again, I thought, no. It's too even, too consistent; it doesn't have the changes, like clouds crossing the sun on a ragged-sky day, of moods. Ten fights, it's been, nearly three months; they said the first slight effects would show by now. It's the *grium*. My mouth went dry and sour. At first I tried to fight off the fear; then, as the night before Riji, I let it take me, until it went through me.

Kurkas invited me for dinner again, to congratulate me on my win over Riji. "Well, you almost lost the ransom money there," I said to him, in mock sympathy. "Yes," he said, taking it for real, "but oh, the excitement! The drama!"

This time we played chess, on a set on which the kings' and princes' crowns had real diamonds and rubies. He beat me—I had only just learned—and, with the glow of victory on his wide face, went on to discourse ad nauseam on how civilization proves its superiority over barbarism in every contest. Then raising his empty goblet of sparkling clear crystal, he declaimed on how the Empire of Arko, the spirit, the essence, the ideal, was like this glass, pure, unblemished, incapable of staining, and a vessel for the noblest virtues—I'd noticed, he had a penchant for glass— and like this glass would last beyond our grandchildren and their grandchildren, greater than any one mere life. Barely a moment later, being clumsy-handed, or perhaps having drunk more than he knew, he knocked it off the table, smashing it into a hundred pieces on the inlaid floor. I couldn't help my smirk.

It was at that dinner or another—being all the same they blur together—he showed me what he called his sanctum: a small room, for the Marble Palace, filled with the most precious things he'd collected, all through his life. This at least was interesting. There was a bird's nest with three blue eggs in it, the jawbone of some impossible huge animal and a waxboard with a child's drawing of a bird against clouds, or behind them; one could not tell whether one could see the clouds through the bird or the bird through the clouds. There were also priceless works of art, most of the great ones that one read about or saw replicas of, *The Delights of Celestialis* by Entonnas, *Mankind's Fall* by Soleitzas, Sibbas's *Flying Machine*. His weakness for glass was evident: the tables were all but heaped with glass cups, vases, sculptures, candelabra, figurines, miniature replicas of famous sculpture, pyramids, chess sets, many-facetted balls, even crystals. There was even a model of the city of Arko, done in incredible detail, the interior of every level of every building entirely furnished; the Mezem was certainly accurate. Bright-eyed as a child he showed me how the tall buildings came apart so you could see everything. It looked like decades of work.

At various times in our conversations, and never with

intent to offend but simply because he believed it, he called me simpleminded, weak-willed, conceited, deluded, a crashing bore, and eternally fascinating for reasons beyond him. One day he would say I was clear and pure as that crystal I wore—often when he was treating on his hypothesis of clarity, that only transparent things such as glass or a lake of perfectly pure water have true depth, and that earth would be as Celestialis and mankind risen once again when all the world was glass like his little Arko. The next he would say a thousand brilliant philosophers in a thousand years couldn't understand me. Once I said, "I'll give you a clue: I've noticed many people see themselves in me"; but it went past him.

One thing he never spoke of, nor showed any evidence of, was his work. I'd thought at first this was out of civility or secrecy; but I began to suspect he just didn't think about it much, more intrigued with being Imperator than doing what Imperators do. Perhaps his father had told him he must keep his mind on theory, and he'd taken it to mean leaving no room in it for practice; or perhaps he delegated everything to leave time for drawn-out dinners with expatriate demarch-gladiator-professors and other such luminaries. (I was almost too busy myself for such distractions, and I commanded only a class of philosophy students.)

Interesting to learn: if it were true as it seemed, someone else was really running the Empire. Yet he told me he'd taken the decisions both to betray me and invade my country against his advisors' wishes—"I see clear and above these little things,"—so he was apparently not in their thrall. I casually asked him why they'd been against; all he said was, "Oh, bureaucratic cowardice; you must know about that." What I knew was, if they were good advisors, they'd based the opinion on facts, and those facts I'd have given my sword-arm for.

Once I asked him how he heard the voice of his God; by Arkan doctrine the Imperator is the Son of the Sun, ordained by the Great Father, Muunas, (who is also god of *Aitzas* men). Arko does the Imperator's will as he does the God's will, a chain of command like an army's; I just wondered how the God gave his marching orders.

My jaw dropped at his answer, though I suppose this was naivete. "The voice of my God? You barbarians and your atavistic concepts, you're as good dupes for gods as the uneduc—wait a moment! You're a Yeoli—an atheist. Aren't you? A sophistication I thought we had in common; don't disillusion me, Shefen-kas."

I found myself chilled to the core again, me, an *Athye*, far worse than his following of Arko's creed would have done. At least that way, he'd have been following something.

"I am," I said, "but I don't claim not to be. You accept the title Son of the Sun, you claim to make the laws and dispense the punishments in the name of God, you sustain the temples and the priests, accept the tithes and the prayers; your position flows entirely down from divine right. And you believe in none of it yourself? How can you live such a lie?"

He shrugged, not taking offense at all. "All these things are needful. As for how I can bear it—I'm Imperator. I can do anything, I can bear anything. Nothing is beyond my strength."

That was too much to resist. "Nothing? I think not! In fact I can prove quite conclusively there is something you can't do. Would you like to witness my proof? Care to take a wager?"

He laughed. "You entertaining barbarian! I must see this. What wager? You don't have anything to match what I could stake."

"I prove there's something you can't do," I said, "and you set me free. Immediately, no ransom, no harm, safe out of arrow range on unconquered Yeoli territory. If I fail in proving it, I send the orders to my people to surrender, and Yeola-e is yours. Good terms, I think, especially considering I know full well you'll break your end of the agreement, whatever oath I talk you into swearing, if I win—but I won't break *mine*."

He let that last part pass by, his eyes flashing with want. "Yes! Agreed! Go on, tell me what I can't do! This is rich!"

"By your own strength, without the aid of any other person or device . . ." I thumped my elbow on the table. "Beat me at arm-wrestling."

He stared for a long while, his petulant round blue eyes slowly freezing in a way I had never seen. It defied belief, like a leper appearing from behind a bronze in the Marble Palace. His voice defied belief too, a shriek so fast and hoarse and venomous in the Palace's immaculate silence, like a death-cry in a library. "You *fikken* dirt-brained barbarian backstabber!"

"Here's Yeola-e," I said, tapping my arm, "right here. You said you could do anything; that means you could win fifty chains in the Mezem if you wanted. Next to that, *this* is nothing!"

He sprang to standing, making his chair-legs screech and all his jewels tinkle. For a moment he stood with his breath held, his face blossoming red all over; then he shouted, "*Guards!*" The room was filled with them instantly, as if they'd burst out of the walls. They seemed a little afraid of seizing me, some no doubt being Mezem-watchers, but didn't hesitate; one could imagine what fate they'd suffer for failing him. "*Out!*" he snapped. "*Throw him out!*" I gave myself up peacefully, but tossed back over my shoulder, "We have our proof, it seems." He had no answer but that strange transfixed blue stare.

I am certain that Kurkas, had he been asked, would have said the animosity between us started then.

Certainly he invited me back in two days, and when I declined due to prior commitments, again two days after that. This time he tried to seduce me. "You belong with me," he said. "Forever." I was always sensitive to the state of my body; I knew after a time that what I felt was not natural. He'd had an aphrodisiac slipped into our food; he didn't deny it. Just as if I were his guest, not his prisoner, I drew myself up when he asked, said "No!" and strode out. I got to the main Aestine stairs before the Mahid stopped me.

What he did to me when they dragged me back I won't put my poor reader or myself through, except to say he had a cart rather like a server's, but with wrist and ankle shackles, to hold a prisoner bent over. It was a fine article, made all of silver engraved and polished to a mirror gleam; I remember the pattern of the one shackle, and the distorted image of my own face in it, flashing gold when I bared my teeth. I remember the scent of heliotrope, of which he always wore far too much; and what he said, over and over again, with indignation as pure as that of a baby's scream: "You can't say *no*! You can't say *no* to *me*!"

VIII

Riji was my nineteenth fight. I made twenty, two-fifths of the way. I followed the war in the Pages; of course it bent its accounts to favor Arko, but like Arkans I learned to read between the lines. All winter the war stood more or less still; Tinga-e was under siege, but held.

I made twenty-one. Doing my mail, Skorsas opened a scented envelope with a dried rose on it, and said, "What sort of puerile gibberish is this?" It was a page full of Yeoli shorthand, in the writing of my sister, now First Artira.

She scolded me for not telling how to reply, but no matter; they'd found out. It seemed some Arkan warriors had a habit of wearing Karas Raikas charms into battle, for luck; a Yeoli who'd captured one got intrigued that his charm had black hair, and took a good look at it. Well-crafted ones, such as *solas* can afford, carry a likeness.

As I'd suggested, Artira had restructured things; how, she did not say, of course. Of alliances she wrote nothing, perhaps, I thought, wishing to keep me from knowing that also. If they meant to ransom me, she had not heard it yet. Shaina had given birth safely, to a girl. Kima Imaye, they named her, "keep faith" or better, perhaps, "keep hope." For Yeola-e, they meant, and for me. She was a slight baby, as I had been, but well-colored and lively, with my eyes and hair. Though I shouldn't, I could not help but see her in my inward eyes, hold her in my inward arms.

Enclosed also was a reply to Mana from his mother. He wrote her again, and again I did the border. On the *grium* I told what the Haians had told me, and that I meant to go there; when they offered me for ransom, I wrote, the best thing to do would be to stall for as long as possible, then require them to show me alive.

I thought of trying to write to Astalaz, Kranaj and Ivahn. But even if I could find a way to get those letters through, I saw, I could hardly bargain, only beg; what power had I, here, to promise them anything in return? I was a gladiator, not a demarch.

I made twenty-three; Niku made twelve. It began to be said she'd had too many easy matches, and it was about time a woman got a true test. I think it actually was true they'd undermatched her; being a curiosity she was always a draw, so they wanted her to last. At any rate, to answer the protest they made her fight under judge's clemency, axe and breastplate against spear, sword, dagger, shield and full armor.

They wounded each other, and both fell, he stunned, she bleeding fast from the arm, an artery opened. It became a matter of who could crawl to the other and use a weapon first. I learned then how she must have felt watching me against Riji. Once as she was dragging herself toward him she looked my way; had I shown emotion then, letting her see I'd lost faith in her and was therefore willing to give away our secret, the strength would have gone out of her, and she'd have been done. But I knew the feeling, and did nothing but drum my fingers on the rail casually, while my heart's blood poured out on the sand with hers. He made the mistake of trying to draw his sword; she snatched his dagger out of its sheath and drove it into his throat first.

She was out of training for two eight-days, though, out of fighting for four; that also slowed down the work of her escape plan. In the third eight-day we were lying together, speaking of this and that, I kissing her arm to heal it, when she said, "I dread mornings these days. I wake up sick every time now; I can't even think about food. Do you get that when you're wounded?"

My heart sprang to racing. Perhaps the women in her family didn't get it; Shaina did, terribly, incapacitated in the morning for three solid moons. "Niku—did you bleed last month?"

"No, why? I often miss now and then when I'm in hard training. You think I should ask Iska?"

"No, whatever you do!" I whisper-yelled. "Niku, haven't you heard when women get sick in the morning?"

The whites of her eyes widened, bright against her skin, which night made pure black. "*Ama kalandris* . . . Sea Mother . . . I didn't think of it, *pehali*, I didn't think of it!"

"Neither did I!" In a place of death, surrounded by death, fighting off death every moment, one thinks little of new life, and forgets one's capacity to make it has not died.

I took a deep breath, and summoned calm. "So. You're pregnant. What of it? The whatever-it-is will be ready in two moons, now, you say, and we'll go; it won't even be showing by then."

She sighed away fear; from under it came a white flashing smile. "Child within . . ." she whispered, then stroked my cheek. "And yours, my love, *mi penzi*." Then we threw ourselves together in celebration. For a long time it was, "What will it look like? Like you, so beautiful . . . your first? My third . . . They're a lot of work, you know . . . Girl or boy, I wonder?"

Finally emotion ebbed enough to allow reason. We had barely touched on plans, before; all that had been set was that we would go to Haiu Menshir together, then I must go home. Now we had to face the rest.

She was the wife of my heart, without question. But was I the husband of hers? She would have to leave her home, for I could not leave mine. And certainly she was not the wife of my people's heart. (I could hear Esora-e: "What's wrong with Yeoli women, that you so spurn them?") Yet since I had two pure-blood Yeoli children older than this one, now people who objected to foreign blood in the line would have less to say than they had before.

Though the A-niah, as her people are called in plural, were not warring Arko openly (she'd been captured fighting for the Srians near Tebrias), they had Arkan troubles, harassment that had grown to be all but war in name, last she'd heard. Though she knew her family would think her

dead because of it, she had not written home, because it
had not come clear to her yet why she had been meant to
live. Once she'd seen me to the healers, she must go
home, and see how things were; though she was not a
leader in name, one sensed she would be some day, since
she was in spirit, and her mother was one of their Council
of Elders, chosen by vote. But after that she wanted to
come to Yeola-e and marry me, even if it meant dispute,
which I made no bones about predicting.

So we were planned. Sure enough, she didn't bleed the
next month either. I ceased even thinking of being matched
against her, the thought unbearable. It would be two lives
to my one now, as well as my life's love, my flesh and
blood. And so, when she was a month shy of finishing the
escape-work, we were matched.

It says much for the strength of our habit, I suppose,
that once the Director announced "Karas Raikas against
Niku Wahunai," and went on as if the world had not
changed, and we could have flung ourselves into each
others' arms right there to no detriment, we still gave each
other no more than a glance. Perhaps it was that neither of
us truly believed it yet; or else we both knew what a show
that would have been, and wanted to deny them.

That night, creeping into her room, I said as we seized
each other, "Is there a way it can be done in seven days?"

"Not by one." Her eyes creased, as if at the shifting of a
blade in her. "By two, perhaps." That meant revealing to
me her people's secret. "Maybe I misunderstood what
Lord Friend meant, maybe he will take me now, but child
within . . . Chevenga, hold me, please, *omores*, hold me—"
She clung, as did I, both trembling. For a long time we
did only that, it being all we could do.

When we'd both found calm I began to see specks of
light in the darkness. "Can I help somehow without knowing what it is?" I asked; she answered no, not at this stage;
if only, I thought, I'd said this earlier. "It could be worse,"
I said. "It could have been two months ago." She nodded,
gathering herself. "You must meditate, or pray, or some
such thing, love," I said, "to settle what is best." She did,
while I held her; I kept still and silent. Finally she whispered, "If this is wrong, may full justice fall on me. I'll
give myself to it, at home. *Omores*, can you sew, or is that

women's work among your people?" I could join two edges together, I told her, but was no tailor. That was good enough.

We slipped out into the night, meeting at the edge of the forest. She took me to her secret place, in the midst of thickets so deep one had to climb over them through the tree-branches. There was a fairly wide clearing, that she had hewn out; beneath a thatch of branches was a hole she'd dug, with several long bamboo rods and a chest in it. Before she opened it she looked at me, with last doubts, I guessed; so I swore silence, Second Fire come and Lord Friend Death hear me.

That first night I couldn't divine what it was at any rate; we just sewed wide pieces of silk together, with a strong double stitch like sailmakers use, that she was very careful to see I did properly. She did not tell me what we were making; I did not ask.

Her reckoning of a month had been assuming she'd creep out here as little as she had before, to avoid suspicion; now we ceased to care, and came all day, except for training, and all night except to sleep. Suspicion was roused: in the mid-eight-day Pages someone waxed poetic on the tragedy of our love. To the good: it was assumed we went to the woods to spend our last days together, and when we threatened anyone who followed us with death they thought they knew why. The last two days we skipped training.

We joined the silk scraps—remnants she'd bought from tailors—into a sheet larger than any garment. Like a sail; but I could not conceive of a boat that would float up a cliff. When we sewed it to the frame, which was of bamboo held together by steel wire—no wonder she'd needed money—it looked like a giant kite, but triangular, with two wings like a bird. A kite big enough to lift a person? It would have to have rope for string. But Arko, being in a pit, rarely got a wind strong enough to lift even a child's kite, by my reckoning.

"*Moyawa*," she said. "It means single-wing. Now a foreigner knows, Sea Mother . . ." I didn't, actually. "To fly, *omores*. No, there is no rope; only the wing, and the wind, and you.

"When the Fire fell, the ancestors of my people were in the sky, in a great machine-wing, midjourney. When they touched down, the world had fallen, so never again could the great wing fly, as was the nature of those things; they ceased to move when the old nations fell. But Rojhai, our first elder, still knew the making of the *a-moyawa*, the simple wing, the small wing. We had no boats; we could only flee from the wars to Niah-lur-ana by wing; all who could not fly fell into the sea and were lost, so flying is in our blood from the start. All through the years we have kept our secret, for it has always stood us well against enemies."

I suddenly remembered her once saying her island looked like a hand with five fingers. "There are mountains?" I'd said; one does not think of such shapes, not seeing land from above. She'd said quickly, "Yes," and I'd thought nothing of it.

"But how . . . ? A bird beats its wings; do you flap these somehow?" She laughed; no doubt every Niah was expert at it from young, as horse-peoples are at riding, so I seemed like a child with my questions.

"No. The wind carries you. From a height, we fly, or on rising winds, as from hot fields, or *el brandil sef*, from fire."

"The heat of a fire could carry you above these cliffs?"

"Yes, and the wind much higher than that, if one knows how."

I sat down, trying to keep my head from spinning long enough to think: of Arkans and the great metal birds they thought were the only things that could fly, of what advantages the A-niah had, being able to get out of impossible places, or in, of how they could scout—doesn't every general wish he had birds that could speak?—or attack from above, or drop things; of how they'd kept it secret, for so many centuries.

Now she laid out her plan. "I climb the cliff to the highest point I can—near the Lift Patthine—and we set the fire by the side of the cliff. You do that—I trust you more, love—Mana is waiting a quarter turn around the pit, at the Lift Inodem. You go there, to the bottom, and I, to the top. I kill the guards"—she had a blow-tube and drugs like Mahids'—"and winch the two of you up." It was one of the modern *lefaeti*, with two platforms: one person could lift two quickly by placing weights on the upper.

All that eight-day our fingers flew, like the rabbit's legs fleeing the fox. On the sixth night, the fight to come the day after tomorrow, the device was finished. But it must be tested.

Long past the bead of midnight, while all Arko slept, we took it out to the archery field in the woods at the south end. Folded up, it looked for all the world like a fine quality tent, and was light enough to carry in one hand. Though motley-colored as a beggar's coat, it was a masterpiece of craft, at least where the master's hands had worked as opposed to the apprentice's. A-niah children learn to make them from childhood; one is required to build a skyworthy wing before one is allowed to fly.

At the downwind end of the field, she unfolded it, facing into the faint night breeze, and strapped herself into the harness, which hung just back of the triangle of rods one holds onto. Lifting the whole device on her shoulders, she dashed away. Under the huge batlike shape, her legs flashed pale in moonlight, her shadow brushing across the pale grass. Then suddenly she and it separated; she was in the air, skimming like a heron over reeds, off the ground, flying.

She came back, smiling and saying breathlessly, "A little adjustment here and there and it will be better—but it works!"

"After we escape," I said, "something may part us, one of us might die, life may by some chance never let us see each other again. Let me try this, just once."

It was probably foolishness, when I who knew nothing; to break the wing now would be disaster. But she understood my wish. She made the straps fast around me, and put my hands on the right place on the bar. "The wind has substance, like water," she said. "You see why, if you push the bar away, you rise and slow, or pull it close, you fall and speed? The wind might seize you and throw you high; don't let it take you too high, and don't come down too fast. However you come down, land running." As I lifted it on my shoulders, a breath of wind one could barely feel on one's face moved it enough to almost unbalance me.

I set off running. Wind rushed through the silk, whistled in the wires. When I was flat out I pushed the bar away gently, as she'd told me, felt the wing lift and snatch me up quicker than I'd expected, all my weight on the leathern straps of the harness and my running feet flailing off the ground, almost before I knew it. Blood surged to my head, from sheer joy; overwhelmed, I forgot what she had taught me, and got caught flat-footed coming down. A hillock tripped me; holding the wing high as I could to protect it, I made my landing on something soft: my face. She came running, to find me laughing so hard I cried, in ecstasy. One should never say something is impossible. All my life, I'd been sure humanity would fly again, but never expected to live to see it. Now I'd done it.

The night before fight day was clear, like most Arkan nights, with a thin moon, good for our purposes.

I left a note in one of the drawers for Skorsas to find, apologizing for my abrupt leaving, and signing over what was left of my fortune to him. "I love you in my way," I wrote, my ritual words these days. I left one for Iska too, with a line for Koree: but there was no one else in Arko I cared to wish farewell.

Into our pouches and belts and boots Mana, Niku and I slipped good amounts of jewels and gold; money never hurts, traveling fast over enemy ground. Having been dragged here with what was on our backs or less, we had little to carry out, though Mana and I took our breast-plates, fine Arkan work (we told the Weapons Trust we were going to rough taverns). Niku could take no armor, that being too heavy for the wing.

Near midnight we gathered at the meeting of paths into the woods, embraced each other for luck, and went our ways, to do our parts. Near the Lift Patthine I saw Niku and the wing up the cliff, where talus and footholds make it possible to get a good twelve man-heights up before one comes to the polished stone. As she'd instructed me, I slicked her down with water, and she wrapped a wet cloth around her face, the last expression on those beautiful red-wine-dark lips before they were covered, a flashing grin. Kissing her for blessing, I went down to where she'd told me, and kindled my torch.

It came clearest to me then, how all our hopes rested on one toss of the die, and what a dangerous toss. The fire had to be big enough to send heat the full height of the cliffs, but flames too close to her might melt the silk; the smoke would choke her breathing and blind her eyes; spiralling in and out, as she must, she might hit the cliff, or get too low to return to the column of heat, and come down among trees and rocks, breaking the wing if not her; even if she landed safely, the woods would be crawling with Arkans by then, for they waste no time fighting fires. I must trust her knowledge; remembering her smile, so free of fear, I began touching my torch to the brush she'd shown me.

The night being dry, as it usually is, the bushes flared like tinder, and flame leapt up into the branches of the trees; I kept moving and lighting, for better too big, she'd said, than too little. I did not see her take off, for smoke and trees and darkness, but I heard the cry, from straight above me, "*Meh ish manwia*! Go, love!"

I'd barely run ten steps through the brush, when running Arkan men, but bearing wood-axes and buckets of water, and cursing *okas*-style, were all around me. I rolled under a bush, meaning to hide until they passed; but some *solas* shouted orders to cut a firebreak, here, and they set torches in the ground, and began furiously chopping and slashing where they were.

Just my *fikken* luck, I thought. I couldn't move—there was no way around me that didn't have either a clear space or a man in it—yet I couldn't stay here until they cut my cover away, or down on top of me. Yet if I tried to fight my way out, that would set up a chase, and if I went flat out with a hundred Arkans behind me to the Lift Inodem, it was a hundred-to-one that Mana and I would both be captured, perhaps even Niku too, if the commotion at the bottom alerted the guards at the top.

As blades whacked through wood barely an arm's-length from my ear, I thought of turning myself in, or leading them on a chase all the way to the Mezem gate; I'd be caught for arson, then, but at least Mana and Niku would be out. But I'd get truth-drugged, and then the A-niah secret would be lost. I decided on that as a last resort, though a terrible one; there wasn't another cursed thing I could do. In the meantime, I'd wait for a chance. I lay there for what I imagine was a tenth-bead, about the time it takes to hard-boil an egg, that seemed a century.

Finally one fellow moved enough for me to crawl like a worm through a heap of branches, and away; making so much noise themselves they could not hear me. How long had Niku and Mana had to wait for me? I did the whole distance at a sprint, gasping and cursing my weakness at the end.

One platform of the lift was down; I saw it shining blue-grey in the faint light, where it should never be at night by Arkan law. But Mana was not there; and at the top of the cliff there was too much torchlight and noise, men yelling words I could not make out for the distance. I stayed back, to try to see up, and strained to hear for Mana's or Niku's war-yell; nothing, they must be hiding. Then the lift-rope creaked, taking the weight of the plat-form, which began to rise.

It was one of those choices that has to be made in a moment. So it was: I ran, made a flying leap to barely catch one of the under-struts, swung myself up to grip it with arms and legs like an ape. It was Arkans winching, I knew; but once at the top of the cliffs, I was thinking, I will fight my way past them if there are a hundred. I began to climb out from underneath when it occurred to me that if they saw me on it before it was at the top, they need only stop lifting and lower; so, clipping Chirel into its scabbard, I stayed where I was.

It was as if my heart lifted, with every fingerwidth my body did; as if the air changed as my ears popped, and I breathed what I had forgotten breathing, the cleanness of freedom, from that reeking pit. It was as if I found my-self again with my gaining height, reaching heights of myself that had atrophied, changing from a gladiator into a demarch at every man-length, these things around my neck no longer the marks of deaths by my hand, but plain money; I felt myself welcomed back into the sane world, which since I could not see it from Arko I'd feared no longer existed, but now with swelling heart I felt claim me.

Then with a lurch that turned my stomach, the lift halted. I waited in horror, and heard the sound of metal sliding on rope, and the thump on the planks above me of two booted feet. Someone at the top had thought that just to be safe, they should stop the lift some eight man-lengths from the top, and have someone shinny down the rope just to check underneath. If I killed him, they would know, and lower the lift; if I didn't kill him, the same.

Scrabbling with my fingers through my pouch, I found a gold brooch. Torchlight snaked flickering through the chinks, moved to the edge; I heard him loosen his sword in its scabbard, get down on his knees, then his front. The torch came down past the edge, then the helmeted head.

"Give them the all clear to keep winching," I said softly, before he could cry out, "and I'll give you five hundred gold chains." I slapped the brooch onto the platform next to him. "Take that as a deposit."

"Karas Raikas," he said wonderingly. So: he knew I had the money. I wished I could see his face, whether he looked greedy, or kind, or treacherous, what would best move him; but he held his torch well away, to keep me from grabbing it, I suppose, so his features were in shadow, while mine were clear to him. "Think what you could buy with that," I said, "for yourself, for your family. A bigger house, better teachers for your sons, better marriages for your daughters. . . ."

He said, "So I give the all clear, and you kill half the other guards carving your way out."

Kind, I thought. *He's kind.* "I will kill no one, on my crystal, on my honor. Since you've checked, no one else is going to look under here; I'll just wait until you're all gone."

"On your honor?" he said, doubtfully.

"You think because I am a Yeoli, I have no honor?" I said.

He hissed out a short breath, his mind made up. "You think because I am an Arkan, I have none?" With a stab of his hand he swept the brooch off the edge of the platform, to fall winking into the great darkness below.

My heart gave out then, and so did my arms.

"*Raikas!*" He could have reached me while I clung with hands and feet; not while I dangled upside-down by my knees. There is my answer, I thought, arching back my head to look straight down, though I could see nothing but blackness, for distance, and tears; there, and only there, is my freedom.

"*Raikas, don't!*" He stretched his free arm toward me, fingers outspread. "You're the best, you're the Living Greatest, you'll make fifty! You can do it!" Upward, he yelled, "*Lower! Lower, fast!*" We began descending, at a speed that seemed almost a fall. "I can't free you, I'm sorry, but you don't deserve to die, you don't *fikken* deserve to die, you're too good, you'll make fifty. Somewhere someone must need you."

Who was he? Just a guard, an Arkan like any other; yet his words had the power of life. I curled up and grabbed on with my hands again; and it seemed as if it were he and I alone against the dark, against Shininao, against the uncaring force that makes one fall. He seized my collar, then my belt, in a grip that might have held me if I'd let go again, then with his other hand grabbed the hilt of Chirel. "Come on," he said, and helped me drag myself up onto the platform, keeping a grip on some part of me every moment. I lay face down on the wood, and let him gently put my wrists and ankles in shackles. For the rest of the descent he gripped my hand in sympathy, and I gripped his, in gratitude.

As they led me back into the City with its stink of smoke and madness, there was only one thing I could do: yell up into the sky. *"Niku! Mana! They have me! Go! Go with my love, go for my sake, go for yours as I love you, Niku, go for the child's!"*

"You're pale as porcelain, lad," Iska said, a cup in his hand. "You need this." It was nakiti; he gave me a good long swallow, that burned sham life back into me. "You understand, lad, I have no choice; I can't help but know you are of interest to the Marble Palace." I just said, "I understand." With Skorsas beside me, stroking my hair and holding my *katzerik*, since I was still manacled, I waited for the Mahid to come.

They didn't give me the drug to kill my memory this time, so I remember the full questioning. Under truth-drug, one falls into a strange state of silence, like the clarity of meditation, or drunkenness, but much deeper and heavier. The words of anyone near seem like the words of the God-In-Oneself, surrounding and filling the soul; though one might consider disobeying them, as well fight them as a river-current; the body will do their will even as one is considering, and the considerations show themselves to be distant, piddling, trivial things. Like torture, the drug has the effect of cutting the mind in two, the will in one half and the power of speech in the other, and no bond between them.

So even as all my soul struggled against answering, my lips answered without even tension, for all my soul was now only half. Though I had no memory of it, the feeling was familiar; now I understood what horror I must have felt, to hear my own voice softly give up my true name, then the secrets that would be death to my people, while my will flailed and shrieked uselessly like a bat in a cage. Even my body was not my own, for while it should prick and struggle, to not give up the secret that would be death to Niku's people, it lay boneless and warm, with a sweet feeling all over like the first hint of sleep when one lies down exhausted.

An old Mahid, a Senior, did it. Under truth-drug, one tends to give answers passively: in one or two words, without thinking to explain anything the other might not know. When he asked me how Niku got on top of the cliff, my tongue answered only, "She flew."

He froze staring, for a moment; then asked me again. Three times he asked me. "You mean to tell me," he said, "that this brown barbarian woman somehow acquired a great machine, such as only Arko's forefathers had, and rode it to the top of the cliffs?" I answered the truth: "No."

"Then she is a demon, and sprouted wings?" Again I answered as I must, "No."

"Then how," he snapped, "did she get to the top of the cliffs?"

"She flew."

Deciding that this vial of truth-drug must be bad, he sent for another. On the third dose, though I'd heard that too much truth-drug could cause harm, my will in its cage was laughing. He simply refused to believe me. What truth-drug actually compels the victim to speak is the truth he believes, even if it is false; so he decided that barbaric naivete and wishful thinking had left me deluded. Never did he ask me, "How did she fly?" or I would have explained the whole thing; to ask that he must admit to himself it was possible. The A-niah were lucky I'd been given to an old Mahid, with the ruts in his mind well worn in, the walls iron-clad. One such as Ilesias would have had it out of me.

So, with three doses of perfectly good truth-drug in me, they dragged me back to the Mezem, two young rock-tense Mahid half-carrying me with my arms locked over their shoulders like a drunken comrade, having to talk me through every step. Iska asked me what I was under the influence of; "Truth-drug," I answered. "What? Usually they let it wear off: why didn't they?" I began to say, "They would not believe Niku could—" but he saw, and slapped his fingers to my lips. "You are still, Celestialis bless!" Forbidding Skorsas to ask me anything but what I needed, he sent me to bed to sleep it off.

IX

During the time of my last twenty-one fights, I was at least half-mad.

It didn't seem so at the time; yet a hand underwater doesn't look wet. The string of thoughts follows one after the other; but look back, imagining half a year as a whole, and one sees it as a blackness, just as the thrusts of history only become apparent much later. Yet even in hindsight it is hard to see, in my own case. From then, I remember some utterly trivial things, like a clasp on a belt or the fall of someone's hair, vividly as yesterday; while major ones, such as being tortured, I remember only the skeleton of.

The signs of madness were there, though, enough for me to notice at the time: waking up in the morning and finding my hands shaking, for instance, whether flexed or relaxed, no matter how hard I willed them steady. I went to Iska, who pressed them in his own, his palms warm and gentle, like a father's. "So far you've borne everything," he said. "What have you clung to? Don't tell me; ask yourself. Whatever it is, it's worked; keep clinging to it."

I said, "I don't know that I have the strength." He said, "Nonsense. Certainly you do. You know you're at twenty-eight fights? Better than halfway, you have less left than you've already done. Take it one day, one fight at a time, for that's how it will come at you." In truth I think he

378

wasn't sure I had the strength; but to tell me might give it to me, as I suspect it did.

I also went to Persahis, whom Nemonden had recommended. There was little he could do but remind me by his Haian-ness that the world was much bigger than Arko, and let me pour out my heart on his massage-table. The emotions gather in the body, as Haians say, and I had believed it in a vague way; but never so specifically as when Persahis said, "Let out whatever you feel," and by pressing his fingers into some part of my back seemed to slip them straight into my heart. I lost myself in rage and anguish as purely and wholly as a baby does, and afterwards felt much better. But it was no cure. The cause of my trouble, as we both well knew, was my circumstances, from which neither of us could extricate me.

That was the last time I went out. Orders came down from the Marble Palace through the Director, forbidding me to leave the Mezem for any reason; I came back from training to find workmen bolting bars to my window, and two guards posted at my door. Next time Kurkas invited me for dinner I replied with regrets. He sent two Mahid for me. That, I think, was the time I was shown into the Imperial bath; by bath, I mean a square marble pool the size of a pond, big and deep enough to swim in, all its trim brass and gold wrought into arabesques. I had not heard he was afraid of water, but now saw; his way of entering it was to be hefted in the arms of six burly servants, who lowered him into the water by the stairs a hair's-width at a time while every moment he threatened them with ten day's dying if they slipped. I was surprised he'd show me this, and watch me with nothing more than amusement when I stripped and flung myself in, did water-handstands and so forth; he didn't begrudge himself this fear but instead seemed to rather admire it in himself, as if it were a refined, Imperial sort of trait.

My philosophy students I had to bid goodbye. They'd be seen entering the Mezem. Persahis would borrow the table in the clinic to wring me out; but it was not the same as his Haiu-like office.

For days, my eyes flicked in terror to the colonnade far too often in training, dreading to see Niku or Mana being led in; the longer they did not come, the more heartened I was, for the better it made their chances. Of course the

Pages could not write that they'd escaped; the tale was that they'd been murdered. For a time I was a suspect, and writers kept asking me where I'd hidden the corpses, as if such a thing wouldn't be found out by truth-drug, were it true. Then the tale was, he had been her mysterious paramour, not me, and it had been a love-suicide agreement. I told everyone who would listen that they'd escaped; between me and the guards who'd seen, we got the rumor all over the city in a day.

This, I might add, was at the same time the gossips were saying I was impotent, as if any Arkan should have had occasion to test. I know who started it: a huge baggy satiny woman by the name of Kidella, who boasted that she'd bedded every fighter over ten chains. Niku had offered herself to this person, making her flee aghast, and change her boast to every *man*; I refused her, making her paste herself to me like spit to a wall at every chance. Finally she threatened to spread the rumour that I was incapable, since that was the only possible way I could resist her charms.

After my thirtieth fight, the lie was put to all the stories of Mana's death at least. When I heard he'd been brought in, I made no pretense, knowing he'd be truth-drugged, but went straight into the clinic. He must have fought all the way back, for he'd been whipped so badly it festered; he was half-delirious with fever and only barely knew me or felt my hand. He'd grown his red-brown hair long here; now it was hacked off short again.

The Pages wrote that he'd been miraculously found in a basement after having been kidnapped by Srian-backed terrorists. Iska healed him, he was truth-drugged, then I went to his room. When we were done embracing, I told him all I had seen, and he told me all he had. Niku had killed three guards, but the fourth had run for others instead of fighting; fast as she could she'd dropped the platform, and after waiting a time winched him up, to have help with her. They'd waited; but the reinforcements had come before I could. I should have fought my way out of the fire-hackers, I thought; but the stroke of the past is in the past. The two had lain low, while the Arkans beat the bushes; Niku had considered going back down to find me. Then they'd heard my call, to go.

"She tried to spring up," he told me, "saying she'd

carve your way out or die trying; I held her arm; I took
what you yelled as a command, though it tore my heart in
half. Then you cried 'for the child's sake,' and she gave
over, and knelt beside me weeping. She's carrying your
child, Cheng? I hope one day to congratulate you. . . .
After a little, we went our ways.

"I was heading to Fispur. I don't know, maybe if I'd
tried harder—perhaps somewhere in me I felt it was wrong,
that I should leave you behind, perhaps I feared what
people would say when I told them I'd got out and you
hadn't . . . call me a fool, Cheng; I know I am. Or maybe
it was just chance, I don't know. A cowherd's dog found
me in some woods. The cowherd reported me to the
watch; they had horses, and bloodhounds." More he did
not say. It went without saying they'd learned we were
friends.

Yet even now, he flashed his invincible grin, and said,
"It was one-third successful: or maybe I should say half,
since two out of four got out. Chin up, Cheng. We'll find
another way."

Time went on, and Niku stayed free. She had an easy
way, of course, to not leave a scent-trail. I realized I was
being an idiot again, not to have attempted to write her
yet; what matter if my letter reached her home before she
did? Persahis agreed to send it through Haiu Menshir,
which is close to Niah-lur-ana, for me, on my avowal that
it was nothing political. I addressed it to her mother,
Tanra nar sept Taekun, on the island of Ibresi. It took
several drafts, before I remembered all I should say; my
mind was not the same, these days. I was already writing
everything important down, finding myself forgetting the
most simple things; I'd given up my tactical card game.

I wrote to my sister too. No more letters to Mana's
mother, now; he too had been Mezem-grounded, his window barred; all his mail would be carefully read. In the
end Persahis agreed to sneak it through Haiu Menshir, by
way of the Yeoli embassy, though he knew full well it was
political. He felt for me.

To her I wrote, "Keep stalling, ask to see me alive, and
don't come to an agreement at all in the end. As I should
know, Kurkas is most likely not bargaining in good faith
anyway, but planning some ruse. At some point they will
make a slip when they take me out of the City to bring me

to you; I will try to break loose. If I fail, it will be because
the *grium* has done me too much harm, and I am worth
nothing to Yeola-e anyway. I cannot command you; take it
then as my suggestion, based on what I know that you
cannot, for what is best, and my choice on what is to
be done with my life." So I kissed off what might be my
only hope. The night after I sent it off I had a dream
in which they'd made no mistake; before an army of my
people, they chopped off the fourth finger of my shield
hand, and threatened to take one more for each day the deal
was held up. There stood Artira, her face nearly as pale as
her hair, knowing my wish, that she never agree to it. It
was something to walk off, shake out of one's head, and
forget, if I meant to have no regrets.

In Yeola-e spring had come, and the war began to move
again. Tinga-e fell, the warriors too starved to fight, and
was sacked. When I read in the Pages that the streets had
run ankle-deep in blood, and a hundred thousand Yeolis
had died, I had no way of knowing how much the story
exaggerated. But I could not doubt the city had been
taken; and Arkan warriors encamped for a whole Yeoli
winter will be vengeful.

The first other Yeoli came into the Mezem after my
thirty-second fight; thereafter, because of the war and
a connection some slaver had set up, they came thick
and fast. If they didn't know who I was when they
first saw me, Mana or another would whisper in their
ear.

The first two to get matched against each other came to me.
We were five then. I called Assembly under the stands.

No one wanted to speak; all sat silent, their eyes wide in
the torchlight, begging for answers, all fixed on me. The
demarch speaks last; but the truth of the Mezem had
dashed them down to children who look for a parent, and I
was the highest-chainer. Who has killed most and lived
longest is king, in the Mezem.

I said, "It's not for me to decree what we do. But one
thing I think: whatever we do, whether it's fight or toss a
die for who kills himself or whatever, both should agree on
it. If we fail to agree we must fight." They voted chalk to
that; a choice made, speaking came easier to them, as it will.
The motion was also carried that the winner should see the
loser decently buried, and submit to a branding on the

face. I thought that severe and said so, as did Mana; but the new three were fresher from home, stricter in ethics, more set to keep themselves Yeoli. It made me see what I had lost.

The first pair were strangers to each other; they ended up fighting. You could see in a moment they were only sparring, though; the crowd started flapping its lips, calling them cowards, throwing things. Finally after five rounds, with the crowd calling "Whip-rounds! Whip-rounds!" the Judge concurred, and I got to see what that meant. The rounds are cut to half the time, and on the first rest break both fighters are struck five lashes with the Arkan whip, the break after that, seven, and so on. Sooner or later, mad with pain, they try to kill each other just to escape the whip.

Finally one wounded the other, and put him out of his agony. He might well have cut his own throat, then, had his boy run out to him any slower. I could have set fire to the Mezem and the crowd as one, when, as he lifted the corpse, they broke out into laughter, and mock keening. I drove the writers off him when he went out into the corridor, though I was due in the Ring. "The courtyard," I said. "Lay him there for now, and get to the clinic. And no blades in yourself, remember; we made our law, and you have your due yet to pay." He saluted me like a commander, sobs racking him, and staggered away to Iska, while Skorsas came yelling, "Raikas, you're on! You're on *now!*"; I ran back to my gate, and my fight.

We had not reckoned on how hard it would be, either, to bury a Yeoli in Arko. First off, burning uncured wood in an oven is prohibited, let alone cut logs outside. The city being in a pit where air lies trapped by the wind, it has strict laws on how much smoke can be made; everyone, even the poor, cooks using alcohol, blackrock, charcoal or wood cured outside. Arson is a capital crime; I'd only been spared because of who I was.

The graveyards are full, corpses already heaped six deep, and try to find one that will accept a heathen foreigner. In the end we had to hire a mortuary house to cremate him, outside the City. They charged us our eyeteeth, of course, and then plundered and buried him instead of doing what they'd sworn to, thinking an oath sworn to barbarians was not binding. We were lucky Skorsas, ever cynical, thought to send a spy. I happened to mention this to Norii, who happened to mention it in the Pages; as such businesses live by their name, that did it much harm. The second house we went to exhumed and cremated the corpse properly and were honest thereafter, so we stayed with them. Those of our people who got kicked into the trench by non-Yeolis we bribed the trench-keepers to give us. Mana and I financed it all.

There was one service no Arkan would do: pull out wisdom teeth. That we had to do ourselves. Each was placed in a tiny sack, with the name of the man, his home town and his killer; these I kept, with the pliers, in a chest on the shelf of my wardrobe, waiting for the first of us to make fifty fights and take them home. Skorsas, who could speak blithely of small girls being cut between the legs, turned green when I told him.

It fell to me also to do the branding; and again Arkan fire laws made trouble. We ended up having to bribe the kitchen staff to let us use their leftover embers, at night; the victor and I would creep in when a scullion let us, and brighten up the coals with the bellows. Then the victor would kneel at my feet, crystal in hand. Some of them I thought I might have to pin or bind, changing their minds at the last; we all knew the scar would make a man an outcast perhaps, and certainly unmarriageable, back home, if he were honest about why it was there. But though every one of them wept on the first mark, even Mana, none flinched away. I remembered how he and I had planned to marry together, and I had done otherwise; now no woman would look at him, who loved women so much. I hesitated; he grabbed my hand and said, "The people wills." I remember his tears sizzling and spitting like meat-juice on the iron, as I pressed it to his cheek.

Then I myself was matched against a Yeoli, Chinisenga Kri-o.

He broke our law, not asking my agreement to his act. He strode out while names were still being drawn, and though I followed him, when I came to the corridor I didn't know which way he'd gone; he'd told his boy he'd gone out for a walk in the city, words with excuse written all over them. I got a torch, and ran under the stands, looking all across the floor with its ankle-deep dust, and up into the rafters. Deep in, under the north end, I found him as I'd expected. Very high up; he must have been thinking to make sure the fall killed him if the belt clasping his neck broke. He was still alive then, for his limbs twitched, and some sounds came from his throat; but, imagining how bitter it would be to be saved from this after choosing it, to face what he'd thought to escape, I took my time getting the people and ropes needed to bring him down, and by then his heart was still.

Intrigued, the powers that were matched me against another Yeoli, Inara Merao. He drove a dagger into his own stomach, and died on Iska's table. Seeing a pattern, the Director had the third one, Kyera Shae-Lemana, seized and restrained before his name was announced. No one saw him again until fight-day. Then, two guards brought him to his gate in chains; I could see even across the ring his eyes were bloodshot and staring; his chest heaved and his body pricked like a rabid dog's. They'd fed him a drug to make him berserk; he could not know who or why or where he was fighting.

As the herald readied to strike the gong, I looked to the fighters' box. The Yeolis, as one, stabbed out their hands, chalk.

Kyera almost beat me. His skill was good, the drug made him both fearless and tireless, and my body shrank from fighting him. Now I understood, why no Yeoli balked at the brand; one could comfort oneself, as one looked for openings against another who wore a crystal, that punishment waited. There were no rest-breaks, of course; if he won he'd be brought down with stun-darts. While I circled away from his rushes, my breath coming in tearing gasps, my limbs turning to water with exhaustion, I heard Mana's voice cry, "Do it, Fourth Chevenga! The people wills!" Suffice to say I did it with my hand, so Chirel would stay clean of Yeoli blood, and in such a way he felt only an instant's pain. The crowd roared, delighted to see me have a hard time of it.

In the shower, I looked at my hands and thought, "However much I scrub them clean, they will never be the same." Next I knew marble was sliding cold against my side; I'd staggered into it. The world spun, its hot sparkling rain seeming to spray from all directions; I held myself up by gripping the pipes, one freezing my sword-hand, one scalding my shield-hand, the difference hard to

tell. Head sickness, I thought, not stomach, for I feel no
nausea: *grium.* I tried to shake it off, and felt Mana's hand.
"Under the stands." I whispered back, "The people wills."

I thought they'd convened to decide who was to brand
me. As it was, Mana put his hand on my shoulder, and
said, "Cheng, we were talking in the box. We decided we
shouldn't do it to you."

Memory plays tricks. I can't recall flinging myself in the
dust at all, or trying to clear a spot of floor to beat my head
against; but the voices all around I remember clear as
yesterday. "You were right, saying he'd take this badly."

"Let him work it off, like that little Haian does him,
then he'll be ready for sense."

"Get his head out of the dust so he doesn't choke."

"Cheng, listen! Cheng, your people are talking, shut up
and *fikken listen!*" Finally Mana backhanded me, and said
a fingerwidth from my face, *"The people wills."*

They made me get up out of the dust before they'd
speak. "You're demarch," Mana said. "When you get home,
you've got to fight the war for us—"

"With a clean face and a clean conscience," someone
cut in.

"Shut up, shitbrains!" Mana snapped at him, knowing
me better, as I was drawing breath to answer. "Whatever's
in your heart, Cheng, we know you can't feel clean with
this on you, you're too much a demarch. But also because
of that, you have to give your conscience up to us; remember, the demarch has no honor, but the people's will. We
commanded you to do it, because we need you for the
war. You're the best we've got. Now we command you to
forgo the brand, because to our mind you can only be
judged properly at home, so punishment should be held
off until then. Show him the vote as it was, sibs." Their
hands all came out, chalk.

"Kyera didn't choose," I said.

"He would have consented," they all started saying, "he
would have, if he'd had a chance, Cheng, look what your
first two did."

"He's right," said Mana. "Kyera didn't have a chance
to say. *We* do." He laid one hand on my shoulder formally, took his crystal with the other. "Fourth Chevenga
Shae-Arano-e, if you and I are matched, and they use that
drug, know now that I die willingly by your hand, so you

may live, for the sake of Yeola-e." He stepped back, and looked hard at the others.

Not so easy to say chalk to, as someone else's death; as well, the feeling lingered in some part that the war was my fault; I'd heard as much. They stood blinking, words catching on tongues.

He stood back on his heels, in his way, and his face bloomed with its wildest grin. "Shit-eaters," he said. "You're only facing a roll of the die, you greenhands, he'll most likely be out of here before you get a chance at him. *Me*"—he ran his hand through his chains, and said what I had never been able to bear to. "*I'm* looking at the certainty, unless there's some way out. Haven't any of you noticed, how they're setting us up against each other for our fiftieths?" All along, they'd kept us in pace with each other, in number of fights. Silence fell, as if everyone's breath had been cut off. "Yet I've done this."

It's the best, I thought, who are their best at the worst. He left the perfect pause. "Well, all right, all right. I can't blame you; even knowing one's ear's due to be pecked soon, no one wants to make an appointment. Think of it this way, then. Even you who think the war happened because this one went off on a fool's mission. He's still the warrior and the general people would cut off their sword-arms to have back, in Yeola-e, he's still the one who has all the friends in high places in other countries, who has the name and the nerve to make the alliances, and now the knowledge of Arko too, he's still the one who's capable of carrying our hopes; he's still the only soul on All-spirit's sweet green Earthsphere who could pull our fat out of the fire. Even if it's just possibly, even if you think I'm just his old friend blowing his horn, even if it's just a slim chance—" He touched my chest, over my heart. "Would you stick a sword through that?"

Two raced each other to be first; then, none wanting to be seen as the most reluctant, the rest crowded in. I took it all in silence and calm, as a demarch should, though my heart was water. Afterwards, Mana caught me by the arm when we were alone. "Cheng," he said, his lip quirking, "don't mess up and fail us, all right?" My heart stopped being water instantly; it was just what I needed, inspired as the rest.

Yet though I knew I shouldn't, I used my herb-pipe that

night. It kept Kyera from dying a thousand more times in my mind.

A heart-rending little subplot of the show we made, for Arko. We were matched against each other for about half our respective fights from then on, except for me, who got more. Out of my last fourteen matches, I was set against my people eight more times.

It was then I started letting Skorsas dress me as he would, ostentatiously. Someone must have spoken to him, for next thing I knew he was saying, "I'd thought this would all be you, but it's not," and trying to dress me austerely again. I'd have none of it, saying, "What is me is whatever I want. I am a thousand things."

I said a thousand things, where before I'd been quiet; I turned into a raconteur, keeping up a running patter like a magician on the stage, shot with vicious wit. One thing I love death for, I remember thinking: it is an inexhaustible source of jokes. I began wearing my wristlets everywhere, my chains open, metal jewelry; I stopped praying, for it no longer seemed to serve; I thought and dreamed as well as spoke in Arkan, and it seemed to me I could no longer speak any Yeoli but "Hold still while I brand you." I didn't decide any of these things, I recall, in fact I barely noticed them, aside from admiring the flash of my finger-rings, or laughing hysterically when I thought, "Hear ye, hear ye, Servants of Buzzard Assembly: he's down, should I plug his heart or fling him to the lions? *The people wills. All who command me chalk, speak now . . .*" I decided nothing; it was more as if it slowly dawned on me that it was much easier to let the current carry me than swim upstream.

I could talk with Mana only in the showers; I ceased asking him whether I had changed. I imagine he tried to tell me, but I remember nothing, so I must not have listened, as I know I didn't to Skorsas, Iska, Norii or Persahis. Norii came to interview me for the book as he had every two fights or so, this the last. We'd become friends; I had told him my whole life story and everything on my mind, except that which I would tell no one, of which about an eighth was safe for him to write. I could tell when I went beyond the pale; he'd put his noteboard down. This time I told him that once I was free, I would return with an army and sack Arko.

How did I expect to manage that, he asked; I just

smiled mysteriously and said, "You expect me to give away my plans?" So it reads; in truth, I don't remember the exchange. I do not doubt, though, that I thrust the noteboard into his hand and said, "Go ahead! Quote me, let all Arko know and be damned!" He did.

It came out after my forty-first fight, under the title *Life is Everything*, from something I'd said when he'd asked me why I thought the Mezem was evil, and this killing we did, wrong. He brought me a copy, and signed it with pen as if he'd scribed it, a custom for authors whose words are passed through the machine. I hadn't thought he'd write like the others, but even so I was not prepared for what I read. His words, and my words in his hands—at least half of it was quotes—were magic; they spoke my life here almost more clearly, it seemed, than I had lived it.

That same day, two Mahid came for me; but instead of to the Marble Palace they took me under the stands, where two more waited, stripped me, bound me and worked me over as only Mahid unleashed, as they call it, can. Their leader was Second Amitzas, the head Mahid torturer; young Ilesias was one of the others. They had me for a good two beads.

I will say only that if one imagines a session of torture as a story, the main thread was that Amitzas had a serrated knife covered with the Lakan ointment of pain, *azan akanaja*, and orders to mark me with it once, to show the Imperator's displeasure at my vow to sack Arko; the others had their sub-plots. One of them tore a bite-sized piece of flesh out of my back with his teeth, which even other Mahid find perverse; he got in trouble for it. I still have the scar, to show anyone who thinks Kurkas did me no wrong. It finished with Amitzas saying, "You will remember, every time you look in a mirror," and slashing my right cheek from nose to jawline. The stuff started eating into my flesh instantly, burning like acid. They left me bound in the dust for Skorsas to find.

Iska took two beads stitching, determined that I should be disfigured as little as he could help. I remember weeping when they lowered me into the bath, more in pleasure than pain. No surprise, the bite festered; that in itself kept me in bed and in half-waking nightmares, despite the sedatives, for three days. By the number of times Skorsas said, "You will always be beautiful," I knew my looks were ruined. I had never seen how I took them for granted; though I'd never thought myself as well-favored by the die as my father had been, I certainly had on occasion, as people do, looked into a mirror, posed and thought, "A fine figure this one cuts, yes, not bad at all." Never again. I'd turn my head to see myself in profile, and wish I could enter rooms that way; or think, "On someone else, I'd think I'd say those eyes have seen too much."

I healed. On the first day after, a note came with a very short poem, directing me to find things of mine in a certain place in the woods, signed, "Raven." Skorsas went. It was my crystal and my father's wisdom tooth, both of which the Mahid had torn off and thrown into the dust under the stands, and a lock of my hair, such as they'd all cut from my head as they left, for trophies. I wasn't in a state to notice, still raving, when Skorsas fastened the crystal and the tooth around my neck, but when I could, I thought: Ilesias. He did what was commanded, as he must; but wanted to give me some mercy. I had no use for a curl of my hair; he'd sent it just to show he'd taken it only for appearances. A Mahid by birth but not by nature, I thought, and then wondered how long he would last.

As for how the rest of the city took *Life is Everything*, my discontent came as a shock, of course. The tavern-master of the House of the Mountains accosted me in the colonnade, and threw himself to his knees: apparently the mood of his place had turned so glum that his livelihood was threatened. He begged me to come and say something, anything, to cheer the miserable curly-black-wigged throng, no one having informed him I was grounded.

Hard on his heels came the king of the clan, a thin man with arms of straw whom one could tell was Arkan only by his blue eyes and his speaking; his hair and eyebrows he'd somehow made indistinguishable from mine, and he wore a vein-blood-red Yeoli-style shirt. His Karas Raikas pendant, the insignia of the fellowship, was golden; probably his life savings had gone to buy it. I thought his heart would fail him, just from seeing me close; he was tongue-tied for so long I started feeling awkward myself. Finally he said what he had come to say: that if he could, he would free me, this on behalf of my true followers as well as himself.

From people who'd give their hair to see me fight, I

thought, that means something. On a slip of paper I wrote my name in Yeoli. "Get this tattooed on your shoulder," I said. "Then get those you know who truly would free me if they could to do the same. In the sack my warriors will know by that, who loved me and believed in me." His eyes bugged; then his face took on a glow, like those of people in Arkan paintings who'd been brushed by divine grace (odd-looking under black curls), as if he'd played a part in a legend that would be told for a thousand years.

Others thought I was a poor sport, throwing this pall on Arko's love for me: someone in the Watcher called me cynical and small-minded, someone else a coward. The rest of the city just took it as a stunning new turn of the script, and relished the heightening of the tragedy. I had wondered about Yeoli things becoming the rage in the city that was Yeola-e's deadliest enemy; now it came to me why. Like Kurkas's Tinga-eni wine, we were something to devour; it was whetting its appetite for us, savoring our delights, finding this new flavorful little morsel tasty. No wonder, I thought, Kurkas always licks his lips more at me than at his dinner, even when it comes from a breast.

My scarring was the start of my feud proper with the Mahid. I swore I would never again go peacefully, though Skorsas begged me to, saying resisting them brought punishment ten times worse.

It turned out Ilesias had been seen picking up my crystal and tooth by the one who'd bit me; Barbutas, as he was named, was blackmailing him. In short, he needed a Yeoli crystal and a wisdom tooth, to prove he hadn't returned them to me, which by Mahid measure would have been treason. I gave him back that one, borrowing one from the Yeoli dead until I ordered another, which would take a moon; the tooth I showed him how to get from the lion-trench, not being willing to give up my father's. When he thanked me he made the Arkan prayer-sign, the hands cupped upwards at the temples, as if I were a god.

Then Barbutas wanted one of the gold leaves I wore in my hair, and made Ilesias ask me. As Ilesias requested, I wrote back suggesting he come to the Mezem and try to take one, though he should make out his will first. I didn't think he'd take me up on it, but he did, with five others, none over eighteen, including Ilesias, blackmailed into this too. They pretended as if they were acting on the orders of the Marble Palace, when in truth they were on a hunt, as Arkans call it, a favorite pastime of young Mahid, usually done in the poor quarter.

Three came through the Legion Mirrors while the other three, including Barbutas, preferring to lead from the rear, waited under the stands. I pretended to come peacefully, then turned around before them in the corridor, and hand-heeled the two flanking me. The third was Ilesias. I offered to let him go, but as duty required he grabbed for his dart-tube instead. So I struck him senseless, dragged him inside and bound him to my bed.

I readied for the siege, getting supplies and weapons, and boarding up the window and the door to Skorsas's room, while Iska stood outside pleading, "Raikas, don't do this, please, lad, this is madness"; Skorsas barred and bolted himself in the wardrobe. Wondering what had taken the vanguard so long to make the capture, the rearguard came and knocked on my door. I dared Barbutas to put his shoulder to it, and he was fool enough to listen; I let him in, stunned him with a kick and bolted the door in the face of the other two, who ran for help.

I wish I could say honestly, I never tortured anyone in my life. Barbutas was the first. Not that I did much, a flick of a knife here and there and lots of taunting, but if the degree of pain is to be judged by the degree of expression of it, it was brutal, for he screamed himself blue as a baby. I shouldn't have been surprised, I guess, to find him a coward. In the end it was in disgust more than vengeance, that I put the knife through his heart.

There is little left to say. The Mahid came in force, sent three through my door with nets and hooks; I killed them all too. Then they turned to subtler tactics. Skorsas being the obvious hostage, I'd kept him with me; but I cared as well for Iska. I remember what the Senior Mahid, whose name was Meras, said when I reminded him I had one of his alive in here: "Kill him, then. He is Mahid, he will understand." Then they slit Iska's nostril. I cared more for Iska's life than Meras did for Ilesias's; so they had me. On Ilesias's cheek, though, I left a cut like my own, more to keep him out of trouble for being favored by me than anything else. Then I stripped, since I knew they'd take everything on me but my chains, and gave myself up.

I'll say even less of what they did to me, if I can. I'd killed six of them. They wanted to execute me, of course, but Kurkas forbade it; instead he gave them three days with me. They could not cause me harm that would not heal within an eight-day, but that leaves plenty of leeway, especially considering that I didn't know they weren't to kill me. A favorite Arkan torment is smothering to unconsciousness, since by their creed Hayel, where sinners go, is a place of eternal smothering; each time, of course, they would tell me I'd breathed my last. Meras, a man with eyes that never changed, whether they saw death or blood or ecstasy, like a lizard's, told me I owed him six lives; six times he killed me in spirit, this way. And that was just him. Soon enough I began to wish they were telling the truth.

They twisted out another of my teeth, so I ended with three gold ones. All the bereaved had their turn, the women and children even crueller than the men. Second Amitzas branded his initials, the Arkan letters A and M, above and below my navel. Last came Ilesias, both wounded and bereaved; I'd killed his uncle. He had a vial of Mahid's Obedience, the pain-drug they use in their own training; its effect is to make all the veins feel full of fire. No one can bear it without screaming and convulsing; one must have a gag in one's mouth or break one's teeth. But he did which by that point was almost worse torture: spared me.

I was an eight-day recovering what passed then for my sanity; they were afraid to put me in the Ring for another two. I weapon-sensed a Mahid kit, dart-tube and dagger, in the corridor, and was so seized with terror I threw up, and shook harder than I could stop. But it was Ilesias, come to give me my crystal again, saying it contained his flaw, as he put it; you and I would say his humanity. I promised I would give it back to him when I returned.

I made forty-five fights, and began to see things in my food, as Jinai had predicted, jam with worms crawling out of it to the edge of the plate. I killed more Yeolis; my last four fights, my last five matches, were all Yeolis. I said to Persahis, "I'm mad, I know," and it ceased bothering me. I donated money to the orphanages, wanting to do it anonymously; Skorsas insisted on loudly announcing the Karas Raikas Beneficent Fund. I made forty-six, and as I was coming out of the shower he said Celestialin, as if it were my name. I said, sorry? He answered, Celestialin is the divine hero of Arkan myth, who will save Arko on its day of deepest peril. It had come to him in a flash like the sun's blinding light that I must be him. Save Arko, you've got to be joking, I said. I will destroy Arko, if anything. Besides, how can Celestialin be Yeoli? But he was quite serious; he'd hired a scholar to check through the Book, the Arkan work they claim is the Gods' word, and never does it explicitly say Celestialin is Arkan. It does explicitly say that the Chosen One shall deny he is the Chosen One, so that didn't get me off. Perhaps Arko can only be saved by a taste of fire and a bath of blood, purification, he said. You are too perfect not to be divine.

As the Mahid are trying to teach me, I thought, their will is mine; I belong in their hands, under them. Shininao came to me in my dreams. He was big, big enough for his leather and steel wings, the ribs curved like sword-blades, to enwrap my nakedness, strong beyond imagining, to cradle my weight on onyxine gossamer. His eyes were blue and his beak had the mouth of a woman on the end, a kiss like warm roses, a long wet binding tongue. "I give myself to you," I told him, throwing my head to the side, to open up my right ear. "We've always been close; let's consummate it." We made our pillow-talk, our jokes. I always had to remember to thank him while I could still speak, to kiss his talon for making it so merciful. It was ecstasy beyond ecstasy, the beak pressing deep into my ear, slow as a healer's probe, his tongue sliding tenderly in through my every vein, to freeze my heart in his warmth; that would kill the *grium*, robbing it of its nourishment, and tear away all my cares; I could feel them smooth off my face, as the peace of stillness filled me. No matter that I was in a crypt, stuffed unburned like an Arkan into this great gaudy stone place that had eaten so many; no matter the thousand blood-dripping ghosts seeping from the walls. I threw my arms wide and came and came and came.

I made forty-seven, and read of the Arkans advancing north towards Vae Arahi. The people wills, Cheng, Mana kept saying to me, when he could. The people wills, we need you, hang on, Cheng, hang on. In the same tone, leaves rustle in courtyards. I'll hang on like Chinisenga, I joked, but it fell flat. Celestialin, you must live to save us, said Skorsas.

I made forty-eight, and to my amazement and delight, Kurkas invited me up for dinner; in fact he honored me, entrusting me to join him in his sanctum, so many of the Empire's greatest treasures laid out before me.

There are no guards there, no spring-darts. Even so, he could call them. Once we were sitting I sprang up, and jammed a gold-leafed chair up under the doorknob. To strike him speechless I raised Sibbas's *Flying Machine* in my hands, and flung it straight up against the ceiling, to smash into a rain of shards. It worked; he sat as white-faced and glass-eyed as the dead.

"It is the truth of life," I said, as I crushed the three bird's eggs under my heel, "that all one has can be destroyed. Those you have trusted will betray you, kill those you love, try to tear down what you *are*, in the deepest sense. I have learned that; you have not; you will now. I call you out: be me, Kurkas Aan, be the world that your hands touch so much, and know what they do.

"Your home will be sacked," I said, as I drew the antique sword and slashed the paintings, "all your possessions ruined, all your slaves . . ." I drew the bird out of its cage, screeching and flapping, by the neck, let him think for a while I meant to kill it, then thrust it out the window, and let it fly. ". . .freed!"

"It will die out there," he said, in an ashen, stupid voice.

"As the old saying goes," I said, "if it comes back, it is yours." I have never known joy until now, I thought, shattering a row of glass figurines with one sweep of my foot, while with my hand I held his childhood drawing of a winged lion in the candle-flame. The euphoria of destruction is giddy, wild, intoxicating like a drug; its sweetness increases with the value of the things destroyed. Some warrior-turned-philosopher once said this comes in truth of the delight in throwing off the bounds of the material, in freedom, however short-lived, from the rule that everything has a cost. Perhaps; I'd thrown off all other bounds. I remember how the miniature *Hero* looked with his head, then without, just a pair of godlike shoulders, while the great jawbone in my hands tingled with the stroke, and my laughter filled the air. "All you have created, burned; all you have thought inviolate, violated, all you have collected . . ." I paused before *The Delights of Celestialis*, decided I liked it, unhooked it and stood it by the door to take away later. "Looted!"

With the bone shouldered, I stood over the glass city of Arko. Those blue porcelain eyes poured out silent tears now, like cracked dishes leaking, though still enthralled by horror, and disbelief of a horror so great, like the eyes of people watching a massacre. "You who have wanted to possess me," I said, "know nothing of me, as you are learning now. You who have such power, know nothing of power; that too, you will learn now. It's only by being the other, one truly can." I raised the bone in two hands. "*This* is power." He froze deeper still. "Beg me not to, Kurkas."

His voice came out a rasping scrape. "What I will do to you for this, barbarian, what I will do to you . . ."

"Don't threaten—*beg*! Threats won't touch me; I am free. Threats are for the future; only this moment is now, and we are only here, now. There's only one thing you can do: beg me." With a clarity like a child's, he spoke his heart. "Shefen-kas. I don't know how."

"Too bad then!" A sweet tinkling crash, the tiny glass Avenue of Statuary made. He screamed, as if I'd run him through the stomach. "And one day," I shouted over the din, "this will be the fate of the real Arko!" Three quick hammer-blows, and the Mezem, the Marble Palace and the University were shards and glass-dust. "Hear me, All-spirit! Hear me, you Arkan gods who might be lurking around to listen, with your dog mother! I who know true power have spoken: so it will be, for the real city of Arko, for so I shall make it! Arko will die in flame and blood, will bend to the dust and have its face ground, will kneel to serve the world as it would have had the world serve it! Arko will die, and history will forever remember Kurkas Aan as the Imperator who failed to save it, and Fourth Chevenga Shae-Arano-e as the demarch who destroyed it! Hear me, all the world! *I will kill Arko!*" I left not so much as a tying-post in one piece, eventually tossing aside the bone and doing it with my hands, though they were soon red with glass-cuts; I felt no pain. He threw his head back and screamed with abandon.

When I was tired enough to be satisfied, which because of my Mezem training was a long time, I tucked the painting under my arm and left him howling on the floor, his arms reaching for the shards and ashes and shreds as if by pure wish and tenderness he could repair them. No guards had come, for he had never called them; no one in authority must have been within earshot, and those who were near, too stunned to seek such a person, for I strolled with the painting out of the Palace and to the Mezem unaccosted. In my room I hung it; from then on all who entered complimented me on having acquired such a faithful reproduction.

That night when full darkness had fallen I knelt by the wall naked, and took off my crystal and my father's wisdom tooth. The crystal shattered well against the stone: the tooth I had to grind under my boot-heel.

X

It's not inevitable, Skorsas said to me. You are forty-eight chains, the Living Greatest. For you there is some consideration. Go speak to the Director. Remind him of all you've suffered.

I scratched on his office door. Ah, my boy, he smarmed, Karas Raikas of the smouldering gaze, how kind of you to visit your master! The marble desk, the whole room, was pristine and shining as ant-picked bones, not a scrap of paper or a pen in sight, all of it pure decor. Only one thing lay before him: a palm-sized brass disk with a spinning pointer on it, and segments graven Yes, No, Maybe, Dismiss Someone and so forth, which he twirled absently with his silk-gloved finger, in wait for a decision that needed making.

I said I will not fight Mana the Wolf, die cast gates fast all go home. He said, what? I'd spoken in Yeoli. But then you must die, he said. I know, I said. After all you've suffered, he said, forty-eight fights, Riji Klifas, all the Mahid trouble and anything, you'd throw it all away now? I said, you heard me. Or are you deaf? I will not fight Mana the Wolf. I was afraid he'd throw my duty to my people at me, but he said he didn't understand what it was with me and Yeolis and the Marble Palace and my most brilliant fighter is my most inscrutable enigma, agh, agh, agh.

I said, are you serious? Everyone above and below you knows my real name, who I was—you don't . . . ! He blinked and said, who are you? I almost fell off my chair, laughing. I'm not telling, no, master, you keep your eye on this space for the Serpent's Tale, the Pen that Knows All: as they say, you always hear it there first! He said it must be the madness of genius, as with Riji. Raikas, please understand, he wheedled, Mana is the highest chainer aside from you and think of the *gate receipts*! Then the door opened, and Meras Mahid came in.

Fancy meeting you here, I said. His lizard-still eyes slid off mine to fix the Director's, which widened like a rabbit's. You perhaps recall the Imperator's intentions regarding this very person, Director, Meras said. I have been sent to remind you.

Whatever the Imperator intends between sucklings, Director, I said, I will not fight Mana the Wolf. So I will it, so will it be. He looked from me to Meras and back several times, the rabbit caught between two wolves. The Mahid and I traded looks; it seemed we shared one thing, a measure of the man. I signed at the brass thing. Give that a flick; maybe you'll find your answers there. Was that the faintest twitch of a smile, on that reptile face?

Skorsas knew where one could find assassins for hire in Arko. Get me the best, I said, price is no object. As a matter of fact I'll throw in a chip for the seat, or seats if they want, right beside my gate for my fiftieth fight. His face turning green, a familiar sight these days, he asked me who I meant to kill, afraid it was Kurkas. No, no, I said mysteriously; someone much easier, shouldn't be trouble at all if they're any kind of professionals. Take this letter, that sets it all out.

I made forty-nine. So did Mana, the next fight-day. A last eight-day to draw it out, and then it was announced. All Arko, at least all Arko that watches the Mezem, went mad with expectation, made it into another eight-day festival. One would hope the rest of Arko would sigh, there go those cock-fighting hooligans again; but it tended rather to get caught up, people not usually interested now buying ribbons and pendants and joining in the war-cries of the streets, *Raiiiiiii-kas*! or *Woooooolf*! The going odds for the Battle of the Killer Mountain Boys: five-to-four for me.

My guards were all Mahid now, all armed with stun-

darts. Mana was in one of the cells, and I was not allowed
to speak with him. Still, I got a message through; it's good
having money in Arko. *Don't kill yourself, or worry; I
have a plan. Trust me.* How much he was inclined to trust
the functioning of my mind these days can be imagined;
but he had no choice. I remember his answer, his last
words to me. "Chevenga, whatever happens: I love you as
my heart's brother, always. Spirit infuse you."

I strung them all along, for six days. Barely a moment
before the mid-eight-day Pages deadline, I told half the
writers I would not fight my best friend no matter what it
meant, and sensed by their questions what a beautiful
tragedy they'd craft of it; the other half I told, actually I
might, since Mana and I have had something of a falling
out. You did this just to *fikken* us up, you overrated little
shit, they yelled at me the next day, when the Pages came
out late. The Director summoned me to his office, to ask
me precisely what my intentions were, since the Pages
still had it as a mystery. I did that just to *fikken* them up, I
answered. You know my intentions; I only told you about
five times, but since the sixth seems necessary: I will not
fight Mana the Wolf. And yet . . . well, life isn't so bad,
and there was that girl we were both after when we were
twelve . . . No. I can't. But . . . O dear master, do you
mind if I borrow that brass thing on fight-day?

He slammed his white-gloved fists on the marble, which
is something for an Arkan, and yelled, How in *Hayel* is
anyone supposed to know how much chips for this are
worth, whether it's going to be a non-fight, a drugged
fight, or what? Don't you know the price goes up and
down with every wind from your noisome mouth, you
young savage, and fortunes are won and lost unjustly
every moment? I said, my heart goes out to them, but the
excitement! The drama!

Then, two days before, they announced that due to my
refusal, unless I changed my mind, I would be executed.
Artira must have stalled too long, I thought. But in honor
of my matchless achievements in the Ring, it would be
done painlessly; in fact, it would be done in the Ring, so
my loyal followers could grant me a proper farewell. Well,
Saint Mother, of course, I thought; they've promised all
those poor citizens who've won and lost fortunes a specta-
cle, and by Celestialis they'll give them one. Skorsas!

What shall I wear? He said, Celestialin, you can't die. You have to change your mind.

They filled Mana full of sedative, to keep him from turning his hand against himself. Seeing no chance of speaking to him again, I wrote him a letter, with all my messages to everyone at home. I sent to my assassin with apologies. His services likely would not be necessary now, but he was to keep his chip, and the first half of the payment with my compliments, just in case it was a ruse and I did end up in my gate full of berserker-serum. Then he must give me the slap on the shoulder with the poison thorn between his fingers or whatever he was planning—I'd forbidden him to tell me, so that if my fighting habits did prick up against him, I'd be less ready—upon which he'd be paid in full.

On the eve, there was a party as there had been for Suryar. Whatever inconsiderate things I did to everyone else, I never gave another fighter even a harsh word, so that they'd been concealing more sympathy for me than I had ever expected. That last eight-day, since they need no longer fear me or my opponent, it came out; they hugged me, blessed me, were my brothers, my comrades in arms, and howled with laughter with me at our oppressors, feeling free for once to do it. In fact there was an air of festival inside the quarters as well as out, that strengthened as fight-day came. Some things, I suppose, only gladiators can celebrate.

Yet that party had a darker feel than Suryar's, the intoxication, or self-poisoning, as a Haian would call it, more vicious, being undercut with greater despair and bitterness; in fact, though no one laid a finger on anything belonging to any of the others, the dining-hall, the pantry and the lounge got ransacked. For one thing, though they all knew Mana would likely make fifty now, at someone else's expense, right now he was locked away drug-palsied to keep him from suicide. As well, however full of hope and heart and blessing my farewell speech was, for I made it so, however cheerfully I poured wine into mouths and danced through the splintered pieces of antique chairs, stuffing spilling out like blood, the fighters were still seeing one of themselves who'd struggled through forty-nine fights as well as all the rest come to grief in spite of all. It brought home their own fate.

Sometime around midnight it came into my sodden head I hadn't made my will. So, with much morbid drunken aid, I wrote, "I, Fourth Chevenga Shae-Arano-e, better known around here as Karas Raikas, being sound of mind, or at least faking it well enough to scribe and sign a legal document, and body, as much as anyone can be with the *grium sefalian*, seven cups of wine and three pipes of Arkanherb in him, do by these presents bequeath my entire fortune, whatever amount it may be, to Skorsas Trinisas, *fessas*, as his own property to do with as he sees fit; and hereby appoint Iskanzas Muras, *fessas*, as my executor." I signed it with both my names, then looked about for a witness; best would be a high-caste Arkan. He was at my elbow, I realized; all night, my two assigned Mahid had stuck to me like the shadows thrown by two candles. I got the elder, Solasas, one of the four who'd tortured me under the stands, to do it, and handed it formally to Iska.

Later, when the place was strewn with sprawled bodies like a battlefield, I realized I had not seen Skorsas for a good bead. He'd told me long before that he was getting old for this game; after I'd made fifty, he'd decided, he'd quit and try to get apprenticed to a Haian. I'd written a letter of recommendation that same day; now it was time to give it to him.

Making my farewells I went to our rooms. I found him kneeling by my bed weeping, though he tried to hide it when I came in. That was something; he didn't cry easily, not like me; he'd had a hard life. "I swore I wouldn't," he whispered. "I swore I wouldn't, while you were here. I'm sorry. Forgive me. I'm sorry. Don't be here in the dark with me, go back out and enjoy yourself."

"I thought I should save the rest of the night for you," I said, and held out my arms to him. "Skorsas. I don't mind if you cry; did I when I first came? Go on, lad, do what you feel."

He broke, like a dam, and poured out his soul like a river in my arms. When his words became coherent, I heard, "I'm not mourning you, Chevenga. You can't die, because you're Celestialin; the Gods will save you somehow, you will live. But all the things that have been done to you, all you've suffered . . ."

"And . . ." I said, prompting him. "I know, Skorsas. I

will be gone, either way. You'll have lost me, without ever having had me." He buried his head in my knee, sobs coming afresh.

I leaned, and kissed his hair. His bright head whipped up, the eyes staring stunned, searching mine to see if he'd felt true. I picked up his naked hand, usually hidden so devoutly in silk or linen, and touched my lips to the palm.

Here, I was thinking, now, what reason in the Earthsphere do I have left, for denying him? He's seventeen, he's taller than I, though he hasn't noticed; he's probably less of a child than most twenty-year-olds. I've held off from him from the start; let me make it up to him at least a little, leave him with one sweet night, to show him his love is not entirely unrequited.

For a while he wept, in joy; then he raised his eyes, clear sky-blue even in yellow candlelight, and touched fingertips as delicate as feathers to my face.

I had meant it for him. Soon I learned, it was more for myself than I'd known. When as a thirteen-year-old I'd first heard of whorehouses, I'd been torn between horror, that love-making could be sold for money, and a delicious wondering, at what skill those who made a living at it must have learned. Now I found out. Yet none of Skorsas's old clients must ever have felt what I did; for his skill he gave me with all his passion in it. I can't remember how many times it was, for either of us, though I know it was more for me; my life, feeling itself soon to be quenched, wanted to burn harder for the last, it seemed. I wept, and fainted, and saw colors painted in my inward eyes by his fingers on my skin all through. Afterwards, it seemed to me this had made my life whole; I could look back along the path I had come, and feel it was long enough. I lay my head back on his arm, closed my eyes, and felt as deep and silent and all-embracing a peace as after the Kiss of the Lake. It came to me, I had come to myself.

I felt at my throat. Only chains, heavy as a yoke now; finally I threw them off, let go their weight. "Shh, lie still and bask, heart of the world," he said, understanding. "A moment."

He came back, held out his hand. He'd picked up all the pieces of my father's wisdom-tooth that same night, when I wasn't looking, joined them together again with glue and restrung it. The crystal was the replacement that

I'd forgotten we'd ordered. Iska had kept them in his desk. "We knew you would ask for them, when you were yourself again. You who are and always will be Chevenga."

I kissed his chin, and said, "As opposed to Celestialin."

"No," he said. "You can be both. The Book says he has his father-given name too. So there." He laced his fingers in my hair. "All those little curls, they're all warm and they feel as if they each want to hug my fingers."

"They do, lad—love. My name isn't just father-given, though. They took a vote on it. That reminds me—you'll still have Chirel. Will you find a way to get it back to Yeola-e? To the, well, king, you'd say."

"You know I'd do anything for you. I bet they took a vote on which way to wipe your nose." He kissed it, laughing. "Still, that doesn't mean you're not Celestialin. You are. I know it."

"I tell you what," I said. "Let tomorrow settle the argument. If I die, you'll know I wasn't Celestialin. If I live . . . well, the gods are going to have to intervene to arrange that, so maybe it'll mean something. Fair enough?" He agreed, and we slept.

I was lying half-awake, in the brilliant sun of morning, when Iska peeked in, guessed what had happened from how we lay entangled, and whispered to Skorsas, "That's the best thing in the world you could have done for him, lad." Skorsas whispered back, "He did it for me." A bead before noon, Iska woke me again. I bathed and ate, and he drew me into the clinic, to explain.

It would come before the fights, so I would not get to see Mana's fiftieth; that I regretted. Reminded, I gave Iska the letter, which he put carefully away. It was the Imperial Pharmacist, First Amitzas Mahid, who would perform the execution, in the center of the Ring, by injecting a poison into the vein in the crook of my arm. Two guards would stand near, to help me hold steady. The feeling would be no worse than falling asleep.

Last night had been the celebration; now, as I gave everyone in the quarters my farewells, came the sorrow. One never truly knows the feelings of those near, until one takes one's leave; I couldn't believe how many tears I saw, even among the grizzled old serving-staff who I'd

thought incapable; it moved me to tears myself. No sign of
Mana, though; they didn't trust him for this.

Skorsas hadn't laid out any clothes, not knowing which.
I wore a plain white linen robe, my crystal and my father's
wisdom-tooth, nothing else. He dressed in plain white
too, and took all his jewelry off, to match me. Between the
Legion Mirrors, we could already hear a thunder from the
Ring: thousands of feet stamping the planks. He gripped
my hand, his, steady as oak.

Noon tolled, observance was made; then the din swelled
again. I heard the chant, reminding me I could change my
mind even now: *Raikas! Live!* I heard a hawker bawl,
"Mourning dye! In sympathy, I've marked it down!" We
stepped into their sight. It seemed to triple, as everyone
rose to their feet. Even Mana's followers wanted me to
change my mind, so they could see him beat me. Banners
and kerchiefs waved everywhere, with the same words.

In the Ring, Amitzas stood in his white robe, his things
on a stand, two younger Mahid in armor at his side. They
even had my bier, in my colors, the wood black, the satin
vein-blood red, the braid gold. Kurkas was in his box, as
I'd thought he would be, though he had the glass doors
closed. Minis stood with his hands and nose pressed up
against them, his eyes wide and blinking.

Let fifty thousand Arkans witness: I kissed Skorsas goodbye, long and deep. Then I stepped into the Ring, through
the gate that was usually mine. Amitzas stood spear-straight
as always, the wind ruffling his robe. The two Mahid
came, reaching to take my wrists. I whipped my arms
free. "Try that again and I'll kill both of you," I said. "Do
you think I need to be dragged to what I chose?" While
they stood flat-footed, I strode between them to my place.

I thought we'd do it now; but the gong crashed for
silence, a long time before it came. The Director rose, to
speak.

What he said I've forgotten, not worth remembering.
The gist was what a tragedy this was after my various
victories; but he filled it in with so much pompous chaff
that any power it might have had was lost. I realized he
meant to draw it out in the hope that time would sap my
resolve, when he mentioned for the third time that I could
yet change my mind. A duel of wills that was no contest; I
just stood steady. Finally, when someone nudged him, I

think, he made a grand and frilly finish, and then asked me if I had any words to say to the people of Arko who had stood with me through good and ill all this time.

I looked all round. In the silence they cried out to me, the roar catching through the stands like fire again. I heard the words of those close, as always. *"No, Raikas! You can't die! You can't die!" "Raikas, I love you, please, please don't do this!"*

"Die, and you'll be a damned coward like all the rest of you barbarians!" That one no doubt had a bet on me to live. *"Raikas, we all love you, live and be free, champion of our hearts, live and go home with our blessing!"*

No one is human, who can hear fifty thousand people cry out to him in the hopes of saving his life, for whatever reason, and not be moved in some part of himself, by their sheer number. It is worse for a demarch, I suspect; even though they were Arkans. I felt a voice in me whisper, "The people wills." But I needed only to think and remember, to harden myself again.

I pulled up the sleeve of the robe, and thrust my arm out to Amitzas, clenching my fist to bring up the vein. I'd said enough; this was all I wished now. "Arko," I said with my naked arm, "you call me the champion of your heart, you call on me to flesh out your lusts and dreams, to live the tale you want to see but not live yourself. You claim to love me, to cherish my life. But do you think, because you flinch away from the bare truth, that I, who have had my face ground into it for a year and a half, fail to see it too? Do you think I should not return you in kind? If you wished to save me, you should have treated me better. If you loved me, you should have set me free. Stop lying to yourselves, finally, and see what you do."

The yelling rose to such loudness it hurt my ears, as they made their last desperate efforts to persuade me, or giving up, cried out in anguish, women and men screaming as if in torture. Once they had molded me into a stranger; that was all in the past now. So much greater than their number was the silence in me now, the peace between my thoughts; they could touch it as much as fifty thousand ants could shift a mountain; soon it would outlast them, and spread to them. Still, it took long enough before the last pleas and whimpers faded away, that my arm got tired. For the first time in longer than I'd realized, I heard the voice of the harmonic singer, and the wind.

The time was now, the Director could not hold off any longer. He signed to Amitzas, who had the syringe filled already; *he* never played things out for no reason. He lifted it in his hand, looked into my eyes, took my wrist with the other, feeling my pulse. "Are you all right?" he said, under his breath lest the front rows hear, so quiet it was now. "Do you need to be held?"

"I'm fine, I won't move," I answered. He said, "Good," and took my forearm on his, in his healerly way. "This is easiest for the brave." He touched the needle to my skin and pressed it through quickly, finding the vein on the first try, as was his skill. As the drug went in, I felt it as a cold tingling, rising slowly up my arm. He drew the syringe out, laid it down. "There. It's almost over now, Yeoli. Relax." The guards shifted in close behind me; I almost turned and snapped at them again until it came to me they were there to catch my fall.

The cold fingered inside my shoulder, and I thought, "When it reaches my head, that will be the end." I looked back over my other shoulder, for Skorsas. He stood in our gate, leaning, his hands clenched around the bars. As the cold seeped up my neck, tingling at the end of my tongue, I sent him a kiss and a grin. He answered in kind. The silence in me seemed to suddenly deepen, then turn to darkness over my eyes as if I'd fallen down out of the world into myself, and that was all.

But as life is not so simple, neither is death.

When I could think, I realized I could not see, nor hear, nor smell, those senses blocked or masked or blinded; I could taste only iron, my mouth filled with a blade; I could not move, as if I were encased in rock, or at least every point of movement on me was; yet I felt naked. I could breathe, though; in my panic and confusion it came fast and harsh. Then there was the bee's-wings whirring in my head that I knew: the *grium*. That cannot have followed me into death, I thought; it was a disease, not an entity; it had no spirit to fly after mine and haunt me. All-spirit help me; I'm still alive.

I wept, in rage, in terror, in disappointment, in every emotion but relief to be alive, I think; then a hand lightly

pressed on my chest, feeling it heave, my heart pound,
learning my state of mind. I knew the touch, when the
fingers came delicately to unfasten the clasps of the blade
in my mouth, and draw the plugs from my ears: it was the
last touch I'd felt, Amitzas Mahid's.

"All-spirit," I babbled, when I could; it was all I could
say. "All-spirit, All-spirit, All-spirit . . ." I was alive; but to
Arko, and the world, I had died. It had not occurred to me
before, when I'd been a gladiator, that the Mezem, my
followers, the crowd, were all protection of a sort; that
while I fought my way toward fifty, Kurkas for one was
waiting, and my body and soul must in some ways be left
inviolate, so I had been from many things safe.

I ceased speaking when the Pharmacist lifted the blindfold, and my eyes met his; I was in a social encounter,
then, and began to think of impressions, and become
aware of the wetness on my temples. His ancient eyes, the
pale blue of robin's eggs, looked on me with an interest
which on his fine old features somehow became a strange
sort of tenderness; it was not the typical ivory Mahid face
he'd shown in the Ring, I sensed, because we were in
private. I was on a Mahid table, in a small round room,
that smelled and felt as if it were deep in the earth: an
oubliette.

I said, and my voice sounded strange to me, being a
thing of life: "I can guess the first part. A drug that makes
the victim appear dead. Will you tell me the rest?"

In his impassive Mahid way, as he undid the various
bonds that make up what Arkan torturers call full restraint, he said, "You were buried in the Marble Palace
catacombs, sealed in properly with lead. Your epitaph
reads, 'Karas Raikas, who died for friendship.' In that
particular tomb, on the end opposite to the entrance is
egress. All Arko is mourning you; there's no mourning dye
left in the City even for gold chains; a hundred thousand
people lined up to pass your bier. That's better than even
some Imperators get; you're lucky, to have been so loved."

"How many know I'm not dead?"

"Four, other than yourself. The Imperator, whose
Thought is the Wisdom of the World, myself, and two deaf
and dumb guards." That was well-done, I thought, if it's
true. From somewhere above came the thump of boots on
a ladder, and the feel of swords; the guards came down,

and he signed them close. They put me in leg-irons,
cuffed my wrists behind my back. I was almost too stiff to
walk, when they pulled me off the table. On the ladder, of
course, I could not grip, but must trust Mahid hands
holding my hair and shoulders not to let me fall.

They took me to a gallery over a windowless room; we
were still underground. In a gold-satin chair that must
have been brought down specially, so out of place it seemed,
was Kurkas. We were over a torture-chamber; the white
hoods readied their things. On the table, with more confusion than fear on his face, was Mana. By the fact of his life,
I knew he had won fifty chains.

I threw myself to my knees, as one must wearing leg-
irons, before Kurkas. "My neck is under your foot," I said.
"I am broken. Tell me what I must do to stop this and I
will do it."

He laughed. "Fourth Shefen-kas, who knows power." I
raised my head to look in his eyes. They were those of one
who has come through a horror, been changed by it against
his will, and rebuilt his strength by embracing some strong
resolution, good or ill. "So easy after all. But what do I
say, to the man who offers me everything, and has nothing? You cannot hand Yeola-e to me, now. There is only
one thing you could do; crawl back through the corridors
of time, and repair my sanctum. You did not think you
would ever regret that, I think; do you now?" I told him
the truth, yes, since I could see no gain in denying it.

Then it struck me that Mana would be happier for
knowing I was alive; I called him, then seeing he could not
hear me, leapt to the glass. He didn't look in time. Kurkas
spoke, some Mahid made a sign and the torturer—Second
Amitzas, I knew his hands—took an iron to his eyes.

I can't write more. What more is there to write? A little;
I will force myself. Every time I closed my eyes or looked
away, they stopped, so I had to watch, to make it quicker
for him. He fought to the last sinew, full of spirit, as one
would expect of a fifty-chainer, as one would expect of
him. I can't write more, All-spirit help me. I can't see my
own words; I am writing blind. Ink runs, with tears.
Imagine, if his pain pleases you, if mine does. Otherwise
let it be over, for him, for me.

When it was, they let me sit with what was left of him
for a time, then take one possession of his. I told them the

arm-ring he'd had on his sword-arm, the ebony one he'd said he'd leave me, to match my hair. It was all to hurt me worse, of course; they imagined his death would haunt me more, if I had a token of it. Perhaps; but when the Mahid unchained my wrists to slide it onto my arm, I swore an oath in Yeoli. "All-spirit hear me and witness; soul of Mana-lai Chereda, hear me and witness. This ring is still warm with your life. It shall not grow cool, until I have sacked Arko. Second Fire come if I forswear."

They took me back up to the gallery. Kurkas rose in his ponderous way, signed them to lead me before him. "Do you understand yet what my intention is, regarding you?" he said. I answered the truth, no. He pulled my head back onto his shoulder by my hair, so I could not help but lean on him, my sidelocks brushing his cheek; my nose filled with heliotrope. "In truth, I'm not sure either. If the ransom deal goes off well, so be it. Otherwise, I'll keep you. Either way, I'm going to torture you until you are insane." Putting all else out of mind but to show nothing on my face that would give him satisfaction, I could manage it. He grinned his innocent grin. "You don't believe me. I hate you, Fourth Shefen-kas; but I will make you one I need not hate, one I, who loves no one, can love. You will be mine in the truest sense, and it will be Kurkas and Shefen-kas forever."

To that I had no answer; so in silence, they took me back down into the oubliette.

Thus ends Part I of the Life of Chevenga. Watch for Part II, *Lion's Soul*.

Trouble in a Tutti-Frutti Hat

It was half past my hangover and a quarter to the hair of the dog when *she* ankled into my life. I could smell trouble clinging to her like cheap perfume, but a man in my racket learns when to follow his nose and when to plug it. She was brunette, bouncy, beautiful. Also fruity. Also dead.

I watched her size up my cabin with brown eyes big as dinner plates, motioned her into the only other chair in the room. Her hips redefined the structure of DNA en route to a soft landing on the tatty cushion. Then they went right through the cushion. Like I said, dead. A crossover sister, which means my crack about smelling trouble was just figurative. You never get the scent-input off of what you civvies'd call a ghost. Never thought I'd meet one in the figurative flesh. Not on Space Station Three. Even the dead have taste.

What was Carmen Miranda doing on board Space Station Three?

CARMEN MIRANDA'S GHOST IS HAUNTING SPACE STATION THREE, edited by Don Sakers Featuring stories by Anne McCaffrey, C.J. Cherryh, Esther Friesner, Melissa Scott & Lisa Barnett and many more. Inspired by the song by Leslie Fish. 69864-8 * $3.95